NO LONGER PROPERTY OF
SEATTLE PUBLIC LIBRARY

D0455271

EDGEWOOD

also by kristen ciccarelli

The Last Namsara
The Caged Queen
The Sky Weaver

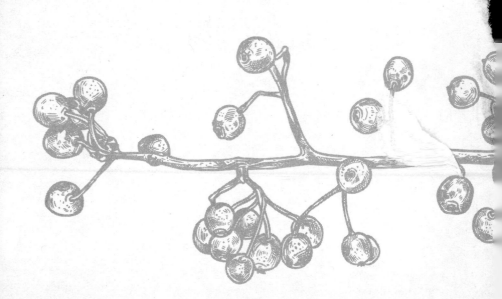

EDGEWOOD

kristen
ciccarelli

W

WEDNESDAY BOOKS
NEW YORK

This is a work of fiction. All of the characters, organizations, and events portrayed in this novel are either products of the author's imagination or are used fictitiously.

First published in the United States by Wednesday Books, an imprint of St. Martin's Publishing Group

EDGEWOOD. Copyright © 2022 by Kristen Ciccarelli. All rights reserved. Printed in the United States of America. For information, address St. Martin's Publishing Group, 120 Broadway, New York, NY 10271.

www.wednesdaybooks.com

Interior and endpapers designed by Devan Norman
Hawthorn branch art © Shutterstock.com

Library of Congress Cataloging-in-Publication Data

Names: Ciccarelli, Kristen, author.
Title: Edgewood / Kristen Ciccarelli.
Description: First edition. | New York: Wednesday Books, 2022. | Audience: Ages 13–18.
Identifiers: LCCN 2021036723 | ISBN 9781250821522 (hardcover) | ISBN 9781250821539 (ebook)
Subjects: CYAC: Grandfathers—Fiction. | Magic—Fiction. | Singing—Fiction. | Love—Fiction. | Fantasy.
Classification: LCC PZ7.1.C552 Ed 2022 | DDC [Fic]—dc23
LC record available at https://lccn.loc.gov/2021036723

Our books may be purchased in bulk for promotional, educational, or business use. Please contact your local bookseller or the Macmillan Corporate and Premium Sales Department at 1-800-221-7945, extension 5442, or by email at Macmillan SpecialMarkets@macmillan.com.

First Edition: 2022

10 9 8 7 6 5 4 3 2 1

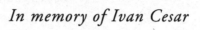

In memory of Ivan Cesar

ONE

HE WOODS CAME FOR Emeline the way they always did: creeping in with the shadows, seeping up through the cracks.

Emeline, they whispered. *Sing us a true song.*

Emeline gritted her teeth, ignoring it. From her perch on the wooden stool beneath the white lights, she continued to croon into the mic, picking the strings of her ukulele, telling herself she didn't care if the ale in the bar taps turned to mucky creek water tonight, or if the cash in the register transformed into crisp golden maple keys. She didn't care if those spongy green clumps currently sprouting up between the floorboards were, in fact, forest moss.

She needed to stay focused.

She needed to not screw this up.

Emeline couldn't give the representatives from Daybreak Records—sitting at the back of this crowded pub—any inkling that freaky things happened when she sang. Nope. Tonight, she was Emeline Lark, folksinger with a pop vibe. Rising star with foot-stomping melodies and a breathy, warbling voice.

Nothing freaky to see here at all.

The lights of La Rêverie were turned down and a real fire crackled and spit from a hearth in the pub's stone wall. Along the opposite wall, round logs for the fire were stacked neatly from floor to ceiling, and oil lamps glowed on wooden tables throughout the room.

It all felt very *hyggely*. Cozy, warm, and dark. Minus the sterile white lights above Emeline. These blinded her, heating her face and making her sweat, hiding the patrons from view as she hurtled towards the end of her final set.

Emeline . . .

As she sang, the scent of damp, mulchy earth festered in the air. Emeline scrunched her nose, trying to focus on the faceless audience beyond the lights. Her leg bounced as she plastered on a smile, cracking jokes between songs, keeping things cheerful and light.

She only played songs her manager approved. Those likely to jive with the Daybreak representatives at the back, watching her. Representatives in a position to offer her a contract.

A contract.

The thought made Emeline crackle and spark with hope.

A contract with Daybreak—one of the biggest record labels in the country—would launch her to the next level of her music career.

But will they see a rising star? she thought. *Or will they see a hack?*

She kept strumming.

When she reached the last song of her last set, the pungent smell of moldy earth made Emeline glance down. The spongy green moss had skulked right up to the scuffed brown toes of her Blundstones and shiny black insects were starting to scuttle out of it.

Just one true song, rasped the woods.

Her spine stiffened as she thought of last Thursday's gig. The woods sent spiders that time. The creepy-crawlies arrived during her third set, crawling up her jeans and falling into her water glass. Drawn to the sound of her voice.

Emeline shuddered at the memory.

She'd found one in her hair later that night, and an infestation in her guitar the next morning.

Don't let it happen tonight.

Before the insects crawled over her Blundstones and up her stool, before green moss could start sprouting out of the mic—a thing that happened a month ago—Emeline skipped the last verse of the song and moved straight into the final chorus.

No one ever noticed the strange things that happened when she sang. Maybe it was because she played so late at night and most people were into their third or fourth beer. Or possibly it was because the lights were always turned down so low. Or perhaps she'd just gotten really good at ending her sets before things got out of hand.

Or maybe it's because you're seeing things that aren't there.

Emeline's last song trailed into silence, ending her set ten minutes short. The forest paused, waiting for her to begin another one.

Not a chance.

Because the moment her set ended, so did the forest's reach. It was something she'd learned after moving away from Edgewood two years ago: the woods—real or imagined—only came for her when she sang.

The problem was: Emeline was always singing.

Music was her life.

The audience applauded. She smiled, hoping it didn't look forced. Thanking them, she wiped her sweaty palms on the threads of her yellow sweater, then let out a deep breath. The house music started up, relieving Emeline of her role as entertainer.

Lifting her ukulele from her lap, she set it on the stand next to her guitar and covertly scanned the room.

The green moss was receding, along with the bugs, taking the scent of the woods with it.

Emeline slumped with relief. She'd done it. Managed to get through all three sets without causing an incident. No one noticed the mossy presence in the room tonight. No one except her.

It made her wonder—not for the first time—if it wasn't all in her head. If her mind wasn't perhaps going the way of her grandfather's.

Maybe I'm crazy too.

Like everyone who lived in Edgewood too long.

An ache flared in her chest as she remembered the last time she'd seen her grandfather. That sterile room. Her shoes on the gray linoleum floor as she walked away and out of his life.

She forced herself to breathe.

You did the right thing. It's what he wanted you to do.

She shoved the thoughts from her mind, but a sharp ache remained.

To soothe her throat—which was dry and parched from singing—Emeline reached for the bright pink Hydro Flask beneath her stool. The one Joel gave her. She'd filled it up with water at the beginning of her last set.

Her fingers grabbed air.

She leaned down, scanning the floor. No Hydro Flask. Emeline narrowed her eyes. She'd put it right there, beneath her stool. But it was gone.

In its place rested a flower. A white anemone, pretty as a star.

What the . . . ?

Emeline pinched the flower's stem between her fingers and plucked it out from beneath her stool. Light caught in the translucent white petals circling the black center.

The sight sent a chill down her back.

"If this is a prank," she murmured to the woods, "it's not your best work."

As Emeline cast her gaze like a net over the pub, her attention snagged on a bright pink water bottle. It was instantly familiar: her missing Hydro Flask.

She glanced from the bottle to the young man holding it. He was little more than a silhouette standing just beyond the reach of the bar's dim lights. Watching her. The shadows hid his face and clothes—but not his tall frame. Nor the intensity of his stare.

Awareness crackled like electricity across her skin. There was something familiar about his presence. Like a book she'd read a long time ago and forgotten.

He lifted her water bottle as if to salute her, then tipped it back, drinking deep.

Emeline's mouth fell open.

He'd *stolen* it. And now he was draining it dry.

Indignation blazed through her. The nerve! It was one thing to lurk; it was another to steal her beverage out from under her and drink it while she watched!

But how had he taken it without her knowing?

Emeline's insides flickered at the thought of him near her, taking her water bottle as if it belonged to him, leaving the flower for her to find.

She forgot all about the Daybreak reps. Forgot about music contracts. Forgot about the woods and Edgewood and everything she'd left behind to pursue her oldest dream.

She would not be taunted by this boy. She would *not* be intimidated. Her grandfather raised her better than that.

Emeline was used to being underestimated. She was a nineteen-year-old girl in a cutthroat music industry—a fact that seemed to give people license to dismiss her. It bothered her, but it also made her grateful.

When people underestimated you, it was easy to turn the tables on them.

Rising from the stool, Emeline stepped out from beneath the bright lights. Keeping her target in view, she zigzagged between tables, closing the gap between her and the bar.

Between her and *him*.

He thought he could stalk her without consequences? She would cure him of that notion.

He set down her bottle on the bar. Even with him veiled in shadow, Emeline sensed the struggle in him. Pleasure that she'd risen to his challenge, unease at her approach.

That's right, she thought. *You picked the wrong girl to mess with.*

She curled her hands into fists, ready to use them if need be.

He made no move to leave. Merely gazed at her from the darkness. Daring her to unveil him. As if he wanted her to.

There was something unearthly about him, she thought as she drew closer. Something that didn't belong in the chic atmosphere of La Rêverie.

She was ten steps away now. Nine. Eight—

"Emeline."

Someone stepped into her path, making her halt. Emeline blinked, jolted out of her tunneled thoughts, her mission interrupted. The young man who cut in was wiry and tall. His dark jeans clung to his lean, toned legs and his blond hair was cropped short on the sides, but long on the top. He brushed it off his pale forehead.

Joel White.

"For you." Joel smiled warmly as he held out a glass of icy root beer. "In celebration."

Emeline paused, momentarily confused by the sight of her manager's son. As if he—not the mysterious stranger—were the oddity here. As if they weren't standing in La Rêverie, but somewhere else entirely. She looked from the glass Joel held out, to his sky-blue eyes, then over his shoulder.

Her stranger was gone.

Vanished.

As if he'd stepped straight out of this world and into another.

Emeline blinked, then clenched her jaw. *Damn it.* Grinding her teeth, she scanned the room, but there was no sign of him.

"Everything all right?"

Fastening on her performer's smile, Emeline took the cold, bubbling root beer from Joel. "Of course." She pushed the stranger from her mind. "What are we celebrating?"

"You." His cheeks dimpled. "Wowing the Daybreak reps."

Emeline stood frozen, her mouth falling open like a hinge. Around them, the dim lights of the pub faded and the house music blurred.

"I overheard them talking with my dad. They adored you, Em."

As the words sank in, her chest expanded with a satisfied warmth. *Did you hear that?* she wanted to say to the woods. *Despite your best efforts, they adored me.*

She took a celebratory sip of root beer. "So, they're making an offer?"

Joel's smile faltered. "Not quite."

Oh.

Emeline's joy flattened like a muted note.

Joel leaned in so she could hear his voice beneath the music. "They want to see how you handle a bigger audience. They're coming to watch you again, at your first tour stop. My dad sent you an email with the details."

Joel tapped his bottle of beer against her glass, clearly unperturbed by this disappointment.

She should have known better. Joel always made things sound sunnier than they actually were. Not because he liked to pretend things were fine; he was simply never daunted by setbacks.

It was probably the reason why, at only twenty-one, Joel was the lead guitarist in a successful indie band, St. Urbain's Horsemen. Their most recent album had won this year's Polaris Music Prize, and he'd just gotten back from touring in Australia. Raised in the music scene, Joel dropped out of college after deciding it was a waste of time and money. Growing up in the industry had given him all the contacts—and credentials—he needed.

"Want to go over your set list tonight? I think a few tweaks is all you need to blow them out of the water." He winked at her. "They should know exactly what they'll lose if they don't offer *Emeline Lark* a contract before she even walks off that stage."

But as Joel pressed his palm to her lower back and steered her towards a table, Emeline thought of the bright green moss creeping up the stage tonight. She remembered the spiders crawling up her jeans last week, her root beer turning to creek water a week before, and the bills in her wallet replaced with leaves. . . .

The forest was more persistent than usual.

As if it was getting desperate.

It's nothing I can't handle, she told herself. *I just need to stay vigilant.*

But what if things worsened while she was on tour?

"What's the flower for?" Joel asked as he guided them through the thick crowd. After three hours spent sitting beneath white-hot lights, sweat soaked her, and Emeline was glad for the sweater shielding his hand from her clammy skin.

Not that Joel minded her sweaty.

"Flower?" Emeline looked down to the white anemone gripped in her fist. "Oh." She'd nearly forgotten it. Already, it was beginning to wilt. "It's nothing. A gift from . . . a fan, I guess?"

Emeline glanced back over her shoulder to the bar, thinking of the stranger in the shadows. Of his lips pressed to her Hydro Flask, drinking her water.

Who is he?

It didn't matter. He was gone—and he had taken her water bottle with him. Deeply annoyed by this fact, Emeline resolved to put the stranger *and* the woods out of her mind.

Finally, she and Joel arrived at a table littered with empty wineglasses and craft beer bottles. Four wooden chairs ringed it. Emeline plunked herself down on the closest one.

"So, your first tour stop is obviously the most important." Joel cracked his knuckles. It was his *getting down to business* move. "Can you pull up your set list? I want to . . ."

The floor should have been sticky with beer beneath her boots; instead, it was squishy. Joel's voice faded into the background as Emeline bent her head to look under the table.

Beneath her Blundstones grew a bed of emerald-green moss.

She blinked, sure she was imagining it. The woods only encroached when she was singing. But there they were: shiny, black, bead-like things emerging from the moss. Scuttling over the floorboards, swarming up the table legs.

Beetles.

She stared in horror at their little black bodies, shimmering and flashing iridescent blue and green. She could almost hear their tiny legs clicking.

The sharp smell of crushed pine bloomed through the air.

It's not possible.

She wasn't singing.

The forest doesn't come for me when I'm not singing.

Emeline shoved back her chair, almost toppling it, then rose and stepped away from the table.

"Em . . . ? You all right?"

Joel's forehead crinkled as he stared up at her. She was afraid to look down, in case the motion drew his attention to the beetles. *Ask him. Ask him if he sees them.*

But what would happen if he *couldn't* see them? It would mean she was losing her mind, just like the rest of them. Pa and Poor Mad Tom and . . .

"Want to get out of here?" Her voice strained over the music. "Maybe go somewhere quiet?"

Not hearing the panic in her words, Joel arched a brow. A small smile curled the edges of his mouth. "Your place or mine?"

"Yours," she said, grabbing his hand and pulling him up. As the horde of black beetles teemed over the edge, flooding the tabletop, she quickly turned him towards the door and shoved. "Definitely yours."

TWO

IN THE DARKNESS OF the cab, Joel traced Emeline's fingertips, callused from her guitar strings. There was no piney scent here—only leather and air freshener. No moss creeping up through the cracks in the floor.

No beetles.

Emeline shivered.

It was just her and Joel and the cabdriver. Perfectly normal. Nothing strange.

She watched Joel's long, tanned fingers trail over her white knuckles, waiting for the relief to wash through her. In the last few months, Joel was the lifeboat she climbed inside when her fears tugged like an undertow: fears of losing the career she'd worked hard to build so quickly, fears of something dark and looming prying her oldest dream out of her tightly clasped hands.

Her delusions of the woods receded when she was with Joel. Sometimes she wasn't sure if it was him that she liked, or the normalcy he represented.

The cab turned down his street. Emeline stared out the window, forcing her thoughts away from the woods, choosing instead to think about Daybreak Records. Of what she'd accomplished tonight. Of how far she'd come since leaving Edgewood.

She would never have made anything of herself in that

backwards town. She couldn't chase her dream there or live the life she longed for.

Two years ago, when she was just seventeen, Emeline packed up her rusty blue hatchback—the one she and Pa saved for years to buy—and drove seven hours to Montreal. She'd had nine hundred dollars to her name, and a lease for a closet-sized room in an apartment shared with three art students.

Back then, Emeline took every gig that came her way—birthday parties, weddings, fundraisers—and when she failed to make ends meet, she busked in the streets. She ate instant noodles and drank instant coffee. She slept on a secondhand mattress on the floor.

She did it because singing was the one thing she was good at, and the only thing in this world she wanted to do. She did it hoping that one day she'd swap out the cold concrete sidewalks for the brightly lit stages of packed-out venues, singing her own songs, making a living with just her voice.

Had she been naïve? A little.

Had she made compromises? Absolutely.

But Emeline's naïveté, her compromises, her sheer stubborn will, had landed her *here*. In just over a week, she would open for her idols, a folk band called The Perennials, on a fourteen-city tour that spanned three countries. If she impressed the Daybreak reps on opening night, she would soon be in possession of a record deal with one of the biggest labels in the country.

If anyone can do it, you can, duckie.

It was what Pa told her in the minutes before she drove away from him and the neighbors gathered on their lawn, all waving good-bye. Back when he was still Pa, not some hollowed-out shell of a man. Back when he still remembered the girl he'd raised.

She withdrew her hand from Joel's, wrapping her arms around herself. Trying to stave off the ache.

Everyone leaves home, she told herself. *Everyone moves on.*

"We're here," said Joel as the cab slowed to a stop, pulling up alongside the curb.

But as he opened the door to step out, Emeline's phone buzzed in her purse, and the sudden smell of earth and moss filled the cab.

Emeline froze, glancing to Joel. But Joel—in the midst of paying for their ride—had discovered the cabdriver was a Morrissey fan. It would be ten minutes before she dragged him away.

As Joel and the cabbie argued in French over which Morrissey album was the *best* Morrissey album, Emeline dug her phone out of her purse.

The name of Pa's neighbor and friend lit up the screen: Maisie Decker. Emeline had given Maisie power of attorney over Pa in order to make things easier for everyone.

She immediately answered.

"Maiz?"

"Hey, baby girl." Maisie's warm voice always made Emeline think of cinnamon rolls. Fluffy and gooey and sweet. But right now she heard the wrongness in it. The tremor. The worry verging on panic.

This is about Pa.

Something was wrong with her grandfather.

Leaning closer to the window, Emeline plugged her ear to block out the conversation between Joel and the cabbie.

"Ewan said I wasn't allowed to bother you. Except for emergencies. But it's been forty-eight hours now, and . . ."

Emeline's body hummed anxiously. "What's been forty-eight hours?"

Joel called her name, motioning for her to get out of the cab. He'd paid their fare, and the cabbie needed to leave. He had other passengers to pick up.

"Ewan's gone, sweetheart."

Emeline didn't move. A chill colder than winter swept through her. Turning away from Joel, Emeline tried to keep her voice calm as her eyes pricked with hot tears.

"Gone? You mean he . . . he's . . ."

"Missing," said Maisie.

Relief slammed into her, stealing her breath. *Not dead.*

"He's been missing for two days."

Missing?

Emeline opened her eyes, staring at the four-story yellow-brick building beyond the cab. Joel's building. An old tannery converted into lofts a few years ago.

"The nurse called yesterday morning. Said he wasn't in his bed. He must have wandered out in the middle of the night and got lost. That's what they think."

They being Heath Manor—the care facility where Pa lived. The one Emeline had moved him into this past April when he fell, broke his hip, and could no longer live in their old farmhouse by himself. Emeline had canceled her gigs, driven seven hours back to Edgewood, packed up his things, and checked him into the closest care home.

Forty-eight hours.

Surely, someone would have found him by now.

Why hasn't someone found him?

Maybe she'd made a mistake, putting him in the closest facility to Edgewood. Maybe she should have found something better. Taken him to the city . . .

"Except the doors are locked at night," Maisie continued, lowering her voice to a whisper. "There are cameras in every corridor. He couldn't have walked out. It's . . . not possible."

Emeline's pulse beat loud in her ears. The back seat darkened as the pungent scent of the forest thickened around her. *You're imagining it,* she told herself. *It's not really there.*

"There's only one explanation," Maisie said.

Joel called her name again, but he sounded a world away.

"Emmie, sweetheart. We think he's been tithed."

Tithed. Frustration sparked through her at the word. The Wood King's tithes were one of many ridiculous rituals she'd grown up with in Edgewood.

The Wood King was an ancient creature who resided deep in the woods—or so Pa and all his neighbors believed. This *king* demanded quarterly sacrifices from those living on the border of his eldritch forest: tithes that kept them safe from him and his bloodthirsty monsters.

Four times a year, the Wood King sent his tithe collector to take offerings from the residents of Edgewood—or so the stories went. Emeline had never seen such a person.

When bad things happened—when cows stopped giving milk, or crops grew diseased, or loved ones went missing—the people of Edgewood didn't consider it the misfortune and unfairness of life. They considered it an unpaid tithe. They believed the Wood King was retroactively taking what was owed him.

It was one of many reasons Emeline left as soon as she could.

And yet, if tonight was any indication, perhaps she hadn't escaped soon enough. Whatever madness had infected Pa and his neighbors was clearly starting to infect her too.

"I'm so sorry, baby girl."

Emeline shook her head.

No. It was ludicrous. Nothing *took* Pa. She'd lived on the edge of those woods for most of her life, and nothing sinister ever came out of them. Her grandfather's mind was fettered by dementia. He had wandered off. That was all. He simply needed to be found.

He's a seventy-five-year-old man. How far can he go?

Emeline thought back to April, the last time she'd seen Ewan Lark. She remembered the confused look on his face as she walked him into the dining area of Heath Manor, then left him there. Remembered the discordant *flop-flop* of her Birkenstocks against the blue tiles as she hastened down the whitewashed halls. Remembered the piercing ache as she stepped out the doors, abandoning the one person she loved most in the world, handing him over to strangers.

Emeline squeezed her eyes shut.

What else could she possibly have done? Pa himself told her to go.

But she'd heard the fear in his voice. He wanted to be home, in his own house, with his vineyards around him. The ones he planted with his own two hands.

He'd wanted to stay in Edgewood.

"Emeline?"

She opened her eyes. Both Joel and the cabbie were staring at her. Joel's hair was damp with the rain that was starting to fall. The cabbie's forehead crinkled with concern in the rearview mirror.

"You okay?"

Her fingers tightened around the cell phone, still pressed to her ear. She heard Maisie breathing on the other end.

I have sets to perform. A tour to prepare for. I can't just leave.

But the thought of her grandfather, lost and afraid, overrode everything else.

Glancing to the driver, she asked in stilted French if he could take her back downtown, where her car was parked. "Pouvez-vous m'emmener sur la rue Sainte-Catharine Est?"

"Bien sûr."

"Em?" said Joel from outside the cab. The rain fell harder, clinking on the pavement. "What's going on?"

"It's Pa."

Joel's brow darkened. He opened his mouth to respond, but they'd had this conversation a million times already. She knew everything he'd say, and she agreed with him. It was why she'd put Pa in Heath Manor. It was the reason she listed the farm for sale.

Emeline couldn't let her grandfather hold her back. It was the last thing Pa wanted.

"I'll only be gone a few days. I promise."

Before Joel could reply, she pulled the passenger door shut.

The cabbie signaled, then started to drive.

THREE

HERE. SEE?"
The nurse's white sneakers squeaked against the clean floors of the hall. Emeline followed, glancing down at the woman's shadow. Checking its shape. A ridiculous habit instilled in her by Poor Mad Tom when she was a kid. *You can always tell a shiftling by their shadow.* Emeline forced her gaze away.

"It's exactly as he left it."

Emeline—who'd driven through the night and arrived late this morning—halted as she stepped into the room.

It smelled like him.

Like *home.*

Pa's bed was made, his forest-green comforter turned neatly down. Its fernlike pattern was so familiar, it filled her with a belly-deep longing for the simple comforts of her childhood.

Beside the bed sat a pair of brown slippers, waiting for him to step into. On the dresser, old picture frames stood in a wobbly row, their glass recently dusted. The photos within all bore Emeline's image—chubby and rosy cheeked at two, gangly and awkward at eleven, lithe and tall at sixteen while she strummed a guitar up onstage.

Emeline wanted to pinch the bridge of her nose. But that

would draw the nurse's sympathy. Instead, she blinked and swallowed, staving off the memories.

"Can I have a minute alone?"

The nurse's round face crinkled as she smiled sweetly. "Of course." She tucked a strand of curly brown hair into her messy bun, then turned to leave. "I'll be down the hall if you need me."

In her absence, Emeline's hands shook—mainly from the extra-large coffee she'd gulped down this morning. The last time she caught a glimpse of her reflection, her eyes were dark and sunken and her black hair hung limp around her washed-out face.

But there was no time to rest.

The sooner she found Pa, the sooner she could return to her life. She'd already emailed her manager, asking him to cancel her gigs this week. She hated leaving people in a lurch. She needed to get back as soon as possible.

It was why she stood here, in Pa's room, searching for clues the staff and police had overlooked. Looking for hints of what Pa was thinking the night he wandered off.

Beside the bed, a calendar hung on the wall. Emeline stepped towards it. A black *x* had been drawn with Sharpie through each day of September. The *x*'s stopped the day before Pa went missing. September 22 was the first box without one.

It read: *Autumn Equinox.*

The season's turn.

When the Wood King collects his tithes.

Before she could reject that thought, the room around her shifted. She stopped looking through the lens of a girl from a big city and started looking through the eyes of a girl who'd grown up in Edgewood.

Things she'd missed at first glance now stood out like tacky cottage signs.

First were the gnarled branches hanging over Pa's door, tied together with twine, their boughs clustered with bright red berries and dark green leaves. Judging by the fresh, sweet smell, they'd been recently cut.

In Edgewood, people hung hawthorn branches over their doors on the night of the Hunt, which happened in early autumn. The magic in the hawthorn's sap prevented the Hunt from entering their homes—or so they believed.

Her grandfather used to make a game of it. When Emeline was little, on the eve of the Hunt they timed themselves, trying to beat last year's record as they ran through the house, bolting windows and doors, hanging hawthorn branches from the nails above the lintels. Afterwards, they inspected each other's work, docking points for sloppiness, giving points for the snuggest lock or most creative hawthorn arrangement. Then Pa made extra-buttery popcorn and together they watched movies with the volume turned way up.

One such evening, a rattling from the other end of the house drew Emeline's attention away. Getting up from the couch where Pa sat engrossed by the film they were watching, his buttery fingers sinking into the popcorn bowl, Emeline sought out the sound.

She followed it all the way to the mudroom, where the door was shaking on its hinges, the handle turning frantically back and forth. As if someone—or something—was trying to get in. Emeline had stood frozen, heart pounding, staring at the knob as a terrible smell seeped under the door. Like rotting wood and old bones. She must have screamed, because suddenly Pa appeared, picking her up and carrying her back to the couch, telling her it was nothing. Just the wind.

Emeline shook off the memory, prickling with unease. It *was* just the wind. Pa himself had said so. Either that, or Poor Mad Tom playing a prank on them.

The second thing she spotted in Pa's room was the empty copper bowl, half hidden beneath the bed. Getting down on her hands and knees, she pulled it out. The bowl's cold, heavy curve—twice the size of her cupped hands—sparked memories. As a child, she often begged to leave a tithe of her own in this bowl. Her favorite dress, or her most beloved doll. Wanting to feel grown-up.

Pa always gave the same answer.

No, duckie. It's my job to protect you. One day, you'll understand.

Emeline ran her fingers over the copper, feeling the rough marks from Poor Mad Tom's hammer. Tom cold-forged all of Edgewood's tithing bowls in his garage-turned-forge. She touched the inscription around the rim. Words she'd traced over and over with much tinier fingers, so long ago.

The steepest sacrifices make the strongest tithes.

Emeline shivered.

The hawthorn branches, the tithing bowl . . . they were like fingerprints at a crime scene. The marks of Edgewood—a place where people believed the forest *took* things from them.

Like last winter, when Cornelius Henrik was convinced it stole one of his horses. It was dusk when Corny saw the shadow skin—a thing of nightmares—come out of the woods and sink its glistening teeth into the horse's throat. By the time Corny ran outside, the monster had dragged its meal into the bare black trees, leaving the snow stained red.

The next morning, Corny found a pearl-like orb sitting in the horse's stall: proof of a tithe paid.

But that wasn't what really happened.

Monsters didn't come out of the woods to eat horses. Starving wolves did. Growing up, Emeline had fallen asleep to the sounds of them howling, killing things in the dark.

The forest takes what it likes and never apologizes, Pa used to say.

Why has it never taken from us?

Because we always pay our tithes.

The summer before Corny's horse disappeared, the forest supposedly took Grace Abel, a girl Emeline's age. It was Labor Day weekend, and Grace's parents had invited all the neighbors over for dinner. It was dusk when Grace's mother, Eshe, saw the flash of black among the forest's green-gold leaves, making her look up from scrubbing the dishes.

While the voices of her tipsy dinner guests wafted through the house, Eshe saw Grace—her thick black curls undone, haloing her head and shoulders—walk into the woods hand in hand with something *else.*

Eshe grabbed her blue knit shawl, flung it over her shoulders, and ran after the girl. By the time she reached the tree line, there was no hint of Grace. Just the trees chattering their warnings . . . and a pearl-sized orb left behind on a stack of Grace's textbooks.

But this, too, was a lie.

The real story was much more mundane.

Grace Abel spent high school getting straight A's. She was accepted into every university she applied to, most offering her full scholarships. Her parents were the proudest people in Edgewood.

And then, a few months before classes started, Grace got cold feet.

Suddenly, she didn't want to go. Not *yet.* She'd spent four years of high school holed up in her room, studying. She'd had no social life, resulting in very few friends, and now she was about to enter university and do it all over again.

Grace wanted to take a year off. Wanted to make up for lost time.

Wanted to *breathe.*

Her parents were livid. They feared if she didn't go to school that fall, she wouldn't go to school ever. They couldn't allow such a thing. Their daughter had worked too hard to let it go to waste.

Emeline heard through the Edgewood grapevine (aka Maisie's gossip) that Grace and her parents fought viciously that summer, and that those fights ended in an ultimatum: if Grace didn't go to school that September, she couldn't stay in Edgewood.

So, the night of her parents' dinner party, Grace angrily packed her things and did exactly what her parents told her to do. No shadowy creatures stole her away. The forest didn't take her. Grace left and didn't come back. Apparently, she hadn't spoken to her parents since.

The forest didn't *take* things—not intentionally. Yes, accidents happened. Sometimes cows went missing or whole flocks of hens didn't lay eggs or entire cornfields came up rotten. But these were just misfortunes. There wasn't anything malicious behind them.

Emeline didn't begrudge her old neighbors their fairy tales, though. She understood why they lied to themselves. Believing in monsters and cruel, fey kings made things easier. It gave them something to blame when senseless disasters struck.

The stories and rituals of Edgewood were touchstones. Ways of dealing with deep losses.

It didn't make her angry, that the neighbors brought Pa superstitious objects. It only made her sad. The hawthorn branches, the tithing basin . . . they were comforts and coping mechanisms. Ways of processing grief. Because Ewan Lark, their neighbor and friend, was slowly losing his mind. And in losing his mind, they were losing *him.*

She understood it.

She simply coped in a different way.

Emeline wrenched herself back to the present. To the sterile room and the task at hand: finding her grandfather.

Something glinted on his pillow then, catching her attention.

Emeline stepped towards the bed. A tiny orb rested in the center of the pale green pillowcase. She picked it up.

The orb was smaller than a marble, but bigger than a pearl, and it was unnaturally cold to the touch. Opal-like colors swirled beneath the surface: pale blues and greens and creamy whites.

Emeline stared for several seconds, unable to catch her breath. *Knowing* what this was despite every part of her that screamed it wasn't true.

The mark of a tithe paid.

FOUR

"IS SOMEONE PUNISHING ME?" she roared into the phone the moment Maisie answered. "For leaving him there? For walking away?"

She sat parked in front of Pa's house, her free hand clenching the steering wheel so hard, her knuckles hurt. The For Sale sign on the lawn glared at her through the passenger window.

"Emmie?"

She'd driven halfway to Maisie's house, then changed her mind and turned down the dirt road to Pa's, afraid she'd do something rash. Like break all of Maisie's china before letting her explain.

"Where are you, sweetheart?"

"I'm at the house," Emeline said through gritted teeth, fury searing her. "I found . . ." She glared down at the pearly orb sitting in the cupholder, gleaming white against the black plastic. The sight made her feel a little sick. "I found a tithe marker. On his pillow. Is this some kind of prank?"

Maisie stayed silent so long, Emeline wondered if the line had gone dead.

"I'm driving Eshe to an appointment right now," Maisie said at last. "We'll come straight over when it's done."

"Fine."

After ending the call, she picked up the tithe marker. An unsettling feeling was taking root in her. Clenching the marker in her fist, she got out of the car. The sweet-sour smell of the grapes, heavy on the vine, greeted her. As her feet touched the earth, the wind picked up, nipping at her bare ankles.

She shivered, then glanced beyond the house. To the dark and looming wood.

Emeline, the forest whispered, just as it had done all her life. *Come and play.*

She thought of her gig. Of the moss and the beetles. The woods had never quite let her escape. Not completely.

Emeline shook off the ridiculous thought. *Don't be crazy.* But maybe it was too late for that.

As she headed for the stone house, she avoided the For Sale sign. Half a dozen people had offered on the house since she put it on the market this summer with help from Corny Henrik, Pa's best friend. Mostly foreign investors. People who weren't planning to move in, only looking for a place to stash their cash.

Emeline turned them all down.

But she couldn't keep turning them down. Pa had almost nothing in the way of savings, and the little he did have was paying for his care at Heath Manor. The only way to keep him there was to sell the house and farm.

One of these days, she was going to have to accept an offer.

Arriving at the door, she punched the passcode into the lockbox where the real estate agent kept the keys, unlocked the door, and stepped inside. Once, dirt-encrusted shoes lay piled to the right. In their place now was an empty rubber mat. Emeline toed off her boots. The tiled floor chilled her feet as she walked from the mudroom to the living room.

No fire burned in the stove. No woodsmoke smell hung in the air. No delicious aroma wafted from the kitchen. The only sound was the ticking of the grandfather clock.

This house—the one harboring her most cherished memories, the one she'd spent nearly all her life in—felt utterly lifeless and cold. Like its soul had fled and only a shell remained.

Emeline called for Pa, checking each and every room. It was pointless, though. Pa didn't know how to use the lockbox. If he'd managed to walk the eight miles here from Heath Manor, he wouldn't be able to get in.

The familiar smells of the house drew a swarm of memories, making her dizzy. Emeline grabbed hold of the kitchen table to steady herself, then sank slowly down into a chair, remembering her last visit home.

They had been sitting at this very table as Emeline explained where he was going: to Heath Manor, to get the care he needed. Pa's leg bounced nervously the entire time she spoke.

He's scared, she realized at the time. So, she'd taken his hands in hers, wanting to soothe him.

Pa pulled instantly away. Like Emeline was a stranger and why was she touching him? He tucked his hands under the table, where she couldn't reach.

Don't be familiar, the doctor had told her. *It will only confuse him.*

But Emeline didn't know how to not be familiar. How was she supposed to pretend Pa wasn't who he'd always been? Grandfather, caregiver, best friend.

Who are you? he'd asked her that day.

The words were like a swift, stinging slap. Throwing her completely off-balance.

At a loss, Emeline had blinked, staring at the man who raised her. Watching him try to recognize her. Watching him reach for memories the way one reached into a river to drink, only to find the bed dry and the reaching hand empty.

He's not the man he used to be, Joel told her at the time. *Don't set aside your dreams for someone who can't remember who you are.*

She shook off the memory.

Is this my punishment? she wondered. *For abandoning him?*

Pa had raised Emeline ever since her mother left shortly after she was born. For all her life, he wholeheartedly supported her dreams. And what had Emeline done to repay him? The moment he needed her help, she'd handed him over to strangers, then put his farm up for sale.

A wave of self-loathing swept through her.

Rising from the table, she pulled her oversized cardigan—one she'd borrowed from Pa and never returned—closer around herself. Her grandfather might not be in his house, but he was somewhere close. He had to be. Old men with bad hips didn't just disappear.

Where else would he go?

She forced herself to look out the kitchen window. Towards the woods. The trees there rose to twice the height of the house, standing like sentries.

Emeline's gaze snagged on the only opening for miles: a space in the hedge. It yawned like a wolf's mouth, marking the entrance to that dark, other place.

Once, a tree stood in the gap. Pa planted it on the day Emeline was born and it had watched over her ever since—or so she used to imagine.

Pa cut it down after she left Edgewood, like a portent of what was to come.

A breeze blew in through the screen, rustling Emeline's hair. A smell slipped in with it: rotting wood and old bones.

She shuddered, thinking of rattling doors and rotating knobs.

Emeline, whispered the woods. *Come.*

The back of her neck prickled, as if she was being watched, and her pulse sped up. She stepped towards the window, scanning the tree line. But there was nothing there. Just the trees hushing and swaying. Whispering her name.

Emeline breathed in deep.

Get control of yourself.

Behind her, someone cleared their throat.

She jumped, heart banging in her chest, and spun to find a middle-aged man standing in the kitchen.

He wore a faded jean jacket, and the head of a wooden tobacco pipe peeked out of his breast pocket. He was tall and sun-kissed and several years younger than Pa. Old enough to be Emeline's father. His dark brown hair was shorter and grayer than she remembered, but the rest of him was familiar.

"*Tom.*" Emeline flung herself at him. Wrapping her arms tightly around his neck, she pressed her face to his jean jacket and breathed in his pipe tobacco smell.

This was Poor Mad Tom, otherwise known as Tomás Pérez. Once a photographer for *National Geographic,* now Pa's retired soft-spoken neighbor. "Poor" because he'd been madly in love with Emeline's mother, Rose Lark, who broke his heart when she went and got pregnant by another man. "Mad" because he truly, deeply believed he was once part of the Wood King's court.

He loved to tell Emeline about his wild adventures when she wandered up to his door as a small, bored child, looking to be entertained.

Tom patted her back gently. "I thought you were your mother."

"Sorry to disappoint you."

He squeezed her shoulder. "You could never disappoint me, kiddo. How's the music thing going?"

She let go to find him smiling down on her.

"Good." She thought of her upcoming tour. Of the Day-break reps and their potential offer. "Really good."

"No surprise there." He beamed like a proud father. "Maiz always says our Emmie has a magic voice. What about that boy-friend of yours?"

"Joel?"

He shrugged. "Whichever one you're on now."

Ouch.

Not that it wasn't true. Emeline went through boyfriends as quickly as she went through guitar strings. Joel once liked to tease her about her cold, ruthless heart.

That was before they started hooking up.

"Joel's . . . good. But he's not my boyfriend." Not *technically.*

Tom studied her for a long moment, then said, more som-berly, "I take it you heard the news?"

Emeline nodded, then dug the tithe marker out from her pocket and held it up to him. It gleamed, frost cold, between her fingers. "Who did this? Do you know? Someone left it on Pa's pillow."

Tom pressed his lips together, looking from her face to the marker and back again. "You know what that is, sweetheart."

"I know what it is," she said. "What I don't—"

"Then you know who left it there."

The silence grew thick and stagnant between them. He watched her, brown eyes quiet, while Emeline seethed beneath the weight of years and years of Edgewood baggage.

"The Wood King has him," said Tom, simply.

Emeline fisted the orb in her hand. The Wood King and his woodland monsters—things like *shadow skins* and *ember mares* and *shiftlings*—were fairy tales she'd left behind when she drove away two summers ago.

"There is no Wood King," she said, even as she remembered

the dark and looming woods stalking her at last night's performance.

Except if the woods really were inside La Rêverie, she told herself, *someone other than me would have noticed.*

But no one ever noticed. Which proved it was a delusion.

And yet, that unsettling feeling was growing like a thundercloud inside her.

Tom looked away, drawing his bottom lip between his teeth. Shoving his hands into his pockets, he stared out at the woods. "If you say so."

She felt irrationally guilty then. But Tom was a grown man, and she wasn't a little kid anymore.

More important: it was going on seventy-two hours now. Pa had been gone for three days. Even Emeline knew that when it came to missing, vulnerable people, three days was too long.

She still had a few hours of sunlight left, though. Stepping around Tom, she started for the mudroom. "I'm going to drive around and see if I can find him."

"Emmie."

Emeline ignored him, feeling herself starting to unravel.

In the mudroom, she grabbed her Blundstones and pulled them on. "What if he's hurt and lying in a ditch somewhere?" The horror of it was sinking in. "What if he doesn't have his hearing aids in and can't hear me calling?"

What if he's dead?

"He's not in a ditch, love."

Tom, who'd followed her through the house at a more leisurely pace, gently touched her arm. Emeline reluctantly turned to face him.

"Maisie and me, Corny and Anya, Eshe and Abel, not to mention the police . . . we've spent the past three days searching. Driving down back roads. Walking through fields." Tom shook his head. "If Ewan tried to leave Heath Manor, the locked doors would have stopped him. If he managed to get through the doors, there'd be footage on the cameras. If he really was wandering around out here, no tithe marker would've been left in his room."

His gaze turned fierce, his voice stern.

"There's only one place he can be, kiddo." Tom glanced towards the distant wood. Almost wistful. "The proof is right there in your pocket."

Emeline followed Tom's gaze towards the windows. What if Pa *was* in the forest? Not because he'd been kidnapped by some fairy king, but because he might have walked all the way home only to find the doors of his house locked and then turned to the trees in his confused state.

"Has anyone checked the woods?" she asked.

Silence rang out as Tom glanced down to his loafers.

No. They hadn't. It was written plain across his face.

"Why don't you get some sleep tonight?" said Tom, evading her question. "And first thing tomorrow, you and I will go out looking again."

Emeline heard the falseness in his tone. He was placating her. Humoring her like a small child.

An ember-red rage flared inside her.

Emeline didn't doubt that Pa's neighbors had searched for him. But what good were their searches when deep down, they all believed he was kidnapped by some wicked forest king? How hard would they look, really, if they thought it a fool's errand?

No one in Edgewood ever entered the woods—not if they could help it. In their minds, nothing but monsters waited beneath those dark boughs. It was the Wood King's domain.

Trespass and suffer the consequences. The warnings of her childhood clanged through her mind. *Set foot there at your own peril.*

Pa's neighbors may have searched everywhere else, but they hadn't searched those trees. Their superstitions prevented them.

It was too much for Emeline. She was so tired of this nonsense. She wanted to yell at Tom. Wanted to curse them all out for letting their ridiculous fears get in the way of finding their friend—a man who was lost and likely terrified.

But she didn't. Instead, summoning the lessons she'd learned as a girl in a cutthroat music industry, Emeline kept her voice sweet and calm despite her building anger. "You're right." She plastered on her best performer's smile—her most winning accessory. "I'll go to bed early, then come get you in the morning."

She didn't need to force a yawn—it came naturally. She hadn't slept since the previous night, back in Montreal.

The tension bled out of the room as Tom relaxed.

He nodded his approval. "Then I'll see you tomorrow."

Not trusting herself to speak, Emeline watched him leave in silence.

Her anger lingered long after Tom's truck disappeared down the lane and the dust from the dirt road settled. Alone now, Emeline slid her phone into the pocket of her jeans and headed for the back door. When she flung it open, a cold wind smacked her skin. It was late September, and the heat of summer had fled.

The moment she stepped onto the bottle-green grass, Emeline heard them: the voices of the trees, whispering in unison.

Emeline . . .

She pulled Pa's blue cardigan closer around her, jamming her hands in its pockets. The sun hadn't gone down yet, but the air glowed gold as dusk approached, catching in the leaves of the giant trees up ahead.

The sight of the woods, watching and whispering, made Emeline prickle with wariness. She thought of her gig last night:

the beetles swarming the table, the moss crawling towards her while she sang.

"Is this what you wanted—to drag me back? To *trap* me here this time?"

Look at yourself. Talking to trees.

But the truth was, just for a moment, she *wanted* to believe the forest was a dark and deadly thing that could steal from her. It would make things so much easier. It would give her something other than herself to hate.

She descended on the woods, letting her feet take her to the tree line.

"I'm going to find him," she growled. "I'm going to bring him home." Her hands tightened into fists. "And then I'm never coming back here again."

She approached the hole in the hedge, where her tree used to stand. The grass was thick and long, as if no tree ever stood there at all. She tried to remember: what it looked like, what it smelled like.

But she couldn't.

The wind rose up, snatching at her hair and stinging her cheeks. The leaves began to flicker.

Beware of the Wood King, Emeline.

"There is no Wood King," she said bitterly.

And she walked into the forest.

FIVE

HE MOMENT EMELINE STEPPED across the tree line, her footsteps slowed. As if her body was having second thoughts.

The wind stopped.

The leaves quieted.

The thick, piney smell of the forest enveloped her.

Awk!

Emeline jumped at the sound, looking up. A large raven perched on the branch of a maple overhead. Its feathers gleamed blue-black in the light of the setting sun, and its beady eyes shone as it cocked its head at her.

It was twice the size of a regular raven. For one silly second, Emeline wondered if it was a shiftling.

Shiftlings were an Edgewood myth—creatures who moved between forms. In Edgewood, people believed that a raven or a fox or a deer might be nothing more than an animal, or they might be something *else*—spies sent by the Wood King himself.

You can always tell a shiftling by its shadow.

Awk! the bird croaked, and flew off, feathers shuffling.

Her skin prickled, as if the raven's call had sounded some alarm and the eyes in the woods were turning to look at her.

Emeline pulled her cardigan tighter and trudged on, her

feet crunching twigs and fallen leaves. Cupping her hands around her mouth, she called for Pa. As she walked, the forest closed in on her like a fist. Her sleeves snagged on thistles and thorns. Clumps of brown burrs collected up and down her jeans.

The trees thickened. Their massive boughs blocked out the sky and the woods grew darker around her. At every creak and moan, Emeline turned sharply to look, only to find herself alone, and the way behind her as tangled and dense as the way ahead.

Will I be able to find my way out?

"Don't think about that. Think about Pa."

She shouted his name, over and over. But there was no answering call, and worse: no sign of him.

Worse still: the daylight was disappearing around her. Emeline needed to head back; she didn't want to be in here after full dark.

Tomorrow I'll go to the police station. If she told the police she believed Pa was in the woods, they'd have to assemble a search team. Wouldn't they?

But as Emeline turned to go back, she found the forest . . . changed.

The trees around her were diseased. The buds on the sumac trees were gray, not red, the hickory leaves were white and withered, and the trunks of the poplars were rotted.

Even the air was wrong. Cloying and moldy and wet.

Emeline turned again, but the lush green forest she'd just come through was gone. In its place was something sick and decaying. The light here wasn't the deep gold of sunset, but the pallid gray of death.

"What is this place?"

The Stain, breathed the trees. *Cursed territory.*

"Cursed?"

But the trees said nothing more. And Emeline, realizing she was talking to inanimate objects, moved quickly on.

Head north, she thought, her skin turning to gooseflesh. *Edgewood is north of the woods.* All she had to do was walk back in the direction she came and she'd get there. Beneath her footsteps, shriveled leaves dissolved like ash. The forest—which had been creaking and moaning—had gone eerily silent.

The voices of the trees turned to breathy rasps: *Something's coming.*

Her skin hummed with awareness as she heard it too: movement in the distance, scraping against branches as it went, air rattling in its lungs as it drew closer.

Go, said the trees. *Run, Emeline!*

But what if it was Pa?

Through the murky gray light, she saw it. Like a shadow, only darker. Black like a cellar with no windows or lights.

As its elongated shape slinked closer, she saw sinewy arms, oddly jointed, and shining white claws crusted with dried blood.

A chill spread through Emeline, like the winter frost sweeping through Pa's garden, killing everything in sight.

She knew what this was.

A shadow skin.

She shook her head, backing away. *It's not possible. . . .* Shadow skins were cunning, ruthless things. Servants of the Wood King sent to terrorize Edgewood. It was a shadow skin that ate Corny's horse last winter. A shadow skin that bled Abel's cows dry two years before that. And when Maisie found one lurking in her shed, she locked it in, intending to burn the whole thing to the ground—only to watch the monster burst through the door and come for *her.*

If Pa hadn't been there that day, hadn't grabbed her and

pulled her into the house, barricading the door, the thing would have torn out Maisie's throat.

But these were only stories.

And if they're not only stories? Emeline thought as the thing slinked closer.

The creature stepped into the clearing, only a dozen paces away. Staring straight at her. Or it would have been, if it had any eyes. Instead, there were just two slitted nostrils and a crack for a mouth. That crack widened, revealing rows of serrated teeth.

It stalked closer.

Run, Emeline!

But it was too late to run.

Sighting a broken white branch on the ground, she reached for it. Her fingers curled around the hard wood. Lifting it furiously over her head, she swung with all her strength.

There was a resonant *thud!* as the branch connected with the shadow skin's palm.

The creature flexed its clawed hand, seizing the branch and snapping it in two.

Emeline stumbled back.

It stood over her now, mouth gaping open, revealing blood-encrusted gums. Strings of saliva glistened between its needle-sharp teeth as its breath wafted over her, smelling like rot.

Emeline felt herself stiffen: muscles seizing, bones locking. She willed her body to move, but it wouldn't. As if someone had taken control of her motor functions.

An unnatural cold flooded her limbs.

And that's when she remembered that killing wasn't the worst of what a shadow skin could do.

You'll never see him again, a putrid voice oozed through her mind. *You'll never hear his voice. When they find him, they'll put him back in that white room, and he'll die there. Frightened and alone.*

She saw Pa then, in a room that wasn't his, waiting for someone who was never coming. She saw him so clearly, as if he were right in front of her. She watched him stand at the windows. Watched him pace the halls. Waiting for his granddaughter. Longing for her to come. Wasting away, a little more each day.

She tried to pull herself out of these thoughts, but resistance only triggered darker, sadder visions. As if something was inside her mind, forcing her down the most heartrending paths.

It was *this* that shadow skins were known for: finding your worst fear and using it to immobilize you.

As the monster clawed through her thoughts and memories, looking for the things she buried deepest, Emeline stared at its gaping maw. She knew that once it was done ravishing her mind, it would sink those glistening teeth into her throat.

Emeline opened her mouth to scream.

Before she could, the sharpened tip of a blade split open the monster's face.

The shadow skin shrieked, relinquishing its hold on her.

Emeline's legs buckled in shock and she dropped to her knees.

The blade vanished back through the shadow skin's skull, but instead of blood, darkness spilled out of the wound. The monster's high-pitched wail stabbed her ears. It lifted its talons, clawing its face as if to stop the flow, then crumbled like dust to the forest floor.

Emeline gaped as its dead form bloomed into poppies, their red petals flickering like drops of shining blood.

From above, a rough-soft voice growled: "You reckless fool."

SIX

EMELINE KNELT IN THE dirt, frozen with shock.

Her rescuer stood two paces away. He seemed close to her in age, with maple-dark hair and skin the light brown of dusk. His feet were planted firmly in the earth, rooting him there like a tree, and he wore a gray overcoat stitched with a subtle pattern of sassafras leaves. Brass buttons ran down the front of the coat, matching the buckles on his dark brown boots, which were scuffed with dried mud.

Emeline remembered the mysterious boy from the bar last night. She hadn't seen his face, but the height and shape of him, the way he held himself . . . there was an uncanny resemblance to *this* boy standing before her.

And yet it wasn't possible, was it? For the stranger from last night to suddenly be here, hundreds of miles away, in the forest bordering Edgewood?

"Have we met?" she asked.

The boy kept his distance, glowering at her. As if Emeline's presence was an unwanted irritation and saving her from a monster was an unpleasant disruption in his day.

"Certainly not." His voice prickled. "I'd remember meeting someone foolish enough to walk alone through these woods at dusk."

Rude. Emeline rose shakily to her feet, then pointed out: "Aren't *you* walking alone through these woods at dusk?"

Her gaze lifted, colliding with his stern glare. His eyes were two shades of gray, like river rocks. One dry and one wet, both ringed in black at the edges. Emeline couldn't help but find them striking.

He studied her back, a little warily, his curiosity getting the better of his restraint. "Why are you here?"

"I'm looking for someone." She glanced to where his knuckles bunched around the pommel of the shimmering blade pointed down to the earth. Frowning, she asked, "Do you always walk around armed with a sword?"

His cool demeanor shifted. He opened his mouth to respond, only to stop himself at the last second and sheathe the blade in the scabbard at his back.

"I suggest you continue your search elsewhere," he said, evading her question. "Night is upon us. The ember mares will be running soon. And who knows how many shadow skins are lurking about the Stain."

Emeline went very still. *Ember mares?* They were horses made of fire, according to Edgewood stories. They galloped through the woods between twilight and midnight, and god help you if you got in their way.

"Who *are* you?" she asked him.

His jaw tightened and he looked away stiffly. "No one of import."

"I'm Emeline," she said. "Emeline Lark."

He nodded, slight and stiff. Not caring in the least. "Let's get you home, shall we?" Glancing over her shoulder, he whistled sharply.

"Wait, no," she said, stepping back. "I need to find—"

Emeline turned around to discover the biggest, blackest

horse breathing on her face. She stared up into enormous golden eyes. Flecks of red dusted the horse's irises, like a fire sparking, and her hot breath smelled like smoke.

Holy hell.

Emeline stepped quickly back—straight into the boy. The scent of him enveloped her: like crushed pine needles and oiled leather.

"This is Lament."

"Uh-huh," she whispered, staring at the massive beast, which was pawing the ground as if to say, *I'm getting impatient! Let us leave!* When she threw back her head, those golden eyes flickered red. "Very . . . pretty."

"Have you ridden before?"

No, and she wasn't about to start now. Certainly not on this thing.

"There's nothing to worry about; you'll be riding with me."

Uh, no. No, she would not be.

She stepped away from the demon horse.

This guy had just slain a shadow skin. If shadow skins were real, the Wood King was too. And the tithe marker in her pocket proved that her grandfather *had* been stolen. That he hadn't merely wandered off.

That Tom and Maisie were right.

As the truth flooded through her, beneath her dread she felt an overwhelming sense of rightness.

She needed a new plan.

As her rescuer reached for the reins of his horse, rubbing the creature's coal-black nose, Emeline asked, "Can you bring me to the Wood King?"

His face darkened. "Don't be daft." He nodded to the north, in the direction of Edgewood. "You need to get out of these woods before something worse than a shadow skin catches your scent. Here." He held out his hand. "I'll help you mount up."

Emeline briefly wondered what was worse than a shadow skin, then quickly decided she didn't want to find out.

"Trust me: I have no intention of staying any longer than I have to. But I think the Wood King has my grandfather." She pulled out the cold, pebble-sized marker from her pocket and held it up to show him.

He lowered his hand as his eyebrows shot upwards, causing his forehead to crease. "A marble? That's your proof?"

Emeline lowered the tiny orb. It wasn't a marble. It was a marker—still cold, despite being in her pocket and close to her body. The colors beneath its surface kept shifting and changing in the murky light.

"It means the Wood King has my grandfather." It was strange to hear the words come out of her mouth, after she'd so vehemently denied them before.

He studied her openly now, as if trying to decide what to do with her. "I hate to disappoint you, but your grandfather isn't here."

But how could he know that?

He couldn't.

"And even if he were in the king's court, there's nothing you can do." His voice was tense as he scanned the darkening woods. "We can't linger here."

He stepped to the side of his horse, waiting for Emeline to join him. As if he expected her to obediently climb onto the massive creature's back. As if he wanted her to go home, forget about Pa, and carry on as if nothing were wrong.

Her temper flared. She wasn't going back until she had Pa with her. "If you won't take me, then tell me the way."

"Get on the horse, Emeline."

So he had been paying attention when she told him her name. She wished he'd given her *his* name so she could use it in the same condescending tone he'd just used on her.

"I'm not getting on your horse. I'm going to find my grandfather. And if you're not going to help me, please get out of my way."

He didn't. In fact, he stepped closer, blocking out the rapidly fading sunlight with his tall frame.

"Do you have any idea what happens to people like you? People senseless enough to wander into these woods?"

Fury boiled in her blood. She held her ground as he bore down on her like a thundercloud.

"There are horrors here far worse than any nightmare. It's only a matter of time before another one finds you. I can't leave you here."

Emeline fell silent. The only thing she knew about these woods was that the longer she was in them, the more she believed the stories she'd grown up with.

"Then don't leave me," she said softly. "Escort me to the king."

His mouth twisted as if he tasted something rotten. "*That* I will not do."

"Fine."

Emeline scanned the ashy grove, searching for a path that might be difficult for a giant horse to follow. She remembered the voices of the trees. The way they'd warned her about the shadow skin.

He was close enough to seize her, and from the look in his eyes, that seemed to be his plan.

"Tell me where to go," she told the trees.

South, they murmured. *Follow the river.*

"Who are you talking to?"

When he reached for her, Emeline dodged and ran.

SEVEN

HE AND HIS HELL-BEAST gave chase, thundering behind, yelling for her to stop. Branches snapped and bracken crunched beneath the horse's mighty hooves.

Emeline flew south, where the silver trail was thinnest between the decaying trees, making it cumbersome for her pursuers to follow.

There seemed no end to this dead place. Ashy white aspens and rotted cedars rushed by as she ran. Too soon, her path arrived at an open thicket. Emeline stumbled, wasted precious seconds regaining her balance, then kept going.

The horse and her rider caught up.

They flew by Emeline's side through the clearing. Labored breaths filled her ears; pounding hooves echoed in her bones. Emeline's legs burned beneath her.

She kept running.

In a burst of speed, the horse rushed ahead. Her black hide flickered as she wove in front of Emeline, who swore she saw twisting flames flare across the animal's flanks. The horse turned to face her, blocking the way. Emeline skidded to a stop inches away from her chest.

Rearing up on hind legs, the horse pawed the air above Emeline's head with ember-bright hooves, eyes raging a hellish red.

Emeline's heart thudded like a kick drum as she stumbled backwards. Her foot caught on a raised root and twisted beneath her. Losing her balance, she fell, hitting the ground hard. Pain flared in her elbows—which took the brunt of the impact—and she hissed through her teeth, "Ow!"

"Are you really such a fool?" Swinging himself down from the horse, the boy advanced on her. "You cannot outrun us. Nor can you be in these woods when night falls."

Emeline tried to scramble backwards, away from him, only to find herself stuck, her Blundstone lodged snugly in the very root system that tripped her.

When she tried to tug herself free, she couldn't.

Dammit.

She maneuvered her foot out of the boot, intending to escape that way, but froze when a cool shadow slid over her.

Emeline glanced up.

He crouched down.

She lay beneath him now, on a bed of ashy leaves, propped on her elbows. He held himself over her as restrained fury blazed across his face.

"Get on the horse, Emeline, or I will be forced to *put* you on the horse."

Above him white branches rattled, and silvery leaves tumbled to the forest floor, like snow falling from the sky.

"I'm afraid of horses," she told him. "I'm not getting on one."

It was mostly true. Certainly true when it came to horses with raging infernos for eyes.

He ran a hand through his dark hair and released an irritated breath. "Lament is well trained and well behaved."

Emeline glanced over his shoulder, to where the golden-eyed horse watched them. *Lament.* A vision of flickering flames rose up in Emeline's mind. Had she imagined that fire as the horse descended on her?

Eyeing the beast—which had to be the size of a small elephant—Emeline said, "I don't know how to ride."

"Not a problem." He rose to his full height, then turned to the twisted, hoary roots where her boot was lodged. With one easy tug, it came free. "You'll be riding with me."

Emeline sat up. "Yes, you said that already. And it wasn't a comfort the first time."

He held out the Blundstone. She stared at her boot, speckled with mud, trying to think of something—anything—to convince him to take her to the Wood King.

She tried to remember Tom's stories about the king's walled city deep in the forest, the gate hidden from human eyes. Tom found a way in—or so he believed. Had he ever told her how?

Emeline wished she could recall more of his ramblings.

"I'd prefer to walk," she said after taking the boot and pulling it on. She got to her feet and dusted the dead leaves from her jeans. "If you could lead me to the city gate, I'll find my way from there."

His knuckles bunched at his sides. "Did you not hear a word I said?"

She shrugged.

He looked truly annoyed. As if he were considering not just abandoning her to the stampeding ember mares but throwing her into their path. "Fine. *If* you get on the horse, I'll take you to the gate. All right? But we cannot tarry here any longer." He pointed to the darkened canopy above. "The sun is down. We must go *now*."

He didn't wait to hear her answer. He simply grabbed her hips in both hands and lifted her without warning. Easily. Swiftly. Up onto the saddle. Startled by his strength, she didn't fight him. Only landed with a jolt, her weight settling on Lament, her legs hanging down the horse's left side.

Unfair, she thought, then froze as the beast swayed beneath her. Fearing a fall, Emeline reached for the saddle's leather edge with one hand and the horse's woolly mane with the other, gripping both very hard.

The whole world looked different from this vantage point.

Mostly more terrifying.

She stared at the ground—far, far below her. Too far. She would definitely break something if she fell.

Lament turned her head, scrutinizing her new rider with one golden eye. Suddenly, all Emeline could think about was the size of those hooves and the sound of her own bones cracking after the horse tossed her off and galloped across her body while she lay sprawled on the forest floor.

She could see exactly how this day would end.

"Are you all right?"

"Um," she managed.

His hands still held her hips, stabilizing her. "Unless you prefer to ride sidesaddle, I recommend one leg on either side."

From atop his demon steed, any desire to defy him fled. Emeline nodded. Willing this all to be over, yearning to be at the king's gate and forever rid of this horse and her rider, Emeline slowly turned herself, lifting her right leg up and over the other side. Both her hands fisted in Lament's mane, the strands thick and wiry against her fingers.

He put his foot into the stirrup. The saddle lurched slightly to the left when he pushed up, making Emeline cling harder. As he settled behind her and his thighs pressed against her own, panic morphed into something else. Her body temperature rose as she became aware of him—how solid and steady and close he was.

One of his hands reached around her to take Lament's reins; the other slid across her waist, pulling her gently against him.

A startling warmth spread through her belly.

"Are you ready?"

No, she thought, relieved that he couldn't see her blushing face.

He was escorting her to the gate, she reminded herself. She could ride with him if it meant finding the Wood King and bringing Pa home. And then she would never have to see him again.

"Okay. Yes. I'm ready."

With a simple nudge of his heels, the horse lurched forward. Emeline's grip tightened in Lament's mane, every muscle in her body going rigid as they began to trot through the silvered trees.

Lament's trot soon became a canter. Her canter, a gallop. The forest blurred around them as they picked up speed, blazing through copses and thickets, the rhythm of the horse's hooves drumming like thunder.

Despite the stinging wind rushing past them, it wasn't cold. Heat radiated from Lament's black coat, and when Emeline looked down she found red flames flickering in the horse's mane. Tongues of fire engulfed Emeline's fingers, licking her skin. She jerked her hands free, staring in horror. But her fingers were unsinged.

Holy cats!

Was Lament an ember mare?

It was impossible. The wild, unearthly horses were forged of fire and said to be uncatchable. Untamable. In no story she knew had one ever been ridden.

But Emeline had thought shadow skins impossible too.

The pungent tang of smoke smoldered in the air. They were out of the Stain—nothing dead surrounded them here. The forest was lush and green and living. But in the distance, Emeline saw red.

Fire.

It surged towards them from the right, spreading quickly. Emeline was about to cry out in alarm, in case the boy at her back hadn't seen it, when she heard the sound of hoofbeats. Hundreds of them. Pummeling the earth in time with Lament's.

Wait.

Emeline squinted into the distance.

It wasn't a forest fire advancing on them. It was a massive herd of ember mares. Their black bodies raged red, like burning coal, and their manes smoldered with bright flames. They were stampeding, headed straight for Lament with no sign of slowing or stopping.

Lament picked up speed. But even Emeline could tell she wasn't fast enough. In mere seconds, they were going to be trampled. As if sensing this, the rider at her back leaned forward, his arm tightening around her waist.

Emeline reached again for the horse's fiery mane—which was warm, but not blisteringly so. Her hands remained unburnt. Holding on tight, she squeezed her eyes shut as her heart hammered in her throat.

The galloping hooves roared in her ears. The encroaching heat of their bodies seemed to scorch her skin.

Any moment, Lament would be broadsided. They would be trampled.

"Emeline," a rough-soft voice whispered in her ear. "Don't be afraid."

Don't be afraid? Now was exactly the time to be afraid. She opened her eyes intending to tell him so, but the words died on her lips.

All around them, ember mares rushed *alongside* Lament. They had never intended to trample her but to join her. The graceful rhythm of their muscular bodies, the thunder in their hooves as they ran . . . they mesmerized Emeline. Moving as one, they reminded her of a cresting wave. A sea of fire.

And beyond their blazing splendor, all was black.

Night had fallen in the woods.

In the steady rhythm of Lament's gait, Emeline heard assurances she'd been too frightened to hear before. *I have you,* Lament's hooves pounded out. *I am steady and true. I won't let you fall.*

Emeline calmed, leaning against the boy at her back. Her vision filled with flames as the sheer joy of the run infected her, making her grin.

"Still afraid of horses?"

When he wasn't being surly, his voice was resonant and deep. A pleasant baritone.

She looked over her shoulder to see his mouth quirk upwards in the light of the horses. Her eyes lifted and their gazes caught. No trace of anger lingered in him, as if the heady rush of the running horses had pierced his hard exterior and he'd been forced to let down his walls.

Why do you feel so familiar? she thought as she studied him.

Too soon, the herd began to slow, then fall back, whinnying as they did. One by one, the horses turned west. Lament didn't go with them; she kept to her path, running north.

The thunder quieted. The darkness returned. Soon, Lament was slowing.

Then stopping.

Not at any gate, though.

Emeline frowned as the horse stepped across the tree line and out of the woods, shaking her black mane. Her breath puffed like smoke, her haunches steamed like hot stones, but the flames in her eyes were gone.

Looming before them was Pa's house—the kitchen lights on from when Emeline left in a rush. The sleeping garden was quiet and still.

"But . . ."

Behind her, the boy dismounted, leaving her alone in the saddle. Emeline's thoughts spun, trying to make sense of it. His two strong hands clasped her waist and dragged her down.

"You said . . ."

As her feet hit the ground, realization set in. That startling joy from a moment ago shattered like glass.

She spun to find him already remounting.

"You *lied* to me."

"Think of it more as a favor," he said, back astride his horse. The moon and stars sparkled in the sky above him, making him appear more majestic than he deserved. "You're looking in the wrong place."

"You're lying to me still!"

The only place Pa could be was in those woods. She knew it now. After being attacked by a shadow skin, after riding with ember mares—Emeline was certain.

She needed to get him back.

Fury and anguish warred within her. She seized Lament's bridle, stopping the boy and his horse from retreating. Her grip tightened around the straps.

"Tell me your name." The words were bitter in her mouth. "So I can find you and pay you back for this."

He leaned over the saddle, staring down at her. His face was inches from hers as he said, "Go home, Emeline."

He clicked his tongue twice. In response, Lament reared up, reminding Emeline that this was no ordinary horse. She swiftly released the bridle and stepped back.

Turning Lament, he disappeared through the space in the hedge, where Emeline's tree was once rooted.

His words floated back to her from the darkness: "Live your life. Forget the woods."

The night was suddenly silent and still around her.

As if he'd never been there at all.

EIGHT

EMELINE WANTED TO SCREAM.

Instead, she picked up a rock and threw it at the gap in the tree line. She threw a second rock. Then a third. When none of them made her feel better, she turned and marched around the side of Pa's house, storming into the garage.

Horrible, wretched boy. She would not let him stop her. She'd return to the woods, find the king's gate, and bring back her grandfather. *Tonight.* Because after she'd faced down a shadow skin and ridden an ember mare, Emeline had to believe that Pa was in the hands of the Wood King—and she was going after him.

Mounds of boxes bordered the walls, all of them full of her and Pa's belongings, hastily labeled and packed by Emeline when she'd first put the house on the market. She moved past them, heading for Pa's workbench, trying to remember where he kept his yellow flashlight.

Halfway there, her phone buzzed several times from her back pocket. Emeline paused and pulled it out.

Notifications flooded the screen, mainly texts from Joel. But the most recent was an update from Elegy—the app she and her songwriter used to share music files back and forth.

The notification read: *Chloe Demarche uploaded a file to your shared folder.*

Chloe was her songwriter. Emeline hadn't written—or performed—a song of her own in almost two years. These days, she only sang Chloe's songs.

Emeline swallowed the bitter taste that accompanied this fact, then nudged the notification aside and quickly scanned Joel's texts.

The first read: *Great news! The Perennials added another stop to your tour!*

The second: *Did you get Edwin's email?*

Edwin was the drummer for The Perennials and also Joel's best friend.

He wants you to read through the revised schedule and make sure you're good with the new date.

Joel's last text simply read: *You okay?*

She decided to respond later—she had a flashlight to find. As she slid the phone back into her pocket, it buzzed again. Emeline fished it out.

Incoming call from: Joel White

Heaving a sigh, she pressed TALK and lifted the phone to her ear.

"Hi," she growled, pulling open drawers.

"Wow, nice to hear from you too."

She winced, paused her searching, then rubbed her forehead with her free hand. "Sorry. I . . . It's been a rough day. I'm sorry."

"Everything okay?"

She shook her head, suddenly wishing he weren't seven hours away and instead was right here so she could pretend everything was fine. Just for a minute. Pressing her hip to the bench as she leaned against it, Emeline hooked her free hand around her waist. "I wish this were over."

She should be at the Merchant Alehouse right now, singing.

She should be crawling into Joel's bed later tonight, safe in his arms.

That's how you felt about the last guy too, said a voice in her head. Craig. The brown-eyed fiddler in the Irish trad band. She came for his fiddling, stayed for his dimples.

It's how she felt about all the others before that. Others who never lasted long.

"How about I finish up here," Joel was saying, "and then I'll hop on a train tomorrow."

"No," said Emeline, a bit too forcefully, remembering why she'd come into the garage. She needed a flashlight. She supposed she could use her phone's flashlight app, except it would drain the battery. And if she got lost in the woods, she'd need her phone to call for help. "I'm fine. Besides, don't you have a show this weekend?"

"We'll be back in time for my show."

Would they? She touched the tithe marker in her pocket. She had no idea how long it would take to find the King's City and get Pa back.

She pulled out another drawer, shoved aside boxes of nails and screws and oil-stained rubber bands, then shut it. She pulled out the next one.

Ah-ha!

There was the flashlight. Sitting between an old ball of twine and a measuring tape.

Emeline pulled it out and shut the drawer.

There were the shadow skins to contend with too, though. She'd run into one tonight. What if she ran into another? She needed to arm herself. But with what?

Pa used an ax to split wood. If she could remember where he kept it . . .

She heard Joel crack his knuckles on the other end of the line, then stretch. "Besides, I deserve a few vacation days."

Emeline paused, hearing the resolution in his voice. Panic pricked her like a needle. When Joel made his mind up about a thing, there was no changing it. He did what he wanted to do. Always.

"Don't come all the way out here," she said, walking over to where Pa's tools hung in neat rows down the wall. "I know you have these quaint ideas about small towns, but trust me: they're not your style."

She stood a little beyond the light of the workbench, remembering where the ax usually hung: below the hammers. Emeline scanned down the row. But the space beneath was empty. The ax was gone.

Emeline chewed her lip. *Where would he put it?*

"Fine," Joel huffed. "But if you change your mind, even if it's three am, call me, all right? Call me if you need me."

"I'll call you if I need you," she repeated.

"I love you, Em."

Those words froze her in place.

Emeline only ever spoke those words to the rare few who deserved them: Pa, Tom, Maisie. People who'd raised her and loved her unconditionally. Saying the words to Joel would turn their casual hookups into something very different. Something she didn't want.

Too much time had passed. Emeline needed to say something back. But all she could manage was, "Okay. Thanks."

Joel sighed from the other end. "Try to get some sleep."

The moment he hung up, Emeline pushed the conversation out of her mind and gripped Pa's flashlight hard in her hand. She needed to find that ax and get back to the woods.

South, the trees had told her. *Follow the river.*

She didn't stop to think about how taking directions from trees was not something rational people did. If she thought like that, she might not go back in. And Emeline knew in her blood and bones and sinew that Pa wasn't on this side of the tree line. So, if she needed to take directions from freaking trees, that's what she would do.

"Where the heck is that ax?"

"This ax?" a voice said archly from behind her.

Emeline spun, her heart pounding.

A figure stood in the doorway leading out of the garage. The shape of Pa's wood-splitting ax hung loose at their side. Emeline held up the old yellow flashlight and pressed the ON button. It clicked, but nothing happened.

She pressed again.

Still nothing.

Because of course.

"What exactly do you plan on using it for?" The figure raised the ax, turning it back and forth in their hand, examining its sharpened edge.

"Who are you?" Emeline demanded.

The figure stepped out of the doorway and into the garage. Emeline stepped quickly back and bumped into the corner of Pa's workbench. It shuddered. Loose nails scattered and fell, clinking to the floor. Emeline glanced to the wall lined with tools. If this person came any closer, she would lunge for one of the hammers.

They didn't come closer. Instead, they reached up and tugged. The lightbulb overhead *flick-flick-flickered* to life, revealing a boy standing in the glow.

A glossy black raven perched on his shoulder.

He was tall and thin, all straight lines and elegant edges. Thick obsidian hair fell into his eyes, which were deepest brown, and his clothes were the same polished black as the raven's feathers.

His shadow gave him away. Twisting behind him, the dark outline revealed an inhuman shape: a winged and taloned form.

You can always tell a shiftling by their shadow.

The corners of his mouth danced with mischief. "My name is Rooke. I hear you're looking for passage to the king's gate."

NINE

"I CAN TAKE YOU STRAIGHT to the Wood King, if that's what you desire."

Emeline yearned to say yes, that was exactly what she desired. But she didn't. Because the back of her neck was prickling. She remembered the ember mare and her rider—the nameless boy who'd tricked her. *Lied* to her. Would this shiftling do the same? He might lure Emeline into the woods with a promise of taking her to find her grandfather and lead her somewhere else instead. To her death, maybe.

"I know what you are." Emeline watched the ever-changing shadow on the floor as she grabbed one of Pa's hammers, her fingers tightening around the smooth wooden handle. "Why should I trust you?"

Rooke stared her down, crossed his arms, and smirked. "Because if you don't, you'll never get to the King's City alive."

It was the same thing the liar had told her: *There are horrors here far worse than any nightmare. It's only a matter of time before another one finds you.*

Emeline could go in alone, follow the trees' directions, and hope she didn't run into another shadow skin. Or get trampled by ember mares. Or . . . worse. Whatever worse was.

Or she could go with this shiftling, who may or may not intend to betray her.

If Rooke was trustworthy, joining him was the preferable option, obviously. If Rooke was a shiftling, he would know exactly where the Wood King's palace was. It was her best chance of finding Pa.

And if he isn't trustworthy?

Emeline would need to keep her guard up. If she got a whiff of treachery, she could always lose him. Run. Find the river and follow it. She just needed some kind of surety. . . .

Emeline set down the hammer on Pa's workbench.

"I'll come with you on one condition." She nodded to the ax in his hand. "You let me carry *that*."

"Take it then." In one fluid motion, he flipped the ax, caught the sharpened head, and held it out to her. "Now let's go."

EMELINE SLID HER THUMB carefully across the ax's paper-thin edge. Judging by its sharpness, someone had recently honed it. Tom, maybe? Tom was the kind of man who took care of his tools. He'd been chopping wood for Pa, along with doing the other farm chores, for several years, steadily taking on more the less Pa could do.

If Tom did it, Emeline silently thanked him. Because the deeper she followed Rooke into the forest, the warier she became, and the more comfort she took in its sharp edge. Night cloaked the woods in darkness and Emeline had left the defunct flashlight behind, which forced her to follow this shiftling nearly blind. Worse: judging by the stars flickering above—

disappearing as the leafy canopy grew thicker, reappearing as it thinned out—they were *not* heading south.

Rooke's raven companion flew ahead, cawing back at him every few minutes, acting as some kind of lookout. Rooke paused when he heard the bird's call, then advanced or pivoted depending on whatever instruction it gave.

It was eerie and animal-like, the way boy and bird conversed without words.

When they were well and truly off course and Emeline was fairly certain the shiftling was leading her into some kind of trap, she halted. "Why are we heading west?"

From up ahead, Rooke said, "Trust me. This is the quickest route."

Emeline's grip tightened around the ax's wooden handle. "Except the gate is south."

"You want to take the gate? Be my guest." She could almost hear him shrug. "It's a three-day walk from the tree line, and you'll likely be eaten before you arrive."

Emeline frowned. Was he lying? Or had the trees failed to mention that part?

"If you'd prefer to remain alive, however, there's an entry point just ahead. We'd be there already if not for your dawdling."

Entry point?

Suddenly, Rooke thrust out his arm and Emeline walked straight into it.

They stood at the edge of a wooden platform that jutted out over a stagnant swamp, the surface of which was broken only by dark, twisted stumps. Pale starlight flooded down, unimpeded by any canopy, reflecting off the murky water.

"Stay quiet," said Rooke. "I'll do the talking."

His footsteps echoed on the wooden ledge, the muck sucking softly on its edges. The water shifted suddenly, and Emeline got the eerie impression they were no longer alone.

"*Trespasser!*" hissed a wet and rushing voice.

"Settle down, Bog." The damp, sour air muted Rooke's voice. "It's me."

Silence bled around them.

"*Rooke?*" The thing called Bog slurped his name, almost affectionately.

Up from the mire, Bog came. As if it were pulling itself together from the swamp bed. Its crude shape mimicked the body of a person—only it was thrice as big as a person—with lumps for shoulders, stones for eyes, and a gaping mouth.

Emeline stared at the muddy form rising out of the sludge, suddenly realizing what this was. *An earth spirit?* The only thing she remembered from Edgewood's stories about the damp, crotchety things was that if you wandered into their territory without an offering, you weren't wandering out again.

"*What tasty morsel have you brought me?*"

Bog smacked its muddy lips, swishing closer to the ledge.

Tasty morsel?

You've got to be kidding me.

This was why Rooke wanted her: he needed an offering to get past Bog. Rooke was going to feed her to this earth spirit.

Emeline stepped back quickly, gripping the ax in both hands, raising it in front of her.

"*I will crunch her bones . . .*" Bog's voice rushed across the swamp. Mud rose up over the ledge of the platform, coming for Emeline, rising over her boots and up her ankles.

"*. . . and suck her marrow . . .*"

Before Emeline could turn and run, muddy hands grabbed hold of her calves, pulling her towards the swamp. She threw out her arms for balance, nearly dropping the ax, then felt a swift yank. She fell, bottom first, into the sludge covering the platform.

"*. . . and slurp her blood.*"

Bog dragged her towards the edge. It was going to suck her down into its depths.

At the last moment, Rooke stepped in front of Emeline, planting his feet in the mud between her and the swamp. "Not tonight, I'm afraid. I'm bringing her to the king."

The pulling stopped.

With nothing to struggle against, Emeline fell back into the slop. It was cold and thick and smelled like rancid leaves. Struggling to sit up, she shoved muddy strands of hair off her face. *Gross.*

Bog turned his attention on the shiftling.

"*You think to get free passage from me?*"

"I'm paying the entry price," said Rooke with a sigh. "For both of us."

Before Bog could protest, Rooke drew a small knife from his belt and swiftly slashed the edge of the blade across his palm. He crouched down, held his thin hand out over the swamp, and squeezed it into a fist. Blood dribbled down, like a spool of red thread, unwinding into the water.

Immediately, Bog's shape crumpled, seeping back into the swamp. A second later, its head came up—just below Rooke's fist.

Bog surged upwards, locking its muddy claws around Rooke's pale wrist, drawing his hand to its mouth. Emeline scrambled to her feet, watching in disgust as it sucked and sucked and sucked. Gorging on Rooke.

A sick feeling twisted in her stomach as Rooke's thin shoulders hunched and his eyelids drooped, the life draining out of him. From nearby, a raven cawed anxiously.

Rooke leaned slowly forward, losing consciousness, looking as if he were about to tumble face-first into the swamp.

It's going to drink him dry—

"Stop!" Emeline grabbed Rooke's bony shoulder and yanked him back, away from the earth spirit. Surprised, Bog released the shiftling's wrist. "I'll supply the rest."

Rooke murmured a protest, barely conscious. Emeline wiped her muddy palm on a clean patch of cardigan. Lifting the ax, she pressed its freshly sharpened edge to her skin, then pushed down and sliced hard.

Pain flashed as the blood welled up. Red and bright and glistening.

Emeline stepped to the end of the ledge and held it out for the earth spirit to take.

Bog's cold, wet grip tightened on her arm. Emeline watched as it drew her whole hand into its dark mouth, greedily sucking. The blood rushed out of her with startling force and Emeline had to bite down on her lip to keep from crying out.

Too soon, she felt weightless. Dizzy. The woods began to spin and Emeline felt herself tip. Surely, Bog had taken enough. She was going to faint if it didn't stop soon.

She tried to tug her wrist free, but her strength was draining away, and Bog only clasped her tighter.

Awk!

Rooke's raven friend careened out of the trees, inky feathers winking in the starlight as it dived at the earth spirit, taking angry slashes at Bog's muddy face with its talons.

Awk! Awk!!

Bog spit out Emeline's hand. *"Bah!"* It swatted at the bird, which soared in circles, dodging the blows.

"Enough, then!" Bog grumbled. *"The price is paid."*

It lowered itself back into the swamp. And then, as if drawing up its skirts, the earth spirit pulled back its fens. The brown tepid water retreated to reveal two wooden steps leading down to a rotting boardwalk. It curved out over the water, disappearing into the distant trees.

Still feeling light-headed, Emeline crouched to help Rooke up. Pulling the shiftling's arm around her shoulders, she rose to her feet, bringing him with her. He was thinner and lighter than she realized, his bony frame reminding her of a bird.

He was also a bloody, muddy mess—they both were. But she'd worry about that later.

Emeline's soggy boots squished beneath her as she slowly helped Rooke down the steps and along the rotting boardwalk. Soon, the trees crowded in close.

Hoary gray vines sagged from their branches. As Emeline ducked and batted them aside, she caught sight of Rooke's hand, where mud and blood were already drying in the cold night air.

"Why are you helping me?" she asked.

Rooke stiffened against her. "Are you sure that's what I'm doing?"

Despite his obvious fatigue, he pushed away from Emeline. He looked formidable, suddenly. Like something straight out of one of Tom's stories.

"You might think differently once this night is through."

Emeline's footsteps slowed. *What is that supposed to mean?* She wasn't sure she wanted to know.

They soon arrived at a particularly thick patch of vines, hung like a curtain across their path. Rooke pulled it aside and bowed his head to her.

"After you."

When Emeline passed through, she didn't step onto boardwalk, but flagstones. She paused, disoriented. The darkness of the woods morphed into soft, dewy lamplight and the sourwater smell of Bog was replaced by the perfumed scent of late-blooming roses.

They'd stepped out of a swamp and into . . . a city.

Before her lay a quiet, cobbled street lined by white row houses, many of them creeping with green ivy. The city stretched out, its streets rising and twisting towards the top of a lush green hill thick with trees. Emeline caught glimpses of rust-red rooftops and stone bridges over steep canals, of a white-bricked bell tower and a wide blue lake.

At the crest of the hill, a fortress crowned the city, gleaming like ivory in the starlight.

It was just as Tom had described it.

"The Wood King's palace," she whispered.

TEN

AN UNKINDNESS OF RAVENS flew overhead as Rooke escorted Emeline through the dark and winding streets of the King's City. Few people were out at this hour of the night, but those who were kept stealing glances at the mud-coated shiftling and his human companion.

Am I dreaming this?

Maybe she hadn't escaped Bog. Maybe she was still back in the swamp, unconscious from blood loss, and all of this was a hallucination.

Except her hand throbbed from where she'd sliced it with Pa's ax and she could feel the mud hardening and cracking, drying out her skin. She couldn't hallucinate those details.

When they neared the palace, the path turned to shining white pebbles bordered by rows of weeping willows as high as three-story houses. A white wall encircled the palace, creeping with lichen and moss and rising to twice Emeline's height. It was set with a copper gate, shut tight. The ravens flew towards it, their black forms settling on its copper ligaments as Emeline and Rooke approached. In the middle, a crest was cast in silver portraying a crowned willow sprouting from a seed.

Four armed guards—*hedgemen,* Rooke told her—stood outside the entrance. Their hammered bronze helmets were shaped like milkweed pods, and the halberds gripped at their sides rose ominously upwards, the steel tips shimmering strangely.

"This borderlander requires an audience with the king," a muddy Rooke explained.

The guards exchanged cautious looks. "Is he expecting her?"

Rooke ignored their question. "I doubt very much you want to delay her."

Two of the guards crossed their arms, their gazes narrowing. As if they were well acquainted with Rooke and didn't trust him for a second. "And why's that?"

"She has something the king desperately needs."

What? This was news to Emeline, who turned to study the boy beside her. His expression was opaque as marble, giving nothing away.

Was he lying to get her inside?

Rooke held up a hand, studying his mud-encrusted finger-nails. "You know how unstable he is these days. *I* wouldn't want to cross him. But perhaps you—"

The creak of copper interrupted him as the gate slowly swung inwards.

"This way," said one, leading them both inside as another followed at their backs.

They swept down alabaster hallways lit by candles, their flames burning like fireflies as wax dribbled down their sides. Rooke fell silent beside her, chewing his lip and tapping his fin-gertips anxiously against his thigh. When he glanced at Eme-line, his expression turned apologetic. As if he was suddenly having second thoughts.

Emeline, who had heard the gate shut and lock behind them, knew it was too late to turn back. Not that she wanted to. She'd made it this far; she wasn't leaving until the king gave her grandfather back.

Emeline reached inside her cardigan pocket and squeezed the cold tithe marker. Yesterday, she didn't believe in a king of the wood, or that her grandfather had been tithed. Didn't believe in ember mares, or shiftlings, or earth spirits. Pa was simply an old man with dementia who sometimes wandered at night.

And today?

She wasn't sure what she believed today.

Emeline couldn't remember when, exactly, things changed. Only that a moment ago she was walking down palace halls and now she walked a dirt path beneath a midnight sky. Tulip trees lined the path, their flowers unfolding like burning yellow crowns among their green leaves.

The farther they walked, the taller the trees grew, until they were impossibly tall. So tall, they seemed to brush the stars.

The path ended in a grove of silver birches. Moonlight pooled in from the canopy above, illuminating a bone-white throne and a man seated upon it. Atop his head sat a crown of rosebud thorns.

His skin was sunbrowned, his hair moon pale; and instead of robes, water adorned him. It flowed in rivers from his hair, over his neck and shoulders where it began to gush, like a waterfall, down the rest of his body. Emeline could see no glimpse of skin beyond the cascade, but at his feet water pooled and sank into the brown earth. Wherever it touched, gray and purple thistles grew.

The Wood King.

Their guards stopped them ten paces from the throne and bowed low. Rooke poked Emeline hard in the back, making her wince before she realized that she, too, was expected to bow.

When the hedgemen stepped back, the Wood King leaned forward in his throne. His liquid gaze slid over Emeline before darting to the shiftling at her side.

"What have you brought me?" His voice sounded old, like dust and earth.

"*This*"—Rooke swept out a slender hand—"is Emeline Lark."

The king's honed gaze felt like an arrow pulled taut across a bowstring, aimed straight at her heart. Beneath it, Emeline felt like cornered prey. Vulnerable and exposed before this ancient thing.

"Come closer."

She did as he commanded, her footsteps crunching the fallen yellow leaves on the path. The cloying smell of magic swelled in the air here, like rotting bones.

When she stopped three paces from his throne, she saw that the king's eyes were the color of liquid ink from corner to corner. Instead of irises, a white crescent moon burned at the center of each eye.

"Why have you come here, dustling?"

There was something cold and dead in those eyes. It made her throat shrivel. Unable to summon her voice, Emeline pulled the small orb from her pocket and held it out to him.

A rippling murmur echoed through the grove behind her. Emeline turned to see people emerging from the shadows of the trees, gathering to cluster and stare. Clothed in leather and fine wool, delicate lace and soft silk, they held themselves with moonlit grace. Their eyes shone too bright and their shadows twisted behind them, hinting at other shapes.

They were . . . not quite human.

Remembering Tom's stories, Emeline knew this was the shiftling court.

I'm really here, she thought, resisting the urge to pinch herself. *All the stories were true.*

Emeline turned back to the king. He held out his palm, which was lined and weathered like an autumn leaf, his nails thick and chipped like bark. As water streamed down his wrists, dripping to the earth below, Emeline willed her hand not to shake as she placed the tiny orb onto his palm.

He raised it to catch the starlight. It glowed milky white.

"You came all this way . . . to return my marker?"

"No," she managed. "I've come for my grandfather."

Those eerie eyes narrowed. His fist closed hard and swift, swallowing the orb.

"And with what do you intend to barter?"

Barter?

Emeline tried to remember the stories she'd grown up with. But in no story had anyone ever sought out the Wood King to demand back their tithe. She had no idea what to offer. Tithes were, by definition, a sacrifice. They were supposed to *cost* you something. Your favorite milking cow. Your best and only three-piece suit. The last note your mother ever wrote you before she died.

What are my most precious possessions?

"My guitar," she realized aloud. It was a Taylor, top of the line, and given to her by an anonymous fan. The instrument had been delivered to the green room before her very first music festival, with wildflowers woven through the strings. Emeline had assumed it was a gift from Pa, except her grandfather couldn't afford such a gift and when she called to thank him, he didn't know what she was referring to.

She loved her mysterious Taylor like a pet, and more important: she needed it to do her job. But she could buy another. She would just have to put it on credit and pay it off gradually. "I can give you my guitar."

Several people in the crowd behind her laughed nervously, the sound chiming like discordant bells.

Heat crept up Emeline's cheeks.

"Or my car?" she blurted out. The one she and Pa saved up to buy before she moved away.

That car had taught her the value of hard work and sacrifice. And, in its way, represented the love of her grandfather, reminding her of him every time she got in—like his cardigans, which she borrowed and never returned. More than this, though: She needed it for her out-of-town gigs. To drive her to and from festivals.

The Wood King continued to stare at her, eyes narrowing. "These things are of equal value to your grandfather?"

What?

"Of course not. No."

Nothing was of equal value to Pa. That was the point. It was why she was here, demanding him back.

But what else could she offer?

"I have a proposition," Rooke interrupted from behind her.

The king did not look away from Emeline. His prolonged attention made her skin prickle.

"Proceed."

Rooke stepped up beside Emeline, brushing his black hair out of his eyes. "I have it on good authority that Emeline is a singer of some repute."

The king's head swung towards Rooke. "Is this true?"

Emeline was about to answer yes, that singing was how she made her living, then quickly stopped herself.

What if the Wood King took her voice?

Can he do that?

She hesitated. Was she willing to exchange her voice—the very thing she used to make her living, to pursue her passion, to realize her dreams—if it meant she could take Pa and go home?

Without her voice, what would she have to go back to? Not a singing career. Without her voice, her whole life would cease to have meaning. Her biggest, oldest dream would be smashed on the rocks.

She'd thought none of this through. She hadn't considered what, exactly, might be taken from her in exchange for getting her grandfather back.

"Yes," she said, ashamed of the tremble in her voice. "I can sing."

A smile bent Rooke's mouth, as if he was playing some game neither she nor anyone else was in on. "Well then. I believe I've found your solution."

Sweat beaded down Emeline's spine.

Please no, she thought, looking from Rooke's twitching lips to the king on his gleaming throne. *Don't take my voice.*

"You're in need of a new court minstrel," Rooke continued. "Seeing as the last one—"

He cut himself off as the king's gaze darkened and those bark-like hands coiled into ragged fists.

"What if," Rooke moved quickly on, "in exchange for her grandfather's freedom, Emeline Lark takes his place in your court—as your new singer?"

"What?" Emeline whirled on him. "No. I can't . . ."

She had a life to return to. Weekly gigs. An upcoming tour opening for The Perennials. And a contract with Daybreak Records hanging in the balance.

It was everything she'd worked so hard for.

"I can't stay here," said Emeline. "I *won't* stay here."

The Wood King's lip curled as he sat back in his throne. "If she were a human male, of course I would consider it. But seeing as she's . . ."

"Forgive my impertinence, my lord, but perhaps that's the problem: you only ever take the men, and they only ever displease you."

Emeline stared at Rooke. What did *that* mean?

The air tingled then, making her skin itch. The damp, rotten smell of magic intensified. She took a nervous step backwards, wanting to put distance between her and the king, but her shoulders brushed against the armor of the hedgeman she hadn't known was standing behind her.

She glanced back. The guard grinned beneath the rim of his helmet, revealing rows of sharpened teeth.

Emeline shuddered and stepped quickly forward again.

"Why not try her?" Rooke pressed. "If her singing displeases you, you can do away with her like all the others." He flicked his fingers, as if flicking away a bug. "You have little to lose."

Do away with me? She glared at Rooke. But he had warned her, hadn't he? Back in the swamp, when she'd thanked him for his help.

The king drummed his fingers slowly, the cracked nails clicking on the arm of his white throne. He looked from Rooke to Emeline.

Meeting his cold, calculating stare, she managed to say, "And if I refuse?"

Silence followed her question. The courtiers gathered at the edges of the grove stopped talking.

Suddenly, the king threw back his head and laughed. The sound boomed through the clearing like thunder, shaking the earth at her feet. Rooke glanced her way, and there was pity in his gaze.

The Wood King snapped his fingers at something in the distance. Emeline turned to find armed hedgemen dragging someone out of the crowd of murmuring courtiers.

"N-no," stammered a too-familiar voice. "S-stop. W-where are you t-taking me?"

The guards shoved their prisoner into the middle of the grove. The old man stumbled in the starlight. His gray hair was mussed, his blue shirt wrinkled.

Pa.

"W-where's Rose?" Her grandfather's voice was loud and frantic. "Where's my Rose?"

Her heart snagged in her throat. He always asked for Emeline's mother when he was frightened and confused.

When she caught sight of the thick green vines binding his wrists, anger flooded her. He was a harmless old man. There was no need to restrain him.

"Take those off!"

When no one did, Emeline moved to do it herself. The guard at her back grabbed her wrists, halting her. Hot fingers dug into her skin.

She tried to twist free. Tried to elbow her captor in the ribs, but the guard only yanked both arms up her back. Pain lanced like lightning from her fingers to her shoulder blades, shocking her into submission.

Helpless, she watched Pa cower before the advancing guards. Two stepped forward, forcing him to his knees in the dirt with their spears.

"Don't touch him!"

She struggled, but the guard only tightened his hold.

"Emeline." Rooke's voice was edged with unease. "Don't make this worse."

"Help him," she breathed. "Please. Help him."

"Only you can help him now."

Her eyes filled with furious tears. Her grandfather blurred before her.

"Choose, Emeline Lark," the Wood King boomed. "Be my minstrel and save his life; or refuse and watch him die."

Die? Emeline shook her head. Her next words sounded small and scared: "You can't . . ."

"Can't? Am I not *king of the wood?*"

His voice grew shrill as a whistling wind as he rose to his feet, the water gushing faster and thicker around him, flowing down the steps of his throne, rushing over the grass like a tide. Something desperate and wild scrabbled through her as the king stepped down, moving towards Pa. Like a predator closing in on its quarry.

Her grandfather lifted his head, blue eyes wide with fear as he knelt in the shadow of the king.

"You *will* be my new court minstrel, or I will take him into the Stain and feed him to the shadow skins while you watch."

Emeline's spine straightened. The very thought of that thing she'd met in the woods tonight, inside Pa's mind, killing him slowly with his own terror . . .

She would never let that happen.

But staying here in the Wood King's court? Forever?

It would require giving up *everything*: the life she was building, her budding music career. She'd worked so hard to get where she was; she couldn't give it up now.

Maybe there's a way to do both.

To save her grandfather and keep her dream.

If Emeline agreed to be the king's singer, Pa would go free. Once he was safe, all she'd need to do was find a way to escape. Rooke had gotten her inside the city; surely, Emeline could find a way to get herself out—preferably before her tour started.

Maybe she didn't have to lose everything.

Maybe she could save Pa *and* herself.

She calmed her trembling voice until it was smooth as a river stone. "I'll stay and be your minstrel. Just let my grandfather go."

Emeline's guard loosened his grip on her wrists but didn't release her.

The king's crescent pupils burned into her. "You do not make commands," he said. "Your grandfather will remain here until you demonstrate your suitability for the position. When I am satisfied that you are sufficiently biddable, and your singing acceptable, *then* Ewan Lark will return home. You have one week to impress me, singer. If you fail, I'll feed you both to the shadow skins."

One week?

This was bad.

The bronze-armored hedgemen grabbed Pa beneath his armpits and hauled him to his feet.

"Wait! Where are you taking him?" At her voice, Pa turned his head. From the look in his startled eyes, he didn't recognize her. His mind was too clouded by terror.

"H-help me," he begged her.

Emeline struggled against her guard's hold, but his grip was a vise, forcing her to be still. She held her grandfather's gaze and made herself sound certain and calm.

"Everything is going to be okay. I'm going to get you home. I promise."

They shoved him onwards. Pa stumbled and looked down to his feet. Emeline watched as they led her trembling, stammering grandfather out of the grove, down the lantern-lit path, and into the night.

The moment she couldn't see him anymore, Emeline's guard released his grip on her. The shock set in, and her legs gave out. She fell to the cold ground, hands planted in the dirt.

What if I fail?

She couldn't fail. That was clear. Emeline needed to find a way to please the king and prove herself suitable—long enough to save Pa, at least.

And then she needed to escape. Somehow.

You are a professional musician, she told herself. *You can do this.*

"Emeline." Rooke crouched down beside her. "If you're ready, I'll take you to your rooms."

She glanced up into his pale face. His dark brown eyes shone with something like regret.

"You." Her hands fisted in the dirt. "This was your plan all along."

"Something like it, yes."

"But *why?*"

"You want to save him, don't you? This is the only way you can."

A sudden movement interrupted them, fluttering at the edge of her vision. Murmurs rippled through the crowd of courtiers.

"What is this?" said a rough-soft voice.

Emeline looked to find the crowd parting and someone familiar striding through. Maple-dark hair. River-rock eyes. The same boy she'd met in the woods earlier tonight. The one with the ember mare. The one who'd *lied* to her.

At the sight of Emeline, he halted, the lines of his body drawing tight and tense.

Dirt spilled from her fingers as she rose to her feet.

"Emeline," said Rooke, rising alongside her. "This is Hawthorne Fell. The king's tithe collector."

The words made Emeline's heart skip.

Tithe collector?

But that meant . . .

It meant the boy before her was the very one who'd whisked her grandfather away. The one who left the marker on Pa's pillow and then, when Emeline had pulled it out to prove he'd been stolen, pretended like he didn't recognize it.

He told her Pa wasn't in the woods. He told her she was looking in the wrong place.

How many times had he lied to her tonight?

Her blood turned to fire in her veins.

"You didn't tell her," Rooke murmured, seeing the murder in Emeline's eyes.

Trembling with anger, she jabbed her finger in the air towards the gray-eyed tithe collector. "This is *your fault,* asshole."

If he hadn't taken Pa, neither of them would be here, imprisoned in the Wood King's court.

None of this would have happened.

"My fault? If you . . ." Hawthorne's words faltered as his gaze swept over her muddy form, catching sight of the bloodied cut on her left hand. A frown thundered on his brow as he turned towards Rooke, who was also caked in mud. "Did *you* bring her here?"

Suddenly, a girl stepped up to Hawthorne's side, equal in age. Her russet-brown hair was pulled off her face in a messy braid. She was tall and lean, and her golden eyes shone in the darkness. Two long blades were sheathed at her back in a crisscross, and the sleeves of her rust-colored shirt were rolled to her elbows.

She looked almost feral, more wild creature than girl.

Emeline glanced to her shadow. Sure enough, the dark shape behind her had wolflike ears and sharp fangs.

A shiftling.

"Emeline," said Rooke. "This is Sable Thorne. Sable, this is Emeline Lark. The king's new singer."

"*What?*" Sable and Hawthorne said in unison. The former, shocked; the latter, furious.

Sable moved like the wind, grabbing the lapels of Rooke's coat and nearly lifting him off his feet. "What have you done?"

Rooke seemed entirely unfazed. As if he was used to being manhandled by Sable. Emeline couldn't tell if they were good friends, or mortal enemies.

"I'd love to catch you up, but I'm sure Emeline wishes to see her grandfather."

"*Rooke.*"

"If you'll excuse us." Peeling Sable's hands off him, Rooke turned towards Emeline, took her elbow gently between his fingers, and began leading her away.

Emeline glanced back once, shooting a murderous thought at the boy responsible for the mess she was in. *I will pay you back for this.*

He stared after her, looking far less sure of himself as he ran both hands uneasily through his hair. As if Emeline's presence here wasn't just unwelcome, but something far worse.

ELEVEN

ROOKE LED HER INTO dark rooms lit by dozens of candles, their flames illuminating a four-poster bed draped with white curtains. Its softness beckoned, reminding Emeline that she hadn't slept in forty-eight hours.

Next to a bay window seat inlaid with green and gold cushions sat a writing desk, and on the wall opposite the bed, musical instruments hung from copper pegs. Emeline found a seemingly endless assortment of guitars and ukuleles, as if the collection had been curated just for her. She tore herself away from the beauty of them.

At least my imprisonment will be comfortable.

In the center of the room, three attendants of varying sizes awaited: tall and solid, wispy and lithe, short and plump. Their skin tones ranged from chestnut brown to dewdrop white, and as soon as Rooke left, the women grabbed her wrists and pulled her into the washroom.

"Wait . . . no . . . I'm supposed to see my grandfather. . . ."

Emeline tried to fight them all the way to the copper tub, where they stripped her, then pushed her into the steaming rose-scented bathwater. It surged up and over the sides as Emeline fell in, splashing onto the tiled floor. Soft pink petals floated on the surface of the water, gathering around Emeline's shoulders and knees.

They forced her head under.

Emeline came up spluttering and gasping.

When she tried to escape, they did it again and again, until Emeline yielded and let them wash her. They soaped her mud-encrusted hair until her eyes burned with suds. They scrubbed her skin until it was raw.

"Where's my grandfather?"

They ignored her.

After they toweled her off, Emeline grudgingly let them dress her in a pale gold gown that fell to the floor. A trail of delicate poplar leaves was sewn into the bodice. The leaves, stitched in ivory thread, trailed gently along the boatneck collar, as if blown there by a breeze. They were so finely wrought, she could almost see them moving.

Next, the women braided her black hair into a knot at the nape of her neck, lacing it through with sprigs of Queen Anne's lace.

Last, they took her sliced palm and carefully salved it, then wrapped it tight with slender strips of gauzy white cotton, fastening it with a golden pin.

"There," said the curvy brown attendant, her voice like summer rain. A smile ghosted her soft lips as she turned Emeline to the gilt mirror. "Look."

In the polished smoky surface, Emeline found a stranger staring back. Gone was the broke musician who desperately needed new jeans, who wore her grandfather's oversized cardigan to keep him close, and who rarely remembered to brush her hair.

The girl standing in the mirror had stepped straight out of a story. Her black eyes were dark pools in her pale face, and her cheekbones were dusted with gold to match her dress.

She looked utterly foreign and strange.

Her eerie reflection reminded Emeline that once, she'd believed all of Edgewood's stories alongside Pa and Maisie and everyone else.

When did I stop believing them?

She couldn't remember.

While her attendants beamed at their finished work, nodding with approval, the pale, willowy woman opened the door leading out into the adjacent rooms. The other two slid Emeline's feet into silken white slippers, then ushered her through the door.

On the other side, two hedgemen stood guard. Each raised a finger to his lips.

A moment later, Emeline realized why.

Loud snores echoed throughout the warm room filled with growing green plants. On a table nearby sat a stack of newspapers and a deck of what looked like worn playing cards. Near the fire crackling in the hearth, bundled in a thick blue blanket, a gray-haired man slept in a rocking chair. Head slanted back, mouth hanging open.

Pa.

Emeline stepped quietly through the room, which smelled like burning spruce. Standing over him, she noticed how thin he'd become these past few years. He was sallow as a candlestick, and the color had been sapped from his hair.

Still, her heart swelled at the sight of him.

He used to do this when she was younger. Exhausted from working in the vineyards all day, he'd collapse in front of the television after dinner, fall asleep in his chair, then wake up grouchy and disoriented the next morning.

He seemed so peaceful, she didn't want to startle him. Not after the terrifying night he'd had. Instead, she quietly pulled up the second rocking chair and sat down, watching him sleep. His big, clasped hands were spotted with age and veins flowed like rivers beneath his skin—a testament to his hardworking life.

You could read that life in his body if you knew how to look. Emeline looked. She loved every crease in her grandfather's face, every spot of age. She loved the strength in his arms when they hugged her, crushing her breath from her lungs.

I miss you, she thought, her eyes prickling with tears. *So much.*

But it wasn't this man she missed; it was the one he'd once been. A man who remembered her name and whose eyes lit up at the sight of her. A man who made her peppermint tea when she was having a bad day, and sang her lullabies when she was scared of the dark, and carried her to bed when she fell asleep by the fire.

That man was gone.

Emeline bit down on her lip, willing herself not to cry as she rose to her feet. After snuffing all but one of the lamps, she came back and bent over his sleeping form. His gray hair glistened, still wet from a bath, and his skin smelled like soap.

"It's my job to take care of you now," she whispered. She'd done a shit job of it so far but was determined to do better.

Bending, Emeline gently kissed the top of his head.

Pa's snoring faltered and he jerked awake, sitting up in his chair.

"What . . . ?" He pulled away from her, confusion clouding his eyes. "Who are you? W-what are you doing here?"

Emeline drew immediately back, realizing her mistake. She'd startled him, and without the light of the lamps it was difficult for him to see.

"It's me." She tried to smile, hoping he would hear it in her voice. "Emeline."

His forehead scrunched into a nervous frown. *"Who?"*

"Emeline. Your—"

"You're one of *them*." His spotted hands gripped the blanket, bunching it hard, shaking ever so slightly. As if he was afraid of her.

An icy unease bled through her body. "Pa, no. I'm—"

His gaze darted fearfully around the room, searching the shadows. "Rose?" His voice shook. But it was only the two of them, and silence answered. *"Rose!"*

She flinched at her mother's name.

Emeline had never known her mother. She'd barely been a week old when Rose abandoned her, leaving in the middle of the night. Her mother packed no bags and left no notes. Ewan Lark found newborn Emeline alone in Rose's apartment, screaming in her cradle.

Now, Pa struggled to get out of the rocking chair. Emeline didn't know if she should step forward and help him, or if that would scare him further.

"Rose isn't here," she said softly. "She left, remember? Rose left us nineteen years ago."

As soon as the words were out of her mouth, Emeline wanted to push them back in.

It was the wrong thing to say.

As the flames flickered in the fireplace, Pa's face changed, turning white with fear. He pushed himself out of the rocking chair, stumbled, and nearly fell. The chair bounced furiously in his absence.

"I'm waiting for my daughter." He'd backed himself into a corner. "Rose is coming to take me home. I just want to go home. Please! Leave me be!"

Grief stabbed like a knife. Emeline tried to tell him again that it was her, his *granddaughter*. But at the terrified look in his eyes, her voice caught and her chin trembled.

Emeline could say it over and over, but it would do no good.

"Please, stay away from me!" He held up trembling hands. "Don't come any closer!"

The guards at his door moved towards Pa.

"No," said Emeline, throwing up her hands. "Please. I'll go. I'm the one he's afraid of."

Before the hot tears spilled down her cheeks, Emeline turned on her heel. Wrenching open the door between their rooms, she stepped through and shut it tight behind her. Sucking in a lungful of air, she fell back against the wood.

The man you knew and loved is gone, Emeline.

She shook Joel's voice from her head.

It isn't his fault. She gripped her arms, hugging hard. *He's frightened.*

But Emeline was frightened too. Not so long ago, it had been Pa who chased away her fears. Who told her she wasn't alone. Back when it had been just the two of them against the world.

And now?

With her shoulder blades pressed against the door, Emeline sank downwards until she hit the stone floor. Drawing her knees up to her chest, she buried her face in her soft silk gown.

An overwhelming wave of loneliness crashed through her.

I want to go home too, she thought.

This yearning, this ache—for someone to take her in their arms and tell her everything was going to be okay—was it so wrong? Was it weak to want to be taken care of, just for a day, or an hour, or even five minutes? The way Pa used to take care of her. *Before.*

Memories flooded her then, of the old Pa. The Pa who was not just a grandfather, but a father and teacher and friend. Strong and stern, loving and tender. Cleaning and bandaging a scrape on her knee. Letting her fall asleep in his lap while they watched movies together, then carrying her to bed. Teaching her how to prune and pick grapes. Trying his best not to cry as she left him to chase her biggest, oldest dream.

The strangest thing was, all those nights when she fell asleep in his lap, he'd whisper, *One day, you're going to forget me, duckie.*

How wrong he'd been.

TWELVE

HE NEXT MORNING, SHE woke to the sound of someone knocking. Emeline pulled the covers over her head, willing the noise to go away. After the horrors of yesterday, she wanted to sleep for a hundred years. Wanted to dream this all away.

The knocking turned to pounding.

She forced her groggy eyes open, then pulled back the white canopy. The golden sun was only just cresting the trees outside her windows. *Dawn.* The time she usually fell into bed.

"Please go away," she croaked, turning over and pulling a pillow over her head.

The pounding continued.

Emeline groaned, threw back the covers, and hauled her tired body out of bed. Halfway to the door, she passed a mirror and stopped dead.

Squinting hard, she found a miniature nightmare staring back. She'd fallen asleep in the pale gold dress, which was now a rumpled mess. Her long black hair was as tangled as a bird's nest, and her face . . .

Bloody hell.

The deep, dark shadows beneath her eyes were hardly the

worst of it. Gold dust smeared her right cheek; her left was creased with pillow marks.

She briefly considered trying to make herself presentable but decided not to. People who pounded on other people's doors at this godforsaken hour deserved to be greeted by small horrors. Gritting her teeth, Emeline swung the door open.

Hawthorne Fell stood in the frame, arms crossed, scowling down at her.

Apparently, he wasn't a morning person either.

"What are *you* doing here?" She tried to sound scathing, but her voice came out soft and croaky from sleeping.

His eyes darkened as he took in her rumpled dress, wild hair, and mismatched cheeks. There was probably drool on her face. She quickly swiped at her mouth.

"Where are your attendants?" He scanned the room and then, to her astonishment, let himself in. "I told them to wake you before dawn. You should be dressed."

Emeline moved quickly out of his way, trying to will herself to full wakefulness. She shook her head and pointed to the door. "Get out of my room, you lying jerk."

Ignoring her, he approached the dark wood armoire in the corner. Its doors were each fastened with copper plates, the surface stamped in an elegant design of yarrow flowers. Emeline stared as he wrenched open the armoire doors and began pawing through it, his movements calm and efficient.

"You want to save your grandfather, yes?"

Emeline crossed her arms over the bodice of her rumpled gown.

"I can help with that." He caught sight of an article of clothing that apparently pleased him, because he pulled it out. "Most of the king's minstrels don't last more than a few weeks here. Some only last a few days."

A few days??

"In order to survive, you'll need an edge."

"What kind of an edge?" Emeline asked, intrigued despite her annoyance.

"The king had a favorite minstrel, once. A human with a magical voice. He was known as the Song Mage, and he died a long time ago. The king's been searching for his replacement ever since."

"I don't understand what this has to do with me."

Hawthorne thrust a pair of thick wool leggings with long leather patches on both inner legs towards her. "Put these on."

When Emeline didn't uncross her arms, he shot her a withering look and lowered the leggings to his side. "The sooner you dress, the sooner we leave. If we want to be back before nightfall, we need to leave now."

"*We?*" she choked out. "I'm not going anywhere with you." *A liar, and the reason Pa's imprisoned here to begin with.*

"Don't be daft. The king grows crueler by the day. If you have any hope of surviving this place, we need to fetch the Song Mage's sheet music *today*. You must learn it before your first demonstration."

Emeline shook her head. "I can't read music. I can only play songs by ear."

He seemed completely unfazed by this. "Someone will teach it to you."

She frowned. "And if you're wrong about all of this?"

He paused but didn't glance her way. The sunlight spilling in through the windows glowed warmly against his skin as he stared into the armoire. "I have watched dozens of minstrels die for offenses as petty as singing a single note off-key. Or forgetting half a verse of music. Or wearing a color the king didn't particularly fancy that day."

Um, what? This was vital information Rooke had definitely forgotten to mention.

"The king is mad and longing for his long-lost Song Mage—a man who's been dead for years. That's why he only ever takes human men. Until you. Thanks to Rooke." Hawthorne ran his palm across his forehead. "If you want to survive here, this is your best chance."

Seeing the wisdom in this, Emeline nodded. "All right. Tell me where this sheet music is and I'll get it myself."

Hawthorne pulled out two more pieces of clothing—a saffron yellow camisole and a dark brown sweater. "Getting there is a half day's trek on an ember mare, three days on a regular horse. You won't make it alone, and no one else is willing to escort you, trust me. Not to the aerie. Put these on."

Emeline crossed her arms harder. "I'm not going anywhere with someone who lied to my face."

He pulled out one last item from the armoire—a pair of gray woolen socks—and added them to the growing pile. "If you had listened to my lies, you wouldn't be in this predicament."

Emeline glared at him, her body buzzing with anger. "I'm in this predicament *because of you.* You're the tithe collector. Whatever Pa tithed to the Wood King, you could have decided it was sufficient. Or you could have taken something else. You didn't have to take *him.*"

The tithe collector had been doing it all her life: Punishing her neighbors for insufficient tithes. Stealing their horses, or their herds, or their daughters. Inflicting pain because he could.

But Pa had been dutifully paying his tithes for as long as Emeline could remember. And now that he was old and forgetful, this boy was going to punish him for it?

"Just know that I hold you responsible," she growled. "For all of it."

"Right." His cheek twitched as he stared emptily into the armoire. "It's my fault you returned to the woods immediately after I told you to leave. It's my fault you marched yourself straight up to a cursed king, demanding back a tithe. And it's *my fault* you bartered your life in exchange for Ewan Lark. Yes. I see how I am utterly to blame here."

Emeline's hands tightened into fists.

He turned fully, crossing the room in three easy strides to stand before her. The heat rolled off him, warm like a wood fire.

"Do you know what else I see?" He glared down at her. "A girl who is in far over her head, and too foolish to know it."

He stepped closer, bringing the smell of the woods with him, along with that delicious warmth. Despite herself, Emeline wanted to step into it.

She shook off the urge.

"No one else can help you fetch the Song Mage's music." His voice was a warning. "And if you don't fetch it, you will never learn his songs, and if you don't perform them for the king— and in so doing, please him—your skull will join the wall of others belonging to minstrels who fell before you. And you will *certainly* never bring your grandfather home. Is that what you want, Emeline Lark?"

Emeline's mouth opened and shut. She swallowed her anger, looking to the windows.

His name suited him perfectly, she decided. Hawthorn trees were prickly, gnarly, horrible things—just like him.

And yet he seemed to be trying to help her.

He'd been trying to help her last night too, she realized, when he tricked her out of the woods. She didn't have to like him, though. She didn't have to forgive him for bringing her grandfather to this wretched place. But she could take what he was offering her if it meant getting Pa out.

She gritted her teeth and said, "Give me the clothes."

A small smirk tugged at the corner of his mouth, as if he'd won some great victory. It made her blood boil.

Oh, she would dress. She would go with him to fetch this music. She would take his advice: learn this dead man's songs, perform them in order to please the king, and then, when her grandfather was safe, she would make her escape.

That's what this is. One step closer to going home.

"Turn around," she said after seizing the stack of garments from him.

He tipped his head in a mocking bow, then did as he was bid. It wasn't until he faced the wall that she turned to the window and set the clothes down on the bed. But when she started tugging at the dress, trying to pull it over her head, she realized she couldn't: it was laced too tightly at the back. Frantically she tried to undo the laces. She contorted herself, bending her arms up her back and then down over her shoulders, trying to reach. *Desperate* to reach.

But she couldn't.

"Something the matter?" he asked, impatient.

An embarrassed heat flooded Emeline's body as she became aware of what she needed: help. The soft silk of her dress crumpled in her fists as she squeezed her eyes shut.

He must have sensed her drowning in her own humiliation, because she heard him turn.

"Oh," he said after a moment. "I see the problem. I can help, if you'll let me."

Steeling herself, Emeline turned her head. She spotted his reflection in the mirror, his gaze on the back of her dress. Coolly, she said, "If you think you can manage it, sure."

His eyebrow cocked, as if she'd issued a challenge. But he said nothing more as he strode across the room. The heat of his body spread across her back as he stepped up behind her. They stood before the bed, its canopies drawn to reveal the windows facing the gardens.

First, he swept aside her hair. Emeline kept her attention fixed straight ahead as she felt his gaze trail downwards, stopping on the nape of her neck.

Next, he reached for her laces, his fingers a hot graze on her skin as he pulled them loose, slowly and steadily, knowing precisely what he was doing. Emeline wondered if helping girls out of their clothes was a regular occurrence for him.

She quickly stuffed that thought down deep, where it would shrivel and die.

When the bodice slackened fully, his hands paused, then fell away. But he didn't step back. His breath was warm on her neck as he asked, "Can you manage from here?"

She nodded, wordless.

"Then I'll wait in the hall."

The cold rushed in as he left her.

THIRTEEN

FTER DRESSING IN THE warm, practical clothes he'd dug out of her armoire, Emeline quickly braided her tangled hair, trying to banish the memory of him gathering it up in his hands. Trying to forget the sensation of his fingers deftly undoing her gown.

What is wrong with you? She glared at her reflection, wiping the remaining gold dust from her cheek. *He's the king's henchman and the reason Pa's trapped here. Pull yourself together.*

Her face was flushed, so she splashed cold water on it. Before joining Hawthorne in the hall, Emeline paused, glancing to the door adjoining her and Pa's rooms. Wondering if she should say good morning.

He's probably not awake yet. And even if he is . . .

She'd frightened him last night. He hadn't known her, and he might not know her this morning either. What was the point in saying hello?

Shrugging off the sting of that question, Emeline stepped out into the hall, where Hawthorne waited.

He sat on the floor, his back to the alabaster wall, bent over a sword. The long steel shaft lay across his lap as he slowly ran a sharpening stone down its edge. With every stroke, the steel glimmered—as if enchanted.

His movements were pensive, almost sorrowful. They tugged at Emeline, who found herself wanting to write them into a song. It was an urge she hadn't had in a very long time.

He glanced up at her.

"I'm ready," she told him.

He rose to his feet, sheathing the blade over his back. "Let's get this over with."

In the king's stables, Lament awaited them in a stall, saddled and ready to go. The black mare snorted at their approach, golden eyes flashing red as she pawed the ground, annoyed at being made to wait.

Emeline mounted first, with the help of a stable hand. Hawthorne followed her into the saddle. As he reached around her to take the reins, his crushed-pine smell enveloped her. It seemed completely unfair that he should smell so good—like the woods on a sweet summer day.

She tightened her grip on Lament's wiry black mane, forcing herself to remember who, exactly, this was. The boy behind her had tormented Edgewood all her life. He'd stolen her grandfather. He'd lied to her face.

Don't forget.

They rode on in stony silence.

NEAR MIDDAY, AFTER THEY raced through endless silver forest, the ground began to rise. Lament slowed, climbing upwards through the sickly trees. The air was wet with rot here, and everywhere Emeline looked there was gray ashy *deadness*.

"Why is it like this?" she asked. It was the first time either of them had spoken since leaving the city.

Hawthorne shifted behind her. "The Stain?"

She nodded. From Edgewood, the forest looked green and alive. You would never guess it was rotten inside.

"It's the curse—it poisons every living thing in the woods. It's been spreading for years, from the heart of the forest outwards, and the more life it takes, the more powerful it grows."

Emeline frowned, remembering what the trees had called the Stain: *cursed territory.* But none of the stories she'd grown up with had mentioned a curse.

"How long has it been this way?"

"As long as I've been alive."

How long is that? she was tempted to ask. Hawthorne seemed close to her in age. *If shiftlings even age the same as humans.*

She didn't actually know if he was a shiftling, though. Emeline made a mental note to check his shadow the next time they were in full light.

"The curse is why the king is . . . the way he is. He's tied to the woods, and what poisons the woods poisons him. The curse has twisted his mind, turning him into the horrifying creature you met last night."

It grew quiet around them. The only sound—aside from Hawthorne's resonant voice—was the gentle rhythm of Lament's hoofbeats on the forest floor.

"He's the only one who can slow it down. It's why he takes tithes from the borderlands every season. Every tithe is a sacrifice, and sacrifices have power. The tithes allow him to keep the curse at bay—or they used to. They have less and less effect these days. The curse has simply grown too powerful."

As they reached the top of the escarpment, the forest transformed into a sea of gray below them, shifting to green closer to the King's City—which was a mere speck of white in the distance.

When Emeline looked north, towards Edgewood, she found no trace of her home.

Hawthorne swung down from Lament. The stones crunched beneath his boots as he turned back to Emeline, raising his hands to help her dismount. She would have preferred to get down herself, but Lament was so huge, even the stirrups were a mile high, and warring with her desire to be independent was a desire to not fall face-first into the dirt from such a height.

Reluctantly, she pushed herself to the edge of the saddle. Just as reluctantly, Hawthorne's hands clasped her hips, pulling her down. When her feet touched the rocky ground, Hawthorne let go and they stepped quickly away from each other.

He looked to where the escarpment dropped, turning into sheer rocky cliff. "Claw should be asleep when we get to the aerie. But if for some reason he wakes . . ." His jaw hardened as he turned to her. ". . . you mustn't listen to a word he says."

Oh? Emeline canted her head. "Why not? Who is he?"

Hawthorne reached for the biggest, bulkiest saddlebag. Unbuckling it, he drew out a massive coil of thick golden rope. "Claw can . . . see things. The future, the present, the past. He just can't tell you which is which. Not anymore." He walked towards a leafy linden tree near the cliff edge, unwound the coil, and looped one end around the tree's trunk. "Those who take his prophecies to heart tend to go a little mad."

"What is he?"

Bracing one booted foot against the linden, Hawthorne tugged hard on the loop, testing its strength. Satisfied, he turned towards Emeline. "A watchdog of sorts. After the Song Mage's death, the witch who killed him wanted to prevent his music from ever being sung again. Claw stands guard over it here."

Here appeared to be the edge of a cliff.

Why would anyone want to destroy the songs of a minstrel?

Why would anyone want to kill a minstrel?

She was about to ask about this homicidal witch when Hawthorne stepped abruptly towards her, looping the opposite end of the rope around her waist. She stiffened as he pulled her in close, but then realized what he was doing and lifted her elbows so he could tie the rope snugly over her hips into some kind of harness.

"And whatever you do, do not make any deals with him." His hands deftly secured the rope with a knot. Emeline noticed that the fingers of his right hand were smudged with a steel-gray shine. It reminded her of Maisie's fingers after she'd spent an afternoon sketching flowers in Pa's garden.

Graphite, she thought. *From drawing?*

"Claw is fond of tricks and games, and he never plays fair." When he finished tying, Hawthorne tugged hard on the loop, testing it. When it held firm, he let go and turned to the cliff edge. "In fact, if he wakes up, just leave the talking to me."

Emeline joined him at the cliff edge, peering over. It was sheer gray rock until about fifty feet down, where a smooth shale ledge jutted out. From the way Hawthorne eyed it, the ledge was their destination.

"Where's *your* rope?" she asked.

"I don't need one."

It was a long way to fall without anything to catch you. If he missed the ledge, it was several hundred feet to the bottom.

Not that she cared about his safety. But she did, unfortunately, need him to find her way back to the palace. Emeline didn't think she could manage an ember mare on her own.

Hawthorne started down, his feet finding footholds. It was then that Emeline noticed the unlit torch swinging from his belt. He must have taken it from one of the saddlebags.

Pausing, he looked up at her. "Don't fall, all right?"

She patted the complicated loop of rope he'd tied around her waist. "I have my trusty harness, though."

His head disappeared as he descended, but his voice floated upwards. "Even with your trusty harness, a fall will be unpleasant."

She got down on her knees, then followed him over the ledge, her stomach flip-flopping at the drop below. *It's only rock climbing,* she told herself. An activity she'd done a grand total of one time. In phys ed class. In a well-padded gymnasium.

Emeline counted to three, then started downwards. Holding tight to the top of the rope, she let the slack fall below. Leaning back, she ever so slowly let the rope move through her hands and began to rappel down the cliff, the hot sun cooking the back of her neck as she did.

Emeline only made it halfway before her arms and legs started to burn with the exertion. She never used these muscles, a fact that was quickly becoming apparent. When her arms shook and her palms began to sweat, Emeline's grip on the rope slipped.

The rope scorched her skin as it slid through her palms. Her feet—which had been planted firmly on the rocky cliffside—skidded out from under her as she slid downward. In order to stop her plummet, she grabbed for the rocky cliff with one hand.

"Emeline!"

Her fingers clung to a small handhold. Abandoning the rope, she wedged her other hand into the crevice. Hanging flat against the wall, she dangled dangerously, high in the air. Stones scattered down the cliff as her feet struggled to find footholds and couldn't. *Shit, shit, shit.* Her hands desperately gripped the rocky fissure she'd placed them in while her arms trembled and burned from the burden of bearing all her weight.

"Hold on." Beneath her, Hawthorne's voice grew nearer. "I'm coming. . . ."

Her fingers started to slip. Clenching her teeth, Emeline glanced to the rope swinging next to her, wondering if she should reach for it. If she missed, she would lose her hold for good.

Even with your trusty harness, a fall will be unpleasant.

Emeline squeezed her eyes shut, knowing her overexerted muscles couldn't hold her any longer. This time when her sweaty hands slipped, the rock disappeared from beneath her fingertips.

She dropped—straight into Hawthorne.

The air seemed to *whoosh* out of his lungs as her body careened into his. Somehow, he managed to grab the taut rope with one hand and her waist with the other as they fell. When her momentum slammed them into the rock wall, Hawthorne took the brunt of the impact as he clasped her to him, his grip tightening on the rope as they skidded to a stop.

They swung, suspended in the air. Emeline felt his muscles strain to keep them both aloft and knew he wouldn't be able to hold on for much longer. If he fell, he had no harness to catch him.

Humiliated by her uselessness, she prodded the cliff with her foot, searching for something steady, wanting to relieve him of her weight.

"You're doing great," he said through a clenched jaw, face pressed into her hair, barely holding on.

"You are such a liar."

His mouth curved against her neck in the whisper of a smile. For some reason, it gave her renewed strength. Taking hold of the rope again, she planted her feet on the wall.

Back in position, Emeline loosed a shaky breath. "Okay. I'm good."

Hawthorne let go of her waist. Clinging solely to the rope now, he found his own hand- and footholds in the rock. When he was secure against the cliffside once more, he pressed his forehead to the shale, eyes closed, taking a second to recover before continuing downwards.

Emeline followed.

When her boots finally hit the rocky platform, she leaned her aching body against the warm rock and breathed a sigh of relief.

"Thank you," she whispered.

When Hawthorne didn't answer, she turned to find him facing down a dark cavern—one as wide and high as a small house. *The aerie,* she assumed. He had just lifted a finger to his lips when a massive shape materialized from the darkness, glinting as it stepped into the sunlight.

Emeline gaped up at it.

A silver sharp-toothed snout emerged first, elegant nostrils sniffing the air. The snout alone was roughly the size of Emeline's hatchback. The rest of a head emerged, revealing filmy white eyes and gray tufts where ears should be.

Was this . . . Claw?

If so, he was definitely awake.

His massive paws were tufted too and tipped in sharp nails, reminding Emeline of a lion. But his wings were like that of a snowy owl, tucked primly against his sides. Feathers and scales rippled over his body, the color of silver coins.

A watchdog, Hawthorne had said.

More like a watch*dragon.*

FOURTEEN

HAS THE WOOD KING *sent dinner to my door?*" the dragon rumbled. *"How thoughtful."*

Despite stepping into the sunlight, Claw continued to sniff, following his snout. He trod directly between Hawthorne and Emeline, separating them.

Emeline stepped slowly backwards. Away from those lethal paws. As pebbles crunched beneath her boot, Claw's head swung to stare at her. Emeline froze. The dragon cocked his head, listening. As if he couldn't trust his filmy eyes.

Because he's blind, she realized.

The scales of his belly rasped on the rock as Claw drew himself up on all fours. Gray lips drew away from blackened gums and yellowed teeth in the mockery of a smile.

"There you are." The dragon crept towards her. *"My, you smell familiar. What are you?"*

Panic sparked in her blood. Emeline was running out of ledge to stand on. Only a few more feet and she'd be at—no, over—the edge.

"It's true," Hawthorne called from the other side, drawing the dragon's attention to himself. Emeline held herself still, not breathing as she glanced to the boy standing tall and calm as an oak. "The Wood King sent us—not to be eaten, mind you. We've come for the Song Mage's music."

Displeasure rippled through Emeline's mind, as if the dragon had growled right into her head. Claw whirled on Hawthorne and the dazzling sunlight glinted off his silver-gray scales.

"*Song Mage?*" He spit the words, stalking towards Hawthorne. "*More like Curse-Bringer. Good riddance to him! If I weren't bound by my mistress to guard his music, I would burn it to ash.*"

Curse-Bringer?

What did that mean?

"Nevertheless," said Hawthorne, catching Emeline's gaze. "We're here to collect it." He silently motioned for her to *go back up*. To climb the cliff and get to safety.

But as Emeline stepped towards the rocky wall, the dragon heard. Remembering the first thing that caught his attention, Claw swiftly turned his head towards her.

Emeline fell still.

"*What is it? That thing over there.*"

Black smoke plumed from his snout.

"Nothing to concern yourself with," said Hawthorne, mouthing the word *Go!* to Emeline. "Now let me pass so I can do as my king bids me."

"*Why should I care what the mad king bids?*" Claw clearly had no intention of letting Hawthorne pass. "*And if it's nothing to concern myself with, why did you bring it?*"

They were at an impasse. Hawthorne was trying to distract Claw from Emeline, so she could escape. But Hawthorne clearly had a plan for fetching the music. It should therefore be Emeline who distracted the dragon while he put his plan into action.

She gripped the rough rope around her waist. Several feet of slack lay on the ground.

"I'm the one who needs the music," Emeline said, ensnaring Claw's full attention with her voice. "That's why he brought me."

Hawthorne shot Emeline a look that said, *Are you simple? I told you to climb.*

"You?" Claw purred, abandoning Hawthorne entirely. *"For what purpose?"*

The aerie's entrance grew less and less guarded the nearer Claw came. Since the dragon couldn't see her, Emeline held Hawthorne's furious gaze and pointed to the opening.

I'll handle this. You go.

"I have a deal with the king." She tiptoed towards the rocky wall. If she climbed far enough outwards, past the ledge, she might be able to distract Claw while staying out of striking distance. "If I please him with my singing, he'll set my grandfather free."

"How curious."

When she glanced back, Hawthorne had disappeared inside the cave.

Claw crept closer, his sharp nails clicking on the rock with every prowling step.

Emeline needed to get out of striking distance. Fast. But she *also* needed to keep Claw's attention away from the aerie.

"My companion believes the king will be less inclined to kill me if I sing the Song Mage's songs." Running her hands over the sun-warmed rock, Emeline found sturdy crevices with her fingers. "Is that true, do you think?"

The smell of smoke wrapped around her as Claw drew nearer.

"The king is mad. Never make a deal with a madman."

Well, it was too late for that.

Pulling herself up, she shuffled outwards, away from the ledge. After her near fall, her feet carefully tested each and every foothold. By the time Claw reached the edge, Emeline was ten feet out, hanging off the cliff face.

Not seeing where the ledge ended, Claw stepped onto air. Stumbling, he quickly drew back, spreading his feathered wings for balance.

"Where are you, creature?" Hissing, he turned back in Hawthorne's direction.

If Claw sensed the tithe collector's absence, he would certainly look for him in the aerie. Hawthorne would be cornered.

Thinking of Hawthorne's warning, she blurted out: "What if you and I made a deal?"

Now that she'd given her location away, Claw swung back.

"I don't make deals with my dinner." But his tufted ears perked upwards, as if intrigued.

Emeline peered around Claw, towards the dark maw of the aerie. Hawthorne hadn't reemerged. She needed to buy him more time.

Keep talking.

"Let's pretend that you do. What would you want in exchange for the Song Mage's music?"

The dragon narrowed his eyes. *"I'm not giving you the music."*

Leaning back on his haunches, the dragon sat like a cat, staring in her direction.

"What if I could prove myself worthy? Of the music, I mean."

Claw's attention was slipping. Bored with his uncatchable prey, his body twitched towards the aerie. She needed to get this conversation back on track before she lost him entirely.

A ridiculous idea struck. It was out of her mouth before she could stop it.

"I could sing for you."

Claw cocked his head like a crow. His scaly tail lashed, scraping back and forth across the rocky ledge, as if he was thinking—about her proposition, or about how to prepare her for supper. Difficult to say which.

"You won't be disappointed," she said, stalling for time. Where the hell was Hawthorne? "I promise. Music is the only thing I'm good at."

Claw peered over his shoulder, towards the cave entrance.

Man, he had the attention span of a toddler.

"How about this: If you *don't* detest my singing, you let me borrow the music. Just until I learn the songs."

"And if I do detest it?"

"Then you can eat my companion."

"The one currently rooting through my cave like a little thief?"

Emeline blanched, remembering what Hawthorne said about Claw: he could see the past, present, and future—but sometimes got them jumbled.

Those gray lips curved in a hungry smile. *"He can search all he likes. He won't find what he's looking for."*

Emeline froze, her fingers clutching rock. "Why not?"

"I think," said Claw, *"I will indulge you. Let us play this game. Sing me a song. If I like it, I won't eat you. If I dislike it, I will eat you both."*

Emeline swallowed hard. "And the sheet music?"

"I've just offered you your life. Don't get greedy."

There was still no sign of Hawthorne. How deep did that cavern go? Would he keep searching until he found the music? If Claw spoke the truth, he'd be searching for ages. Emeline couldn't keep Claw distracted forever.

She had to warn Hawthorne. But there was no way to do that, trapped as she was on this cliff wall, with a dragon between them.

"Well, creature? What will it be?"

She couldn't sing from out here, desperately clinging to the side of a cliff.

"I need your word," she said, thinking of Hawthorne's warning. "That you won't hurt me before I finish."

"You have it."

Breathing in deep, Emeline shuffled back to the ledge. She moved slowly, to buy Hawthorne more time. Shale crumbled beneath her feet, scattering softly down the cliff face.

"My patience is wearing thin," growled Claw. *"Hurry up before I change my mind."*

When her feet landed on solid rock again, the dragon rose from where it sat up on all fours, nostrils flaring as he followed her scent. He stood over her, the way an ocean liner towers over a rowboat. He was so impossibly huge, he blocked out the sun. Emeline shivered in his shadow.

"Begin," he growled. *"Now."*

Emeline's fingers itched for her ukulele. She curled them into her palm. She'd have to make do without.

Letting habit guide her, she shuffled through invisible set lists in her mind, searching for the right song.

The air felt charged suddenly, like the moment she got up onstage, before her fingers started to strum and her voice started to sing, pulse humming, stomach clenching. Wondering what kind of crowd it would be, and if she could woo them. Everything resting on her and her voice.

Taking a deep breath, Emeline closed her eyes and began to sing.

She chose Leonard Cohen's "Hallelujah." It was a cover she used at almost every gig. Not only was it a crowd-pleaser; it was one of Pa's favorites. He used to sing it to her when he put her to bed as a child. Like a lullaby. And perhaps, deep down, that was why she chose it: because of the memory it contained.

Songs, for Emeline, were like time capsules. They always had been. For her, every song contained a moment from her past trapped inside.

This song—"Hallelujah"—made the cliffside and the rocky

ledge and the forest disappear. *This* song smelled like the scent of laundry detergent on her pillows. It sounded like Pa's deep voice, singing off-key as he sat at the edge of her bed, rubbing slow, comforting circles into her back as he tried to lull her to sleep.

She often played this song during gigs to keep the loneliness at bay. She played it because it took her to a place where she still had her grandfather . . . and he still had her.

Claw yawned as she sang the first verse, then folded in on himself, curling up beside her. His scales and feathers rippled as his body softened.

As the second verse flowed out of her, Claw's eyelids drooped. His serpentine tail whooshed softly across the rock, lazy and slow.

When Emeline reached the bridge, still trapped in the memory of Pa singing her to sleep, Claw's jowls went slack, gray lips resting on the ground, as if he was utterly at his leisure.

Emeline sang on.

Only when she reached the end, voice trailing into silence, did the memory release her from its hold. Emeline clung, grasping at it, not yet ready to let go. But the song was over, the memory gone. And as it left, something else left with it. She felt it pour out of her, leaving her empty.

She shook off the feeling as Claw's snores rumbled through the rock beneath her. Emeline looked down to find the dragon's eyes closed, his chest steadily rising and falling, and his gray tongue lolling out of his half-open mouth.

She'd sung him to sleep.

A laugh bubbled up at the absurdity of it. She quickly swallowed it down. They weren't out of this yet. Emeline's fingers pulled at the rope looped around her waist. Hawthorne's knots were tight and secure, but she figured them out. When the rope unraveled, she stepped out of it—slowly, lightly, so as not to wake the sleeping dragon.

But as she stepped into the aerie, an odd heaviness sank into her bones, dragging her down. As if the song had taken a toll on her.

Don't be silly.

She was obviously exhausted from the climb down.

Emeline paused at the entrance, trying to shake off the feeling, then continued into the cavern. Cold, damp air kissed her skin. When she whispered Hawthorne's name, he didn't respond.

Emeline strode onwards until her boot kicked something in the darkness. She tripped, nearly fell, then crouched to look.

A sea of yellowed human bones lay scattered at her feet.

She abruptly stood, swallowing down the sick feeling pushing up from her stomach.

Find Hawthorne, she told herself. *And get out of here.*

But the deeper in she went, the darker it grew. Not wanting to wake the sleeping dragon outside, Emeline called Hawthorne's name as loudly as she dared. Had he fallen down some crevice? Was he dead?

Suddenly, a torch flame appeared in the distance, farther up the cavern. The orange smudge of it bobbed in the dark, growing larger as it drew near.

"What are you doing?" he called out. "You're—"

"Claw's asleep," she whispered back. "We have to go. The sheet music isn't here."

As he came closer, she saw twin flames reflected in his eyes. The light of the torch limned his face with black shadows. "How—"

"No time." She grabbed his arm, tugging him back towards

the entrance. "Claw knew you were in here. He said you wouldn't find the music."

Hawthorne lowered his voice to a whisper. "And where is he now?"

In answer, something moved in the darkness, rasping against the stone floor. Goose bumps rushed across her skin as a cold awareness set in. Hawthorne stepped in front of Emeline, shielding her as he raised the blazing torch, its glow radiating outwards.

When silver scales flashed in the dark, Emeline felt the sudden heat of a massive body. And then: Claw stepped into the light, snarling as he loomed over them.

Hawthorne pressed Emeline back just as Claw lashed out. One massive paw hit Hawthorne square in the chest, sending him sprawling. He grunted as his shoulders hit the floor.

The dragon pounced, pinning him beneath sharp claws. As Claw's jaws slid open, gobs of drool dripped from his teeth.

The torch rolled away from Hawthorne's hand, guttering.

"No!" Emeline snatched up the torch and the flame flared anew. "We had a deal!"

"*Indeed,*" Claw rumbled. "*You sang me a song I did not detest. So I will let you walk away with the sheet music.*" The dragon stared at the boy pinned beneath his paw. "*You. Not him.*"

Suddenly, Claw's body shivered, then clenched. A liquid noise surged from his stomach as he heaved. Drool bubbled along his lips.

He looked like a cat that was about to vomit.

Up it came, like some kind of giant hairball: a dark brown satchel coated in glistening saliva. It landed with a sticky *thud* at Emeline's feet.

"*Take it and go.*"

She picked up the satchel, trying not to gag. It smelled sour, like stomach acid, and stuck to her hands like tree sap. She untied the slippery twine and pushed back the leather flap. Milky sheets of vellum lay within. Across their translucent surfaces, elegant black notes tumbled from bar to bar, untouched by saliva.

The Song Mage's sheet music.

Claw turned back to his prey, increasing the pressure of his paw. Emeline glanced from the music to Hawthorne, who arched his throat, straining against the dragon pushing down on his chest.

Claw was going to crush him to death.

"I need him," she burst out. "To get me back to the palace."

"Is there not an ember mare waiting atop this cliff? Take it and return to the palace yourself." Claw flexed his sharp nails and dark red blood bloomed across Hawthorne's shoulder. *"Trust me, singer. You don't need this one."*

That might be true. But Emeline couldn't abandon him.

Hoisting the satchel over her shoulder, she came to Hawthorne's side. Gripping the torch tight in her hand, she thrust the flame into the paw keeping him pinned, searing the dragon's scaly flesh.

Claw hissed and withdrew, limping backwards.

"Horrible creature!"

Hawthorne drew in a staggered breath as Emeline fell to her knees beside him. He sat up, wincing, while she held the torch aloft, illuminating the dragon in the shadows.

Claw's murky eyes narrowed in the light of her flame. Getting to his feet, Hawthorne drew the blade at his back. Its steel edge burned red in the light of the torch.

"You will let us pass."

"And if I don't?"

Hawthorne gritted his teeth, betraying the pain he was in. "Then you and I will slay each other here, and Emeline will leave with the music."

Claw hissed, glancing between them, as if thinking through his options. Finally, the dragon drew back.

"Go, then. You will not live long, Tithe Collector. I've seen it: my mistress's curse will swallow the King's City and everything in it."

The words chilled Emeline.

Hawthorne didn't sheathe his sword. Just held out his hand for Emeline to take. As her cool fingers slid through his warm ones, Hawthorne kept himself between her and the dragon while Claw watched and waited.

Halfway to the cave entrance, that growled voice no longer echoed on the rock walls but glided through Emeline's mind. Like water over stone.

And you, singer.

She paused at the entrance, glancing behind her before stepping into the sunlight. A low growl rumbled through the cavern, and from the darkness, the dragon hissed into her mind:

Beware of this one. He betrays you in the end!

FIFTEEN

HEY RODE HARD THROUGH the woods, arriving back in the King's City just before sundown. The gate slammed closed behind them, ringing like a tune. Outside the king's stables, Lament came to a halt. She shook her black mane and stomped the ground, sparks flaring beneath her hooves, as if calling for attention.

Hawthorne dismounted, his movements heavy and sluggish.

Emeline sat frozen in the saddle, clutching the leather satchel to her chest, tacky with dried saliva. Claw's last words swirled around her mind, like water in a draining sink.

He betrays you in the end!

What did it mean?

Claw knew Hawthorne was searching his lair, just like he knew Lament stood waiting at the top of the cliff. So why did Hawthorne tell her that Claw got confused?

Claw can see things. The future, the present, and the past. He just can't tell you which one is which.

Unless Hawthorne lied.

It wouldn't be the first time he lied, and it would make a kind of sense. If Hawthorne intended to betray Emeline, he wouldn't want her listening to an all-seeing dragon who might spill all his plans.

You mustn't listen to a word he says, he'd told her before they climbed down to the aerie.

If Hawthorne had malicious intent, if he knew Claw could see the future and might tell that future to Emeline, wasn't that exactly what he'd say?

For a fraction of a second, Emeline wanted to dig her heels into Lament and gallop back to Edgewood. She wanted to *run.* Except Hawthorne still gripped the reins and Lament was spent. Sweat glistened across her back and foam glazed her lips.

Most of all, though: Pa was still a prisoner.

Calm down. You can handle this.

It didn't make sense that Hawthorne would endanger her. He'd saved her from a shadow skin, then put her on his horse to prevent her from being trampled by ember mares. Today, he'd given *her* the rope and caught her when she fell.

She was sure he didn't want to harm her.

But he had deceived her. And he clearly didn't want her here, in the Wood King's domain. Perhaps that's the type of betrayal Claw meant—one that would sabotage her ability to come through on her deal. One that would prevent her from bringing Pa home.

Emeline watched the tithe collector press his hand to the stable wall, wincing at whatever pain Claw had inflicted.

One thing was certain: if Hawthorne was planning to betray her, she needed to be ready for it.

THAT EVENING, AS THE moon rose in a black sky, Emeline's attendants swarmed her as she stepped out of her bath. She was too tired to fight them off.

Her body ached. She never rode horses. Riding one for a whole day—not to mention scaling up and down a rocky cliff—had taken its toll. Muscles she didn't even realize she had screamed at her.

But her sore body was the least of her concerns.

Now that she'd obtained the Song Mage's music, she had a week to prove herself to the king and, after Pa went free, find a way to escape. If she didn't escape, she'd miss her tour.

She remembered the schedule sitting in her inbox. The one Joel had told her to review and send back to The Perennials.

Emeline grabbed her cell phone from where it lay on the dressing table, amidst combs and pins and ribbons, but there were no bars.

She tightened her grip on the phone. Of course. She was trapped in a strange, fey world with no cell towers or wireless internet. But if a week went by and neither her manager nor Joel heard from her, they would do any number of things: they would think her missing; Joel would come looking for her; her manager would cancel her tour—he'd have to.

The thought gave her heart palpitations.

It was her first major tour, and she'd worked her ass off to get it. To cancel now was to say good-bye to all of the exposure, sales, and income from each show. She would tarnish her reputation as a professional musician, and worst of all . . .

They want to see how you handle a bigger audience, Joel had told her. *They're coming to watch you again, at your first tour stop.*

If she wasn't at that first stop, Daybreak *definitely* wouldn't offer her a contract.

Emeline had worked too hard for too long to make it this far. She couldn't let it all fall apart now. If she could somehow tell her manager she was fine, that she'd be back soon—if she could tell him not to cancel her tour—maybe her career would still be intact when she got back.

Except how was she supposed to tell him all that from here?

A pang of homesickness pierced her. She wanted her life back. The ordinary, familiar one where dragons didn't want to eat her and boys weren't waiting to betray her and the only strangeness in her life was the woods appearing at inopportune times.

She missed the lights and sounds of Montreal. She missed her late-night gigs. She even missed her cramped apartment.

Emeline's attendants fluttered like moths as they dressed her, oblivious to her unhappiness. They helped her into a midnight-blue gown with two glittering cicada wings stitched down the back in gold thread, cascading from the middle of her shoulder blades to the tops of her thighs. The attendants undid her braid, then brushed out her hair. As they tugged at the knots, a knock sounded at the door, breaking up her thoughts.

"Be right there."

Finished with their fussing, her attendants removed themselves, opening the door as they fled.

Rooke stood in the frame, sidestepping the women. He looked tall and slender in a midnight-black overcoat that came to his knees, and over his heart a silver feather brooch winked in the light.

"I've been charged with escorting you to dinner." He gave a roguish grin as he held his arm out to her. "Hurry now. Else we'll be late."

With her hand tucked into his elbow, Rooke led Emeline down halls awash in the golden hues of sunset. Vases bordering the windows sprouted green pine boughs and branches of bright red sumac. As Emeline quickened her pace to match his long strides, the fabric of her dress whispered against the floor.

"I must say," said Rooke as they passed window after window looking out over the dusk-drenched city, "it's a pleasure to see you're still alive."

Emeline shot him a look, remembering what Hawthorne said—about her predecessors and their untimely deaths.

"You might have mentioned the dangers *before* I agreed to be the king's singer," she said as they arrived at the end of the hall, where two large arching doors were flung wide and bordered by hedgemen in bronze armor. The smells of roasted meat and pungent spices wafted out, followed by clinking silverware and conversation.

"Would it have made a difference?"

Before she could answer, Rooke pulled her into a darkened ballroom.

The ceiling was the height of her grandfather's barn, and Emeline counted four exits, each one guarded by a pair of hedgemen. Candles burned along the walls in iron brackets, their honey-colored wax dripping to the floor. Long tables set with food were arranged in a circle, and in the center a band of musicians played while couples danced. Over their heads, fireflies flickered intermittently.

As Rooke led her towards the tables, conversations quieted around them. Eyes widened and heads turned as the dining courtiers whispered behind their hands, watching the king's new minstrel.

More than once, Emeline heard her name.

Placing bets on how long I'll last?

Rooke sidestepped benches and bodies, maneuvering Emeline towards a nearly full table close to a massive fireplace set into the far wall. Emeline spotted Sable Thorne first, seated near the crackling fire, its flames setting her golden skin aglow. Her russet hair was unruly, but someone had managed to pin it up, tucking a sprig of rosehip into the brown folds.

She looked . . . wild and pretty.

Beside her sat Hawthorne.

His gray woolen shirtsleeves were rolled to his elbows, showing off darkly tanned forearms. Both he and Sable sat on the bench against the wall. But while Sable leaned into the shadows, one arm looped around her knee, Hawthorne leaned over his drink, listening to a young woman across from him, her hands animated and her face alight.

"Friends!" Rooke roared over the din of their conversation. "Meet the king's new minstrel: Emeline Lark."

The whole table went quiet at their arrival, turning. Some lifted their drinks in welcome; others smiled wine-bright smiles behind their goblets; still others stared, their hungry eyes searching her. Emeline's skin warmed beneath their gazes as Rooke pushed her towards the one empty spot on the bench, right next to Hawthorne—who quickly glanced away from her. But not before Emeline glimpsed something wild flash in his eyes.

The only other person who didn't look her way was Sable.

"Good evening, singer," said Hawthorne, staring firmly into his cup as she shuffled in beside him.

"Hello, Tithe Collector."

In the cramped space beneath the table, their knees brushed, and the jolt of it startled Emeline. Like two polarized magnets, they simultaneously leaned away from each other.

Rooke slid in on Emeline's other side, trapping her between them. Hawthorne shot Rooke an accusatory look. Ignoring it, Rooke shouted to Sable, "Where's Grace?"

Sable pointed her thumb in the direction of the dancers.

Hawthorne reached for a copper pitcher filled with a honey-gold liquid that smelled like wine.

"I'm afraid I have unfortunate news." It took a moment for Emeline to realize Hawthorne was talking to her and not to the pitcher of wine as he filled her glass. "Your singing instructor was attacked by shadow skins on the road. She survived, but her horse did not. I've sent an armed guard to escort her. Depending on what they encounter on the way, it could be a few days before she arrives in the city."

Emeline reached for her glass, cupping it with both hands. "But if I need to learn the songs within the week . . ."

He nodded. "It won't be enough time." He refilled Sable's glass, Rooke's, and finally his own. After setting the pitcher down, he said, very softly, "I could do it in the meantime."

She turned to stare at him. *"You?"*

"I can read music," he said, not quite meeting her eyes. "Which, I understand, is all you need."

The prospect of working one-on-one with him made her break out in a hot rash. Claw's words echoed through her mind: *He betrays you in the end!*

"Is there no one else?" She pointed to the musicians currently playing a waltz in the middle of the room. "One of them, maybe? Someone who . . ." *Isn't you.* "Someone who knows what they're doing?"

He opened his mouth to answer, then closed it instead.

"There are many capable musicians in the king's court. Unfortunately, none of them are willing to risk their lives for what they consider a doomed cause. It's why I had to reach out to another court. Calliope has agreed to be your instructor at great risk to herself."

Emeline frowned. *What risk?*

"If you'd prefer to wait until she arrives . . ."

"You said you don't know when that will be."

He nodded.

"And I only have a week to learn the Song Mage's music."

"Correct."

"Which means I don't really have a choice, do I? If I want to learn the songs, I need to get started as soon as possible. And if you're the only one willing to help me . . ."

It has to be you.

"I suggest we begin at dawn tomorrow," he said, sensing her defeat. "I'll tell your attendants to take you to the conservatory first thing in the morning."

Hawthorne turned away from her then, signaling the end of the conversation, and returned to the girl across from him, who Emeline heard him refer to as Aspen. The girl smiled sweetly as they resumed their chat.

Could this day get any worse?

Someone farther down the table cleared their throat. "Tell us, singer. How did you vanquish him?"

Emeline looked up to find most guests at the table setting down their silverware and leaning in. As if they'd all been waiting for this.

The question came from a freckled young man whose large brown eyes reminded her of a fawn. His shaggy hair framed his pale face, shining like copper. "No one has ever come back from the dragon's aerie. But here you are."

No one? She stole a pointed glance at Hawthorne.

"It's true," said a girl with foxlike features and hair as white as frost. "The king has made several attempts to retrieve the music. The men and women he sent never returned."

"Oh. Well, um, I didn't *vanquish* Claw."

"Then how are you sitting before us? Hawthorne says you successfully retrieved the music."

They all murmured their assent, staring at Emeline as if she were a god who'd waltzed straight out of a Greek myth. Like golden Artemis striding out of the woods after a successful hunt, a prize deer slung over her shoulders.

She shook her head. "I only sang to him."

Puzzled silence filled the table. Emeline felt the sudden weight of Hawthorne's stare. She didn't meet it.

"I . . . sang him to sleep, I mean."

It sounded absurd to her now, as gazes met over goblets and plates of food. *They think I'm making it up.*

Except no. They didn't.

The freckled young man raised his glass. "To Emeline Lark," he said softly. "Conqueror of dragons."

One by one, the rest of the table raised their glasses, echoing his toast. Reverently whispering her name like she was some kind of hero. Heat crept into her cheeks. She tipped her face to her empty gold-rimmed plate. "I didn't . . ." But no one was listening. They were all chattering excitedly in the wake of her story. Emeline could already hear them embellishing the details.

"Don't mind them, dearie," chimed a singsong voice across from Emeline, cutting through the noise around her. "It's been years since they've had good news."

Emeline looked up and found an owlish face peering straight into hers. Tawny hair curled in short ringlets around the girl's head, and her amber eyes were a little too big for the rest of her dainty features. "I'm Nettle."

"Lovely to meet you, Nettle."

"Are you enjoying your stay?"

Emeline blinked, not sure how to answer. *Yes,* she thought, sipping her drink. *It's so fun being imprisoned by a creepy king, nearly eaten by a crusty old dragon, and utterly cut off from everything I love.*

She thought of her phone. Without a signal, she couldn't contact Joel, and soon her battery would be dead. But maybe it wasn't the only way to reach him. Maybe someone here could help her.

"I would enjoy my stay more if I could get a message to someone. So he knows I'm all right. Is there a way to do that? Send a message home?"

If she could get a message to Joel explaining that she was . . . temporarily detained . . . he could tell his dad not to worry, that she would be there ready to go on opening night.

Nettle reached across the table, taking Emeline's hands from where they cupped her glass and clasping them in her own. Her fingers were rough, and a little curved. Almost like talons. But when Emeline looked . . . no. They were definitely fingers, with perfectly rounded nails painted in gold. She shook off the disorienting feeling as the shiftling leaned in.

"Poor thing." Nettle's voice turned whispery. As if they were friends confiding in each other. "This young man you left behind, is he . . . a lover?"

Beside her, Hawthorne choked on his wine.

Emeline blushed red. "Um."

Nettle tsked sadly. "They often have lovers, the singers who end up here."

Alerted by Hawthorne's choking, Rooke leaned in. "Don't mind Nettle. She hasn't been properly socialized."

Tugging her hands free from Nettle's, Emeline took a big, long sip of her drink and desperately wished this conversation was over. From the look on the shiftling's face, however, she was still waiting for an answer.

Is he a lover?

The night she first invited Joel up to her hotel room, it was because of the woods. She'd been traveling the summer festival circuit, trying, as always, to outrun the dark thing chasing her. But it always caught up, creeping through crowd after crowd, slinking towards the stages where she sang.

But it wasn't only the relentlessness of the woods; it was the ache that seemed to grow with every performance. That cavernous gap between her ribs, as if something there was missing, only she didn't know what. It made her feel like a puzzle with a lost piece. Sometimes after a gig, she would lie awake in her bed, rubbing at the place in the middle of her chest where she imagined the hole to be.

She'd grown so tired of running from it—the woods and the ache. Joel was there, and he wanted her. He'd made that very clear. Always texting and flirting and inviting her out with his friends, coming to all her shows, then walking her home when they ended.

So, just like all the others before him, Emeline let Joel in, erecting him as a shield between herself and the things she was running from, using him as a way to feign normalcy.

"You poor, poor thing." Nettle patted Emeline's hands, deciding the answer to her own question. "So tragic." She sighed, almost happily, as if she relished a good tragedy.

"Save your pity." Hawthorne's voice was barbed. "Emeline was warned. I actively dissuaded her from coming."

Emeline scoffed. "Actively deceived me is more like it."

His gaze cut to her, gray eyes flashing silver in the dusky light. "The singer didn't heed me," he continued as if she hadn't spoken. "Now she's suffering the consequences."

Emeline's hands dropped to her dress, where they clutched the fabric, wrinkling the midnight-blue silk. "If you hadn't stolen my grandfather," she hissed under her breath, "I wouldn't have had to heed you. I would never have come to the woods at all!"

Before he could answer, the girl he'd been conversing with earlier cut in.

"Couldn't you deliver the message, Hawthorne?" She was long boned and delicate, with white-gold lashes and eyes like soft gems. She glanced to the ring on Hawthorne's hand, a stark white band against his light brown skin. Emeline hadn't noticed it before. "You're the tithe collector. You can walk deep into her world whenever and wherever you want."

"Yes, Hawthorne," said Sable, crossing her arms. A small frown creased her brow as something unspoken passed between them. "Couldn't you do it?"

Hope flickered inside Emeline. *Could he?*

Hawthorne stared straight ahead, at no one in particular. "I believe I just gave my opinion on the matter."

"Your opinion," said Emeline, suddenly desperate to convince him. Her career depended on it. "But not your answer."

He shot her a piercing look. "I'm not delivering a love letter to your boyfriend. Is that answer enough?"

"It wouldn't be—"

"Emeline." He ground out her name through the stubborn clench of his jaw. "Don't ask me again."

Rooke narrowed his eyes. "Really, Hawthorne. Must you be so disagreeable?"

As the two boys glared at each other, Nettle quickly smiled at Emeline. Only the smile was all wrong. It curled in a way that suggested she was something playing at being human. "Don't mind him, dearie. Hawthorne was in love once too." That smile turned into a slithering, snakelike thing. Lashing out to bite. "Weren't you, Tithe Collector?"

A muscle jumped in Hawthorne's jaw. He stared at the ceiling, like a wild creature suddenly realizing it was trapped in a cage.

The table went silent around them. Tension radiated off

Hawthorne like steam as he gripped his glass tightly. To no one in particular, he said, "Excuse me."

In one fluid motion, he rose from the bench, pushed away from the table, and left his empty cup behind. Emeline stared after him.

What the heck was that about?

Sable and Rooke exchanged glances.

"I'll go," said Rooke, a frown bending his mouth. Rising from the bench, he strode after the tithe collector weaving through the thickening mass of guests in the hall.

Nettle tutted sympathetically, watching them go. She leaned across the table towards Emeline. "They say it was a human who made him so horrible. Broke his heart right in half. He's never been the same."

"That's enough." Sable's voice slashed the air like a knife, her golden eyes glowing brightly as she leaned in from her place by the fire. "Go spread your poison elsewhere, Nettle."

The owlish courtier bristled. She looked ready to lash back when a shadow fell across the table. Sable glanced up, and whatever she saw made her soften like warm butter.

"*Emeline?*" said a feminine voice. "Emeline Lark?"

Emeline's gaze shot upwards. Confusion clouded her mind at the familiar face looking down on her. For a moment, she didn't understand who she was seeing.

And then: "*Grace?*"

Emeline rose to her feet.

Standing at the edge of the table was Grace Abel. The girl who left Edgewood last summer, after her parents gave her an ultimatum: go to university, or find somewhere else to live.

Grace's night-dark curls gleamed around her face and shoulders, luminous in the candlelight. Her hips were fuller and her nut-brown cheeks rosier than the last time Emeline had seen her. She wore a flowing silk shirt tucked into fitted cream trousers, and a simple iron ring adorned her finger.

What the hell are you doing here? said the look on Grace's face.

The exact same question echoed through Emeline.

Stepping closer, Grace drew Emeline out and away from the table, then into a tight hug. She smelled like lavender. But her grip on Emeline was too tight, and her voice was a warning. "Come with me. *Now.*"

Before Emeline could react, Grace drew back. She smiled brightly at those still seated. Her voice was liquid sunlight with no hint of any secrets as she held her hand out to Emeline and said, "Care to dance?"

SIXTEEN

EMELINE BIT BACK A multitude of questions and took Grace's hand, leaving the table behind. Grace's fingers tightened as she led them closer to the dancing.

"Stay away from Nettle," she said sternly. "She's a cat who likes to play with her prey before she kills it. She didn't give you anything back there, did she? Like wine? Or whiskey?"

"No. Why?"

The air was much warmer here and the music beat loud, drowning out their voices. Grace slowed, leaning in closer so Emeline could hear her.

"It's Nettle's favorite game: she enchants her friends by spiking their drinks with spells. Last month she threw a party and everyone who attended fell in love with their worst enemy for a day."

What? Emeline's eyes widened. "She does that to her *friends?*"

They entered the crowd of clapping, stomping dancers. Many of the faces around them were like Nettle's: Features too askew to be precisely human. Eyes too big—or too small—for the faces they were set in. Smiles full of serrated teeth. Hair hiding tufted ears.

Grace didn't stop walking. Just dodged and sidestepped the shiftling dancers, moving through the circle and out the other side. Taking Emeline with her as she strode towards the exit.

The hedgemen in their hammered bronze armor and helmets shaped like seed pods stared straight ahead as Emeline and Grace walked between them and out into the hall. When they were free of the ballroom, Grace let go of Emeline's hand and kept walking.

"You're his new minstrel. Aren't you?" Her copper-brown eyes were bright with concern. "Are you all right?"

"Am *I* all right?" Emeline spluttered. "What about you? What are you doing here?"

A confused wrinkle creased the skin between Grace's eyebrows. "I was tithed last summer. Didn't Maisie tell you?"

It's what everyone in Edgewood told her—that Grace had been tithed. Emeline just hadn't believed it. "I thought you ran away."

Grace shook her head, sending her black curls bouncing. "Not . . . exactly. Anyways. That's not important right now." She turned sharply at a stone staircase, her feet hurrying down the steps. "This way. You need to see something."

When they hit bottom, darkness seeped in and the temperature dropped. Emeline shivered and rubbed her arms, trying to stave off the chill. Up ahead, a large wooden door was illuminated by two brightly burning torches set into sconces on the wall. Lifting one of them, Grace pulled on the door's iron ring, then stepped through the opening.

Emeline followed her.

It was black as pitch within. Their footsteps hushed against the stone floor, which was carved up into slabs, smooth with age, and imprinted with words. In the flickering light of Grace's torch, Emeline caught names. Dates. Inscriptions.

Tombs, she thought. *We're in a crypt.*

Emeline glanced around, slowing as the realization sank in. In the darkness, she could almost make out the shapes of statues carved from marble, and doorways leading into alcoves, holding the dead within.

Grace was several yards ahead now, standing before a white wall, the torch held high over her head. Emeline hurried to catch up, not wanting to be left in the dark.

"Why are we . . ."

The question died on her lips as she drew nearer to the wall Grace stood staring at. It only looked white, she realized, because of the rows and rows of human skulls. Hundreds of skulls. Teeth bared, sockets gaping. So many, they filled the wall from floor to ceiling, end to end.

"They're the king's singers . . . as well as their instructors."

An icy chill seeped into Emeline.

It's why I had to reach out to another court, Hawthorne had told her. *Calliope has agreed to be your instructor at great risk to herself.*

"Shit." This was way worse than she thought. "Do *any* survive?"

Grace shook her head.

Between them and the wall was a marble podium that rose to the height of their chests. Upon it, a crimson velvet pouch sat untied and open. Nestled inside its red folds was one more skull.

Emeline stepped towards it, touching the words on the bronze plaque. "'The Song Mage,'" she read.

"What's left of him," said Grace. "They say the witch who killed him delivered his head to the king in that pouch."

Remembering what Hawthorne said about this same witch—who'd given Claw the Song Mage's music to guard— Emeline wrinkled her nose at the thought of it: blood dripping through the fabric, leaving a smear of red across the palace's polished floors. "She must have really hated him."

"Apparently, she loved him. But he didn't love her back." Grace turned away from the wall of death. "So she killed him."

Emeline's eyebrows lifted in astonishment. "Seems reasonable."

The corner of Grace's mouth tipped upwards. But she quickly sobered, looking back to the skull. Emeline looked too, studying the remains of the king's beloved singer. The small teeth, the yellowed bone, the shadowy gaps. "What was so special about *you*?" she asked it.

"He was originally from our world," Grace said. "A human singer renowned for his captivating voice. But then he came here, to the King's City, and didn't want to leave. So he traded his voice in exchange for a place in the court."

Emeline cocked her head in confusion. "How could he sing with no voice?"

Grace shook her head. "His voice *beyond* the woods. He could speak and sing here, but the moment he stepped back into our world, he fell mute."

Emeline reached for her throat. To not be able to sing . . . "It would have ended his career."

Grace nodded. "Beyond the woods, yes. But here, in this world, there's magic in sacrifice. His gave him power. A lot of power. It transformed him from court minstrel to *Song Mage*—a man who used his magical voice for the betterment of the woods. The Wood King's reign was prosperous when the Song Mage was the court minstrel. It was a golden age, or so people say."

"And now that golden age is over," said Emeline, "because the Song Mage is dead."

"And the woods are cursed," added Grace. "Which is why you can't stay."

Emeline remembered Claw's last words to Hawthorne.

You will not live long, Tithe Collector. I've seen it: my mistress's curse will swallow the King's City and everything in it.

"Hawthorne says the curse is poisoning the woods."

Turning away from the skulls, Grace nodded as she led Emeline back through the crypt.

"The curse has three parts," she explained. "The first is the Stain. It's rotting the woods from the inside out, gaining more ground every day, spreading its poison closer to the King's City.

"With the Stain comes the shadow skins. Every week, there's another attack in the woods, and more are crossing the tree line, wreaking havoc on Edgewood and the other borderlands. Feeding on people's fears before feasting on their flesh.

"But worst of all: the curse turns everything back to its true form."

Emeline jerked her eyes to Grace's face, illuminated by the flame of the torch. "What does that mean? And why is it the worst?"

Grace nodded as if she, too, had once needed to have it explained to her.

"A shiftling, for example, has two forms. Rooke, Nettle, Sable . . . you know them as one thing. As human, or at least human*like*. But that's not what they really are. Every day, the curse forces more and more of them into their true forms permanently, preventing them from ever turning back. Every month, the city grows emptier as the curse gets stronger."

When they arrived at the door they'd come in through, Grace turned to Emeline.

"This is why you can't be the king's minstrel." Grace's eyes were bright, almost feverish in the light of the orange flame. "The curse grows more powerful every day. You need to escape this place before it devours us. You're in too much danger here."

Emeline's brows lifted. "And you're not?"

That small frown appeared on Grace's forehead. "I—"

Whatever she was about to say was cut off by the crypt door swinging open.

They both jumped back, hearts hammering.

On the other side stood Sable, her eyes luminous in the dim light. "There you are." Her lean shoulders sagged with relief at the sight of Grace. "I've been looking—"

At the sight of Emeline, though, Sable stiffened and stepped back.

"Emeline," said Grace, "this is Sable. Sable, Emeline."

Emeline nodded. "We've met."

Grace glanced to Sable, her eyes darkening with confusion. Her mouth hardened into a line as a bright emotion flickered across her face. "You've met?"

Sable's lips parted, as if to speak, but Grace cut her off, speaking once more to Emeline.

"Listen." She handed her torch to Sable, then held the door open for Emeline to pass through. "There's a pub in the city called The Acorn. Sable and I and a few others go every Friday night." As Sable replaced the torch in its sconce, Grace and Emeline started up the steps. "Meet me there at sunset on Friday, okay? We can make a plan."

"Sure," said Emeline, despite the fact that she was going nowhere until her grandfather was safely out of the Wood King's clutches.

"We'll find a way to get you home." At the top of the stairs, Grace paused, waiting for the golden-eyed shiftling trudging up the steps behind them. "Ready?"

Sable nodded.

To Emeline, Grace said, "See you Friday. Try to stay alive until then, okay?"

The two girls walked away, in the opposite direction of the ballroom, their hushed argument echoing back to Emeline: Grace's raised voice, followed by Sable's curt answers.

"You didn't think I'd want to know?"

"I only found out last night."

"And you couldn't have found the time to tell me between then and now?"

When they turned a corner, the hall fell silent.

SEVENTEEN

HE NEXT MORNING, EMELINE'S attendants brought her to a domed room for her first singing lesson. The bowed walls were made of glass, giving her a bird's-eye view of the city below. Cobbled streets glided snakelike beneath terracotta rooftops all the way to the city wall. Beyond it, the tops of the autumn-touched trees spilled outwards as the woods stretched as far as she could see.

Emeline looked north, in the direction of Edgewood, but there was no sign of her world.

Suddenly, someone cleared their throat behind her. Emeline stiffened, turning towards the sound.

Hawthorne stood in the center of the domed room, bathed in sunlight. He wore a navy-blue knit sweater and his hands were clasped behind his back. The usual thunder darkened his brow.

She crossed her arms at the sight of him, still angry that he'd refused to take a message to Joel.

"I've just been informed that the king wants a demonstration at midnight tomorrow."

"*Tomorrow?*" Emeline's arms fell to her sides. "But we haven't even started."

Hawthorne nodded. "Which is why there's no time to lose."

He turned to the delicate sapling growing in the center of the room. The tiny tree was shaped like a music stand. On its leafy branches rested a stack of vellum: the Song Mage's sheet music. Elegantly inked bars and black notes scrolled across the milky surface, with lyrics written underneath. "If you can learn three or four songs before tomorrow, it should suffice. All he wants is proof—of your talent, and your obedience."

Swallowing her disappointment, Emeline nodded. "Then let's begin."

They spent all morning in that domed room, with the sunlight flooding the crystal windows and the woods spilling out in all directions beyond the walls.

Emeline found herself pleasantly surprised by Hawthorne's enchanting baritone. He was a little rusty—clearly he hadn't sung in quite some time—but the rawness of his voice only made it more endearing.

She had never been here before, with Hawthorne in the Wood King's palace, singing a dead man's songs. Yet the moment he started singing, a dizzying sense of déjà vu struck Emeline. A memory prodded at her mind while he sang, but when she tried to reach for it, it eluded her.

Soon, they fell into a comfortable rhythm. Once Hawthorne taught her the notes and breaths, Emeline joined her voice to his, matching him note for note, breath for breath, memorizing the patterns and fluctuations.

Hawthorne sang verses; Emeline echoed them back. When she had trouble with a progression, he made her repeat it, mercilessly, until she got it right. When she got it right, he immediately moved on to the next part, never giving an inch.

He set the standard high, and Emeline met it.

See? she thought. *You're wrong about me. I'm not some fool in over my head. This is what I'm good at.*

If she softened beneath the pressure he exerted, if she melted under the heat of his demands, it was only because her life—and Pa's—depended on her learning these songs and pleasing the king.

It had nothing to do with the admiration burning in Hawthorne's eyes. Nor the smile he hid when she hit a note exactly right. Nor the way he glanced sharply away when she looked up to find him staring.

Pitchers of water appeared at Hawthorne's request, to keep her hydrated. Midday came and went. There were eleven songs in all. She wanted to learn three today, if she could.

When the late-afternoon sun shone through the glass, raising the room's temperature from warm to *too warm,* Hawthorne reached for the hem of his sweater and started tugging it off.

"We should stop soon. I don't want to overextend you."

As he pulled up the sweater, the shirt underneath came with it, giving Emeline a glimpse of toned abdomen. She looked away quickly, feeling suddenly too warm herself.

He wrenched the shirt down, then finished wrestling the sweater over his head.

"I sing for a living." Emeline put her hands on her hips, staring intently at the floor. "I know my limits. I need to keep going."

As if to contradict her, Emeline's stomach grumbled loudly.

Hawthorne arched a brow, his hair gently mussed. He ran his fingers through it, smoothing it down. "It sounds like what you need is something to eat."

She opened her mouth to say she was fine, except she couldn't remember the last time she'd eaten.

"I can make us dinner while you continue practicing." He stretched his neck, then rolled his shoulders, wincing a little as he did, clearly stiff from standing all day—or possibly from the damage Claw had done the day before. Wiping the back of his hand against his gleaming brow, he looked to the glass walls around them. "Besides, I could use a change of scenery. My house isn't far from here."

With his blue knit sweater thrown over his arm, he collected the sheet music from the stand and turned to leave the domed room.

Unsure if she understood, Emeline called after him: "Is that a dinner invitation?"

Without stopping, he said over his shoulder, "If you want it to be."

Emeline's pulse quickened.

He was a fiend in the Wood King's employ. She shouldn't be having dinner with him. Not alone.

But Emeline had learned only two of the Song Mage's eleven songs today. If her demonstration was tomorrow at midnight, she should try learning at least one more before the night was out. She could then spend tomorrow perfecting all three. Hawthorne was the only one who could help her do this.

Her stomach rumbled again, snapping her out of her thoughts.

You can't survive on songs alone. You also need to eat.

"Coming?" Hawthorne called from the doorway.

Summoning her courage, Emeline followed the tithe collector out of the room.

It was only as she left the glass dome that she realized the woods hadn't come for her while she sang. No horde of insects swarmed. The sheet music hadn't molded over. The woods had been absent the entire time.

Odd.

Perhaps it was because they'd gotten their wish: Emeline trapped within their borders. But if that was true, why did they want her here so badly?

Emeline turned the question over in her mind but found no

answer. Shaking off the ominous feeling threading through her, she hurried to catch up with Hawthorne.

FROM THE PALACE GROUNDS, Hawthorne led her down a dirt path through a quiet wood leading away from the city center. The path took them to a small stone bridge over a gurgling creek, and by the time they reached it the sun had almost set and the trees had grown dark beneath their canopies.

Hawthorne's house stood on the other side of the bridge, green ivy creeping up the dusty stone and swerving around the window shutters. Its yard was bordered by a drystone wall speckled with moss.

Hawthorne opened the door and stepped through first, moving into the darkness. Emeline stood frozen on the threshold, Claw's warning suddenly clanging through her like a gong.

Beware of this one.

A sudden realization—that she was alone with him, far away from the eyes of the palace—turned her legs to jelly. She pressed her hand to the doorjamb, steadying herself.

A match flared nearby.

"You look terrified," Hawthorne said as he lit the lamps. "I'm not going to murder you, I promise."

"The promise of a liar," she said, forcing herself to step into the dark and shut the door behind her. "How comforting."

Candles and lamplight soon softened the darkness, allowing Emeline to see her surroundings. The pine floorboards beneath her feet were swept clean, and the house smelled of flour and yeast, as if someone had recently made bread.

It didn't seem like the house of someone dangerous.

But appearances could be deceiving.

While Hawthorne started a fire in the hearth, Emeline scanned the room, looking for clues. Anything that might give her insight into the king's tithe collector, his motives and secrets. A worn harvest table stood wedged between two benches near the window. On its surface, a lamp burned low, illuminating the book there. It had a crimson cover and a cracked slender spine. She wandered over to it.

Twenty Love Poems and a Song of Despair, the title read. By Pablo Neruda.

Why would Hawthorne be reading a book from her world?

He'd lit several lamps scattered around the room, and in the golden glow of their flames Emeline saw the shelves were crammed full of books.

Hundreds of books.

Sorted alphabetically, by author.

Drawn to them, Emeline lifted her fingers, reading the worn spines. Her fingertips swept across the works of Rumi, Christina Rossetti, and W. H. Auden. She found *Antigone* and *The Iliad. Meditations* and *War and Peace. East of Eden* and *If Beale Street Could Talk.*

On one shelf was an entire row of books with blank, smudged spines. *Sketchbooks?* It made her think of the graphite she'd seen on his fingers yesterday.

She turned to look at Hawthorne, who crouched before the hearth, blowing into the flames, trying to make them catch. His gray wool shirt stretched tight across his back, revealing the wings of his shoulder blades beneath.

He seemed so human, here in his house.

On either side of him, two moss-green armchairs faced each other, with more books stacked on the tables beside them.

Above, a vivid painting hung over the fireplace. Inside its frame, a woman was transforming into a tree.

The lower half of her body was bark and roots, plunging into soil, while her waist and chest arched upwards and her outstretched hands reached for the sky. The nymph's dark hair was a knotted mass of branches around her head, sprouting bright green leaves.

It was the myth of Daphne—the nymph who begged the river god to save her from Apollo and was turned into a laurel tree.

"It must be a terrible thing to lose," Hawthorne said, making her jump.

He looked up from where he crouched near the fire: to the woman in the frame. His left forearm was streaked with black ash.

"What's a terrible thing to lose?"

Hawthorne's eyes glittered as he studied the nymph. "Your humanity."

"But it was her choice," said Emeline, feeling defensive of Daphne. If the river god hadn't turned her into a laurel, she would have fallen prey to Apollo. "She asked to be saved."

Firelight flickered over Hawthorne's face as his gray-eyed gaze caught hers and held it.

"Saved," he murmured, considering this. "Is that really what the river god did? As a tree, her life is forfeit. She'll never be human again. She'll never laugh or sing, ponder or love, again. Don't you think she would have preferred the river god defeat Apollo, or at the very least warn him away, instead of taking something so precious from her?"

Emeline stared at him, wordless. His attention was intent on her, as if willing her to hear something he wasn't saying. As if he was no longer talking about Daphne, but something—or someone—else.

Her skin prickled as she tore her gaze away from him. "At least she's safe. As a tree, nothing can hurt her."

Hawthorne said nothing.

In the kitchen, Emeline shook off their strange conversation about Daphne and insisted on doing her part. A plan was forming in her mind. Here, in his home, Hawthorne seemed . . . softer. More at ease. If she, too, lowered her defenses, if she proved herself friendly and helpful, she could try asking again about the message to Joel. She could explain why her career depended on it. Maybe he'd be more understanding this time.

Hawthorne passed her a wooden cutting board and two white onions for chopping.

She sliced herself almost immediately.

"Darn it."

Bright red blood seeped up from the cut on her index finger. Hawthorne glanced up from where he stood roasting tomatoes on the woodstove.

"I should have warned you." He came towards her. "Sable's blades can sever fingers in one stroke. Let me see."

Emeline contemplated the knife gleaming on the wooden countertop. It was a beautiful blade, with a razor-thin edge and an elegant rose pattern carved into the ebony handle.

"Sable made that?"

She remembered the way Sable rose to Hawthorne's defense at dinner last night. *They must be friends.*

Hawthorne arrived at her side just as Emeline hooked the tip of her finger into her mouth, sucking gently to stop the blood flow. The taste of salt bloomed on her tongue.

Hawthorne fell instantly quiet.

"She's the king's bladesmith," he murmured, watching her.

When she withdrew her finger, Hawthorne reached for her

wrist and drew her hand closer to examine the cut. "Let me bandage this."

It was only a thin red line now, so Emeline shook her head. "It's fine."

Letting go, Hawthorne stepped back and put the contaminated knife in the sink. After reaching for a new one, he quickly and efficiently chopped her onions.

"Why don't you do what you're good at." He nodded to the sheet music resting on the countertop. "And leave the chopping to me." He scraped the onions into the pot, then reached for a cord of purplish-white garlic bulbs hanging down from the window over the sink.

She crossed her arms. "You don't think I can do this."

"Do what?" He broke off a flaky bulb, peeled four cloves, then started to crush and mince them.

"*This.* Cook."

He paused his chopping and raised an eyebrow. "Can you?"

The last thing she'd cooked herself in Montreal was a package of instant noodles. She glanced away, reaching for the stack of music. "I'm not great at it, no."

"Well, I happen to be good at it. So relax." He nodded to the windowsill above the sink, where a mason jar perched. Another object from her world. *Curious.* "Have some of Rooke's moonshine, if it will help. Then sing through those two songs. By the time you finish, this soup will be simmering, and I can assist with the next one."

Emeline hoisted herself onto the pale wooden countertop and reached for the jar of moonshine. Twisting the lid off, she brought it to her nose, sniffed, then raised it to her lips. As Hawthorne scraped the garlic in with the onions, she took a sip.

The liquid burned like a wood fire on its way down, all smoke and heat, the warmth of it flooding her.

"Oh," she murmured, surprised by its strength.

As the smell of cooking onions flooded the kitchen, she took a fuller sip, leaned her shoulders against the cupboards, then did as Hawthorne suggested: with the Song Mage's music on her lap, she sang though the songs she'd learned.

Both were ballads about a woman "marked by the moon." In them, the Song Mage praised his muse, describing her midnight hair, her rosebud mouth, her rocky spine. They were odes to her unparalleled beauty.

"He's a little obsessed," said Emeline when she finished singing. "Even her *teeth* enchant him." She browsed through the next ballad—also about his moon-marked woman. "And she must have had some pretty sexy ankles, because there's an entire verse devoted to them in the next song. . . ."

The corner of Hawthorne's mouth turned up. "Maybe ankles were his weakness."

Emeline glanced up at the boy cooking her dinner. He was like the forest, she thought. Quiet and steadfast in the way he held himself, with secrets hidden beneath.

What's your weakness? she wondered.

Emeline cleared her throat, trying to ignore the heat creeping across her cheeks. She took another sip of Rooke's moonshine. "Everything about her appears to be his weakness. It seems too good to be true."

Hawthorne, absorbed in his work, said nothing.

As the alcohol hit her bloodstream, Emeline grew warmer. Brighter. Watching Hawthorne cook, it struck her again how human he seemed. Thinking of his concern over Daphne's lost humanity, she glanced to his shadow. It didn't twist like Rooke's and Sable's. It didn't hint at any other form.

She decided to brave a question. To test the waters before she asked about Joel.

"Hawthorne?"

"Hmm?"

"What are you?"

Hawthorne—who was in the middle of turning the roasted tomatoes over with a wooden spoon—froze. "I'm sorry?"

She thought of the books on his shelves.

"You live here, in the Wood King's court. But you aren't a shiftling." She nodded towards his normal-shaped shadow stretching across the floorboards.

He lowered the spoon. "I'm human," he said stiffly. "Like you."

"Then how did you become the king's tithe collector?"

Quiet, he studied her. His walls were going up, those gray eyes turning cold and wary.

Before he could withdraw completely, Emeline took another sip of moonshine—to give her courage—and slid down from the counter. She walked over to the stove and pressed the jar into his hand.

"I saved you from a dragon yesterday, Hawthorne Fell. You could at least answer my question."

His gaze trailed over her, leaving her skin warm in its wake. Taking the moonshine, he brought it to his lips and tipped it back, taking a long swallow. Returning the jar to her hand, he wiped his mouth on his wrist. "I'm no one. Trust me."

But I don't trust you.

He'd been keeping secrets from the start.

Hawthorne turned back to the tomatoes, which were starting to blacken. "I'm almost done here," he said, as if the topic was closed. "And then we can work on the next song."

Letting him evade her—for now—Emeline lifted herself back onto the counter, considering him as he added the tomatoes and some fresh basil and salt to the pot.

"Here," he said after a long while. Dipping the spoon into

the soup, he cupped his hand beneath it as he walked over to where she sat on the counter. He blew on it softly, cooling it for her as he stepped between her knees.

At his closeness, all of Emeline's senses came alert. He was pressed against the counter, his hips wedged between her legs. If she scooted forward a few inches, her body would be flush with his.

Her heart kicked.

He lifted the spoon to her mouth. "Tell me if you like it."

She opened for him. He put the roasted tomato soup on her tongue, watching her lips close over the spoon.

Mmm, it was good. His soup tasted like comfort and warmth. Like being bundled up in blankets next to a blazing fire on cold winter days, watching the snow fall outside.

She looked up to find Hawthorne staring at her mouth. Like soup was the last thing on his mind.

Heat sparked between them. The moonshine hummed in Emeline's blood. It made the room beyond them soften, putting him alone into sharp focus. She'd drank too much too quickly, on too empty a stomach, and now her blood was turning to fire.

It made her reckless.

"Let's play a game," she whispered.

Hawthorne's mouth curved. Setting down the spoon, he braced his hands on the edge of the countertop, gripping it on either side of her. "What did you have in mind?"

She tipped her head back against the cupboard, gazing up at him. "I ask a question, and if you refuse to answer, you take a swallow." She pointed to the mason jar. "Then we switch."

He considered her for a moment, as if sensing the folly of such a game. But he didn't step away. Only leaned in closer, his gaze hungry. "All right. You start."

He betrays you in the end! Claw's voice hissed in her mind.

Emeline didn't know how to reconcile that boy—the one she

first met in the woods, the one Claw warned her against—with this one. A boy who liked to read, and kept his house cozy, and made his guests soup from scratch.

It was as if the rope he'd secured her with at the aerie was still looped around her waist and he was tugging on it. Pulling her towards him.

Maybe Claw's wrong.

But even if he was wrong, Hawthorne still took Pa and lied about it. Which was, indirectly, the reason she was stuck here. And if she couldn't get a message to Joel, Hawthorne would be—indirectly—the reason her music career crashed and burned.

"Why won't you deliver my message?" she asked as he frowned. "I don't think you understand—"

"I understand perfectly." Where a moment ago he'd been loose—almost liquid in his movements—his limbs had gone taut and stiff. But he didn't pull away from her. "And I already gave you my answer."

She reached for his sweater, which he'd pulled on during the cold walk here from the palace, and bunched it gently in her hand. The knit wool scratched her skin. "I was hoping you'd reconsider."

Their faces were inches apart. His gaze swept down her, and a startling heat flared in his eyes. Her body responded with an echoing warmth, rushing from her cheeks to her toes.

"Perhaps you're the one who should reconsider," he murmured, wrapping callused fingers around her wrist. "If you're this desperate, deliver the message yourself. Return to him."

He issued it like a challenge.

She narrowed her eyes. "You know I can't leave. Not without Pa."

"Then this discussion is over." His expression shuttered as he abruptly let go of her wrist and stepped back. Out of reach.

She bristled, glaring after him.

Another, deeper question surged up inside her.

"Why did you do it?"

The room was starting to spin a little from the moonshine.

"Do *what*?"

"Why did you take my grandfather?"

Hawthorne went stiller than stone. She watched those walls go up. High, high.

"You're the tithe collector," Emeline pressed, scooting to the edge of the counter. "Whatever Pa tithed to the Wood King, you could have decided it was enough. Or you could have taken something else. You didn't have to take *him*."

He shook his head, taking another step back. "Let's not do this."

She pushed herself down. "I need you to explain. You could have taken pity on him. He's just a harmless old man who's forgetting everything." She was walking him backwards, towards the kitchen wall. "Why would you steal him from the safety of his own bed and lie to me about it?"

A muscle in his jaw twitched.

"Tell me."

He halted, holding his ground. "It wasn't his own bed."

She stopped a few inches away from him. "What?"

"It was a bed he'd been forced to sleep in." He looked away. "He didn't belong there. He belongs in his house, on his farm, close to the people who love him. Not trapped behind locked doors, waiting for someone who isn't coming to rescue him. So yes. I took him. I took him because *he begged me to*."

The words were like ice water dumped over her head.

What?

"Ewan Lark tithed *himself* to the king."

Emeline stared at him, wordless. Her body growing hot, then cold.

"You're lying."

"Am I?" he whispered, refusing to look at her. "That man loves you more than his own life."

Emeline's eyes burned.

"And you put him in that place to forget him."

"Stop it."

"You should have seen the way he paced those halls, looking for you. The way he stood at the windows, watching for you. The way he sat near the phone for hours on end. But you never even called."

A hot coal simmered within her. She wanted to shove him. She wanted to sink to the floor and cry.

"Why call him when he doesn't even know who I am!" she shouted. "He doesn't remember me! Last night, when I accidently woke him up, he was terrified. Of *me*. His own granddaughter." Her hands balled into trembling fists. "He thought I was a stranger coming to hurt him."

The tension in the room snapped like a too-tight guitar string. Hawthorne stepped back as hot tears tracked down Emeline's cheeks. She spun away, walking out of the kitchen, palming her face in swift strokes.

"Pa asked me to put him in that care home," she whispered. "It was his decision."

It was true and not true. Pa had asked—for her sake. He wanted his granddaughter to be free of the burden of him.

"Emeline . . ."

She couldn't stay here, in his house, knowing that Hawthorne thought her a selfish, coldhearted girl—and wasn't she exactly that? Wasn't that why she felt so guilty?

"Emeline, wait."

Moving for the door, she said, "I'll let myself out."

Slamming it behind her, she escaped into the night.

EIGHTEEN

HE NEXT MORNING, AS she awaited her lesson beneath the crystal dome, Emeline paced the room, her nerves flickering. She hadn't slept at all last night. She kept going over their argument in her mind.

She'd drank too much. Gotten too bold. She never should have pressed him.

Her face heated as she remembered the words he'd thrown in her face.

I took him because he begged me to.

The shame of it scorched her. Pa, forced to tithe himself because she'd abandoned him in that place. Because being imprisoned in the Wood King's palace was better than being alone.

Sorrow welled like a rising tide. Emeline stopped pacing to press her hands to her face.

Her phone buzzed, jolting her back to the present.

She pulled it swiftly out, thinking maybe, *miraculously,* a text had come in. That she had stepped into some kind of magical hot spot and Joel was trying to get through to her, worried to death and wanting to know where she was.

When she glanced at the cracked screen, her heart sank.

It was only an automatic notification from Elegy, her music app.

She glanced to the upper corner of the screen. There were still no bars. No way to contact Joel. And her battery was almost completely dead.

At the sight of the background image, Emeline gripped the screen hard, staring. An old photo of her and Pa stared back. He sat in the driver's seat of a tractor and the trailer behind him was piled high with sun-bleached baskets of grapes, green and glistening. A five-year-old Emeline sat on his lap, turning towards him. Her small tanned hands were cupped to his ear while Pa grinned at whatever secret she was telling him.

Emeline swallowed down the lump in her throat.

How can so much change in so little time?

Marring the image was the notification from Elegy. It read: *Chloe Demarche uploaded a new file to SHARED FOLDER 3 days ago.*

She'd ignored the notification when it first came in. But since she was trapped here, waiting for her lesson to start, Emeline opened the app—which made its files accessible offline—and started to scroll.

All of the music files were written by Chloe, her songwriter.

Instead of opening Chloe's new file, though, Emeline scrolled all the way to the bottom of the list, stopping at a familiar password-protected folder.

The folder was full of her old songs, many she'd written as young as fourteen, before she'd ever driven away to the city with a dream in her heart and a tune in her throat and the stubborn belief that she could find success playing her own music.

The songs in that folder were less polished than her current sound. If she could even call it her sound.

A few months after moving to Montreal, when she was feeling the weight of her choice, struggling to pay her bills and two months late on rent, her manager convinced her to use a writer.

Someone with a commercial ear who could write more marketable songs.

Emeline was reluctant. She wanted to sing her own songs. Ones that *meant* something. But her bills were piling up. She'd nearly maxed out her credit card simply by keeping her car insured and putting gas in the tank. Emeline didn't know how much longer she could keep herself afloat.

She finally understood how young and unprepared she was. So she caved.

Her sound changed overnight. She started getting more gigs and exposure. People liked her new music. She signed with a small label and put out a professional album. Suddenly, Emeline could keep her bills paid. Suddenly, she was on an upwards curve instead of a downwards spiral.

Suddenly, she could breathe.

Back then, Emeline had recorded rough tracks of all her old songs, uploaded them into the folder, and locked it. Hoping that maybe, one day in the future, she would come back to those and sing them again.

Ironically, in the time since she'd locked them away she'd forgotten the folder's password. Probably her subconscious telling her to *let go and move on.*

But sometimes—if she had time to kill before a gig and needed to calm her nerves—Emeline would open up Elegy, scroll to the bottom, and try guessing the password until it was time to go onstage.

Nothing she thought up ever worked. She couldn't even remember why she'd titled the folder "Forgetting Is So Long."

Emeline tapped on the locked folder. A notification popped up.

You haven't accessed FORGETTING IS SO LONG in 546 days. Do you want to delete?

She hit NO.

This folder is password protected. Enter the password now.

Emeline's fingers hovered over her screen.

In the end, she didn't guess it. Just canceled and returned to Chloe's new song. Hawthorne hadn't arrived yet. She might as well listen to the file. She had a tour soon—one she fully intended to go on, the Wood King be damned—and she needed a few more songs to add to her set list.

This song could be just what she needed.

Before her phone's battery croaked, Emeline found the new audio file and tapped PLAY.

Chloe's raw, smoky voice came through the phone's speaker as she crooned long and low about an unrequited love. It was classic Chloe. Contemporary pop, with a dash of country drawl. It wasn't Emeline's style, but she understood why people liked it. Emeline smiled as she listened once, twice, three times, then started making edits in her head.

Soon, she was singing along, tweaking the song as she watched the sun rise over the King's City below. As she sang, her gaze wandered over the shining white walls of the palace beyond the dome. She thought of the Wood King sitting on his white throne. Of candlelit halls and attendants fluttering like moths. Of Claw's silver snout emerging from the shadows, and Rooke falling to his knees before Bog, and that creepy wall of skulls in the crypt . . .

It was habitual. Whenever she sang a song for the first time, she sealed a memory inside the melody. Like a gift she was packaging for her future self. She'd been doing it for as long as she could remember.

From now on, whenever she sang this song, she would come back to this moment, looking out over the King's City. She would remember the things that happened here.

If she survived, that is.

When she'd fashioned Chloe's song into a shape she liked, Emeline sang it back one more time—without Chloe's original cut—hitting RECORD as she did, then uploaded the file to her set-list folder.

"Did you write that?" said a voice from behind her.

Emeline spun. Hawthorne stood in the doorway, leaning against the jamb, arms crossed firmly over his chest.

Her insides sparked at the immediate tension in the room. She felt exposed beneath his piercing gaze. Tucking her phone into the breast pocket of her rose sweater, she forced the tone of her voice to match his: cool and uncaring. "I didn't realize I had an audience."

He remained in the doorframe. "That song isn't you."

Um, what? Emeline stared at him. "I'm sorry?"

Pushing away from the jamb, he stepped slowly into the room. "Is everything you sing like that?"

She crossed her arms over her chest, temper simmering. "Like *what*?"

"Dull and shallow."

The words stung.

No. This was perfect. The Wood King's henchman was back to his callous, surly self. That suited Emeline just fine. She didn't need his friendship. She only needed his help learning the Song Mage's music.

He took another step, coming farther into the room. "Like I said: not very *you*."

Emeline's fingers dug into the sleeves of her sweater. "You don't know a thing about me."

He didn't answer. Only looked beyond her, to the city below, his jaw clenching. "Should we begin? Your demonstration is tonight."

He didn't get to do that. Didn't get to provoke her, then move on as if he'd done nothing wrong. But their squabbling was cutting into her lesson, and her demonstration *was* tonight. They needed to get down to work.

Emeline tamped down on her anger, picked out the next song from the Song Mage's stack of music, and handed it to him. Keeping the growl out of her voice, she said, "Start with this one."

ALL THROUGH THE LESSON, the tension between them remained. Emeline's emotions bubbled, threatening to spill over. Anger, shame, and something else. Some fragile, shimmering thing she needed to keep contained.

Hawthorne, too, was off his game. Now that she was looking, there were dark smudges beneath his eyes, and his maple-dark hair was wild as a raven's ruffled feathers, as if from running his hands through it.

Maybe she wasn't the only one who couldn't sleep last night.

In yesterday's lesson, he'd been a model of restraint. Controlled and in charge. Leading her through the first two songs.

Today, there was a fault line running through him.

But they forged ahead, untangling the difficult knots of the next two songs together. When Emeline found the heart of each one, when she carried the notes *just right,* she looked—despite herself—for that slight nod of approval, that tiny hint of a smile that told her he was impressed.

Instead, she found him coming undone: hands clenched, eyes thirsty. As if he wanted to drink in the sound of her voice. As if he wanted to drink her down to the dregs.

When their gazes met, he tore his away, face shuttering closed, entombing himself within a wall of stone. As if her voice did something to him that he didn't want it to do and he was trying his best to ward himself against it—and failing.

As if yesterday he'd been holding himself in check. Reining something in.

The idea of it—that *she* could get past his defenses—made something swell inside her. Part delicious challenge, part revenge for his refusing to deliver her message to Joel, Emeline yearned to smash down his walls, just to prove she could. She longed to strip down his defenses and force him to face her head-on.

"Again," he commanded when she got the notes wrong. Still pushing. Still demanding her best.

Emeline sang it again, then again.

This time, when their voices aligned, Emeline's blood hummed like a tuning fork. She could feel herself on the cusp of something.

Sensing it, Hawthorne hesitated. His voice wavered as he pulled back, about to close himself off.

Don't you dare. She stared him down. *We aren't done.*

Emeline had an intense urge to *force* him to stay with her. Letting go of her temper, she reached for him with the melody, fixing him in place with her voice. Needing to know what lay beyond those walls of his. Wanting his secrets.

Face me.

Her voice held him hostage.

Let down your walls before I break them.

To her surprise, he didn't pull back. Instead, he rose to meet her. Their gazes locked. Their voices mingled and fused, growing into a crescendo. But as their voices became one, so did other things.

A startling warmth flooded her, heady and strong. With it came feelings of happiness and pride.

She isn't only learning this song; she's transforming it into something beautiful.

Emeline faltered. It was his thought—spilling into her. Like a tipped cup of hot tea.

Her voice knows its shape better than the notes on the page.

She should have let go right then. Should have broken off the song, for his sake.

But she didn't.

Emeline dug deeper, to the thing buried beneath his thoughts. Something with bottomless, thirsty roots. Something one pruned and cut and tried to dig up—but never got all of. So it kept coming back, thirstier than ever, until it was a bitter, unquenchable yearning. An ache with no balm . . .

"Enough!"

Hawthorne wrenched himself out of her thrall. The sudden shock of it made the room spin. Emeline reached for the music stand, gripping it until her knuckles whitened, trying to steady herself.

A heavy cloak of exhaustion fell over her, as if breaking down his defenses had taken more strength than she realized.

Hawthorne stepped back. Away from her.

Emeline's gaze lifted to find his eyes wild and his breath coming fast. Spots of color appeared high on his dusky cheeks as he blushed the way magnolias bloomed, realizing what she had done.

Her voice had stripped him down. Peered straight through his skin to his core. *Stolen* something he hadn't wanted to give her.

"Hawthorne . . ."

The room shrank around them. Too small and cramped

despite all the space. It was dark, she realized. The moon was high.

How long have we been here?

"I think I've reached my limit today." His anguished voice tore at her like a jagged knife. "You're ready, and it's nearly midnight. You have no further need of me." His face was unreadable. "I wish you luck tonight, singer."

Before she could stop him, Hawthorne turned.

"Wait. . . ."

The desperate thud of his footsteps rang out through the dome as he moved past her.

"I'm sorry," she whispered.

But he was already gone.

NINETEEN

BEFORE HER DEMONSTRATION THAT night, Emeline's attendants braided her dark hair into a crown, then wove garlands of silver stars through it. They rubbed rouge on her cheeks and lips, then dressed her in black, with more tiny stars clustered at the hems of her sleeves.

As they worked, Emeline stared at the reflection in the smoky mirror, thinking of her voice tangled up with Hawthorne's. Of the song binding him to her. Of his thoughts spilling into her mind, followed by that hot ache of longing.

She had done that. Somehow.

If she was being honest, there was something incredibly satisfying about it. Hawthorne had wielded power over her—first by lying and tricking her, then by refusing to send her message to Joel. Emeline had simply repaid him in kind, by tearing down his walls.

But there was something unnerving about it too. She remembered the shadow skin reaching into her mind against her will, taking things it had no right to take, using those things against her. . . .

That thought frightened Emeline. Surely, she would never go that far.

Whatever she had done to Hawthorne, she could never do it again.

Soon, two hedgemen came and delivered her to the grove where she'd first confronted the Wood King. The trees were just as tall, rising up towards the night sky, but their leaves had transformed from green to gold. The tall lampposts had been lit and night bugs chirped in the shadows. Like in her first meeting with the king, courtiers gathered at the edges, this time seated at elegant tables awaiting her demonstration.

Hawthorne wasn't among them, but Emeline sighted Pa and his attendant sitting at a table near the middle. Someone had recently washed and combed Pa's gray hair, and he looked handsome in a pressed shirt.

She'd been avoiding her grandfather ever since scaring him the other day. But he seemed himself tonight. Calm and content as he sat among the courtiers.

When he caught sight of Emeline, she could tell from the look in his eyes that he was fighting to place her, watching her cross the grove like he knew she was important; he just couldn't remember why.

Emeline smiled at him.

I love you, she thought. *I'm sorry for getting you into this mess.*

He smiled slowly back.

If everything went as planned, Pa would go free soon.

And I'll be stuck here, she thought, soberly. *Alone.* Until she found some way to escape. If that was even possible. And if it was, how long would it take?

She thought of her tour. Of the Daybreak representatives. Of Joel, wondering where she was.

If Hawthorne weren't so stubborn, she thought, her anger rising. *If he'd simply agreed to deliver one little message . . .*

But Hawthorne had no intention of helping her. If she

wanted to save her career, Emeline would have to take matters into her own hands.

Up ahead, the king rested on his frost-pale throne, bathed in starlight. He wore a robe of blooming white flowers and Emeline watched in disbelief as the delicate petals unfurled while others shriveled, browned, and died away.

Two hedgemen flanked him, standing straight as birches.

Gathering her courage, Emeline walked out into the center of the clearing. The breeze ruffled her hair and cooled her skin.

"Good eve, singer." The Wood King's voice rushed through the clearing, like a wild wind.

She bowed her head to him. "Sire: before I begin, I have a favor to ask."

Her voice rang through the clearing. The king watched her, his face unreadable. With a flick of his fingers, he motioned for her to go on.

"I've been in your court for several days," she said. "No one knows I'm here. People will be thinking the worst by now."

When the king didn't interrupt her, she took a step forward.

"All I need is to send one message home to let them know I'm safe." She would send it to Joel, explaining things and asking him to tell her manager to please *please* not cancel her tour, because she'd be back soon.

But she left this part out.

Silence fell over the grove. In the stillness, the flowers cloaking the king stopped blooming. Instead, the petals curled in on themselves, tightening into buds.

"You may ask my tithe collector to send a message for you."

Emeline's hands bunched the fabric of her dress. "I've asked him, sire, and he refused."

"Then there's nothing more I can do. My tithe collector is

the only member of my court able to pass beyond the border-lands. Please proceed with the demonstration."

Emeline's blood sparked. *Can't you force him?* she wanted to say. *Aren't you king?* But it was written straight across his face: he didn't care. She'd been a fool to think he would.

This was the creature who'd tormented Edgewood all her life. Emeline was nothing to him. She was utterly powerless here.

Except for one thing.

She lifted her chin as the Wood King waited on his pale throne. Her anger made her reckless—but so did her experience. Years as a musician had taught Emeline there was no reward without risk.

"I fetched the Song Mage's music from Claw—a feat no one else in your court has accomplished for you." She tried to keep the anger out of her voice. "I've been learning your beloved min-strel's songs in order to please you, my king. Send a message for me, and I will happily sing them for you."

The unspoken threat was clear: *no message, no songs.*

The audience behind her murmured. The king's black eyes narrowed.

Like a shadow moving slowly up a wall, he rose from his throne. "You think to bargain with me further, dustling?"

The hair on her arms prickled. This was dangerous ground she was standing on, but Emeline held firm. Both Hawthorne and Grace had said the king longed for his Song Mage. Emeline was in possession of the man's music. She'd learned four of his eleven songs in only two days. That had to be worth more than the favor she was asking.

The king prowled towards her. Dead, shriveled petals scattered across the earth in his wake. Standing before Emeline, the shadow of him cloaked her, cold as winter, and his gnarled fingers curled into lumpen fists, like knots in a tree.

"Sing," he commanded, lips pulling back from chipped, woody teeth. Beneath the scent of him—all earth and moss—Emeline smelled decay.

She held his dark gaze. "I will," she promised. "Once a message is sent."

His hands shot out. Before she could move, those coarse fingers grabbed her throat and *squeezed.*

The strength of him stunned her. Ice spread through Emeline's body as she gasped for air, but none filled her lungs. She grabbed his wrists, trying to dig her fingernails into his toughened flesh, trying to force him to let go. But his limbs were hard as tree trunks.

She heard shouting. Saw Pa rise from his chair, yelling her name. Saw her grandfather stumble shakily through the courtiers, trying to get to her.

But if he did, the king would hurt Pa too.

What had Hawthorne said? *The curse has twisted his mind.*

The king squeezed harder. Any more force and he would snap her neck. Her lungs burned, starved for air. Pain made stars pop before her eyes, which were tearing up. Her grandfather disappeared as the grove blurred.

Only the king's white pupils stamped her vision now, their moon shapes thicker than before. As if they waxed and waned with the lunar cycle.

She'd made a grave mistake. She'd dared to defy the Wood King, and she would pay the price, dying here while her grandfather watched, his terrified yells the last sounds she heard.

She couldn't breathe.

Couldn't breathe.

Couldn't . . .

From a world away, a smoky voice said, "Damage her vocal cords and she'll be of no use to you, sire."

"She already is of no use to me!"

"I must respectfully disagree, sire. Not only did she liberate the Song Mage's music from Claw, she sang the dragon to sleep. I think she will prove quite valuable . . . if you let her live."

The iron grip around Emeline's throat suddenly loosened. Cold air rushed into her lungs as she collapsed to her knees. The ground was solid and cold beneath her as she gasped, gulping down air while the world came back into focus. First the Wood King above her. Then the tall trees of the grove. And last, her grandfather's face as he ran towards her.

When her gasps turned to coughs, Pa reached her, yelling at the king. His trembling arms came around her as he sank down beside her, pulling her into him. Emeline pressed her face into his shoulder, letting him hold her. Silently cursing her own defiance.

She now knew the limits of the Wood King's mercy.

Only when her coughing subsided did she search for the owner of the voice. Sable Thorne stood between Emeline and the Wood King. Barely restrained. Eyes blazing with golden fire. The tight lines of Sable's body said she was prepared to draw steel if her king touched Emeline again.

But why? Sable had barely even met her, and all but ignored her when they were around each other.

At the presence of his bladesmith, the feral look in the king's eyes dispersed, like fog in warm sunlight. His robe of flowers began blooming once more as he rubbed his hand across his eyes, as if waking from a dream.

"Go *now*," said Sable to Emeline without taking her eyes off the king. "Get yourself and Ewan out of the grove."

TWENTY

BACK IN THE SAFETY of her rooms, Emeline took Pa out onto their shared terrace beneath the stars—to soothe them both. The garden was aglow with fireflies, and alive with the chatter of night birds. But the night was cold. After seating Pa in a chair, she tucked a thick blanket around him, then went to fetch one for herself.

When she returned, stepping out through her door and onto the darkened terrace, Pa jumped.

"Who's there?"

Emeline hesitated, frozen between the door and her grand-father. "It's just me. Emeline."

Her voice scratched like sandpaper. Startled, she reached protectively for her throat, rubbing it gently to assess the damage. She remembered the feel of the Wood King's hands. The painful squeeze. The terror of gasping for air to find there was none.

I need to get Pa away from this place.

But even here, there were hedgemen stationed at the doors of their quarters as well as patrolling the garden, their gazes glued to Emeline. Even if she could get past them—even if she could get *Pa* past them—the palace gate was even more heavily guarded.

And then there was the city gate to get through. . . .

"Emeline, yes." The night hid Pa's face from her. "Of course I know who you are."

The admission shocked her. *You do?* she thought, lowering herself into the chair next to his.

"I planted a tree for you. On the day you were born." He smiled at the memory.

Her heart skipped a beat.

"Whatever happened to that tree?" he asked, suddenly frowning. "One day it was there and the next it was gone."

Emeline glanced away from him. "You cut it down after I left."

"What's that?" He turned sharply towards her. His face was all shadows. "Why on earth would I cut it down?"

Emeline shrugged. She'd believed it was because he forgot her and, with her, the reason he'd planted it.

She'd loved that tree as a kid, climbing up into its boughs, telling it all her secrets and singing it her songs. It had been like a good friend.

"Listen, duckie, I know I'm losing my mind," he spoke into the darkness. "I'm forgetting things. I *know.* But I would never cut down your tree."

There was something about the way he said it that made her look at him. He was strangely lucid, remembering her name and who she was. Remembering her tree.

"That tree was an offering," he said softly, as if to himself. "A gift to the Wood King. If I wanted the forest to keep you safe, I had to offer something in exchange."

Emeline frowned. He'd never told her that before. But it made sense: the residents of Edgewood were superstitious people. It was no different from hanging boughs of hawthorn over their lintels to protect themselves from the Hunt.

Emeline and her grandfather fell into a companionable silence. It made her long for her guitar, in order to imprint this moment into a song. The way his eyes recognized her. The way he spoke her name—warm and familiar. Like before.

"Emeline," he said, breaking the silence. His blue eyes were earnest as they peered into hers. "I want you to do something for me. I want you to get out of this place."

She nodded. "As soon as you're safe, I will. But I need to get you home first."

He turned fully towards her, leaning across the arm of his chair. She studied the familiar lines of his face, the cowlick in his gray hair. "My time is running out, duckie. But yours . . ." He looked down at his open hands. "I never wanted this." He shook his head. "It's my fault that you're here."

She was about to argue when he reached across the space between them, taking her slender hands in his big ones.

"I want you to leave me here and go home, Emeline. I want to live out what little time I have left knowing you're happy and safe." He smiled a sad smile. "Will you do that for me?"

Emeline swallowed the lump in her throat, then squeezed his hand.

She couldn't leave him again.

You should have seen the way he paced those halls, looking for you.

A sudden knock echoed from inside her room, saving her from answering his question.

"Emeline?" a voice called out from the other side of her door.

This is it. She pulled her hands from Pa's. *The king's guards are here to drag me away.*

"It's Sable."

Oh. Emeline pictured the golden-eyed girl stepping between her and the king, like a shield. Putting herself at risk by challenging him.

Why?

Walking back through her rooms, Emeline swung the door open.

Sable leaned against the adjacent wall, her head tipped back to the ceiling, her body radiating tension. When the door opened, she snapped to attention. Like a cornered wolf, she seemed suddenly wary.

Until her gaze fell on Emeline's bruised throat.

The wariness fell away. Frowning, Sable pushed away from the wall. "Hawthorne never should have denied you."

In one hand was a rolled piece of parchment; in the other, a black fountain pen. "Here." She held them out to Emeline. "Write your letter."

Emeline stared as the words sank in. "Is this a trick?"

Sable shook her head. "No trick. Hawthorne will deliver it tonight. I've ensured it."

A featherlight feeling whooshed through Emeline. Maybe she could save her career after all.

Taking the parchment and pen, she ran to the desk near the windows, pulled out the chair, and sat on its green velvet cushion. Drawing in close, she pressed the parchment flat against the dark wood and wrote quickly.

She kept things vague: telling Joel she was safe, that she'd found her grandfather, and that she needed to *take care of some things*. She told him she'd be back before her tour and to please tell his dad not to do anything other than cancel her gigs before then.

Emeline blew on the ink, then folded the parchment once it was dry. Rising, she returned to Sable and handed it over.

"Rooke has persuaded the king to give you another chance," said Sable. "But there's one condition: he wants you to perform all eleven of the Mage's songs."

Eleven songs. She only knew four right now. "How much time do I have?"

"Your final demonstration will be at midnight in three days."

Seven songs in three days.

Her heart plummeted into her stomach.

But if it would make up for her disobedience tonight, if it would set Pa free, Emeline would do it. She had to.

If the Wood King was willing to give her a second chance, Emeline wouldn't screw it up. She would learn the rest of the Song Mage's music, prove herself to the king, and save her grandfather.

And then she would escape.

Before turning to leave, Sable paused in the doorway. "My advice? Don't defy him again."

THE NEXT MORNING, EMELINE'S fingers trailed the cool stone walls of the palace, her breath bunched tight in her chest as she walked to the crystal dome. She'd been practicing what to say when she saw Hawthorne. He would have delivered her letter to Joel by now, so it seemed only fair that she apologize for what happened in yesterday's lesson.

We started off on the wrong foot, she would tell him. *Let's start over.*

But when she stepped into the sparkling sunlight of the domed room, it wasn't Hawthorne who awaited her. It was a small woman with bark-brown hair shorn close to her face.

"Emeline Lark?" The woman's ochre eyes folded into half-moons.

Emeline nodded, scanning the room. There was no sign of the tithe collector.

"I'm Calliope." The woman clasped her small hands in front of her. "Your singing instructor."

"Oh." Emeline stopped scanning. This was the woman Hawthorne had been temporarily filling in for. The one who'd been waylaid by shadow skins on her way to the city.

Emeline forced a smile as she stared at the spot near the music stand, where Hawthorne had stood these past two days. Feet planted firmly. Arms tightly crossed. Watching her sing.

"It's nice to meet you."

This was good, she told herself. What had she been thinking, anyway? That she and Hawthorne could be *friends*? The idea seemed absurd to her now. All they ever did was argue.

No, the more distance she had from the tithe collector, the better.

"Shall we begin?"

TWENTY-ONE

CALLIOPE WAS AN ALTOGETHER different sort of teacher. Where Hawthorne stopped Emeline mid-song, making her repeat the trouble spot until she smoothed out the snags, Calliope waited until she finished, then pointed out her weaknesses, offering suggestions. Hawthorne demanded, pushing Emeline to her limit. Calliope coaxed, allowing Emeline to find her own way.

Emeline was happy to have Calliope's guidance, but by the end of their lesson she found herself craving the pressure. She missed the stern intensity of Hawthorne. She yearned for that moment when their voices aligned in a harmony so perfect, it made her body hum.

No, she thought, remembering the look on his face as he wrenched himself out from under her voice's spell. *Not that.*

"Very good," said Calliope, looking to the sun's position in the sky. It was late afternoon, and their shadows stretched long across the dome. "I'll meet you back here tomorrow."

That's it? Emeline watched her instructor pull on her yellow coat. They'd only gotten through one new song today.

Before she could beg for more time, Calliope said, "Oh, Emeline? I noticed there are some sheets missing. From the last song." She tapped the stack of music resting on the sapling stand with the tips of her willowy brown fingers. "Do you happen to know where they are?"

"What?" Panic flickered through her. Emeline stepped forward and shuffled through the pages. "That can't be right. . . ."

"I'm certain they'll turn up," Calliope said kindly, her hands starting to fasten the buttons of her yellow coat. "Perhaps they're in your rooms."

Before leaving, she flashed Emeline a quick smile, then turned on her heel and went out.

Alone, Emeline came to the last song—or rather, what was left of it.

It was as Calliope said: several pages were missing, including the title page. Hoping they'd gotten mixed in with earlier songs, Emeline went through the whole stack, sorting out each song, stacking them in separate piles on the floor.

Over and over, the last song came up short. Only the two final pages were there; the first four were gone.

Emeline's heart pounded against her ribs.

Don't panic. Calliope's right. They're probably in my rooms.

Emeline went and searched. She turned over furniture. She checked under the bed, in the armoire, and on the desk.

She didn't find them.

Dread crept through her body like frost across a pane.

If she couldn't find the missing music, she couldn't sing the last song. And if she didn't sing all the songs for the king in two days, Pa would never be free. And who knew what the king would do to Emeline.

Where else could it be?

She'd brought the music to Hawthorne's house the night he made her dinner. It was possible she'd dropped a few sheets in her rush to leave. Perhaps they were there.

Throwing on a coat, she pulled on her Blundstones and set out for his house.

Yellow leaves spilled like gold coins across the path through the trees, flickering in the light of the setting sun. Trees hushed and swayed around her, too big and too thick and too tall. Here in the quiet, she could almost hear them breathing. Deep, steady breaths that sank all the way down to their roots.

Emeline followed the path through the quiet wood to the small bridge over the creek. After crossing it, she walked up to the stone house and rapped her knuckles on the wooden door.

"Hawthorne?"

No one answered.

She knocked harder. "Hawthorne!"

When nothing happened, she tried the knob.

Locked.

Emeline growled, then stepped back, scanning. "Where are you?" she whispered. She'd only learned one song today, the last one was missing, and her demonstration was just two days away.

I need you.

But no smoke plumed from the chimney and no lamplight warmed the windows. The house looked sleepy and dark.

Hawthorne wasn't home.

Who else could help her? She thought of Sable and Rooke but had no idea where either of them lived.

She thought of Grace.

There's a pub in the city called The Acorn, Grace had told her. *Meet me there at sunset on Friday. We can make a plan.*

It was Friday today. So that's what Emeline set out to do.

AFTER AN HOUR OF wandering the city's lamplit streets, asking for directions (twice) and getting turned around (twice), she finally spotted the sign for The Acorn swinging above a door. It was nut shaped and forged of tarnished copper. The windows of the pub glowed gold, illuminating the packed house inside.

Emeline stepped through the door and into the warm, rowdy space. Lamps glowed dimly and it smelled faintly like beer. A pair of fiddlers dueled in the corner, bows slashing their strings, feet stomping in time with their tune, mouths grinning as their duet sped faster and faster towards its end while the audience cheered them on.

Emeline scanned the tables crammed full of people and caught sight of Rooke first. He sat near the very back, his dark eyes twinkling as he told Grace some raucous joke from across their table. With them sat Aspen, Hawthorne's friend from dinner the other night. The girl with the gemlike eyes and delicate features. Beside Aspen sat Nettle.

Emeline made her way towards them, then sank down on the bench next to Rooke.

"Emeline!" He grinned, throwing an arm around her shoulders. His breath smelled like ale, and his smile was bright white. "Let me buy you a drink. What do you fancy?"

He was already on his feet.

"Um . . . you choose?"

When he left, Emeline glanced to Grace. "Have you seen Hawthorne?"

"He's visiting a friend," Aspen answered from farther down the table. "He'll be joining us later."

A friend? "Are you sure?"

Aspen's unbound hair glittered in the lamplight. "That's what he said over dinner last night."

The image of Hawthorne making the beautiful Aspen dinner flooded Emeline. She couldn't get it out of her head: the two of them alone, eating together by candlelight.

Was it just dinner? Or something more?

The thought snarled her stomach up in knots.

Startled by her own reaction, Emeline swiftly buried it.

What is wrong with you? It didn't matter what Hawthorne and Aspen did together. It was none of her business.

Just then, Rooke returned. Handing her a glass of whiskey, he squished back in beside her.

Grace cocked her head, studying Emeline. "You all right?"

Emeline shook her head.

Sweat beaded down her neck from wearing too many layers in too warm a place. As she unbuttoned her coat and shrugged it off, she explained her predicament: the king's second chance, her need to learn all eleven songs, and the missing pages.

"I don't know what to do." Thinking about it more, if the missing music *was* at Hawthorne's house, wouldn't he have seen it and brought it to her? She was certain he would—he'd wanted her to learn the songs as desperately as she did. "I only have two days to find it."

She took a long, burning swallow of whiskey, trying to numb the panic sparking through her.

"This is exactly why I back up all my files," she muttered. On her Elegy app, in the cloud, and sometimes, if she was feeling especially paranoid, on a USB key.

"Maybe the Song Mage did too," said Grace, who was dressed in a periwinkle shirt with lace sleeves. Her copper-brown eyes glittered in the lamplight. "Even if he didn't, there are probably rough drafts, right? Maybe at his house?"

Grace was a genius. Of course there would be rough drafts! As a last resort, she might be able to piece together notes and lyrics in lieu of the finished song. If she could find such things.

Hope sparked inside Emeline. "Does anyone know where he lived?"

The table went dead quiet.

Aspen stiffened. Rooke's smile faded right off his face. It was Nettle who leaned in eagerly, her eyes going round as moons. "The Song Mage's estate lies just outside the city, due west from the gate."

"It's more of a shell than a house," Rooke interjected. "Like all of the settlements beyond the wall, the curse has claimed it. No one goes there anymore."

"Because it's haunted," added Aspen.

Emeline glanced down the table. "Haunted?"

"By the Vile," said Nettle. Her smile was too big and too bright. It reminded Emeline of Grace's warning: *She's a cat who likes to play with her prey before she kills it.*

Emeline looked to Grace for clarification. "What's the Vile?"

"The witch I told you about," said Grace. "The one who delivered the Song Mage's head to the king in a velvet pouch."

"She was desperately in love with him," said Aspen. "But he spurned her; he loved another."

"So she cut out his heart," said Nettle. Her amber eyes gleamed, as if this thrilled instead of saddened her.

"She's a horror now," continued Rooke. "People believe she created the shadow skins and that they do her bidding."

"It's why you can't go to his house," said Aspen. "She's not something you want to meet."

Rooke nodded his agreement.

And if I have no choice? Emeline didn't voice this thought. From the looks in their eyes, she doubted she'd get any encouragement. Except, perhaps, from Nettle.

Suddenly, the music changed. The fiddles in the corner slowed, their song morphing into a waltz. Grace rose, her eyes on Emeline.

"My usual dance partner isn't here tonight," she said, that iron ring winking on her finger. "Do you mind? I need the practice."

"I . . ."

There was a secret blooming in Grace's eyes. And from the way her brow lifted, almost like a dare, Emeline wondered if she wanted accompaniment for something other than dancing.

Emeline rose from the bench and went with her.

"I don't know how to waltz," Emeline admitted as they left the table behind.

Grace waved her hand, as if this were nothing. "I'll show you."

When they entered the crowd of dancing couples, Grace turned to face Emeline, her lavender scent warring with the smell of sweat and beer, her eyes bright with concern.

All at once, the dancers around them started to notice the king's singer—who'd conquered a dragon and defied the king. She heard their whispers and felt their stares.

Grace ignored the onlookers. Her hand settled on Emeline's shoulder. "Everything looks the same in the Stain. It's easy to get lost there," she said, leading them in the steps of the waltz. "But Sable has dozens of maps of the woods. She won't notice if one goes missing. I'll bring it."

Emeline frowned, her hand on Grace's waist as she tried to follow the pattern of Grace's feet. "What do you mean?"

When a pair of dancers came too close for comfort, Grace steered them away, out of hearing distance, and lowered her voice. "I'm coming with you to the Song Mage's house."

Emeline slowed, nearly tripping over Grace.

"When does your singing lesson end tomorrow?"

Judging by today's lesson with Calliope? "Late afternoon."

"Perfect. We can be there and back before nightfall."

Her words rang with authority, reminding Emeline that Grace was the eldest of three sisters and used to getting her way.

"Are you sure? You heard them." Emeline nodded towards the table at the back. "It sounds dangerous."

Before Grace could answer, the waltz ended and one of the bartenders stepped up beside them. He was tall and thin, with sea-blue eyes and shoulders that hunched like a hawk's. Around his waist was a checkered apron.

"Fortification," he said, holding out a glass of what looked like the whiskey Emeline had left behind at the table. "From a friend."

Thinking that friend was Rooke, Emeline thanked him. Taking the glass, she slanted her head back, downing the drink in one swallow. It wasn't nearly as smooth as the moonshine sitting on Hawthorne's kitchen sill, and a strange aftertaste bloomed in her throat: like flower petals and honey. A sudden queasiness turned her stomach, and she pressed her hands to her abdomen, sure she was going to be sick.

But all at once, it passed.

When she looked up, she found Grace glaring hard over her shoulder. Emeline turned to look.

In the corner, at the table they'd left, Rooke leaned towards Aspen, deep in conversation, with Emeline's drink still beside him. It was Nettle who watched them. Nettle's owl-like eyes stared at the empty glass clutched in Emeline's hand as she smiled that too-strange smile.

It's Nettle's favorite game, Grace's words rang through her mind. *She enchants her friends by spiking their drinks with spells.*

Emeline's blood hummed.

Grace's face darkened.

"What should I do?" Emeline whispered in horror.

"Go." Grace's voice prickled like a thistle. "Sleep it off. I'll come get you tomorrow afternoon, and we can leave from there."

Emeline thought of Hawthorne, who hadn't turned up yet. She still wanted to ask him about the missing music.

But did she really want Nettle's spell to manifest with Hawthorne in the room?

Hell no.

She headed straight back to the palace.

TWENTY-TWO

EMELINE SANK INTO THE hot bathwater, her blood brimming with whatever spell lay dormant inside her, put there by Nettle's enchanted drink. She intended to hide here, in her bath, until her skin turned wrinkled and white.

Until she *soaked* the spell out.

When the water finally grew tepid, Emeline lifted herself from the tub. As she toweled her hair dry, muffled laughter drifted through the walls between her rooms and Pa's.

Odd. She tilted her head to listen. Who was visiting Pa at this hour?

The laughter came again. Wrapping herself in a silk robe that ended just above her knees, she padded barefoot across the floor, leaving puddles in her wake, and stood at the door leading to her grandfather's rooms.

After silently turning the crystal knob, she opened the door to listen.

"Who are you again?" she heard Pa say.

A rough-soft reply followed. "I'm Hawthorne."

Emeline froze.

Peering through the crack, she spotted both Pa and the tithe collector sitting in two armchairs facing the fire. They held steaming mugs in their hands.

It stunned her.

What was the tithe collector doing with her grandfather?

He's visiting a friend, Aspen had told her.

"Well, Hawthorne. Have you ever stopped to wonder: What's the point?"

Emeline winced. It was Pa's most-asked question. He'd probably asked it three times already while she was in the bath. But if he had, Hawthorne was unbothered.

"I do wonder that," he said, surprising her. Usually people checked out the second time Pa asked it. "All the time, in fact."

"Have you come up with anything good?" Pa leaned in as if they were old friends sharing a secret.

Hawthorne smiled, too, mirroring Pa. He sipped his drink before answering, "There's this book I've been rereading lately. More of a long poem, really. It's called *Beowulf.* Do you know it?"

Pa shook his head. "Can't say that I do."

"Well, there's a phrase in Latin, *ubi sunt,* which describes the spirit of the poem. It translates to a question. Something like: *Where have they gone?*"

Emeline's heart hammered in her chest as she listened. What, exactly, was happening here? Was the Wood King's henchman . . . hanging out with her grandfather? Discussing poetry with him?

"Where has who gone?" asked Pa.

"The ones who've come before us," said Hawthorne. "In *Beowulf, ubi sunt* means . . . or at least, I think it means . . . 'What's the point of courage? Of fighting off monsters? Of doing your best? What's the point of any of it, if we're all going to die in the end?'"

Pa sat back in his chair, pensive.

"It's not an answer to your question," Hawthorne said, raising his mug. "But it means you and I aren't alone in our quest."

Pa lifted his mug, clinking it against Hawthorne's.

When he yawned a moment later, Hawthorne drained his drink. "It's late. I should be going."

Pa nodded as they both rose to their feet.

"I'll see you tomorrow."

Tomorrow? How often did he visit?

The way Hawthorne smiled at her grandfather, so full of admiration and respect, made Emeline's pulse kick. She gripped the knob of the door until her knuckles hurt. The boys she'd brought home in the past never treated Pa like this—like someone they wanted to be friends with. Like someone worthy of the utmost respect.

With her heart pounding in her ears, she shut the door before they saw her, then leaned her back against it, her entire body crackling and alert as she listened to Pa walk him out.

Soon, she heard Hawthorne's footsteps echo in the hall. Emeline tightened the sash of her silk robe and went after him.

Outside her rooms, she saw him several paces down the candlelit corridor, the small flames illuminating his dark form.

"Hawthorne, wait. . . ."

His footsteps slowed.

Still dripping from her bath, her wet feet padded against the cold marble. As he turned, she stopped abruptly and slipped. Hawthorne reached for her elbow, steadying her.

He wore a dark green sweater tonight, the color complementing his skin tone. Like spruce trees in late autumn.

"Emeline. What are—"

His gaze fell instantly to her bruised throat. Storm clouds moved swiftly in and a sharp line appeared between his brows as he studied the marks on her skin. Stepping towards her, he lifted his hand, silently asking permission.

She gave it, baring her throat to him. "It's not as bad as it looks."

His fingers traced her bruises, achingly tender as they glided down her neck. Emeline's heart beat strangely fast beneath his touch.

"Do you have to be so reckless?" It sounded like more of a plea than a question.

"Maybe it's in my nature."

He moved closer, bringing his fire-like warmth with him. "Maybe so." He cupped the back of her neck with his palm, fingers sliding through the small hairs there as he raised her chin with his thumb, continuing to examine her. "You should be far away from here, Emeline Lark. Somewhere safe."

"Hmm," she said in vague agreement. When his thumb stroked softly along her jaw, her blood sparked, and she whimpered. Mistaking the sound, he withdrew his hands and stepped back.

Before he could turn and leave, she reached for his forearm. "Wait. I came to thank you."

His brow knit. "If this is about the letter . . ."

She shook her head no, remembering the sight of him before the fire, enjoying Pa's company. "You treat my grandfather like he's important."

Silence descended between them.

His voice went soft and careful. "He *is* important."

Emeline closed her eyes at those words, afraid he'd see what they did to her.

She shouldn't like this boy. Shouldn't like the sound of his stubborn voice, or the startling gentleness of his touch, or the heady strength of his presence. Hawthorne Fell was not for her. He did the Wood King's bidding. He was from another world.

He was definitely not boyfriend material.

And Emeline was with Joel. Sort of.

Most important: this was a nightmare she was getting out

of very soon. As soon as she saved Pa, Emeline would leave this behind and return to her regular life.

Hawthorne's gaze swept slowly over her. Lingering on her wet hair, trailing across her collarbone, then skimming downwards to take in the sheer silk robe clinging to her curves, revealing too much.

Or, from the look flaring in his eyes, revealing exactly enough.

A startling warmth bloomed in her belly, followed by a strange sweetness in her throat. Like honey and flowers.

Emeline's senses heightened. She was suddenly fully aware of his pine-forest scent infusing the air, of just how close he stood to her.

The heat in her belly turned to fire.

Shit.

Nettle's enchantment.

"You're shivering," he said, frowning.

Shivering? Emeline felt hot with fever. She peered down to find her skin covered in goose bumps.

"It's cold out here. You should go back to your rooms, where it's warmer."

Come with me, she thought.

She wrestled the thought into a cage. *He's right: go back. You're not in control of yourself.*

Hawthorne was saying something else, but the words blurred in her ears. She heard her name, and the enchantment tightened around her, wrapping her up in a slow, silvery web.

I'm about to completely humiliate myself, she realized.

But instead of stepping back, she stepped closer, drawn to him like a bee to pollen. Unable to help herself.

"Hawthorne?"

He fell quiet as her palms skimmed up his chest, over the

fine wool of his sweater. His fingers wrapped lightly around her wrist, but he didn't stop her. He didn't say a word.

Warn him. Now. Before it's too late.

Emeline leaned in. The bridge of her nose slowly grazed the edge of his jaw. Hawthorne drew in a sharp breath, his fingers tightening around her wrist.

"Hawthorne, there's something I—"

Before she could finish, his free hand slid behind her neck. Emeline melted beneath the heat of it. He bent his head to hers, eyes dark with desire, and the sight of it—the *wanting*—snapped something inside her.

She took his face in her hands and kissed him.

Hawthorne didn't hesitate; his kiss burned through her like wildfire. Her body blazed with it. But instead of quenching her greedy hunger, it made her ravenous.

She pushed him back against the hall wall, running her hands along his shoulders, feeling the bones and muscles there. He captured her waist with one arm, dragging her against him, needing her closer. His free hand trembled as he traced her jaw and throat and collarbone, as if searing her into his memory. As if she were a balm for some hidden ache.

As Emeline deepened the kiss, though, Hawthorne suddenly went rigid, pulling back like he tasted something bitter. His fingers dug into her shoulders, wrenching her away.

Emeline sucked in a ragged breath. Forced out of a dream she would much rather remain in, she reached for him, wanting it back.

"No," he said. "I can taste it on you."

She blinked, trying to get this crazed yearning under control.

"You're enchanted." His gaze was thunderous. "Who did this?"

But Emeline didn't care. She wanted his kisses back. Wanted those warm, strong hands on her . . .

"Emeline." His grip on her shoulders tightened, and it made the fire in her roar louder. "Give me a name."

"Nettle," she murmured, her skin hot in all the places he'd touched her. "She gave me a drink."

Hawthorne's eyes blackened.

"I'm going to kill her."

TWENTY-THREE

EMELINE SLEPT TERRIBLY THAT night. Her dreams were full of Hawthorne. Hawthorne untying her robe and sliding it off her shoulders. Hawthorne in her bed, his body flush with hers. Hawthorne whispering sweet things against her skin.

Emeline pressed her palms to her eyes, trying to grind the dreams out of her head.

How am I supposed to face him? Last night was too embarrassing to come back from.

Maybe they could pretend it never happened and move on. *It was only an enchantment, after all.* Maybe nothing needed to be weird or awkward. They could simply avoid each other until Emeline saved her grandfather and escaped. After which, they'd never see each other again.

Emeline pushed Hawthorne out of her mind in order to focus on her lessons. She spent that morning and afternoon with Calliope, pushing hard through the Song Mage's music. Countering her new instructor's patience with an unyielding drive to learn as much as she could.

The songs were more of the same: odes to the minstrel's muse, the moon-marked woman whose beauty had utterly bewitched him. Emeline was starting to wonder if he'd made this woman up. She was so . . . perfect. No woman was this perfect.

By midafternoon, she'd managed to learn two new songs, bringing her count up to seven. That left four songs to still learn—one partly missing—before tomorrow at midnight.

She had no idea if she could do it.

So much depended on what she found at the Song Mage's house today.

IT WAS THE WITCHING hour when Emeline and Grace arrived at the Song Mage's estate. Despite the iron gate hanging open, their horses refused to tread any closer. They were in the Stain here, and the sickly trees looked bleached in the sunlight filtering down from the sky, their leaves silvery with corruption.

"This is it?" Emeline stared across the curse-bitten earth, past the black stagnant pond, to the end of the path leading towards the towering manor. Darkness clung to the house. Dead moss covered the sunken roof like a carpet, and cobwebbed cracks scarred the windowpanes.

It certainly didn't seem livable. Not even for a witch.

"According to Sable's map, yeah." Rolling up the map, Grace thrust it back into the canister buckled to her saddle. "This is it."

The trees of the Stain murmured anxiously around them. *Beware.* They brushed their leaves across Emeline's cheeks. *Horror lurks within that house.*

Neither of them swung down from their horses.

"Well," said Grace, chin in the air, clearly working up the nerve to dismount. "Probably best not to linger."

They left the horses, stepped through the gate, and warily approached the house. Corrupted elm trees bordered the path, watching Emeline pass beneath them, whispering as she approached the door.

Turn back, Emeline.

She glanced to Grace, who either didn't hear the warnings or was ignoring them.

The rotted wood was slick with damp and the doorknob was ice-cold beneath Emeline's fingers. When she turned the knob and pushed the door open, she found the air within even colder. Unnaturally so.

Grace shivered. "What are we looking for again?"

"Sheet music. Rough drafts of songs. Any musical notes left by the Song Mage."

"Right. Got it. Let's be quick about this."

Emeline eyed the hilt of a short sword strapped to Grace's boot. *Just in case we run into trouble,* Grace had told her earlier.

The floorboards sagged beneath their footsteps, mushy with rot. Furniture lay smashed and overturned around them, while years of moisture flecked the windowsills with mold. Meanwhile, the late-afternoon sun beamed cheerfully though the windows as if it hadn't gotten the creepy memo.

Emeline's heart sank. If the sheet music was here, it was likely damaged, or decomposed.

Grace waded through the chaos. "This will go faster if we split up."

Emeline nodded. "I'll search upstairs. Call me if you . . . see anything."

"Like a bloodthirsty witch?" Grace smiled, trying to lighten the mood. Except a sudden breeze rattled the windowpanes, making them both jump.

Emeline's footsteps creaked on the wide staircase leading up from the front entry. She paused at the top of the stairs where yellow wallpaper hung in ribbons down the walls, shredded. As if something had scraped sharp claws down it. Portraits that once hung along the corridor were smashed and discarded on the floor, and a sour odor lingered.

Emeline searched room after room and found more of the same: destruction. She pulled out rotting drawers and looked in damaged cupboards. Finally, Emeline stepped into something that looked like a conservatory. A wide glass wall faced the back of the house, giving her a panoramic view of the Stain. Inside the room a harp lay overturned in the corner, and a guitar had been twisted until it snapped, its fragments scattered across the stained carpet.

She searched through the mess, but all she found were a few crumpled scraps of paper and a waterlogged notebook. The writing inside was smudged so badly, she couldn't read a word.

"Emeline?"

Grace's voice sounded faint and muffled from the floor below.

"You might want to get down here."

Emeline retraced her steps back downstairs. Grace stood in front of the fireplace, clutching a matchbox in one hand and a match in the other. Frowning hard.

"There's dry ash in the fireplace," she said. "And dry logs over there."

Grace motioned with her chin towards a basket of kindling. Beside it, a dozen cut logs were arranged neatly in a pile.

"These should be too damp to light." She struck the match and a flame immediately flared. Her eyes met Emeline's. "Someone's been here recently."

"The Vile?"

Grace stared at the dying match, saying nothing.

Maybe coming here had been a bad idea.

"There's something else." Grace glanced down to the floor, where a rug was folded back, revealing an iron latch secured to the floorboards underneath. Crouching, she reached for the cold black ring and pulled.

A section of the floor lifted up. Beneath it, wooden steps led down into the darkness below.

Emeline and Grace exchanged glances.

Lifting an oil lamp from the shelf above the fireplace, Grace struck a new match to light it. When a flame glowed softly within the glass, she handed it to Emeline. "After you."

Taking the lamp, Emeline started down into the damp, heavy darkness. A feeling of foreboding settled over her skin and she had to run her hand down her arm to flatten the rising hairs there.

To keep her mind off her fear, Emeline whispered to Grace, "You never answered my question in the crypt."

"What question was that?"

A familiar smell wafted towards them. Like fermenting grapes in Pa's cellar.

"Why do you stay here? With the king being the way he is, and the curse coming . . . why not escape the city?"

For a moment, the only sound came from the wooden steps creaking beneath their feet. "I don't want to escape," Grace said.

Emeline glanced back in surprise. The light of the lamp made Grace's eyes shine and her skin gleam. When she tucked a curl of hair behind her ear, the iron ring on her left hand winked.

"Even if I did want to, I can't. I tithed my old life to the king. I can never go back."

"Why would you do such a thing?"

Grace ducked her chin, a secretive smile adorning her lips. "For love, of course. What else?"

Love?

Grace continued on. "Humans aren't allowed to reside in the King's City anymore. The curse makes it too dangerous, and few exceptions are given. So, I made the Wood King an offer he wasn't likely to refuse. I tithed the most powerful thing I owned: my entire life beyond the woods. My family. My *future*." She swallowed softly. "For love."

Emeline ducked her head to keep it from hitting the ceiling as she continued downwards.

"That's how this world works," Grace said, her voice heavy with longing. "You have to give up something precious if you want something precious in return."

Emeline's foot suddenly hit hard, packed earth instead of a wooden stair. The darkness congealed around her. Lifting the lamp, she squinted, deciphering their location: a damp underground room with dirt floors. Two slotted wooden racks ran the length of the walls on either side, filled with grass-green bottles.

"A wine cellar?" Grace mused.

A shape in the darkness, near the back of the cellar, caught Emeline's eye. She moved towards it until the lamp's glow illuminated a mattress covered in blankets. A bucket stood beside it. From the dark substance glistening at the bottom, Emeline had the distinct impression it was used as a kind of chamber pot.

"It looks like wine isn't the only thing she keeps down here," said Grace, her voice strangely flat, staring at a spot on the wall above the mattress.

Two heavy iron shackles dangled down the bricks, fastened with chains.

"It looks like she keeps *people* down here."

A chill swept through Emeline, making her shiver. She was about to turn around. To tell Grace they were leaving—right now—when something made her pause.

"Hold this?"

Handing Grace the lamp, Emeline stepped closer to the mattress. It looked like it was decomposing, the moldy insides crumbling out of its seams and onto the floor. The blankets, too, were damp and old. And when she examined the manacles, she found them rusted shut.

"I don't think anyone's been down here for a very long time," she said.

A tiny object glittered near the floor. Emeline picked it up to find a copper hairpin pinched between her fingers. It was twisted and bent out of shape, as if used to pick a lock.

The pin had the dull quality of something mass produced. Something that might come in a package of ten at the dollar store. There was a copper butterfly at the end of the pin, with little swirls in the wings, and it was achingly familiar to Emeline.

Only she couldn't think why.

A door slammed in the house above, making them jump. She met Grace's gaze over the lamp flame as slow, squeaking footsteps echoed overhead, followed by a low murmuring.

We left the latch open.

The footsteps moved to the stairs, descending slowly towards them, the murmuring growing louder.

Pocketing the pin, Emeline quickly scanned the room. There was no other exit than the way they'd come. Grace pointed towards the two wine racks along opposite walls. There was space beneath each for one person to lie down.

Seeing her plan, Emeline nodded, quietly moving for the farthest one. Down on her hands and knees, she lowered herself beneath it. The earth was packed hard beneath her palms, damp and cold beneath her cheek. As she pushed herself as far back as she could, cobwebs brushed across her skin and stuck in her hair. She tried not to shudder.

When they were both good and hidden, Grace turned out the lamp.

The cellar went dark—except for the bobbing light coming down the stairs.

"Come out, come out," rasped a scratchy voice. "I can hear your beating hearts."

TWENTY-FOUR

HE MONSTER WAS IN the cellar with them.

The creature set down her candle on the dirt floor, giving Emeline a perfect view of Grace stretched out on her back beneath the wine rack, her face tilted towards the ceiling, fists tight at her sides.

The Vile—if indeed this was the Vile—was a black shape in the darkness. Emeline caught a whiff of a familiar smell: rot and bones. It reminded her of nailing up the windows with Pa, and double-checking the locks. The front door, rattling and shaking. The knob, turning and turning. Something trying desperately to get in.

Emeline saw a flash of gray tendons and gleaming black claws as the Vile moved towards Grace. If the Vile heard their hearts beating, of course she knew where they hid. Grace and Emeline were sitting ducks.

This is my fault. Emeline watched, frozen in terror, as the Vile crept closer to her friend. *Grace wouldn't be here if not for me.*

But what could she do? Panic immobilized her, stiffening her limbs, turning her to stone. Her heart thumped painfully fast as her body refused to do as she bid. She couldn't move.

Even if she could, she had no way to stop this monster.

Maybe I don't need to stop her, she thought, watching the Vile creep closer towards Grace. *Maybe I only need to distract her long enough for Grace to run.*

As the Vile lowered to look beneath the opposite wine rack, already reaching for her prey, Grace scrambled back, gasping as she tried to stay out of reach.

Do something, Emeline commanded herself. *Draw her attention away.*

She did the only thing she could think of. Reaching for an old song, Emeline started to sing.

"Que sera, sera. . . ."

The Vile straightened. Abandoning Grace, she turned slowly, eerily, towards the source of the singing.

Emeline paused her song to hiss, "*Grace, run!*"

Grace didn't hesitate. Pulling herself out from under the rack, she fled into the darkness. The monster let her go, more interested in *singing* prey. Moving into the light of the candle, the Vile crept towards Emeline, murmuring under her breath.

Terror zipped down Emeline's spine. And she *still* couldn't make her body move.

Her fear held her trapped.

Desperate to calm herself, to loosen her limbs and drive out the panic, Emeline closed her eyes and continued singing. She'd chosen this song for a reason, after all.

The memory trapped inside the song flared to life within her.

Emeline was seven. She'd woken from a nightmare and screamed for Pa in the darkness. She remembered his heavy footsteps thudding quickly down the hall. Remembered the switch flicking on, flooding her room with light.

Hush now, duckie. I'm here. You're all right.

He was warm and strong as she crawled into his lap. His voice was a beacon in the dark as he cradled her in his arms, singing her nightmares away. Soothing her with this song.

Que sera, sera. . . .

It reminded her of all the good days that were gone. Of the man who raised and protected her. Of how much she loved him.

Her voice trembled but didn't waver. Didn't stop.

The Vile, however, did.

Emeline opened her eyes to find the monster's hunched form hesitant, her face blank. As if she, too, was remembering. Like she had some kind of history with this song.

The Vile stepped back, shaking her head, covering her ears. Trying to stop the song filling her mind.

Watching the monster, Emeline was reminded that her voice sometimes did strange things. Like summoning the woods against her will. And lulling dragons to sleep. And tearing down Hawthorne's mental walls, laying his innermost thoughts bare.

Suddenly, a clawed hand grabbed her shirt, nails pricking her skin. The Vile dragged her out from beneath the rack, raised her up, and rammed her into the shelved bottles.

Pain burst up her spine, stunning her.

The Vile's ice-pale eyes stared into Emeline's. That translucent skin revealed the blue-green veins beneath, like a creature who lived so deep in the woods, the sunlight never touched it.

"So noble," rasped the Vile, grinning like a child who was about to do something very wicked. A horrible stench rolled off her, like blood and rot, making Emeline's stomach roil. "After I pick my teeth with your bones, I will hunt down your friend and—"

A clanging *thud!* made the Vile tip forward, blinking dazedly. Another *thud!* echoed as something metal swung again—and then again—at her head.

Letting go of Emeline's shirt, the Vile stumbled and fell to all fours.

Grace stood behind the creature, the bucket from beside

the mattress gripped firmly in her hands, its glistening contents spilled at her feet. From her knees, the Vile moaned, stunned and staring at the floor. Dropping the bucket, Grace scooped up the lamp, grabbed Emeline's hand, and said, "*Come on.*"

They ran.

Up the stairs and into the house.

When they stood before the fireplace, Emeline swung down the trapdoor with a *slam!*

"Go, go, go!" said Grace, already out the door, down the path, racing for the horses waiting in the silver trees. Emeline kept close on her heels, heart pounding, adrenaline making her run faster than she'd ever run in her life.

They swung themselves up at the same time, then kicked the horses into a gallop. The ground thundered beneath them, hooves pummeling the earth, taking them far away from the Song Mage's estate.

They rode hard all the way to the city.

Only when they were safely inside the walls did Emeline realize they hadn't found the missing pages.

STILL ON HORSEBACK, PROTECTED now by the city walls, Grace led Emeline through a quiet neighborhood overlooking the king's vineyards. They stopped before a large black gate, its wrought-iron bars forged to look like roses climbing upwards, their blooms getting fuller the closer they grew to the top.

Grace dismounted from her speckled roan mare, then unlatched the gate. Emeline swung down from her borrowed horse—one of Sable's—and followed Grace through.

A flagstone path lay before them, cutting through lush green grass. At the end of the path sat a two-story house. Dusty rose shutters bordered its windows and a white dormer jutted over the front door.

Emeline's mouth hung open. This gorgeous house was where Grace lived?

In answer to her unasked question, Grace led Emeline around to the back. A stable stood in the distance, its pasture bordered by weeping willows. But it was another building that Grace moved towards, one made of white stone.

The air around it shimmered with heat, and it smelled like smoke and steel.

At the sound of their horses' hoofbeats, someone strode out through its open door. Her russet hair was a wild tangle, barely scraped back off her face, and her face was red from the heat. *Sable.* When her strange eyes alighted on Grace, she wiped her soot-stained hands on the leather apron tied around her waist.

Letting go of her horse's bridle, Grace ran for Sable, nearly barreling the girl over upon impact. "I'm sorry," Emeline heard Grace murmur as she burrowed her face into the shiftling's throat.

Sable's brow creased, but she said nothing. Only looped a protective arm around Grace's waist, pulling her snug, then slid a hand into her dark curls with startling tenderness.

It was then that Emeline noticed the iron band on Sable's ring finger. An exact copy of the one on Grace's.

Oh, thought Emeline. *Oh.*

I tithed the most powerful thing I owned, Grace told her. *For love.*

The softness of Sable's embrace, the desperate way Grace clung to her . . . Emeline couldn't look away from them.

She'd never held anyone like that.

Suddenly, she was back on the road this past summer. That too-familiar ache of longing, of *loneliness,* haunting her. Roaring to life at the most inconvenient of times. In the green room, up onstage, at the bar with other musicians. It was what drove her into Joel's arms last summer, and the arms of countless others before him.

The ache had always been there. A sign of something missing. *You don't need someone like that,* she told herself.

She had her music. She had a rising career. That was all she needed.

"What's this?" came a mischievous voice.

Rooke stepped out of the forge. His hands, too, were creased with black soot. As if he'd been helping in the forge.

Behind him were Hawthorne and Aspen.

Emeline's stomach squeezed at the sight of the tithe collector.

Something sparked as their gazes collided. The air turned electric, like the moment before a lightning strike, forcing Emeline to remember their kiss in the hall. The heat of his mouth against hers. The strength of his chest beneath her palms. The way she'd *thrown* herself at him, sick with desire.

Was it Nettle's enchantment that had compelled him to kiss her back? Or had he kissed her because he wanted to?

It doesn't matter. Stop thinking about it.

She'd been under a spell. That was why Hawthorne's kiss filled up her hollow places. That was why, even now, she wanted to do it again.

A blush bloomed in her cheeks.

You were enchanted. It wouldn't be the same. You would definitely hate it.

Panicking, she looked to Sable. "Thanks for lending me your horse." Her voice sounded tinny in her ears.

Sable's eyebrows lifted, making Emeline remember that Sable didn't know about their trip to the Song Mage's house. That Grace hadn't told her and probably hadn't asked to borrow her horse.

She would let Grace explain.

Grace reached for the mare's reins. "I'll take her."

Emeline released the horse. Sensing Hawthorne's gaze, she was about to turn and leave *immediately* when Grace touched her elbow. "Thanks for sticking your neck out for me."

Emeline swallowed, nodded, then said good-bye and started walking. She needed to put as much distance as she could between herself and Hawthorne Fell.

TWENTY-FIVE

THE **NIGHT PRESSED IN** around Emeline as she traversed the city's cobbled lamplit streets trying to find her way back to the palace. She scanned the façades of the white row houses on either side of her, hoping for a familiar landmark.

As she walked, Emeline ran her thumb over the twisted shape of the copper butterfly pin. Trying to remember why it was so familiar. So much of what they'd found in the Song Mage's house didn't make sense. The mass-produced pin. The manacles in the cellar. The way her song seemed to provoke the Vile.

The Vile had been terrifying, but it wasn't her monstrousness that captured Emeline's thoughts again and again. It was the moldy mattress. The rusted chains fastened to the wall.

As she traced the shape of the pin in her pocket, she wondered who had been kept down there.

Suddenly, she was standing before The Acorn, its copper nut-shaped sign hanging over the door, its windows bright with lamplight.

This was the third time she'd passed it.

Emeline hugged her arms. It was getting colder and darker by the minute, and she was clearly . . .

"Lost?" said a familiar voice from the shadows. It sent a wave of sensation rushing through her. She was suddenly back in that hallway, pressing him up against the wall, running her hands over him. . . .

She straightened, swallowed, then smoothed out her voice. "What are you, stalking me?"

"Don't flatter yourself. Rooke and I are here for a drink."

She turned to find both Hawthorne and Rooke stepping out of the shadows. *Oh.*

"We *might* have been following you." Rooke grinned. "In case you got lost on your way back."

"Well, I'm not lost." Avoiding their skeptical gazes, she turned back in the opposite direction, quickening her pace along the cobbles.

She heard Rooke say something to Hawthorne, who growled something in response.

Seconds later, Hawthorne caught up to her. Easily. She glanced over her shoulder to see Rooke enter The Acorn without him.

"I'll walk you back."

Please no, she thought. *I don't have the strength.*

"You're having drinks with Rooke," she pointed out, still walking.

"Rooke doesn't mind."

His voice was colder than steel. She dragged her gaze upwards to his perfect scowling mouth. It told her that he knew everything: she'd gone to the Song Mage's house against the advice of his friends, she'd endangered Grace, and she'd barely escaped with her life.

And for what? She had nothing to show for it. No missing sheet music. Just a tarnished hairpin.

Emeline was exactly what he'd accused her of being: a reckless fool.

And he was here to rub it in her face.

She felt like an exposed nerve. A sparking wire.

"Why didn't you tell me you were going to the Song Mage's house?"

Emeline shoved her hands into her pockets. Ran her thumb over the butterfly pin. "You would have stopped me."

"Of course I would have stopped you."

A rowdy group of friends started towards them on the sidewalk—likely heading for The Acorn.

"I was looking for the missing sheet music. Which I would have told you about if I'd been able to find you." Except she did find him—in the hall outside her rooms last night. Where she'd made a complete and utter fool of herself.

Humiliation scorched her. She lowered her voice. "I'm sorry for involving Grace."

The group drew closer, shouting and laughing, giving no sign of letting her and Hawthorne pass. His warmth swept up her side as he pressed his hand to her lower back, dodging the group by cutting down a narrow alley and bringing her with him.

"Grace assured me she was a willing participant," he said when they were alone. "According to Grace, *she* convinced *you* to let her come." His fingers closed around her elbow, turning her to face him. "I'm talking about you, Emeline. Throwing yourself into harm's way. Over and over again." He pinned her in place with his furious gaze. "Do you have such little regard for yourself?"

"Little regard?" She glared up at him. Three nights ago, in the middle of his kitchen, he'd accused her of being the most self-centered person he knew. "I abandoned my grandfather so I could selfishly pursue my music, remember?"

"Right," he said. "*Your* music."

Emeline's temper spiked at those words. "What the hell is that supposed to mean?"

He quickly looked away from her, mouth twisting. "Nothing." Releasing his grip, he returned to the now-quiet street.

Emeline stormed after him. "Tell me what you meant."

He stared into the distance. "How can it be your music when you only sing other people's songs?"

Ouch. Thinking of the music locked away in a folder on her phone, she murmured, "No one wants to hear my songs."

Turning away from him, she continued to walk.

"According to who?" His voice sparked with anger.

"According to everyone. Joel, my manager, record labels, *everyone. That's* why I have a writer." She bristled. "Can we drop this? I don't want to talk about it."

But Hawthorne did. "So that's your big dream? Singing someone else's inferior songs, night after night, up on stage? It's the shadow of a dream, Emeline."

She stopped walking. It was absurd that he could affect her like this, but there it was: the words hurt. As if it mattered, what he thought. As if *he* mattered.

"Fuck you," she said, rounding on him. "You don't even know me."

He opened his mouth to respond, but she cut him off.

"I've done what I've had to do." Her voice was too high and shaky. She fisted her hands, trying to control it. "I couldn't stay in Edgewood, so I ran. I couldn't face my grandfather's forgetting, so I put him in a home. My songs weren't good enough to pay the bills, so I sing someone else's."

It was as if he'd ripped off a scab and she couldn't stop the bleeding.

"It's just me, alone out there, Hawthorne. I have no one to help me. No one to turn to when things get hard. The only person I've ever loved doesn't remember who I am. Can you imagine what that feels like?"

At that question, a wild emotion flickered like lightning across his face. But before she could decipher it, he'd caged it.

"I know I'm a coward, okay?" Her throat tightened. Her eyes heated. "Trust me, I know it."

He stared at her, wordless, then took a hesitant step.

Emeline stepped quickly back.

Because the truth was, deep down, she *wished* she could sing her own songs. More than anything. She missed it: Drawing words up from her depths, like water from a well. Putting them together like pieces in a puzzle. Finding exactly the right tune to match.

She hated that he'd fished it out of her.

"Emeline . . ."

Another thing she hated? The way he said her name. The way his voice seemed to summon her very soul to the surface of her skin.

He was supposed to be out of her system.

"Forgive me." His eyes glimmered in the near dark. "I shouldn't have said that."

This time when he stepped towards her, she didn't step back. He didn't touch her, but he stood so close, he might as well be touching her. She could smell the woods on his skin. Could feel his warmth seeping into her.

The air heated as their gazes met.

Suddenly, she noticed they were no longer surrounded by lamplit streets, but the walls of the king's palace. The full moon didn't shine above them; instead, the light came from lit candles all down the halls.

As if by magic, he'd walked her straight up to the door of her rooms. Like this was a date and he was a gentleman.

"I knew a girl once," he said softly, "whose songs helped her stand against all the forces stronger than she was." Hesitantly, he reached to touch a wisp of hair escaping Emeline's messy bun. As he did, the plain white ring on his finger winked in the candlelight. "Sometimes, you remind me of her."

She went still, watching him.

"Singing was like breathing for her." He smiled at the memory. Like he could see this girl singing in his mind. "When she sang, she went somewhere no one could touch her."

Was this the person Nettle mentioned? The one who broke his heart?

"What happened to her?"

This question shattered things. His hand fell quickly to his side and he moved back, as if stepping out from under a spell.

"Where did she go?"

He lowered his face. "Away from me."

The silence stretched heavy between them. Hawthorne cleared his throat.

"Sleep well, Emeline."

And then he turned and was gone.

LYING IN BED THAT night, Emeline tried to remember her younger self. What would that girl think of herself now, burying her own songs in a locked folder and singing someone else's?

Emeline's fingers prickled, yearning for strings. She suddenly wanted those old songs. But she could only ever recall snippets of lines, a half-remembered chord progression. No matter how hard she tried, they eluded her. Locked away behind a password she couldn't remember.

"Forgetting Is So Long."

What kind of a hint was that? Emeline scowled, annoyed at herself for picking something so obscure.

She sat up. The moon was full, glowing bright white through the skylight above. Rising from the bed, she walked to the wall lined with instruments, scanning its contents, passing over the guitars until her gaze settled on a handcrafted ukulele. Fashioned out of pale maple, it was more finely made than even her Taylor. A leather strap embossed with roses was fastened to each end.

She thought of the missing song pages. They might not turn up before tomorrow night, and even if she managed to find them, she had less than twenty-four hours to learn three other songs besides.

What if I rewrite it tonight? She had the final pages and therefore knew how it ended. She also knew it was a waltz. She could write new lyrics, fashioning them in the style of the Song Mage's other songs, with her own personal twist. The king was mad; he likely wouldn't even notice. His Mage had been dead for ages, after all, with the music hidden away inside Claw's stomach.

It was a backup plan, at least.

But it's been so long since I've written a song. What if I don't remember how?

Still. She could *try*.

Emeline took the ukulele down from the pegs. Sinking onto the gold velvet cushions inside the bay window, she started tuning it. As her fingers picked the strings, Emeline thought of Pa. Of who they used to be to each other. Of the terrifying power of forgetting.

She started to play, her voice testing out words:

"Breathing slow and steady
Sleep has settled in
I trace the pathways, midnight blue
That run beneath your skin"

She tweaked it as she went, rearranging words and lines. Matching them to chords.

"Some spirit I have lost somewhere
I search for it in vain
Some beauty I've forgotten
Since you forgot my name"

It took her all night. By morning, she had a nearly finished song and her whole body glowed from the inside out. It had been too long since she wrote something of her own. She'd forgotten how it felt.

It feels like this, she thought, smiling as her attendants got her ready the next morning. Bathing and scrubbing her. Combing out her hair until it shone like a river in the noonday sun.

It felt like the world had come to a standstill. Like everything weighing her down was suddenly featherlight. Like she was equal to whatever task lay before her.

It made her wonder why she'd ever stopped.

TWENTY-SIX

EMELINE BUSTED HER ASS learning the remaining songs that day. Realizing the king's minstrel had mere hours left before her final demonstration, Calliope took pity on Emeline and stayed well past sunset to ensure her pupil knew them by heart.

After her lessons, Emeline returned to her rooms, ate dinner, and went through every song one final time. The last song—the waltz she'd rewritten—was by far the roughest. It needed more practice.

Two hours before her demonstration and tired of pacing her rooms, Emeline pulled the ukulele strap over the shoulder of her dove-gray dress—one with delicate white trilliums embroidered along the collar—and went for a walk.

Her bare feet trod the cool floors of the Wood King's halls and her voice echoed softly as she strummed, treading out the song. When she arrived at the glass-domed room where her singing lessons took place, she stepped inside.

Standing beneath the dome, she recalled Grace's impromptu waltzing lesson at The Acorn and let her feet find the rhythm. With the ukulele in her arms, Emeline closed her eyes, making her feet go through the steps while she hummed the tune, trying to smooth down the roughness.

When she finally stopped, satisfied, someone cleared their throat.

Startled, Emeline opened her eyes. Hawthorne stood half in shadow at the entrance. No lamps were lit; only starlight illuminated them. But she could still see his charcoal knit sweater, and the dark hollow at the base of his throat.

"You keep rushing the first beat. Try drawing it out more."

Emeline's grip on her instrument tightened. *Of course* he came to correct her form. "I thought you weren't stalking me."

He emerged from the shadows and held out his hand. "I can show you, if you'd like."

Emeline froze like a startled deer, staring at his outstretched palm.

Was he asking her to dance?

Here? In the dark?

His eyes were earnest as he waited. Swallowing tightly, Emeline flipped the ukulele over her shoulder, so it hung flat across her back, and placed her hand in his.

Hawthorne's palm settled against the curve of her waist, his skin warm through her silk dress. Emeline placed her hand on his shoulder, the fine wool of his sweater scratching her palm.

"You're too far away," he said, drawing her closer. His smell was everywhere: leather and wool and pine. Ensnaring her. "We need a tempo. Can you hum the song you were singing?"

A blush crept up her neck. How much had he heard?

"It's one of yours, isn't it?"

Emeline's blush deepened. Her face was certainly crimson now. To hide it, she stared down at her bare toes peeking out from the hem of her gown.

"I liked it," he said. "Very much."

Her pulse quickened at the compliment.

"It's not entirely mine," she admitted.

Instead of pressing her, he nodded, then began waltzing to an invisible tempo, emphasizing the first beat. In the silence, he danced her around and around the room.

"Joel seems nice, by the way."

Emeline stumbled. That was the last thing in the world she expected him to say.

Hawthorne waited for her to recover, then continued. "Handsome. Suave. Good with a guitar."

"What are you talking about?"

"Your boyfriend. I met him the other night when I delivered your message."

Oh. The thought of Hawthorne meeting Joel—of them talking to each other—made her feel weird.

"He's . . . not my boyfriend."

Hawthorne arched a brow. "Are you certain of that?"

She shot him a look. Which was a mistake. It only encouraged him.

"We spoke of you. According to Joel, you make him *very* happy."

She bristled at his mocking tone but couldn't help the blush creeping up her neck. "Bite me, Hawthorne."

The corner of his mouth curved upwards. His eyes glittered, as if he was imagining doing exactly that.

In the silence, his gaze traced over her. Moving slowly across her jaw, down her throat, and along her collarbone, stopping to linger on the curve of her shoulder. As if showing her all the places he longed to bite most.

Emeline couldn't help but imagine it: His teeth on her bare skin. Soft little bites in between kisses.

Heat bloomed through her. *Is he messing with me?*

She glanced quickly away, staring straight over his shoulder.

"You're not going to like what I have to say next," he said, still spinning her around the room.

"How is that different from any other time you open your mouth?"

Both corners of his lips curved now. Emeline decided that she liked what smiling did to his mouth.

"Right. Well, hear me out."

She eyed him, suspicious, but motioned for him to continue.

"The king is getting increasingly unstable," he said. "I'm worried about what he'll do tonight, if you can't sing him the last song."

"What are you suggesting?"

"That you leave."

Emeline fumbled the steps. *"What?"*

His hands tightened, steadying her.

"I can help you." He lowered his voice, gaze darting to the shadows around them. "You'd have to go now, though. Before the demonstration."

She didn't understand. There were guards everywhere—in the palace, patrolling the streets, standing guard at the city gate. "How?"

"There's a way," was all he said.

She stared at him, her steps slowing, forcing him to slow too. "And Pa? Will you help him too?"

He looked down at his feet. "Ewan tithed himself. I can't interfere with a tithe. It goes against my oath to the king. If I did . . ." His throat worked audibly. "It would not go well for me. But *you.*" He looked up. "I have no such oath where you're concerned."

"You expect me to leave him *again?*" She shook her head. She wouldn't. "I'm not running."

Not with a curse devouring the woods. Not when I'm this close.

"Ewan agrees with me," he said softly. "He's the one who brought it up. I told him I'd do my best to convince you."

She opened her mouth to say she didn't appreciate him going behind her back—except Pa had told her this exact same thing three nights ago.

And Hawthorne wasn't finished.

"You'll have your freedom." He stared at her with a startling intensity. "Nothing will hold you back. It's what you want, Emeline. It's what Ewan wants."

They'd stopped dancing. The glass room continued to spin around them while Emeline and Hawthorne stood still, their hands falling away from each other.

She studied him in the starlight. He stood mere inches away from her. But she knew the taste of him now, knew the warm trace of his hands on her skin, and it wasn't close enough. He was a drug and she was slowly becoming addicted, needing a higher and higher dose.

"Is that what *you* want? For me to leave and never come back?"

He drew in a breath.

"Yes," he whispered. "That's exactly what I want."

But Emeline had learned the shape of his lies. She knew the strain of his voice when he told them.

She thought of the Wood King, wild-eyed and cursed.

I have watched dozens of minstrels die for offenses as petty as singing a single note off-key.

She thought of those bark-hard hands closing around her throat, choking off her air, squeezing until it hurt.

Emeline shuddered. No. That wouldn't happen tonight. She had a plan. She'd learned ten of the Mage's songs and rewritten his missing waltz. The king would be pleased—he had to be. If he was as unstable as Hawthorne feared, if his mind was as twisted as Grace said, he wouldn't even notice the changes she'd made.

Once she finished her performance, Pa would finally go home. And *then* she would take Hawthorne up on his offer.

But if I escape tonight—without Pa—I'll never see him again.

That thought pierced like an arrow. Emeline shook her head. She'd abandoned her grandfather once; she wouldn't do it again.

Pushing herself onto her toes, she pressed a kiss to Hawthorne's cheek. "Thank you for the offer," she whispered. "But I'll take my chances with the king."

Letting go, Emeline left him there beneath the crystal dome and walked back to her rooms, where her attendants waited.

TWENTY-SEVEN

UST BEFORE MIDNIGHT, PA escorted Emeline to her demonstration. She kept close, in case he teetered, her arm tucked inside his elbow. As they walked, he hummed the tune of "Goodnight, Irene," transporting her back to a time when he would play this song on his accordion while she did homework by the fireplace.

Emeline held on tighter.

Soon, they stepped into the king's grove. The night sky was clouded overhead, and the giant birches were leafless around them. She helped Pa to one of the empty tables, where courtiers gathered.

He squeezed her hand before she walked away.

The hard earth crunched beneath Emeline as she moved to face the king. She'd worn a knit shawl to ward off the night's cold bite, but it was mild in the grove. The air shimmered as she walked, making Emeline wonder if the king enchanted it to stay warm.

Finally, she stood before the Wood King. He was clothed in moths tonight. Thousands of them crowded his body, their creamy wings folding and unfolding, like hundreds of blinking eyes. Behind him, black mold speckled his white throne, and the grass at his feet was gray and dying.

The smell of magic hung thick in the air here, making her dizzy.

The king leaned forward on his throne. "Are you ready, singer?"

"Yes, sire."

"Then let me hear the songs."

It was difficult at first, with the full intensity of the king's gaze fixed on her face. She was used to being blinded by lights, unable to see her audience. But so long as she focused on the song instead of her surroundings, the king and the courtiers and the grove faded away.

The Song Mage's music was the only thing that mattered tonight, and she soon found her rhythm. Her body hummed with warmth as her heel tapped out a beat on the ground, and the lyrics spilled from her lips: Odes to a woman marked by the moon. Songs that immortalized her midnight hair and cobalt eyes.

As Emeline sang, a familiar longing swelled within her.

I miss this.

The raw energy of a room. The way every crowd was different. The way it kept her on her toes, wanting to please them.

It made her come alive.

She yearned to be on tour, going from city to city, stage to stage. A new audience every night. Her name in bold letters, lit up by bright white marquees.

Soon, she thought. *Soon I'll be home, and this will be my life again.*

The king smiled as he listened. Tipping his head back, he closed his eyes, falling under the spell of Emeline's voice.

At the sight of it—their king, soothed—the watching courtiers relaxed, sinking into the songs. Nodding along to the beat. Tapping their toes.

She'd done it.

She'd pleased the king of the wood.

Emeline grinned, happy. Her face warmed as she sang on, and her hairline beaded with cool sweat. Soon there was only one more song to sing, and then Pa would be free.

She started the last one. *Her* song. The one she'd written to the tune of the Song Mage's waltz.

"Breathing slow and steady
Sleep has settled in
I trace the pathways, midnight blue
That run beneath your skin"

When the song began, the king was clear-eyed and quiet. As she continued, though, his soft edges began to change.

Or maybe she was imagining it.

"Some spirit I have lost somewhere
I search for it in vain
Some beauty I've forgotten
Since you forgot my name"

By the time she finished the second verse, the king's eyes had narrowed to slits and his bark-like hands curled into claws.

Fear nipped at her.

The king is getting increasingly unstable, Hawthorne had said. *I'm worried about what he'll do tonight. . . .*

As she waded into the third verse, the king rose to his feet, his face full of fire. The moths clothing him opened and closed their wings erratically. Some flew off and darted into the shadows.

"You dare defy me *again,* singer?" His voice was harsh, like the caw of a crow.

A chill swept through Emeline.

"I rewrote it," she explained, backing up as he stalked like a wolf towards her. "There were pages missing. I wouldn't be able to sing it otherwise."

"Seize her."

"But I—"

Hands clamped down on her arms.

This was going all wrong. So completely wrong.

Had she really underestimated him again?

"You have greatly displeased me, Emeline Lark." The king stood over her, the smell of him enveloping her like dirt and rot. Like he was decaying from the inside out. "I asked for my Mage's songs. *Not* yours. You think your music, your talent, could possibly compare to *his*?"

Her throat stung at the insult. It was nothing she hadn't heard before—her songs weren't good enough; *she* wasn't good enough—but it still hurt. It always hurt.

His black gaze fixed on her like a viper waiting to strike. "As punishment for your defiance, you will be executed. Tonight."

Emeline's blood turned to ice. *"What?"*

At the edge of her vision, she saw movement in the crowd of courtiers. She looked for Pa, but the crowd was blocked by a row of hedgemen moving into formation, trapping Emeline inside the clearing.

When she turned back to the king, she found instead the biggest, burliest man she'd ever seen stepping into the circle with her. He wore the same helmet and livery as the other hedgemen, but instead of a spear, his hand gripped a massive cleaver. Moonlight glinted off the blade.

Emeline's palms grew damp.

My executioner, she thought, unable to take her eyes off the cleaver. Hawthorne had warned her about this exact scenario. As had Grace. *Will he lop off my head in one stroke? Or will it take several?*

She nearly turned and ran.

Little good it would do her. She was completely surrounded by guards. Instead, she started backing away from the man with the cleaver. Immediately, four hedgemen stepped out of their positions with steel-tipped spears pointed directly at her, corralling her back towards the executioner.

"Step away from her," said a rough-soft voice.

Emeline looked to find Hawthorne wrestling his way through the circle of guards, with Rooke and Sable on his heels. Rooke's dazzling smile was gone, and Sable's mouth was curled in a snarl.

All three were armed. As if they'd expected trouble.

Hawthorne strode to Emeline's side. Sable and Rooke positioned themselves behind her, like shields at her back.

Emeline glanced up at Hawthorne. "What are you doing?"

They were putting themselves at risk by coming to her aid.

"What does it look like?"

He stood strong and still and rooted beside her, his face hardened by fury as he stared at the executioner bearing down on them.

"He'll only kill you too," she said.

"There's a curse coming for us all. We're doomed either way."

Before she could respond, Hawthorne drew the sword at his back. The steel scraped the scabbard, *hushing* as it came forth.

The executioner paused, suddenly uncertain.

"*What is this?*" the Wood King hissed from atop his throne, where he'd returned to watch the spectacle. As he rose sharply to his feet, the moths cloaking him scattered completely, taking to the air and fluttering off into the night. "This is how you repay me? After everything I've done for you?"

Emeline shot Hawthorne a look. What had the king done for him?

The king's eyes were daggers, aimed at his tithe collector.

"With all due respect, sire: enough blood has been shed in this court. I cannot stand by and let more of it spill."

"You think to stop *me*? I am king!" His voice scraped like dead branches across a sidewalk. *"Seize them all."*

The circle of hedgemen constricted, armor clinking as they caged in their prey.

Emeline stepped closer to Hawthorne. *Think!* What could possibly save them? What did the Wood King want more than anything else?

To have his Song Mage back.

She couldn't give him that. But in lieu of it . . .

Her version of the Mage's waltz had enraged the king; he'd wanted his precious minstrel's song, not hers. If she could somehow give him the dead man's missing song, would it be enough to get them out of this mess?

She had to try.

"I know where the missing sheet music is," she blurted out.

"Emeline!" Hawthorne hissed from beside her, sensing the lie.

Since his entire plan involved brandishing a sword and hoping their enemies—who vastly outnumbered them—backed off, she ignored him. Emeline stared down the Wood King, who'd wrenched his gaze from his tithe collector.

All she had now was her fear and her wits. She clung to them.

"Let me fetch the missing music for you," her voice rang out, strong and clear as a bell. "Give me one more chance. If I succeed, you'll have every last one of your beloved Mage's songs. Then, if I displease you again, your next minstrel can sing them for you."

"Tell me where the music is," said the king, hunger in his gaze.

"In the borderlands," she lied. "Let me go, and I'll bring it back to you."

The king narrowed his eyes. "Tell me where they are, and my tithe collector will fetch them."

She shook her head. "Only I can find the sheets."

"You think me a fool? That I trust you to return of your own free will?"

"Then compel her to return," said Hawthorne. She glanced up at him, surprised. "Let me stand surety for her."

Surety?

The king fell silent, considering the two of them. Some of the moths that had flown off earlier returned to tentatively resettle on his shoulders and head, opening and closing their wings once more.

"So be it." The king's voice had taken on a deadly edge. To Emeline, he said, "I will allow you to fetch the sheet music from the borderlands. And if you do not return"—he glared viciously at Hawthorne—"your surety will pay the price for your defiance."

Pay the price? "What does that mean?"

"Just agree, Emeline," said Hawthorne from beside her.

Annoyance rippled through her. No. She needed to know exactly what she was getting into, in case there was some trick.

"What price will Hawthorne pay if I don't return?"

The king smiled. "If you don't return, Hawthorne will be killed in your place."

Her stomach bottomed out. *Killed in my place?*

She shook her head. "No. No way." She didn't even know where the sheet music was! There would be no bringing it back in time to save him.

"What other choice do you have?" said Hawthorne. "Either we all die here tonight, or you take this offer." She glanced over her shoulder to where Sable and Rooke were also surrounded.

They'd valiantly come to her defense tonight. She couldn't let them die here.

But she refused to let Hawthorne die in her stead, and if she didn't know where the sheet music was, that meant she'd have to return and take the punishment herself.

She swallowed, then glanced to the crowd of courtiers again, searching for her grandfather. There was still one more person she needed to save.

"Fine. I agree." Her gaze found Pa, staring at her from behind the line of hedgemen. "But only if my grandfather comes with me." She turned back to the king. "And once he's free of the woods, I want your promise that you'll never touch him again."

The Wood King's eyes sparked like black fire. But whatever anger she provoked, he kept it coiled. "Very well. It will be done. You have three days, Emeline Lark. If you are not back through my gate by sunset on the third day, your sentence will be carried out with Hawthorne standing in for you."

He motioned to two guards, who started towards Hawthorne. Seeing them, Hawthorne sheathed his sword, unbuckled it, and handed it over. The two men forced him to turn, then bound his hands behind his back.

"Emeline . . ."

She nodded. "Sunset in three days. I know. I'll be back before then."

"No." The word was firm, compelling her to look up at him. "If you have any sense, you'll be far, far away by then."

Emeline frowned. Was he telling her to run and let him perish?

"I'm not leaving you here to die."

He looked down to the grass between them. "I'm too valuable to the king. He won't let me come to harm."

But the king was cursed and unstable—Hawthorne had said

so himself. And if the king's behavior tonight wasn't proof, there was the wall of skulls in the crypt, bearing witness. Emeline had no doubt the king would come through on his threat.

Hawthorne was lying in order to save her.

Angry that he would try to trick her *again*, this time at the cost of his own life, she gritted her teeth and stepped closer. "One of these days, your lies are going to catch up to you, Hawthorne Fell."

His mismatched eyes lifted to hers, taking her in. "Trust me, darling. They already have."

When the guards yanked him back, tearing him away from her, Hawthorne didn't take his eyes off Emeline. There was something sorrowful in his gaze. Something that reminded her of the way she looked at Pa, on his worst days.

It was an odd thought to have as they marched him away. Yet it lodged like a leaden weight in her rib cage.

IT WAS ALMOST DAWN by the time Lament delivered Emeline and Pa to the tree line. The sky lightened above them as Emeline dismounted. After she helped Pa down from the saddle, they turned towards the farmhouse together.

She almost didn't believe it.

Emeline breathed in the smell of the farm, letting its calm wash over her. The sun hadn't quite risen yet, and there was a glow in the air, like a promise. Her heart hummed with it.

Home.

And yet it was a bittersweet sight. Instead of feeling free of the Wood King's court, she felt as if invisible shackles had locked around her ankles, the chains of which led all the way back to the king.

She'd lied to him. She had no idea where the missing music was and doubted completely that it was here beyond the woods. Now, if she didn't return in three days with the music in hand, Hawthorne would be executed.

Her heart twisted.

At least I set Pa free, she thought, watching her grandfather cross the tree line and move towards the house.

But if in three days she was dead, who would make sure he was taken care of?

She started to follow her grandfather when Lament bit her sweater, preventing her from moving forward.

Emeline frowned up at the horse. "What is it?"

Letting go, Lament nudged a small saddlebag with her nose. As if to say, *Open it.*

Emeline undid the brass buckles and reached into the leather bag, pulling out a small bundle wrapped in midnight-blue silk and tied with a gold ribbon. Curious, Emeline untied the ribbon. The silk fell away to reveal a small, sheathed knife. The same size as the utility knife Pa once carried on his belt while working on the farm.

Emeline's fingers curled around the leather sheath, which had been oiled and stitched with care, then drew out the knife.

The handle was carved out of a ruddy wood—cherry, maybe—with a knot left in at the base, giving it an elegant strangeness. But it was the blade that held her attention longest. The surface glimmered in the same way as Hawthorne's sword. As if it contained some spell.

With it was a folded piece of paper. Unfolding it, Emeline read the shaky script:

Normal steel can't cut through shadow skins, but this can.
Keep it close.
—Sable

Emeline thought of the golden-eyed shiftling and quickly glanced back into the trees, which were only just starting to lighten. But there was no one there.

Feeling unworthy of such a gift, she said to Lament, "If you see her, thank her for me."

The ember mare snorted in response.

With that, Emeline turned and left the woods.

TWENTY-EIGHT

WHEN MAISIE FOUND OUT Pa was home, a feast was planned and their neighbors were invited over for dinner.

Now it was nearly sunset, and Pa's farmhouse was bustling.

Conversation rose up like puffs of smoke as neighbors—the men and women who'd helped raise Emeline—sat around the table stretched across his dining room. The smell of rosemary potatoes and roasted lamb made Emeline's stomach grumble. She rubbed at her eyes, feeling like she hadn't slept in a week.

"Emmie!" Corny shouted from down the table. He was an enthusiastic man with an athletic build and a voice that boomed when he spoke. He and his wife owned the winery in Edgewood. "Ewan's been telling us strange tales. Maybe you can fill us in?"

Emeline glanced around the table, remembering how—only a week ago—she hadn't believed the stories these very neighbors had raised her on. Stories of a cruel king and his court of monsters. She'd thought them nothing more than delusions. Uneducated ways of coping with the unfairness of life.

She believed them now. And as Emeline told the neighbors about Pa tithing himself to escape Heath Manor, about how she only narrowly saved him from the Wood King—who wanted her for his minstrel—they believed her too. Without a second thought.

After she finished, Anya, Corny's wife, leaned forward, peering around her husband. Her wispy, reddish hair fell into her eyes. "What's it like, riding an ember mare?"

After Emeline told her, Abel, Grace's father, said from across the table, "I saw an ember mare once. It was eating apples straight from the trees in my orchard. I thought one of Corny's horses got loose from its pasture, but when I went out to catch it for him, it looked straight at me, and its eyes were red as fire."

This prompted more questions. "How did you escape the shadow skin, Emmie?" "Did you meet any shiftlings?"

The questions were followed by more stories.

Eshe, Grace's mother, told them about the first time she ever saw a shadow skin. The way it prowled around her house, trampling the flowers in her garden, peering in through all the windows while she hid upstairs.

Anya spoke of her last shiftling sighting. Coyotes had been terrorizing their horses and, after spotting one near the stables, she grabbed Corny's rifle and tracked it into the woods. When she finally caught up to it, she found not a coyote, but a child with lupine eyes and wild black hair.

As more and more of them offered up stories, Tom leaned back in his chair, remaining quiet, staring into his wineglass. It struck Emeline as strange. Tom was the only one who'd ever been to the Wood King's court. Or so he'd told them. Emeline supposed he had more stories than any of them.

Eventually, dinner resumed, and conversation turned to other things.

"Ewan!" Corny pointed his fork at Pa. "Where's your button box? Are you going to play for us?"

Pa fiddled with his watch. "Bah. You don't want to hear an old man play."

"Yes we do!" Corny's face was a little red, making Emeline wonder how much wine he'd already had. "Where is it? I'll get it for you."

"After dinner, Corny." Anya, who didn't look up as she spoke, continued sawing through her lamb.

"What are you doing?" Corny asked Pa quietly. "Why do you keep looking at your watch?"

A wall-sized painting of the farm hung above Pa's head. In it, the vineyards were half hidden by the reddish-brown barn, and beyond the farm loomed the woods.

Pa shook his wrist, then turned the little brass knob. "I think it's broken."

"What does it say?" Corny peered down at Pa's wrist.

"Eleven thirty."

"Let me see. . . . It says . . . seven fifteen." Corny's mouth turned down a little as he glanced from the watch to Pa's face. But his bright smile returned. "Same as mine. No worries. It's working fine!"

Pa frowned deeply, studying the glassy face of the timepiece. Emeline's heart twinged as she watched, but Corny seemed unfazed and unembarrassed for his friend.

Just then, Emeline heard a knock at the door, half drowned by the conversation. Rising, she went to answer it.

She was not prepared for the person standing on the other side.

"Joel?"

The glow of the porch lights caught in his blond hair and illuminated his long jaw and cheekbones. Behind Joel, his bright red Volkswagen pinged in the driveway, the engine cooling from the drive.

"Thank god. I've been trying to call you for days!" Joel pulled her out of the doorframe and into his arms, crushing her in a hug. With him came the smell of strong coffee and Old Spice and everything familiar. Reminding her there was a whole other world out there. *Her* world. A world she desperately wanted to get back to.

"Did you drive all the way here from Montreal?" she asked, stepping out of his arms. It was almost October, and their breaths puffed like clouds in the crisp air.

"Yeah. I was worried sick." His sky-blue eyes examined her. "I knew something was wrong as soon as that weirdo showed up with your note."

Emeline froze. *He must mean Hawthorne.*

"Are you okay?"

She swallowed down the thought of the tithe collector and nodded. "You didn't need to come here. I told you in my letter not to worry."

He shrugged. "I wanted to see you."

Emeline should have been happy to see him. Instead, she felt . . . nothing at all. Guilt twisted her gut.

He cocked his head. "Am I going to get invited in?"

"Oh. Sure." She stepped back through the door. "We're just having dinner."

Joel followed her inside. Slipping off his coat, he threw it on the back of a chair and kicked off his tan chukkas. "Who *was* that guy who delivered your note? He wouldn't stop scowling at me. I'm not sure what I did to make him dislike me so much."

"He scowls at everyone. I'm sure you're overthinking it." She turned away, leading him through the house. In the dining room, she pulled up an extra chair, made introductions, then fetched an extra plate of food.

Joel seemed about to continue their conversation when Corny burst through the doorway.

"Ewan! I found your button box!"

"Corny, seriously . . ." But his wife's voice drifted off as Pa slowly pushed out his chair, getting to his feet.

Joel leaned in towards Emeline. "This is . . . lively."

Emeline nodded. Dinners in Edgewood always were.

"I'm not sure how much I remember," Pa said, coming to take the thick scarlet straps from his friend.

Corny hesitantly held up the silver and white music box, unsure if Pa could handle the weight of it. "Do you need help?"

Pa shook his head. "No, no, I'm fine." He slid the straps over both his shoulders, so the accordion hung across his chest, and moved into the adjoining sitting room, where there was more space.

As he stood in his dark gray cardigan, with everyone's attention on him, Pa's right hand came to rest on the black and white keys running down one side of the instrument while his left went to the silver pushbuttons on the opposite side.

He hesitated only a moment before he started to play. Eyes closed. Head tilted back.

With the red velvet straps looped over each arm, he stepped slowly. His fingers moved firmly over the keys, pressing buttons as he tugged the accordion open and closed, the box fanning out and in, the red interior flickering like a tongue.

Song after song he played without faltering.

It astonished her. Watching him, Emeline remembered only a few minutes before, when he'd forgotten how to read his watch. Yet here he was, after not picking up his instrument in what must have been years, playing five songs in a row. How could he do that but not remember something he knew how to do yesterday?

On the sixth song, Pa's fingers fumbled and his breath quickened. He played the same part twice.

Seeing it, Corny moved towards him. "Ewan! That was great!"

As Pa slid off the straps, Corny caught the heavy box and let it sink to the floor. While Corny helped his friend back to the table, the room erupted in applause.

A slow smile spread across Pa's lips and he took a playful bow.

Joel slid his arm around Emeline's shoulders. "Want to get out of here soon?"

Emeline frowned up at him. She'd only just arrived.

But Joel didn't know that. Nor did he know she had limited time left to spend with the people she loved. She'd mentioned nothing of the Wood King or his court in her letter. As far as Joel knew, she'd been here all week and was probably desperate for an escape.

"I'd like to stay, if that's okay."

"Come on, Em. I haven't seen you in a week." He ran the backs of his fingers up and down the side of her neck. Her skin prickled beneath his touch, mildly irritated. "I just drove seven hours straight to see you."

Despite my asking you not to, she thought.

"I'd like you to myself for a little while." Reaching for the beer she'd grabbed him from the fridge—some brand Pa and Corny liked—he took a sip. His nose promptly wrinkled in distaste. Eyeing the can, he set it down. "You only have two days until you're away on tour, and then who knows when I'll see you next."

Her tour! She'd been so consumed with learning the Song Mage's songs, she'd almost forgotten.

In just a few days she'd be opening for The Perennials. She'd be up onstage with them, traveling across three countries with them, for almost a month straight.

Except . . . no.

That would never happen. Not unless she miraculously found the Song Mage's missing music. *Either that, or I do as Hawthorne suggested and never return to the Wood King's court . . . and let Hawthorne die in my stead.*

A chill swept through her, turning her heart to ice. She had to at least try to find the music.

But where was she supposed to start?

As Joel pulled her closer, the smell of Old Spice invaded her senses. Normally, she didn't mind the smell. Tonight, she found it artificial and cloying. As his arm looped around her neck, keeping her close, she suddenly felt trapped.

Emeline shut her eyes and drew in a breath. When she exhaled, though, the feeling remained.

I don't want him, she realized.

This always happened.

With every one of them.

"I'll be right back," she said, overwhelmed by the need to get away. Disentangling herself from Joel, she slid out of her chair and fled the crowded dining room.

She had no plan, just an impulse. It drove her to the garden door, where she slid her feet into someone's insulated rubber boots. Maisie's, maybe, by the size of them. She pulled on a worn wool hat—Tom's, by the sweet tobacco smell—then threw on one of Pa's cardigans.

Outside, the night breathed its chill across her skin. The sky was black as she started towards the trees, their branches rattling and scratching in the wind.

Emeline, they hushed. *Come back to us.*

Emeline wanted to blame the woods for her inability to live a normal life. To not bring the forest with her to every set and stage and gig. To stay attracted to nice, normal guys instead of breaking things off whenever they wanted to get more serious.

But staring into the darkening trees, she wondered: *What if it's not the woods?*

What if it's me?

She stopped walking when she reached the space in the hedge, breathing in the scent of bark and pine, listening to the forest's creaks and calls—so different from the jarring noises and concrete smells of the city.

The forest swelled around her, vast and unpredictable. Here, something nameless and huge lay beneath the bracken, tangling with the roots of the old trees, pulsing beneath the soles of her feet. Here, the hungry song of the woods thrummed like a pulse. Calling to her.

The power of it terrified Emeline.

What if it terrifies me because I want it?

She stepped back, away from the tree line.

No.

Emeline had spent her whole childhood dreaming of big cities. Of the bright lights and the buzzing energy. The city had always cast a dizzying spell over her.

Sure, the sounds and smells were different. And it never got dark. Not true dark. Not dark enough to see the stars.

And yes, there was nothing wild there.

There was nothing free.

But she was a musician, and it was her scene. *This is where the opportunities are,* her manager had told her often enough. *This is where you have to be.* And she agreed with him. Edgewood was a backwoods town no one ever left. She was one of the few who'd gotten out.

So why was it constantly pulling her back?

TWENTY-NINE

HE NEXT MORNING, EMELINE woke to find Joel beside her in bed, checking his phone.

"Morning, beautiful." He reached to pull her closer, still staring at his screen. As his hand slid across her abdomen, the last bit of sleep clinging to Emeline evaporated.

Her whole body tensed up. *I need to break this off.*

Right now.

"Joel."

"Yeah?"

"I can't do this."

Lowering the phone, he glanced up at her. "Do . . . what?"

She stared at the ceiling, diligently finding patterns in the white stucco. "Us."

Joel went silent. The air prickled between them. "You've been through a lot, Em."

True. But that wasn't it.

Or maybe that was exactly it.

"Let's talk about this when we get back to Montreal, okay? When you're far away from this place and back to your normal self."

Emeline wanted to laugh. Her normal self?

Who is that, I wonder?

"I'm not going to change my mind."

He didn't hear her. Or rather, he was ignoring her. He did that, sometimes, when he thought she was wrong about a thing. Like he wasn't going to argue, he was just going to go ahead and do what he wanted anyway.

"I'm sorry," she said again, glancing over at him.

Predictably, he changed the subject. "Is this your mom?" He reached over to the bedside table, where a picture frame stood facing them.

Emeline wasn't ready to let the subject drop. She wanted this done and over with. But as Joel lay back, holding the frame up between his hands, she fell silent beside him.

"I guess we know where you get your good looks from." Joel grinned, then handed her the frame. He kissed her cheek and got out of the bed.

Emeline stared hard into the frame, no longer seeing or hearing Joel.

The photo was of her mother and a much younger Tom at the beach. They stood with their backs to the camera and their faces turned towards each other, giving Emeline a view of their profiles. The sky was pure blue in the distance. Glittering sand stuck to their skin, a gob of white lotion streaked the back of Tom's neck, and a small crescent moon tattoo stood out against Rose's pale shoulder blade.

But what held Emeline's attention was the look on her mother's face.

Inside the frame, Rose Lark was staring up at Tomás Pérez. Smiling like her heart would burst from happiness.

Emeline had seen a smile like that before: on Grace Abel's face when she looked at Sable Thorne.

Her hands gripped the frame so hard, her fingers hurt.

She and Tom never spoke of it, but Emeline knew it all the

same: Tom and her mother had history. Once, when Emeline was younger and baking pies with Maisie and Eshe, she overheard Maisie whisper to Eshe that Tom and Rose dated for years. Everyone thought they were solid—until Rose broke his heart, getting pregnant by another man. A man she refused to name.

Back then, Tom was constantly on the move, traveling from place to place, taking photos for *National Geographic*. When he heard the news, he took on a project halfway across the world and didn't come back for a long time.

No one had seen or heard from Rose Lark in nineteen years. Not since the day she walked out on her newborn baby, leaving Emeline wailing in her crib.

It used to make Emeline sad, that story. Now she was numb to it.

What was this photo doing on her bedside table? It should be in the garage, with all the other personal items she'd boxed up before putting the house on the market.

Her gaze fixed on Tom, remembering how quiet and withdrawn he'd been last night. It was Tom who'd described the King's City to her as a child, Tom who taught her how to tell a shiftling by their shadow.

If Tom had spent time in the Wood King's court, he might know something about the Song Mage's missing music. It was a long shot. But even if he didn't, he would know other things. Things that might help her.

Red letters blared on her old alarm clock: 12:13. After noon.

She'd slept through the entire morning.

Surging from the bed, Emeline threw on a fresh pair of jeans and a floral button-up, then hooked Sable's sheathed knife onto her belt. After creeping past the washroom where Joel was showering, she went to find Tomás Pérez.

THE DIRT PATH WAS warm beneath her bare feet as she followed it alongside Pa's vineyards, carving across the back of Eshe and Abel's farm. It was the path she'd trod as a child, running back and forth to her neighbors' houses, and it faithfully delivered Emeline to her destination: a white clapboard house at the edge of the woods.

Tom's garage door gaped open and the metallic, oily smells of his shop wafted out. Emeline started forward, pivoting when she saw a figure standing out behind the house and heading towards him.

At the sound of her footsteps, Tom turned. His chest rose from the breath he drew in, as if he were seeing a ghost.

"Emmie." He shook his head. "For a second, I thought . . ." The wind had swept back his dark hair, and his cheeks were ruddy with cold. "You remind me so much of your mother these days."

Emeline wrinkled her nose. She didn't want to remind anyone of the woman who walked out on her baby without looking back. So she changed the subject.

"When you were in the king's court, did you ever meet the Song Mage?"

Tom's shoulders tensed. "Of course, kiddo."

"What do you know about him?"

Tom rubbed a hand across his eyes. "That he's invaluable to the Wood King. That he isn't just a minstrel, but a kind of magus. If the king needs something done, the Song Mage does it using the magic in his voice."

It was strange how Tom spoke as if the man weren't dead.

He turned back towards the woods.

"But he sacrificed something precious in exchange for his power. He tithed his voice to the woods, and if he ever wants to return to this world, he'll be mute. A shade of his once-famous self.

"The last I heard, he'd started to regret his decision and felt more like a prisoner. Like the role he'd been given—doing the king's bidding—wasn't a gift but a burden."

"How do you know all this?"

Grimacing, he looked away. "Your mother told me."

Emeline stared at Tom. "*My* mother? What do you mean? How would my mother know anything about it?" And because he was still talking as if the man were alive, she added, "The Song Mage is dead, Tom."

He turned sharply to look at her. "Dead?"

"A witch called the Vile killed him."

His brow creased. "*Dead.* It can't be. Are you sure?"

Emeline nodded and pressed on. "You said my mother knew him. How is that possible?"

Tom breathed deep, running one hand through his wind-swept hair. "No good will come of this, sweetheart. Leave it be."

Emeline stepped between Tom and the woods. No way was she leaving this be. Digging the folded photograph out of her pocket, she unfolded it and thrust it at him.

"The back is dated a year before I was born. How can she be looking at you like that—like you are everything she wants in the whole world—*mere months* before she gets pregnant with someone else?"

Tom's fingers gripped the photo. As if he were drowning and it were a life raft.

"I wanted to impress her," he whispered. "Or maybe I wanted to impress *them.*" He glanced to the woods. "I don't know." His Adam's apple bobbed as he gulped. As if getting the words out was a fight he was losing. "I took her to the King's City. I wanted her to see it. To love it the way I loved it. And she did. But she also . . ."

Folding up the photograph, he handed it back to Emeline.

"You need to tell me all of it." Emeline stared him down. "She was my mother."

He nodded, eyes shining.

"She fell in love with someone else."

"Who?"

"She wouldn't tell me." From the look that darkened his eyes, though, he had his suspicions. "She was utterly enchanted by him. She stopped showing up for her shifts at the diner. Like she didn't care anymore. She'd forget to eat. Wouldn't sleep. She was . . . unreachable. Living in a dream. So, when she came home pregnant after months of being at court, I couldn't bear to see her. I . . . I left."

"Because the baby was his," Emeline murmured.

But that meant . . .

My father came from the woods.

She suddenly felt unbalanced.

Tom touched her arm—as if to steady her. The sorrow in him fled, replaced by a warm tenderness. "When I got back after those three years away, I didn't want to look at you. I avoided Ewan's house for months. I avoided everyone's houses—in case you were there. And then one day, Ewan stormed over. 'Enough is enough,' he said. 'This is Emeline Lark, my pride and joy.' I took one look at you, and it all went up in smoke. One shy smile, and you melted my anger away."

Emeline's eyes burned as he pulled her to him, hugging her tight.

"Why did no one tell me any of this?" she whispered against his jacket, breathing in the familiar tobacco smell.

"She didn't want anyone to know. So I promised to keep her secret."

Emeline pulled away, glancing up at him.

He was staring into the woods again, eyes clouded. "Sometimes I wonder if I misinterpreted the signs. She looked so . . . *hollow* by the end. Like love was eating away at her. Making her forget all the things that were once important to her. Almost as if . . ."

Tom shook his head like he was trying to shake away a bad dream. "I'm sure I was imagining it. Just seeing what I wanted to see. And anyway, it's over now. Rose made her choice."

"Did she go back to him? After she left me?"

He raised his hands, palms upturned. "I assume so. I've always thought she was living happily with him in the King's City." Without Emeline. Without either of them.

They both stared into the trees.

Was it possible her mother was still there?

Grace had told her that humans weren't allowed to reside in the King's City, and few exceptions were given. Emeline was under the impression that she, Grace, and Pa were those exceptions. But maybe there were others. Maybe Rose Lark was living in the King's City, too.

"If she's there," said Emeline, "I'll find her."

THIRTY

TOM'S WORDS TRAILED HER like a shadow as she skirted around Eshe and Abel's orchards. The sun hung low in the sky as she hurried past Pa's vineyards, turning their green leaves to gold.

Her second day was almost over, and Emeline was no closer to finding the missing sheet music. She would have to go back to the king empty-handed. And once he realized she lied to him . . .

Emeline would never get the chance to find her mother.

If she's even in the woods at all.

She opened the folded photograph, scrutinizing Rose Lark's profile as she walked. Her mother had irises as blue as robins' eggs, raven-black hair, and a lovesick smile.

But it was something else that caught and held Emeline's attention. Her gaze dropped to the small black tattoo on her mother's pale shoulder blade: a crescent moon.

Her footsteps slowed.

Marked by the moon . . .

The farm shrank, like the end of an old movie, the edges contracting into the center, the image narrowing to a pinpoint. The songs she'd spent the last week learning were all about the same muse: a woman marked by the moon.

It's just a coincidence.

But the more she stared at her mother's tattoo, the louder Tom's confession reverberated inside her, and the less sure she was.

Was my mother the Song Mage's muse?

Her heart was thudding hard when she arrived back at Pa's house. Instead of going inside, however, she walked into the garage.

Towers of boxes loomed before her. Emeline waded into them, searching for one in particular. She pulled them down, one after another, reading their labels and shoving them aside.

She was down to the last few when she found what she was looking for: a rectangular box marked *ROSE,* written in black Sharpie.

Emeline pulled it to the floor.

She had packed this box. After rounding up remnants of her mother lingering around the house, she'd taped it shut. Taped it *too* well. Almost as if she never wanted it opened.

Luckily, she had Sable's leather sheath fastened to the belt of her jeans. The enchanted knife sat snug against her hip.

Drawing it, Emeline sliced through the tape, then resheathed the blade. Sitting cross-legged on the cold cement floor, she pushed back the cardboard flaps.

Inside were photos, jewelry, and a few summer dresses. All things that once belonged to her mother. Emeline started taking them out, not sure what she was looking for exactly, only that she was looking for *something.* Some clue.

In one photo, her mother's head was thrown back as she laughed. Her long, lush hair hung loose and her cheeks were pink with joy. In another, she was grinning so hard, you couldn't see her eyes. In a third, she'd just tackled a young Tom, whose back she now hung from as he recovered, grinning.

All too soon, the woman in the photos changed.

She was pregnant in these. Her cheeks hollow, hair stringy, eyes dull. That joyful spirit was gone, snuffed like an unwanted fire.

Did I do that to you? thought Emeline, touching the round bump of her mother's belly. *Did you not want me?*

But of course she didn't. It's why she left Emeline screaming in her crib without a backwards glance.

Emeline set aside the photos, then pulled out more items. A bright yellow sundress. A fake pearl necklace. A handwritten note from Tom she didn't read out of respect for his privacy.

Soon, she came to the bottom, lined with papers. A vehicle registration. Bills for the apartment she lived in. Why hadn't she thrown these things out? Emeline was halfway through the papers when she spotted one last object, half hidden in the crease of the box: a copper hairpin.

Is that . . . ?

Emeline picked it up, staring hard at the tiny butterfly on the end.

She thought of the Song Mage's cellar. Of the twin butterfly pin she'd found on the floor, and how familiar it had been. Of the moldy mattress and the bucket and the manacles.

A sick feeling twisted her gut.

No.

It was too horrible to consider: That her mother had been trapped in that cellar. That she'd been the one to pick the locks of those chains. That *she* had slept on that moldy bed.

Emeline recalled Aspen's words about the Vile: *She was desperately in love with him. But he spurned her; he loved another.*

"My mother," Emeline murmured aloud. "He loved my mother."

So she killed him, Grace's voice seeped up in her mind. The

Vile killed the Song Mage because he loved Rose Lark and not her.

Did the Vile lock my mother in that cellar to punish her for being the one the Song Mage chose?

The world fell away beneath Emeline. But no—it was just the papers in her hands, slipping through her unmoving fingers, scattering across the floor.

And that's when she saw it. There on the cracked cement.

Sheet music.

Four pages of it.

Emeline's hands shook as she bent to retrieve them. One, two, three, four pages. She stared down at the first one. In the same script as all the other songs she'd been learning, the Song Mage had written the title of his very last song: *Rose's Waltz.*

It would have been the last song he ever wrote before the Vile killed him.

Is that why . . .

Was the man Rose loved already dead when those photos of her, hollowed out and pregnant, were taken? Did she look so lost because her heart was so utterly broken?

Was the reason she never came back for her baby because the Vile *imprisoned* her?

If so, where is she now?

The sound of shattering glass jolted Emeline out of her thoughts, followed by a shrill scream. Both came from inside the house.

Emeline's heart beat swift and hard.

Pa.

Her mind ran through every worst-case scenario. With the sheet music gripped in her hand, she ran for the front door and flung it open.

She found Joel standing in the middle of the living room,

backing slowly towards the wall, staring wide-eyed into the kitchen.

Pa stood between Joel and whatever lay in the kitchen.

"Stay back, Emeline." Her grandfather's voice shook, even as he tried to sound strong.

Emeline moved past them to find Maisie backed against the sink, a wineglass smashed at her feet. Tears streamed down her cheeks as she stared, horrified, at the thing before her. As if caught in some kind of awful trance.

A shadow darker than midnight rose above Maisie, hunching over her, as if about to feast on her. At the sight of its elongated form and claw-like hands, Emeline's footsteps halted.

A shadow skin.

What was it doing in the house?

Get Maisie out of there.

Emeline moved towards the horror. A broken shard of glass sliced her heel, sending a stab of pain through her foot. She grabbed her neighbor's arm, pulling her away from the monster and stepping in front of her like a shield. "Go, Maisie."

Maisie shook her head. "W-what . . . ?"

"Get Pa out of here."

The shadow skin didn't stop Maisie from escaping. Only fixed its attention on Emeline. It had no eyes, and yet it seemed to see her. *Know* her. As if she and it had some score to settle.

As if *Emeline* was the reason it was here.

She reached for the knife block next to the sink, pulling out the biggest blade. When the shadow skin saw it, that crack of a mouth grinned.

She swiped. The knife skittered off the shadow skin's chest. She tried again, stabbing this time. The blade shattered on impact. As if the monster was fashioned not of flesh, but solid night.

Drop it. The voice oozed like blood through the cracks in

her mind. To her horror, Emeline watched her fingers loosen. Watched the knife clatter to the floor amidst the broken glass.

There was a sudden commotion in the living room. But Emeline couldn't turn to see. Cold fingers were slithering through her mind, and horror froze her in place. Like a fingertip running over the pages of a diary, it sifted through her secret thoughts and fears and desires.

The shadow skin grinned wider, until its mouth was a cracking line splitting its face in two.

Emeline tried to reach for something else—a pot or pan. Anything to defend herself with. But before her hands could grab hold of something, a flood of images made her stiffen.

A young man was before her. With mismatched gray eyes and maple-dark hair, he stood tall and strong as an oak. *Hawthorne.* They were in his kitchen, and she was sitting on his counter. He was so real, she could smell the woodsmoke on his clothes. Hawthorne leaned over her, his warm hands cupping the backs of her bare calves. His mouth crooked at the side, as if he had mischief in mind.

Suddenly, the scene changed. His kitchen disappeared, replaced by a moonlit grove. Hawthorne was taken from her by two armed hedgemen and forced to his knees. They pressed his cheek against the surface of a gray stone slab, holding him down.

The Wood King appeared over him. Gray lichen wrapped around the king's woody body like rotting flesh, and in his gnarled hand was the cleaver.

Emeline tried to move, to come to Hawthorne's aid, but her body refused to obey. Fear rippled through her as the blade lifted, catching the moonlight.

But I have three days!

Unless . . .

Unless the night of her performance counted as the first day. If so, *today* was the last day. It was exactly the kind of cruel trick she should have suspected from the Wood King.

The sudden weight of it—*Hawthorne, dead*—pushed all the air from her lungs.

Emeline shook off the vision and looked up to find a nightmare standing over her. Past its shoulder, through the windows, the setting sun painted the sky bloodred.

Sunset.

No!

The force of that one little word broke the shadow skin's hold, giving Emeline a split second to remember Sable's knife at her hip. *Normal steel can't cut through shadow skins, but this can.* She drew the glimmering blade from its sheath.

You're mine! the monster hissed, its clawed hands reaching to plunge into her chest and dig out her beating heart.

Emeline thrust the knife into the monster's throat.

The cold voice in her mind went silent. The shadow skin staggered back, dazed, as darkness seeped out of the wound and it fell to its knees before crumbling completely. Within seconds, the dust of its body transformed into bright yellow buttercups, blooming in the middle of the kitchen floor.

The room solidified around her. Pa and Maisie and Joel were all there, staring at Emeline. Maisie had a shovel in one hand, poised as if ready to swing. Joel gripped a crowbar, ready to do the same.

In the sky out the windows, the sunset was bleeding away.

If you do not return, the king's dusty voice thundered, *your surety will pay the price for your defiance.*

With the Song Mage's music crumpled in her fist and Sable's knife sheathed at her hip, Emeline moved barefoot through the kitchen, heading for the back door.

"Baby girl." Maisie reached for her. "Are you all right?"

She nodded, looking towards the woods, to that empty space in the trees. "I'm fine." *But someone else might not be.* "I'll be back as soon as I can."

Joel stared openmouthed at the buttercups.

Emeline hugged Pa tight before tracking blood from her sliced heel across the floor and into the woods—where she ran as hard and as fast as she could.

She didn't feel the pain in her foot. Didn't feel the burn in her lungs.

This way, said the trees. *Follow us.*

They led her to Bog. The nearest entry point into the city.

As the sky darkened, that muddy form rose up from the swamp, dripping as it sloshed towards her.

"I'll give you half the blood I own if you let me pass right now."

"*Pity,*" slurped Bog, pulling back its fens to reveal that mucky boardwalk. "*Your passage has already been paid by Grace Thorne.*"

Paid by Grace? Emeline didn't have time to ask how or why, but a rush of gratitude swept through her. She raced down the boardwalk, ducking beneath hanging gray vines, until at last she pulled the final curtain aside and stepped into the city. The streets were growing dark, and lamps were being lit around her.

Emeline's heart thundered.

She needed to save Hawthorne . . . if it wasn't already too late. She ran.

At the palace gate, the hedgemen led her inside. She didn't wait for them to bring her before the throne; she knew the way. Her bloody heel throbbed as she ran. Through the windows, the sun slipped below the treetops.

The sky was pink as coral when the endless halls finally dissolved around her and the giant white birches of the grove emerged. Emeline advanced towards the king waiting atop his throne.

Am I too late?

Her breath scraped her lungs. Sweat dampened her skin.

"I found your missing pages," she said, chest heaving as she thrust out the sheet music.

Those black eyes peered down at her, the moon-shaped pupils glowing bright white. He held out a gnarled hand that reminded Emeline of a tree branch in winter, stripped of its leaves. She came forward and set the rolled vellum in his palm.

The king unfurled the music, studying it.

Emeline looked around them, but the grove stood empty. No courtiers. No guards.

No Hawthorne.

Did I get here in time?

"Well done," rasped his earthy voice. "I was certain you'd lied."

Emeline opened her mouth to answer him, but promptly decided not to. What good would telling him the truth do?

For several breaths, she just stood there, bracing herself for the moment he decided to gleefully declare that she'd arrived too late and Hawthorne was dead. But the king only held the music back to her.

She took it.

"You've proven your loyalty, Emeline Lark." He reclined in his throne, studying her closely. "You'll make a fine singer in my court."

Emeline had no intention of being a permanent fixture in his court, but kept this to herself.

"And Hawthorne? Is he . . . ?"

"Alive?" An unnerving smile slid across the king's dry, cracked lips. "Go to his house and see for yourself."

Fully dismissed, Emeline fled out of the grove, down candlelit halls, and through the palace gate. She half ran, half limped, down the path to Hawthorne's house and only slowed when she came to the small bridge over the prattling creek— where two armed hedgemen stood guard.

Neither tried to stop her, so Emeline crossed the bridge and ran for the stone house. She didn't bother to knock, bursting through the door.

"Hawthorne?"

No fire burned in the fireplace. A bowl of wild apples sat in the middle of the table. Next to it was a mug of half-drunk tea. Emeline touched the mug and found it cold.

"Hawthorne!"

She moved to the kitchen, but it was empty. Then the bedroom—empty too. She searched every room, opened every door. But he wasn't here. No one was. Her breath came too quick. Her thoughts raced in panicked loops.

I'm too late.

But why wouldn't the king have told her so?

An ax splitting wood broke the silence. Her heart skipped at the sound.

Emeline moved towards the front door, hanging open on its hinges, and stepped outside. When the sound came again, Emeline's pulse sped up and she followed it past the stable, to the back of the house.

Her footsteps slowed as she spotted him.

Hawthorne stood near a long, neatly packed woodpile—very much alive. His pine-green shirtsleeves were rolled to his elbows and both his hands gripped the shaft of an ax. He brought it up over his head and swung it down, neatly cleaving the log in two before replacing it with another. His eyes were dark and his jaw was set, as if chopping wood while he awaited his death sentence was the only thing keeping him calm.

He swung twice more before sensing her in the yard.

Hawthorne looked up, startled by the sight of her. His face changed as his gaze swept down her, taking in her unruly hair and windburned cheeks.

"Emeline . . ."

Something bright and burning flared within her. She stumbled towards him, limping through the pain in her heel.

He lodged the ax head in the chopping block, then turned to her. She threw her arms around him, pressing her forehead into the curve of his neck and holding on tight.

Hawthorne's arms came around her, cocooning her in warmth. He pulled her against him, one hand skimming across her lower back while the other cupped her head, tucking it beneath his chin.

"You're alive," she whispered.

"And you're trembling."

She held him tighter. "I thought I was too late."

All too soon, Hawthorne pried away from her to glance down at her foot. Eyeing her bloody heel, he bent, scooping her knees beneath his arm, and carried her into the house.

THIRTY-ONE

AS HAWTHORNE TENDED HER foot, Emeline showed him the sheet music for "Rose's Waltz," along with the photo of her mother. After pointing out her mother's moon tattoo, she recounted what Tom told her about Rose falling in love with someone in the Wood King's court.

Hawthorne straddled the bench beside the harvest table, facing her. Steam rose from the bowl of hot water in front of him, and on the table was a jar of Rooke's moonshine and clean strips of white cotton gauze. Taking her heel in his hands, he checked for glass shards embedded in the wound before starting to wash it.

"My mother was the Song Mage's muse," she told him. "I'm sure of it."

As he listened, Hawthorne's hands gently wiped the dirt and blood from her foot, avoiding the cut at first, then prodding it carefully until it was clean.

"I think his death broke her. I wish I had the photos to show you. She looked . . . dead inside."

The opposite of how she looked with Tom.

Hawthorne was strangely quiet. He hadn't said one word since she first started talking. He unscrewed the lid from the jar of moonshine. With her foot in one hand and the jar in the other, he glanced up, asking permission.

Emeline nodded, giving it.

Her grip on the bench tightened as he poured alcohol over the wound, sanitizing it. She hissed through her teeth at the sting. When it was over, she sucked in a breath and relaxed.

"My mother could still be in the King's City."

Silently, Hawthorne took strips of gauze and wrapped them generously around and around her heel, pinning them in place. When he finished, he set her foot in his lap and, very gently, dragged his thumb in slow circles around her anklebone.

"I don't know of any Rose Lark living in the city," he said finally. Almost distantly. "But the Song Mage and his consort were . . . before my time. I can ask around. Aspen might know something. Her father used to be the Song Mage's tailor."

It was difficult to focus with his thumb caressing her like that. It made her shiver. Good shivers. Shivers that sank down below her skin.

He fell quiet.

"Emeline?"

She glanced from his stroking thumb to his watchful eyes. There were shadows in them, and a careful cadence to his voice. "If the stories are true, and the Vile was jealous of her . . ." His thumb stopped its gentle motion as his eyebrows drew sharply together. "It's possible the Vile killed your mother too."

Emeline pulled her foot back towards herself, nodding silently. She'd thought of that already.

The twisted butterfly pin was proof that someone had tried to escape that cellar. *But did they succeed?* Until she found evidence suggesting otherwise, Emeline had to hope her mother was alive.

"And if this is all true," he went on, "then the Song Mage was your father."

She nodded again, staring at the pine floorboards beneath

Hawthorne's gray wool socks. *My father.* She hadn't said the words aloud to herself yet. They were too strange.

Was that why her voice did unexpected things, sometimes?

She thought of her last lesson with Hawthorne. Of the power coursing through her as she sang, stripping him bare. Seeing things she had no right to see.

Something dinged in the kitchen. Hawthorne turned sharply in that direction.

"The bread . . ."

He screwed the lid back on the moonshine, then cleaned up the mess on the table.

"I should go," she said, rising. "If I'm going to find my mother . . ." She only had so much time to look. She needed to be in Montreal in two days, for the opening night of her tour.

How she would *get* to her opening night was less certain— she doubted the king would let her leave, even if she had found his missing sheet music. But this was a problem she would deal with later.

Hawthorne reached for her wrist, stopping her. Her skin sparked at the contact. "When was the last time you ate?"

Emeline pressed a hand to her empty stomach. "Not since yesterday."

"Then stay for dinner and afterwards, we can go see Aspen and ask her father about Rose Lark. He won't be home for a few hours yet, so you have some time."

Since Emeline had no other leads, she nodded. "All right." If Hawthorne thought the man could help her, she could afford to wait a few hours.

Gathering the gauze, the moonshine, and the bowl of luke-warm water, Hawthorne brought them into the kitchen, where Emeline heard him wash his hands. When he returned, one arm cradled a ceramic bowl covered in a red-checkered cloth while the other carried a large muslin bag full of flour. He hefted both onto the table. After rolling his shirtsleeves back to his elbows, then sliding that plain white ring off his finger and placing it in his pocket, he peeled the checkered cloth back from the bowl. A pale hump of dough sat nestled inside.

She came to stand beside him. "Can I help?"

He raised a dark brow. "Do you know how?"

Uh, no. The process of making bread was a total mystery to her. But Maisie baked bread all the time. So she rolled up her sleeves and shrugged. "How hard can it be?"

He smirked.

She crossed her arms. "You don't think I can do it?"

"We'll see." He reached into the muslin bag and pulled out a handful of flour, sprinkling it across the surface of the table.

Emeline braided her hair back, then washed her hands in the kitchen sink. When she returned, Hawthorne held out one flour-dusted hand.

"First, you'll need to punch down the dough."

Emeline reached for his hand, determined to demolish his skepticism. His fingers folded around hers, pulling her between himself and the end of the table. The heat of him rushed up her back, spreading like wildfire.

In front of her sat the bowl of dough.

Was she actually supposed to punch it, or was he teasing?

"You're already hopeless," he murmured, his warm breath grazing the back of her neck. "First, make a fist." She heard the smirk still in his voice as his hands folded around her right one, curling her fingers into her palm. "Then, bring your elbow back. . . ."

"Okay, okay," she said. "I know how to throw a punch."

His hand coasted around her hip, settling on its soft arc. "Go ahead then."

Emeline fisted her hand and punched the middle of the dough.

Mmmfff.

The bump collapsed.

Emeline watched it caving in on itself, slowly, like a deflating balloon. Hawthorne's arms came around either side of her, his hands pushing the dough down, flattening it out. She smelled the forest on him, earth and moss and pine.

"Get the air out," he said, stepping out from behind her and flipping the bowl over so the dough spilled out onto the floured table. He started tearing it into six roughly equal chunks. "Take one in your hands and tuck it into itself, like this." He folded his dough, then rounded it into a perfectly smooth circular orb in less than a minute.

But when Emeline tried to copy his movements, hers ended up a lumpy mess that stuck to her fingers.

Hawthorne's mouth quirked again. "You're thinking about it too much."

Or possibly, she wasn't thinking about it enough. She was thinking about his hands, and how efficient they were. How they knew exactly what to do.

His forearm disappeared inside the bag. When it reemerged, his hand held a fistful of white flour. He tossed it across the table, back and forth, like gently falling snow. "Cover it with more flour, then try again."

While she worked on her lumpy mess, Hawthorne finished his second, then third—cupping the dough on both sides and moving it in circles until it was perfectly round. He worked quickly and skillfully. By the time he finished shaping his fourth loaf, Emeline had turned her first back into a sticky bulge.

She pulled her hands away.

"I'm ruining it."

He swapped out her mess with the last chunk of dough, then held out the bag of flour, as if to say, *Again.*

Emeline reached inside, grabbed a handful of flour, and threw it the way he'd shown her . . .

Or not.

She'd taken too much flour, and it slipped out of her fist all at once instead of sparingly. A dusty white cloud billowed up, forcing Emeline to close her eyes.

When she opened them, a white haze coated her eyelashes. Her lips tasted dry and powdery, and her button-up shirt and jeans were dusted in flour. Blinking up at Hawthorne, she found him covered too.

Emeline laughed at the sight of his dark hair speckled with white.

He raised both eyebrows. As if to say, *Oh really.* Reaching into the bag, he tossed a fistful back at her. She gasped as the flour hit, splattering across her shirt like a soft snowball.

A slow grin spread across her lips. *This is something I can beat him at.*

Grabbing the bag of flour, she hoisted it high and dumped the whole thing over his head.

It was like standing in the midst of a snow squall. The room disappeared. Emeline couldn't see the table, or the dough, or even Hawthorne.

And then there he was: lunging at her through the white cloud. Emeline dodged out of reach, shrieking and laughing as she ran for the other end of the house. Halfway to the bedroom, he grabbed her around the waist and lifted her off the floor. "We're not finished."

She attempted to fight him as he half carried, half dragged her back to the table, but she was laughing so hard, she couldn't kick her legs.

He set her down before the table. With his arm still looped around her waist, he held her snug against him, her back to his chest. Laughter softened his voice as he whispered against her cheek, "Try again."

The brush of his lips made a warm ache roar to life inside her, and her laughter fell silent.

"You said it yourself," she swallowed, breathless. "I'm hopeless."

She squirmed free of his hold, turning to face him, and his arm fell away from her.

Only a sliver of space divided them. She leaned back into the table behind her, gripping the edge, peering up at him. He lifted a hand to her face and as his thumb gently smeared flour off her cheekbone, a startling thought flickered through her.

I want him.

Not the way she wanted the others. She didn't want him to *use*—as a shield between her and the things she was running from. To feel normal. To soothe that lonely ache.

She wanted *him*. His sharp edges and surprising tenderness and quiet strength. She wanted him spooning homemade soup into her mouth in his cozy, tidy house that smelled like bread. She wanted him discussing poetry in the dark with her grandfather. She wanted that fervent, desperate kiss in the palace hall.

She wanted Hawthorne Fell. The Wood King's henchman. Not exactly boyfriend material, but still. He called to her the way the forest did. Called to something deep and forgotten. Something that longed to come alive again.

Emeline reached for the hand that had smeared flour off her cheek. He let her take it. Let her turn it palm up between them, tracing its calluses and flour-caked creases.

Such strong, capable hands.

"Emeline . . ."

He was all dark hair falling into river-rock eyes. Eyes that were, at present, captivated by the sight of her. Hot silence simmered between them. She stared at his mouth, so close to hers. Deliriously close. Letting go of his hand, she reached for his face, savoring the roughness of his jawline against her palms.

"Emeline." Her name was a growl. Part warning, part yearning. But whatever he'd been about to say was lost in the softness of her mouth as she arched to kiss him.

Her fingers twined through his hair, pulling him closer.

"We can't do this," he murmured. But his hands slid behind her thighs as he lifted her onto the edge of the table. "What about Joel?"

She gently bit the curve of his jaw. "I broke things off with Joel."

At those words, Hawthorne gave in to her. Securing her legs around his hips, he drew her against him. Desire burned through Emeline. Her blood hummed as he hooked his finger into the collar of her button-up shirt, tugging gently downwards. The buttons opened, one after another, and Emeline sucked in a breath as cool air rushed against her skin. He pushed the shirt down her arms and kissed the smooth curve of her shoulder, his teeth grazing her bare skin.

A low hum escaped her throat.

His eyes glazed over. Suddenly, his mouth was hot against hers, his tongue urgent. She kissed him back, pulling him closer, tighter, and still: it wasn't enough.

She wanted him to lay her down.

She wanted him to . . .

Her hands fumbled with his belt, trying to undo it. Realizing what was happening, what she wanted, Hawthorne stilled. His hands slid away from her. His fingers wrapped around her wrists.

"Emeline, darling." His voice was ragged and rough. "We can't."

A bubble of frustration expanded inside her and she nipped the soft place between his shoulder and throat, showing her displeasure. "Why *not?*"

He didn't answer. Only unhooked her legs from around him and stepped back, looking her over, assessing the damage he'd done. He immediately stepped forward again, his fingers shaking ever so slightly as they buttoned her shirt.

His face was flushed, his hair mussed. He looked . . . undone.

It made her want to kiss him again.

Sensing this, Hawthorne abandoned the buttons and backed away. Emeline pushed herself down from the table. "Tell me why."

He ran both hands through his hair. "If circumstances were different . . ." He glanced away from her—but not before she saw the desire raging in his eyes. "I would happily take what you're offering. More than happily."

Emeline gripped the edge of the table, not trusting herself to let go. What did that mean, if circumstances were different? If she weren't a prisoner here? If she weren't secretly planning to leave all of this behind and escape?

Maybe that's it.

Emeline remembered what Nettle told her the night they met: that someone in Hawthorne's past broke his heart. She remembered the girl Hawthorne had mentioned the night he walked her home.

Where did she go?

Away from me.

"You loved someone, and she betrayed you." Emeline's voice sounded raw. "Is that what this is about?" *Because whoever she was, I'm not her.*

"Yes." His eyes turned to stone. "And no. There are things you don't know."

She crossed her arms. "Then fill me in."

He ran his hands raggedly over his face. He looked everywhere but at her.

"She didn't betray me." He paused for a long moment. When he finally raised his eyes to hers, he said, very quietly, "I betrayed her."

THIRTY-TWO

MELINE STARED ACROSS THE space between them. "What do you mean, you betrayed *her*?"

Before he could answer, the door burst open. A gust of wind howled into the house, sending the sheet music blowing across the room. Emeline quickly did up the last of her buttons as the door swung on its hinges, slamming into the wall with a *bang!*

Sable stepped inside, with Rooke on her heels.

They were both out of breath.

"*Shadow skins,*" Sable managed, her chest rising and falling in heaving gasps. Her russet hair was tangled and wild. *"Inside the city."*

Hawthorne crossed to them in three easy strides, his argument with Emeline swept away by the wind whistling through the house. "Are you certain?"

It was Rooke who answered, pushing his hair off his face. "There's no mistake. The entire city has been ordered to lock their doors and arm themselves as best they can."

"But that's impossible." Hawthorne was already pulling on his boots. "The city walls have never been breached. The king's magic—"

"We've always known the curse is getting stronger," said

Rooke, his dark brown eyes almost black. "The king can't hold it off forever."

"I slew three in the street on the way here." Hawthorne's sheathed sword was gripped in Sable's hands—the same sword the hedgemen took from him when he offered himself up as Emeline's surety. She handed it over. "There's no time to waste."

He buckled it on.

"I'll come with you," said Emeline, moving towards where they gathered by the door. "Maybe I can help."

She still had Sable's knife at her hip. And she'd killed one shadow skin today already.

"You're injured." Hawthorne stared down at her bandaged heel. "It will slow you and us down."

"So I'm just supposed to wait here?"

"Go with Rooke to the palace. Once you're safely inside, stay there."

Emeline was about to argue, except Hawthorne was already following Sable outside. The moment they passed through the door, it shut in Emeline's face.

The tarnished brass knob winked at her and Rooke. The house fell silent around them.

Her hands curled into fists.

He's right, said a voice deep inside her. *What can you do? All you have is one little knife against a forest full of monsters.*

BACK IN THE PALACE, as the silver moon rose in a velvet black sky, Emeline paced, trying to distract herself with "Rose's Waltz." The last thing the Song Mage wrote for her mother. Again and again, she read the lyrics, but the words slipped through her mind like sand through a sieve.

Rooke had assured her that Hawthorne and Sable were well trained and accustomed to dealing with shadow skins. That the king's army would eradicate the threat. That everything was going to be fine.

But his assurances did nothing to calm her.

Just after midnight, Emeline's pacing was interrupted by a knock on her door.

When she opened it, Sable stood in the frame, shoulders hunched, russet hair bedraggled, a bloody cut across her cheek.

"We chased a pair of them into the woods." Sable sounded scared and small and not at all herself. "It was an ambush. Four shadow skins held me down while they dragged him away."

Him.

She was talking about Hawthorne.

"I kept thinking . . . why don't they just kill us? Why leave me alive?" Sable pressed her face into her hands. "It was as if they wanted me to watch him be taken."

Hawthorne. In the hands of shadow skins.

Had they twisted his mind beyond recognition yet?

Had they *killed* him yet?

"Rooke's assembling a search party."

It will be too late, she thought.

"We'll find him."

It's already too late.

The truth washed over her like a cold, powerful sea. Jolting her out of her shock. When Sable left, Emeline pulled on her Blundstones, shrugged on her coat, and slipped out into the hall.

She might not be able to wield a sword. She might not be

trained to fight monsters. But she wasn't helpless. She refused to sit behind the palace walls waiting for worse news.

Emeline limped quickly through the empty streets until she arrived at the city gate. It was locked and heavily guarded by more hedgemen than usual, the air around them tense.

Turning back, she headed for the door that led to Bog's boardwalk only to find it gone. She ran her hands over the white stone wall, retracing her steps, but the door was hidden from her. She realized then that she'd only ever left the city with Hawthorne or Grace. It was possible the king's prisoner was only permitted to leave if she was accompanied. Or perhaps the entrances and exits to and from the King's City were sealed in light of the breach.

She pounded her fist against the wall, frustrated, when something scratchy brushed her cheek. She jumped, glancing up into the branch of a nearby sycamore.

Come, the tree whispered.

The sycamore's bark was peeling, revealing a mottled green trunk beneath, and as her gaze followed it skywards she saw that its uppermost branches towered over the wall. The moon was almost full beyond its branches.

Climb, it said.

After glancing around to ensure she was alone, Emeline strode towards the tree, grabbed hold of its lowermost branch, and hauled herself up.

If she'd been in better shape, she might have scaled it easily. Instead, it took more time than she would have liked to get to the top. Her breath came fast and sweat dampened her skin. Straddling the sturdiest high branch, she used it to shimmy towards the top of the wall. As she neared the flat white stone, the branch bent, and Emeline's heart plummeted, sure the branch was about to snap. She gripped it tight, ready to retreat, but when she glanced over her shoulder she found not the branch bending, but the *tree.*

Go, it said as it delivered her onto the top of the wall. A wall, she noticed, that was starting to speckle with black mold. Emeline wrinkled her nose at the musty, rotting smell, reminded of the moldy walls of the Song Mage's house, deep in the Stain.

Had the curse spread to the King's City? Was that how the shadow skins got inside?

If so, she couldn't worry about it now; she needed to find Hawthorne.

When her feet touched stone, she let go of the branch, teetering a little without its support. The top of the wall was less than two feet across, and when Emeline looked down she found a twenty-foot fall. Her stomach lurched at the sight.

She quickly got down on all fours, avoiding the mold as best she could, then carefully lowered herself until she was dangling on the other side of the wall. "Thank you," she whispered to the sycamore.

She closed her eyes and, after counting to three, dropped.

The ground swiftly rose up to meet her. As her feet hit the earth, she bent her legs to protect her ankles, which still spiked with pain.

"Ow!" she hissed, dropping to her knees, waiting for the sharp sting to subside. When it did, she rose and limped into the woods, noticing that the trunks of these trees were turning silver with disease.

Her stomach twisted with uneasiness.

Patches of starlight flickered through the leafy boughs overhead. "Where is he?" she asked the trees.

They murmured and swayed, as if consulting each other.

This way, they hushed, leading her to a gurgling river, which shone like a silver ribbon beneath the bright moon. *Follow it west.*

As she hobbled alongside its whispering current, the earth began to thunder beneath her feet, as if at the mercy of hammering hooves.

Emeline paused, listening. Were the ember mares running?

Don't stop, said the trees.

Emeline scanned her surroundings. Something red flickered in the distance. She squinted, focusing on it, and found a dozen black mares galloping to a halt in a nearby grove, snorting smoke and stomping their fire-gold hooves, which sparked against the forest floor.

Unlike Lament—who was steady and calm—their whinnies were shrill and piercing, and they tossed their heads restlessly. Unlike the wild ember mares she once stampeded with through the woods, these had steel harnesses welded to their faces, the metal biting into their flesh, leaving raw, bleeding wounds.

Worse, there were shadow skins astride their backs.

Emeline sucked in a breath as the monsters rode their captives slowly though the grove, heads turning back and forth, as if hunting something.

When one glanced her way, Emeline dropped to the underbrush, her pulse pounding. Her breath came fast as she listened, but nothing encroached; there was no sound of fiery hooves or horrifying footsteps.

Hurry, begged the trees.

Emeline crawled forward on her elbows, pushing through leaves and burrs and thorns. If she could distance herself, keep out of sight . . .

A rough-soft voice pierced the quiet.

"Emeline?"

She stopped crawling.

Hawthorne?

"Is that you?" His voice shook, as if he was frightened. He sounded very close.

This shadow skin hunting party—they must be the ones who took him.

"Help me, Emeline."

His panicked voice tugged at her, drawing her towards him. Emeline stood up. She turned away from the river and silently crept from tree to tree, trying to conceal herself as she moved towards the sound of his voice.

No, said the trees.

Sharp branches scraped her cheeks and caught at her hair, as if the trees were trying to stop her. Emeline ignored them as a shape appeared ahead, between her and the captured ember mares.

"Hawthorne?"

The figure halted, swinging in her direction with an unearthly swiftness. Two more shapes stepped out to join it. Emeline went still, staring at the three dark shadows from between the boughs of the spruce she hid behind. Their tall, thin forms were blacker than the night, and they had no eyes.

"Emeline!" Hawthorne's terrified voice knotted around her heart.

She moved without thinking, reaching for Sable's knife as dead leaves crunched beneath her steps. She was about to call out—to tell him she was coming—when a hand slammed down over her mouth.

Someone grabbed her from behind, their arm fastening around her middle, hauling her backwards. She tried to squirm and kick and buck, using her elbows and feet. She tried to scream, but the hand clamped too hard, stifling the sound.

"It's not him!" hissed a voice in her ear. "It's not him."

Emeline breathed in the tang of smoke and steel.

Sable.

When her hand fell away, Emeline insisted, "It is him." She was still fighting as Hawthorne called for her and Sable continued dragging her backwards, into the hollowed-out trunk of an old tree. At the center was an empty hole, letting the stars shine through. "They're hurting him!"

"Hush. *Hush.*" Sable pulled Emeline against her. "It's not him. I promise you." She leaned back against the wall of the hollow and sank down to the ground, bringing Emeline with her. "Stay quiet and still."

Hawthorne's tortured cries drew closer, calling out for her. His voice echoed in this hollow, swelling around them.

Emeline pushed against Sable, needing to get to him.

Sable held on tighter.

When Emeline dug an elbow into her ribs, trying to hurt her so she would let go, Sable started to sing. It began as a hum in the back of her throat, soft as velvet. The way a mother might soothe a crying child.

Emeline fell still at the sound.

But it wasn't Sable's singing that entranced her; it was the song she'd chosen. One of *Emeline's.*

An old song buried in the password-protected folder on her phone.

How on earth . . . ?

The tune was only a whisper, but its familiar rises and falls held Emeline spellbound. She could barely remember this song—nor any of the others she'd locked away. How could Sable possibly be humming it?

Like every other song Emeline had ever heard or sung, this one came with a memory: She was maybe fourteen, sitting on the second-story beam of Pa's barn, her bare legs swinging as she sang. It was the height of summer and everything stuck to her sweaty skin: her clothes, her hair, the dust in the air. And she wasn't alone. There was someone beside her, all stretched out, lying with her back to the beam. A girl with brambly hair and bright gold eyes. She was smiling as she listened, her dirty bare foot bobbing to the rhythm of Emeline's song.

Sable.

The memory burst like a popped bubble.

What??

It made no sense. Emeline and Sable had only just met. Had something distorted the memory trapped in the song? Or had her brain inserted Sable because *Sable* was the one singing it now?

In Emeline's confusion, the terror in Hawthorne's voice stopped tugging. His calls for help quieted, moving into the distance. Finally, she heard the truth in his voice: beneath the familiar cadence was a sick and festering rot—like the curse itself.

It was a trick of the shadow skins. A weapon to lure her in.

Sable hummed until the sounds beyond the hollow trailed into silence. When the shadow skins had moved on, Sable fell silent, letting Emeline go.

Their staggered breaths echoed in the dark space.

"We should go." Sable pushed upwards to her feet. "Before they circle back."

THIRTY-THREE

HOW DO YOU KNOW that song?"

Sable—whose lupine eyes could clearly see in the dark—strode several steps ahead, as if she were trying to put distance between them. As if Emeline were wrapped in barbed wire and if Sable got too close she'd get cut.

"What song?"

"The one you were humming."

It was possible Emeline mistook it. Maybe the tune only sounded like hers and too much distance made her misremember.

But she didn't think so.

Or maybe her fear for Hawthorne, combined with Sable's sudden presence, made her brain alter the memory. Memories were tricky things, after all. Just look at Pa, whose memory had utterly betrayed him.

"I can't recall where I know it from," said Sable, guarded. The snow-white pommels of her long blades gleamed from where they crisscrossed her back. "I panicked. It was the first thing that came to mind."

She hadn't seemed panicked. She'd been so calm. Maybe that was Sable's nature, though: still as a glassy pool on the surface, chaos churning beneath.

Emeline decided to let the subject drop—for now. Not only had Sable saved her, Hawthorne was out here somewhere. They needed to find him.

"Thank you," she said softly.

Sable glanced back. "You're welcome." Her eyes shone like a wolf's in the darkness and she paused, waiting until Emeline caught up.

They continued on in silence, Emeline listening to the trees' directions, then telling Sable where to go. If Sable found it odd that the forest spoke to Emeline, she didn't show it.

All too soon, the trees took on a sickly white translucence, their deadened trunks shining eerily beneath the starlight.

The Stain.

The air was thick and stagnant. No breeze blew. No birds called. No insects croaked.

There, rasped the dying trees.

A cage of bone-white elms stood in the center of a clearing, illuminated by glowing torches lodged in the ground. The elms grew in a perfect circle, with less than a handbreadth of space between each trunk. Six feet from the ground, they bent inwards, twisting together like a knot, trapping the shape within.

Hawthorne.

He lay sprawled in the dirt, hair plastered to his temples, eyes closed. Still as death.

Emeline ran to him.

"Hawthorne?"

He didn't stir.

"Hawthorne!"

Emeline scanned the elm trunks. "Where's the way in?"

"There isn't one," said Sable, walking twice around the cage, her gaze running up and down the trunks.

Emeline reached through the space in the elms, feeling for a pulse. The skin of his neck was cool to the touch, and it took her several tries before her fingertips felt the slow thud of his heart. She let out a shaky breath.

"He's alive, at least."

She reached for a slender trunk and pulled. It didn't budge. She reached for the knife at her hip and was about to start sawing when, on the other side of the cage, Sable tensed, her attention fixing on something behind Emeline.

She spun to face it.

The Vile stepped into the clearing with them. She grinned, her pale gaze fixed on Emeline as if Sable didn't exist. As if *this* was her reason for capturing Hawthorne: he was bait in a trap set for Emeline.

Emeline stared back, hands curling into fists as a cold, dark hatred twisted her insides. *Here* was the monster that murdered her father and imprisoned her mother in that cellar.

Sable moved like the wind, drawing the two blades simultaneously from the sheaths at her back as she stepped between Emeline and the Vile.

"Take one step closer and I'll gut you like a fish," she snarled. The glow from the torches glinted off her enchanted steel.

The Vile sneered, her lips pulling back from sharp teeth. "Your magic steel can't bite me, shiftling."

There came a grotesque cracking sound, like bones snapping and joints dislocating, as the Vile opened her mouth, revealing layers upon layers of those needlelike teeth and bloodstained, rust-colored gums. Her dark maw widened like a cavern, as if to swallow Sable whole.

"Wait." Emeline's voice rang through the clearing. The Vile turned her head, staring. "I'm the one you want. Let them go, and I'll be your prisoner."

Sable shot her a startled look. "You'll do no such thing."

Holding Sable's gaze, she whispered, "Trust me." She'd distracted the Vile once before with her singing, and now that she knew who her father was, how there was a chance she'd inherited some of the Song Mage's magic, she was certain she could do it again. It would at least buy Emeline enough time to run—after Sable and Hawthorne were safely away.

But first and foremost: she wanted to find out what the Vile did to her mother. She needed to know if Rose Lark was alive.

The Vile's pale blue eyes bore into Emeline.

"If you can get him out of that cage before I eat your friend, they can both go free." The creature's attention shifted to Sable and she grinned hideously, taking a clawed step towards the girl.

"Don't worry about me," Sable said as she lifted her blades, knuckles bunching around the handles. "Find a way to get him out of there."

Emeline nodded, turning to the elm cage.

I'm the Song Mage's daughter, Emeline told herself. Her singing summoned the woods. It put a dragon to sleep and stripped back Hawthorne's defenses. It had even held off the Vile, temporarily, down in that cellar.

What else could it do?

She pressed her hand to one of the trunks. A gentle thrum pushed against her palm. Like the faint and sluggish pulse of a dying heart, beating below the bark.

Maybe these blighted trees hadn't quite given up yet. Maybe there was something alive in them still.

Behind her, the air hissed with the swing of a blade. Emeline looked to find the Vile mere steps from Sable—teeth bared, ready to strike.

Her heart sped up.

Focus.

Emeline wrapped her hands around two elm trunks, thinking of the day she'd seen inside Hawthorne's mind. She'd *wanted* to defy him. Wanted to break down the walls he erected to keep her out.

She remembered singing Claw to sleep. She'd been thinking of Pa as she sang it. Pa, singing lullabies.

Maybe intention mattered. Maybe, when her voice did strange things, it did them in tandem with what she wanted.

Emeline. The voices of the trees whispered like ghosts. *Sing us a true song.*

A true song.

But what did that mean?

When Sable's steel whistled through the air again, Emeline stopped thinking and reached for the song she'd written to the tune of "Rose's Waltz." The lyrics were her own. Did that make it true? She hummed the first verse, wading slowly into it, thinking about what she wanted: Hawthorne, free.

The pulse beneath her palms quickened.

She sang louder, letting the song grow, and as it did, the pulse locked away in sap grew with her, drumming loudly beneath her hands, matching the beat of her song. As if it were harmonizing.

It was like singing with Hawthorne—that tuning-fork feeling glowed within her. She could feel their feelings, spilling into her. Flooding her senses. Like they were one, her and these trees.

Unexpected sorrow and longing infected her. Weariness sank down to her roots. The forest was sick and tired and cursed—but holding on. Determined to keep fighting.

Suddenly, it wasn't just Emeline's song flooding out, but something else. A thick and shimmering power gushed out of her, like blood from a wound. Around her, the clearing changed. Pale, dead leaves cascaded to the forest floor like snow. The trunks of the trees changed from powdery white to deep browns and dappled greens, color spreading like a blush from their roots to their branches. New leaves began to bud and unfurl, teeming with life.

Looking back to Hawthorne's unconscious form, Emeline sang louder.

Let him out, she told the trees. *Set him free.*

A moan filled the air, coming from above. At her command, the elms untwisted themselves—slowly, slowly—until they no longer caged Hawthorne in. The trees bent, arching away from each other in a V, giving their prisoner enough space to escape through.

Her song fell silent as Emeline stumbled into the cage. Immediately, the forest spun around her. Exhaustion crashed like a wave onto her shoulders, making her collapse to her knees at his side.

Emeline felt like an old rag, all wrung out.

She tried to wrap her arms around him. Tried to pull him up. But the strength had gone out of her. "Hawthorne," she whispered. "Hawthorne, wake up."

Outside the cage, the wind sighed. The trees were quiet and calm, the starlight soft and twinkling.

But then the air turned sour, and the rot returned—fast, faster, spreading like spilled ink. Emeline felt the trees try to fight it, felt their panicked desperation. But the curse was too strong. It leached them of life, leaving them sickly white.

Emeline hadn't saved them at all.

What did she expect? That just because she was the Song Mage's daughter, she could counter the curse?

Wrapping her arms around Hawthorne's torso, she gave a fierce cry and *pulled,* dragging him through the gap in the trees and out of the cage. As soon as his unconscious body was free, the opening closed behind them.

Emeline collapsed to the earth, utterly spent, then looked up.

Sable drew away from the Vile, whose eyes were darkening with rage. Her veins blackened like ichor beneath her skin as she stared down Emeline like she'd never seen a more loathsome thing.

"I thought so." The Vile's voice scraped like wintry branches on a frosted pane. Pointing a clawed finger at Hawthorne, she hissed to Sable, "Take him and leave!"

A black ember mare came out of the trees, muzzled and ready to ride. Sable paused, reluctant. She clearly had no desire to leave Emeline alone with a monster.

But Emeline needed answers only the Vile could give her. So she said, "Get him to safety." When Sable still paused, Emeline forced herself to rise, despite her body feeling heavy as stone. "Either we all die here, or you escape and bring back help."

Seeing the logic in this, Sable narrowed her eyes and said, "Promise me you'll stay alive."

Emeline nodded. Together they hoisted Hawthorne onto the horse. Sable climbed up after, holding him in place with one arm looped around his chest.

"Sable?" she heard Hawthorne's slurred voice say. "Where are we?"

Sable looked back once before the horse stepped into the darkness beyond the clearing. And then they were gone.

The Vile started forward, examining Emeline like a meal she intended to eat.

Thinking of the cellar, Emeline started to sing in an attempt to fend her off. But the Vile seemed unaffected. She didn't back away this time, or try to shake off the spell of Emeline's voice. Only scowled.

"Song Mage spawn!" hissed the monster before her. "*He* thought the poison in his voice was boundless too. But it wasn't."

The Vile lunged for her. Shakily, Emeline drew Sable's knife from her hip—too late. The Vile batted it easily aside, moving in. One bony hand grabbed Emeline's jaw, gripping her cheeks painfully, while the other wrapped around the wrist that held the knife and squeezed until Emeline dropped it.

The steel fell to the ground with a *thud*.

"It's why he locked me in that cellar. To *force* me to stay. Because whenever the venom in his voice dried up, *I remembered.*"

Emeline frowned, confused. The Vile was the prisoner in the Song Mage's cellar?

The Vile's pupils widened, swallowing up her irises until they were entirely black. Letting go of Emeline's wrist, she dragged translucent fingers down Emeline's cheeks, her touch rough as dried leaves, her sharp nails skimming dangerously against the skin.

"I could never leave him, he said. He loved me so much, you see." Her slitted nostrils flared angrily. "So I killed him."

The Vile was talking nonsense. The Song Mage loved Rose Lark, Emeline's mother. Not this monster standing before her.

But if it was the Vile he imprisoned . . .

She remembered the butterfly pin.

A horrifying thought took root in her.

No . . .

Letting go of Emeline's face, the Vile bent down, her fingers plunging into ashy leaves until they found Sable's blade. When she rose, she lifted the honed tip to Emeline's heart, holding the hilt with both hands, ready to plunge it in.

"I know you're his. You have his eyes. And his blood—I could smell it in that cellar. Just as I smell it now." Her nose wrinkled in distaste. "And that song . . ." She bared her teeth. "Is that why you came to the manor—to finish what he started? To imprison me there for good?"

Emeline's thoughts were spinning too fast. *It can't be.*

It was too horrible.

She shook her head blindly as images of Rose Lark rose up: laughing with her head thrown back, eyes bright with joy; smiling adoringly up at Tom.

You can't be her.

The trees began to hiss around them. The elm tree cage pressed into Emeline's shoulder blades. She wrapped her hands around their thin trunks, leaning back, away from the knife, trying to stop the world from spinning.

She thought of the sycamore, delivering her over the wall. Thought of all the other times the trees had assisted her, giving her warnings or directions.

It reminded her of what Pa said the other night: he'd given an offering to the king on the day she was born, in exchange for the forest's protection.

Was that why the trees were always helping her—they were trying to protect her?

She sent up a desperate plea to the woods. *Help me again now—if you can.*

The wind picked up, rattling through the brittle branches. That faintly beating pulse thrummed beneath the bark, pushing through to her.

A soft rustling sound broke the quiet as something swelled in the earth beneath her feet.

The Vile paused, listening. She lowered the knife as the ground shifted. Rising and dropping. As if something slithered under the newly fallen leaves.

The Vile turned, sensing danger.

Twisting white roots surged upwards, reaching like fingers to wrap around the Vile's ankles and twine up her legs. As they did, the Vile stumbled, losing her balance. Fury flashed across her face. She righted herself, then turned to Emeline—who was still within striking distance.

Run! hissed the trees.

Before the blade lashed across her chest, Emeline ducked out of the way.

The Vile screamed.

Emeline ran—from the rage in that scream, from the edge of that sweeping blade, but most of all, from the realization slamming through her.

The Vile and Rose Lark were one and the same.

That monster is my mother.

THIRTY-FOUR

OMETHING FOLLOWED ON HER heels. Or rather, *many* somethings.

Emeline heard them crash through the thorny brambles behind her. Shadow skins set loose by the Vile. The hooves of their captive ember mares pounded the earth in a furious tattoo, closing the gap.

She counted a dozen nightmares in the darkness.

Emeline waded quickly through the sighing river, its cold water filling her boots. Her legs burned. Her sliced heel throbbed. Her breath scratched her lungs.

Her bad foot snagged in a patch of thorns, and she went sprawling. Emeline turned over, scrambling backwards. But it was too late. The monsters were descending from all sides.

Before they seized her, the starry sky darkened.

A raven cry pierced the night.

Emeline looked up. Hundreds of black shapes blotted out the stars. Ravens, circling. Readying themselves to dive.

But the wolves arrived first.

Emeline heard their growls before she saw them. The leader had russet fur and golden eyes. *Sable?* she wondered, remembering the fanged shape of the girl's shadow. The wolf snarled at the shadow skins, keeping itself between the monsters and Emeline.

The others followed suit as the ravens plunged down from the stars.

Wolves clashed with shadows. Ravens swooped and dived, keeping the monsters away. Beyond them, the trees hissed. *Run faster!* Emeline scrambled to her feet and kept going.

She ran straight into one of *them*.

The shadow skin grinned down at her from its sightless face. Out of its crackling mouth came Pa's voice. Pa telling her everything was going to be all right. The shadow skin's power curled like a snake through her mind until she no longer saw the monster before her, only her beloved grandfather. Pa's arms were outstretched, ready to soothe whatever was hurting Emeline.

Come here, my duckie.

Her traitorous body rose to obey, bringing her closer to the Pa who was not Pa. A flicker of fear raced down Emeline's spine as he reached to pull her into his arms. . . .

And then a glimmering sword plunged through his chest.

"No!" Emeline screamed, despite herself.

Pa's lips parted in surprise and his chin dropped as he stared at the blade protruding out of him, canted down towards the earth.

His form dissolved into a shadow skin falling to its knees.

Emeline stumbled away and looked up to see Hawthorne drawing his blade out of the creature's chest. From atop Lament, who shone like black fire, Hawthorne gleamed in the moonlight, fury blazing across his face. If he was injured from his earlier capture, he showed no sign of it.

Lament regarded her with wide, fire-red eyes. She whickered, nudging Emeline's cheek with her soft nose. As if to say, *Tell me who hurt you, and I'll trample them into the earth.*

That spent feeling was still heavy inside Emeline, making the world blur. She reached for Lament's saddle, using it to stay upright.

Frowning, Hawthorne swung himself down. Sliding a warm

hand behind her neck, he cupped the curve of it, his shadowed gaze drinking her in. "Did she harm you?"

Emeline shook her head. "No. I'm just . . ." *Tired.*

Unnaturally tired.

Sensing it, he reached for her waist and helped her into the saddle.

No sooner was she mounted than Lament reared at the approach of a shadow skin, flashing her fiery hooves. Emeline held on tight to keep from falling as Hawthorne plunged his sword through the creature's heart.

"Ride straight to the city gate," he told her. "No stopping."

She was supposed to run and hide, while he battled shadow skins alone? No. She wouldn't leave him here, surrounded.

At the ring of drawn steel, she looked to find he wasn't alone. Sable was there in human form, swinging her enchanted blade, beheading shadow skins as wolves and ravens lunged for monsters, and claws and fangs collided.

Meanwhile, a horde of hedgemen teemed from the silver trees, their bronze breastplates flickering in the starlight as their spears flew through the air. They drew swords and rushed the shadow skins, swarming the clearing, armor clinking as they outnumbered the enemy, their enchanted steel blades ending the monsters swiftly. Sensing the turning tide, most of the remaining shadow skins fled, and the rest were quickly overcome.

When the woods fell quiet, Emeline scanned the surroundings from Lament's saddle, watching the hedgemen push outwards, searching for lingering enemies. Nearby, Sable ran her fingers slowly over the black wing of a raven perched on her shoulder, as if checking for broken bones. Though she couldn't say how, Emeline knew the raven was Rooke.

"Care to let me up?"

Emeline looked down into gray eyes—one dark, one light.

Hawthorne wiped his glistening forehead and gripped the back of the saddle, wanting up.

She took her foot out of the stirrup and bent forward as he mounted. His arm came around her waist, and he dropped his forehead to her shoulder, breathing deep. She smelled the salty tang of sweat on his skin.

"You shouldn't have come for me." He leaned heavily against her, letting her bear the weight of him. "But I'm glad you did."

Emeline glanced to Sable, who met her gaze. The shiftling nodded, wordlessly telling her to take Hawthorne home. Lifting the reins, Emeline nudged Lament back towards the city, and together they moved through the cursed and dying woods.

EXCEPT FOR LAMENT'S LABORED breathing and clopping hooves, the ride back was utterly silent, leaving Emeline prey to her thoughts.

The Vile's words haunted her, circling inside her head.

Whenever the venom in his voice dried up, I remembered.

She remembered her life beyond the woods, Emeline realized. Remembered the things she'd been stolen from. Remembered the man she truly loved: Tomás Pérez.

Not the Song Mage.

It's why he locked me in that cellar.

He loved me so much, you see.

It made Emeline want to cry.

The Song Mage had enchanted Rose Lark. He'd used the magic in his voice to coerce her, to make her believe she loved him. And when that magic reached its limit, when he couldn't keep her enchanted anymore, he physically restrained her in his cellar—to stop her from leaving.

So she murdered him.

And then she must have cursed the woods.

Had she been a monster when she killed him? Or had the killing turned her into one and the curse did the rest?

If my mother is a monster, Emeline thought, *the Song Mage is something worse.* A monster masquerading as a gentleman. An accomplished singer, highly esteemed in the Wood King's court, hiding a disturbing secret beneath his house.

Curse-bringer, Claw had called him. Because he knew. He'd *seen.*

A terrifying thought occurred to her.

Is this what I'm capable of?

Bile rose in her throat. Because hadn't she used the power in her voice to coerce? First Claw, then Hawthorne, and tonight: the trees caging him in. She had made them all bend to her will.

What if next time she did something worse?

When they dismounted in the stable behind Hawthorne's house, Emeline kept her distance. This new knowledge made her feel like a plague. Repulsive and dangerous. She didn't want Hawthorne around her. Didn't want him to know what her father had done. What she herself was capable of.

"Let me do this," she said, starting to unbuckle Lament's saddle from within her stall. "You're exhausted. Go inside."

If he went inside, she could leave the woods without him knowing. If she left tonight, she could keep him safe from the dangers in her voice. He would never have to know about her twisted inheritance.

Leaving had always been the plan, anyway. Once she ensured Pa's freedom, she'd always intended to escape and return to her real life. It was her search for Rose that interrupted her plan, but that search was complete.

It was the only thing to do.

Leave.

Besides, it was only a matter of time before the curse over-took the King's City.

"I think I'll stay," Hawthorne said, watching her fingers fumble the buckle. The only light came from an oil lamp out in the wider stable, making it difficult to see. "Let me—"

"I've got it."

It took her twice as long as it would have taken him. But still, he stood there.

When she finished, Hawthorne lifted the saddle and went to hang it on the wall outside the stall. In his absence, hop-ing he'd change his mind and go, Emeline pressed her forehead to Lament's flank, breathing in the smells of the stable around them: fresh hay and old leather and wood.

Instead, Hawthorne returned with a wool blanket. His movements were slow as he tossed it over Lament's glistening back, making Emeline wonder if he was in pain.

"I can handle this," she told him. "Go inside."

"I'll go inside when you tell me what has you so frightened." He reached for her hands. "You're shaking. What happened?"

She remembered the hate twisting her mother's face. Re-membered those rough fingers grabbing her cheeks and the nails scraping her skin. Remembered her mother lifting the sharpened tip of Sable's blade to her heart.

Her mother hadn't recognized her. Or maybe she had and wanted her dead anyway—because Emeline was *his*. A reminder of the horrible things he'd done to her.

Of course Rose would hate the sight of her daughter.

Tom would hate the sight of Emeline too, when he found out what she was the product of. Tom would never be able to look at her again.

And what would the rest of Edgewood think?

What would *Hawthorne* think?

That thought made her throat close up. Hot tears pricked her eyes. Pulling her hands out of his, she knotted her fingers together and walked out of Lament's stall to the edge of the stable, where a cold breeze blew in.

She wanted to run far away from here.

She wanted to outrun the truth.

"Emeline." The warmth of him moved up her back. When she didn't answer, he reached for her wrist. *"Emeline."*

But there was something else she wanted. Something deeper, humming like a pulse beneath her skin. She wanted to turn and burrow her face in Hawthorne's throat, breathe in his scent, pull his mouth down to hers, and drown in him.

Is this how my father felt?

The question scared her.

She glanced to where Hawthorne's fingers gently encircled her wrist. "Please don't touch me," she whispered.

He raised his hands, stepping back. "Will you at least tell me what's wrong? Perhaps I can help."

She smiled a bitter smile, turning to face him. "You can't help."

"Let me try."

Emeline swallowed, looking away. She shook her head. If she was leaving tonight, it wouldn't matter, would it?

"What if I told you . . ." But how could she tell him?

Try.

"What if I told you the Vile wasn't the real horror? That the real horror was the Song Mage?"

Hawthorne took a slow, small step towards her. "I would believe you."

The brass buttons of his coat shone in the moonlight. Emeline fixed her gaze on them.

"What if I told you that the Song Mage wanted his muse so badly, he stole her away from everything she loved, enchanted her to want him and him alone, and when the enchantment wore off, imprisoned her in his cellar?"

Hawthorne paused.

"What if I told you"—Emeline lowered her voice to a whisper—"that I'm the outcome? That she—the Vile—is my mother?"

Time slowed around them. The silence blared in her ears.

He'll turn away now, she thought. *He'll leave me here in the dark, disgusted.*

But Hawthorne only took another small step towards her.

"I would believe that too," he said.

Hesitantly, he touched her hip, cupping the curve of it. It steadied her. Rooting her in the stable and the lamplight and his solid presence. His hand glided across her lower back, warm and strong, then curled over her other hip as he drew her slowly against him.

She wanted to give in to the strength of him. To press her cheek against the fine wool of his coat. To let his arms tighten, pulling her snug.

But as his hand stroked her hair soothingly, Emeline remembered that day beneath the glass dome. When her voice smashed down his walls and *took* something from him. Something he didn't want her to take.

It had been so easy.

What if I'm no different than my father?

She wanted Hawthorne. Even now, the press of his body woke a hungry fire in her, stoked with every caress of his fingers. Heat flickered and spread as his jaw grazed her cheek.

She wanted so much more than to be held by him.

How far would that want drive her? Her father wanted her mother, and he'd done terrible things to have her.

What if she didn't stop with Hawthorne?

Emeline shuddered and stepped out of his arms.

If he looked in her eyes now, he might see to the ugly core of her. She kept her face lowered and said, "It would be wise to keep your distance."

Leave, she told herself. *Now. Before you hurt him.*

Nothing held her here anymore. Pa was safe. The Wood King had her father's songs; he could find a new minstrel to sing them. And her mother was a monster that wanted her dead.

More important: Emeline had a life to return to.

It wasn't too late. Her tour started in two days. A major record label would be watching her first performance, and if she wowed them they'd give her a contract. Produce her next album. Level up her career. Emeline simply needed to do what she'd always done: Pretend to be normal. Pretend none of this was real. Pretend there was nothing dark lurking in her depths.

Emeline turned to go, her mind made up. She would head for Edgewood and, from there, drive to Montreal. She would go on tour. Secure a record deal with Daybreak. Save her dream.

She would go back to faking normalcy.

She would bury her secrets deep.

All she had to do was run.

Now.

She moved to step out of the stable. Hawthorne grabbed her wrist. Before she could pull free, he caught her face in his hands and kissed her. Tenderly. His teeth scraped her lower lip, sucking softly, slowly, as his hands slid into her hair, freeing it from her messy bun.

Heat licked through her.

Her shoulders hit the wall.

She inhaled sharply, pulling back. "What are you doing?"

"Being unwise." He pinned her there, eyes glinting.

He kissed her again. This time, her stomach tightened with desire and a soft, hungry sound escaped her throat.

No.

She pressed her palms against his chest and shoved. The force sent him backwards, wincing. She stared at him, wide-eyed and breathless, a reckless need taking root in her.

"My parents are monsters."

"That doesn't make you one."

Before he could kiss her again, before she could give in to her urges and take what she wanted from him, Emeline stepped back.

"Go inside," she told him. He didn't budge. Could she use her voice to *compel* him? She winced at that horrible thought.

But how else could she protect him?

She thought of their first meeting, when he'd lied to her. He'd tried his hardest to stop her from reaching the city and confronting his king, knowing what would happen if she did.

Knowing the danger it would put her in.

Lie to him.

"Don't you get it? All I want is to escape before the king adds my skull to his growing collection."

He paused, hesitating.

"I'm leaving, Hawthorne. Right now. Tonight." She forged her voice into something hard and unyielding. "I don't want *this*. I don't want *you*."

If she stopped now, he might see through the cracks in her words. So she kept going.

"I want my singing career. I want my *real life*. I've worked so hard to get where I am. You think I'd throw that away? For *this* nightmare? For *you*?" She shook her head. "I barely know you."

Hawthorne looked away abruptly.

"Of course not. I would never . . ." He ran his hands through his hair. "I would never ask that of you. Of course you should leave."

He stepped sharply back.

"You deserve to have all your heart's longings." The words lacked any bitterness. As if he truly wanted that for her: *happiness,* or something like it. As if he'd already resigned himself, long before now, to her walking away. "Here. Take this." He tugged something off his hand. Stepping towards her, he reached for her wrist and slid a ring onto her finger. "It will get you safely home. Think of where you want to be, and it will bring you there."

The ring was white and thin and, like a tithe marker, unnaturally cold. It made her skin tingle where it touched.

It reminded her of something Aspen once said.

You're the tithe collector. You can walk deep into her world whenever and wherever you want.

Was this how he did it—using an enchanted ring?

Without another word, Hawthorne turned away and walked towards the house. As if he'd always known exactly how this story would end.

Wait, she thought, watching him leave. *I didn't mean it.*

Heat rushed against her shoulder as Lament snorted, startling her. The mare had left her stall and now stood next to Emeline. The night wrapped cold fingers around both of them, but there was something far colder inside Emeline. A sliver of ice, lodged in her heart. She leaned her cheek against Lament's, and when that didn't warm her, looped her arms around the horse's neck.

They hadn't even said goodbye.

THIRTY-FIVE

FTER PACING THE STABLE for a good ten minutes, trying and failing to talk herself out of what she intended to do next, Emeline followed Hawthorne into the house.

I'm only going to say good-bye, she thought, twisting his ring around her finger. A true good-bye. *And then I'll go.*

A fire blazed in the hearth. Down the hall, she heard rushing water from where he was drawing a bath.

She remembered his hands in her hair as he pressed her up against the wall. Remembered the way he turned her skin to fire.

From the washroom, a buckle rattled as he undid his belt, followed by the whisper of fabric as his clothes fell, piece by piece, to the floor. The sound made her swallow. Water splashed as he stepped into the tub and sank down into the water.

Emeline tugged off her boots and listened, thinking back to the stable. To the heady crush of him pinning her to the wall.

He wanted her. That was clear. It was okay to take what she wanted, so long as he wanted it too. Just once. Just tonight.

And then she would leave.

She and Hawthorne came from different worlds. His world was cursed and dying; hers held her beckoning dreams. They would never work.

Of course she was leaving. There was no question.

She just needed to say good-bye first.

Emeline walked towards the sounds of him bathing, her shaky fingers trailing the walls. She paused before the door, staring down at the sliver of gold lantern light spilling through the crack beneath. Her heart hammered as she took the brass knob in her palm and turned it, pushing the door open.

A window lay straight ahead, framing the white moon in a navy sky. Beneath the pane sat an aluminum washbasin, illuminated by the glowing lantern on the floor. Sitting in the basin, head tilted back, was Hawthorne.

When Emeline shut the door behind her, he lifted his head.

For a moment, they stared at each other.

"I thought you were leaving."

She stepped away from the door. "I forgot something."

"So you . . ."

Holding his gaze, she pulled off her shirt and dropped it on the floor.

Whatever he was about to say dissolved into air. He swallowed instead.

Her heart pounded as she undid her jeans, letting them fall in a heap. When she stepped out of the denim and glanced up, she found him fighting to keep his eyes on her face.

Look, she thought. *I want you to look.*

He gave in, his feverish gaze sweeping down her pale body. His grip tightened on the sides of the basin as she slowly stripped off her bra, then her underpants and socks. The cold air rushed against her, making her skin tighten.

The breath shuddered out of him. Hearing it sent a wave of desire crashing through her.

It drove her towards the tub, her bare feet padding against the floorboards. Warm, soapy water rushed up her legs as she stepped into the basin. With one foot planted on either side of him, she lowered herself down onto his hips.

He inhaled sharply, muscles tightening with restraint.

"Is this all right?" she whispered. "Or do you want me to go?"

In answer, he cupped the wings of her shoulder blades and ran his trembling hands down her back. "Are you mad?" he murmured into her throat, planting a kiss against her skin. "*This is where I want you.*"

His mouth was like a spell, unraveling her. She felt herself coming undone.

It shouldn't be like this. No one should have this kind of effect on her.

She slid her hands firmly up his chest, over his collarbone, then along his shoulders. He half closed his eyes as she traced him, his dark lashes shadowing his cheeks. When she arched against him, his breath hitched and his hands spanned her waist, clasping her tight, pulling her into him.

"*Emeline.*"

The agony in his voice made her ache. She bit his collarbone and clutched his shoulders, rocking against him. Slowly at first. Then faster. Insistent.

Tension hummed through his body. His fingers dug into her hips.

She was breathless with desire. Urgently needing him.

Hawthorne moaned low in his throat. One hand wrapped around her thigh, the other cupped her head, bringing her mouth down to his. He kissed her hungrily, seizing what she offered him as their yearning built towards its crescendo and he quietly called out her name.

When it ended, Emeline fell against him, panting softly as she rested her head on his wet shoulder. Lying curled against his chest, she listened to the slow, steady beat of his heart.

Her whole body hummed with pleasure. She couldn't remember the last time she felt so perfectly happy.

As he leaned his cheek against the crown of her head, Hawthorne's arms circled her, keeping her close as his palms rested on her curves beneath the water.

"Was that okay?" she whispered, tracing his lean edges with her fingertip. So new to her, and yet familiar. Like a puzzle piece she hadn't known was missing.

In answer, he tipped her head back and kissed her mouth, the warmth of his lips parting hers. Before she could return it fully, he rose from the tub, wrapped her in a towel, and carried her to his bed.

Where they did it all over again.

THIRTY-SIX

EMELINE WOKE TO THE splutter and crack of a wood fire. Her nose was cold, but Hawthorne's bed was warm, and she snuggled down deeper. The smell of him on the sheets brought back memories of last night. Of his capable hands and his deep warmth and his soft kisses.

When she reached for him, though, her fingers brushed cold, empty sheets.

Emeline opened her eyes.

On the pillow next to hers, he'd left three sprigs of Queen Anne's lace, tied with twine. The delicate white buds trembled as she touched them. They reminded her of the anemone left beneath her stool that night at La Rêverie. Had that really been Hawthorne standing at the bar, drinking from her Hydro Flask? If so, why? What had he been doing there?

Her mind wandered further back, to the mysterious Taylor sent from an anonymous fan. Wildflowers had been woven through the strings of the guitar. Buttercups and daisies and . . . Queen Anne's lace.

Was that Hawthorne too?

Emeline frowned. It didn't make sense. Both instances were from before they'd ever met.

She decided to ask him about it.

Emeline stretched, preparing to rise. Beyond the bed was a faded blue armchair, her clothes neatly folded upon it.

She had a hazy memory of him sitting in that chair, with a notebook on his knee, watching her sleep.

Sketching me, she thought. *Or did I dream that?*

Emeline sat up, and there on the bedside table was the leather-bound notebook. A smudged gray pencil lay atop it.

Sitting up, Emeline gathered the blankets to her chest, then reached for the book. Carefully, she opened to the first page. There, in soft gray shades, was Lament. Hawthorne's lines had somehow captured the velvety softness of her nose and that impatient, fiery gleam in her eye.

Turning the page, Emeline found a sketched scene of Sable and Rooke, leaning towards each other from across Hawthorne's fireplace. He'd drawn them deep in discussion: the lines of Rooke's raised hands were sharp and rough, as if he was waving them to emphasize his point; Sable's chin was propped calmly on her hands, as if she was plotting her rebuttal. The next sketch was of Grace, smiling and happy, her chin on her fist with The Acorn bustling behind her.

Emeline turned more pages and found more scenes: the tall grove where the Wood King sat upon his throne; the view from the crystal dome over the sweeping forest; a dark raven wing with each and every feather drawn in precise detail.

Emeline turned page after page until she came to the last one.

The sketch was of a bare foot—*her* foot—peeking out from beneath the covers at the bottom of his bed. He'd drawn each of her toes, the gentle curve of her arch, and the line of her ankle.

Even his pencil marks were startlingly tender.

Emeline turned the page, eager for more, but only blank ones followed. Dozens of others lined the bookshelf, though.

She had the urge to take them all in her arms, dump them on the bed, and go through them, one by one.

Part of her recoiled. It would be an invasion of his privacy. Like going through a diary.

Wouldn't it?

Yes. Obviously, yes.

Tearing her gaze away from the sketchbooks, she rose from the bed and started pulling on her jeans, then her shirt. She was about to go find Hawthorne when she glanced at the shelf.

What would it hurt if she peeked at one more? She doubted he would mind.

Giving in to temptation, she grabbed a particularly thick book in the middle of the shelf and pulled it out.

Sitting down cross-legged in the armchair, Emeline hungrily flipped through it. The first dozen pages or so were tree studies, each one labeled with a name: *Chestnut, Ash, Sassafras, Red Cedar*, and more. The leaves, flowers, fruit, and bark were drawn in detail. But the lines of these drawings were shakier, less confident. When she came across sketches of Rooke and Sable again, they looked several years younger.

She kept flipping, skipping through the tree sections, trying to find more personal ones. An image of another face caught her attention, but she passed it too quickly and she had to flip back.

When she found it, her heart thudded to a stop.

There, rendered in dark lines, was a sketch of *her.* In profile. With her hair tied up in a bun and a guitar pick between her lips.

She leaned in, staring.

This Emeline had cheeks much fuller than they were now, and the lines of her face were softer. *It's a younger version of me,* she realized. From three or four years ago.

An Emeline who hadn't met Hawthorne yet.

A cold, prickling sensation spread over her skin.

Her pulse beat hard at the base of her throat as she flipped more pages and found more sketches of herself, scattered among images of the forest. Two, four . . . she counted ten in all. Emeline snapped the book closed, trying to breathe. She stared at the brown leather cover for a moment, then reached for another.

More of the same: Trees, feathers, Lament. Rooke and Sable and scenes from the king's court. And Emeline. Lots of Emeline. Emeline, sitting with her back to the artist. Emeline laughing with her head thrown back—like the photo of her mother. Emeline with a ukulele in her lap, eyes closed as her fingers crept across the strings.

What the . . . ?

Why were there so many drawings of her?

The last one sent a sharp shock slicing through her, like a jagged blade plunged into her belly. Her fingertips dug painfully into the edges of the page as she stared in horror at the sketch.

In it, a younger Emeline sprawled naked across a soft surface. Her elbow was bent, cushioning her head, and one pale arm rested on her bare stomach. There was a liquid gleam in her eyes as her head turned towards the artist and her lips parted sensually.

She looked no older than sixteen.

His pencil rendered everything in perfect detail: her hair fanning out around her head, the gentle curves of her small breasts, the dark curling hairs peeking out from between her legs.

Emeline slammed the book closed, breathing too fast. The room blurred around her.

The rest of the sketchbooks lay in a frantic pile on the bed. Emeline pressed her hands to her face, trying to steady her erratic breathing. But all she could see was her younger body, drawn in Hawthorne's hand, over and over and over.

What the fuck?

Emeline rose from the armchair. Her legs trembled beneath her. Her heart hammered too hard as she made her way into the main part of the house, the last sketchbook still gripped in her hand.

The front door was opening as Hawthorne stepped inside. Emeline froze as sunlight spilled into the room. Silhouetted by the morning glow, the boy whose bed she'd slept in stood in the doorframe, his arms full of wood for the fire.

At the sight of her, his dark brow crumpled.

"What's wrong?"

She lifted the sketchbook in her hand, open to the nude drawing of herself. Her hands shook, making the pages shake too. "What the hell is *this*?"

Hawthorne's lips parted at the sight of the sketch. He dropped the wood in his arms and the logs fell, thudding at his feet.

Emeline threw the sketchbook furiously to the floor. "Why am I in all your sketchbooks, Hawthorne? Why are there drawings of me from before you ever knew me?" *Nude drawings!*

Standing in the midst of the scattered wood, he ran his hands raggedly over his face.

"You were going to abandon your dreams," he said, pressing his palms into his eyes. "You were going to stay. Here. For *me*."

His hands fell to his sides.

"I couldn't trap you like that."

What? She took a step back. "What are you talking about?"

He stared at her like the world was falling apart around him— and not for the first time. He swallowed so hard, she heard it.

"The girl I told you about? The one I betrayed?" His voice cracked. "She's you."

The words made her go cold. An electric kind of cold, starting in her belly and moving swiftly outwards, *That's not possible. . . .*

Emeline suddenly remembered Sable singing to her last night. Singing a song there was no possible way she could know. One with a strange memory trapped inside it.

"Two summers ago," said Hawthorne, "you told me you were giving up on your dream. You said you didn't care about being up onstage because I couldn't be there with you. You were going to sacrifice it all and stay. Here, where there was nothing for you. *Less* than nothing for you."

He looked away miserably.

"I went to the king and asked him to . . . to make you forget. If you forgot—me and everything else in the woods—there would be nothing to stay for. Nothing to hold you back anymore."

Emeline's heart dropped. She took another step away from him.

"Are you saying . . ."

"That you and I—" He shook his head, then started again. "That you've known me for a long time. Why else would you be in my sketchbooks? How else could I love Ewan like he's my own family? Why else would Sable be so protective of you?"

Sable. The song. The memory of the two of them, up in the barn beams. They couldn't have been older than fifteen.

"In making you forget me and the woods, I made you forget her too. I made you forget everything. It's a wrong she'll never forgive me for."

No. It's not possible. I would remember . . .

Except she wouldn't. Not if her memories were stolen.

She thought back to when she first arrived in the court. Sable had kept her distance, and Emeline had assumed the girl was simply shy. Then Sable intervened when the king tried to choke her to death, and Emeline hadn't understood why she would put herself at risk. But if they'd been friends . . .

Realizing that her entire body was trembling, she hugged her chest to try and hide it.

"If everything you've said is true, why would Sable go out of her way to avoid me?" she demanded.

Hawthorne glanced away from her. "For the same reason you avoided Ewan, I imagine."

Emeline bit her lip. She *had* avoided Pa—refusing to visit or call him—because it hurt so much to be forgotten. Still . . . "A real friend would have told me the truth."

"And would you have believed her?"

Emeline paused, remembering all of the times she'd told her grandfather the truth, and how it so often twisted his fractured mind into further chaos—like the night she told him Rose had abandoned them.

Upon arriving in the king's court, would Emeline have believed that a shiftling girl she had no recollection of was, in fact, a long-lost friend?

No, she realized. *It would have sounded crazy.*

Emeline thought of Pa's missing memories. Without them, a part of her grandfather was missing too. That's what Hawthorne had done—taken a piece of Emeline, without her even knowing.

As the truth flooded her, the walls of the house seemed to shrink, with Hawthorne standing between her and the only exit. She suddenly felt like the nymph Daphne. Swallowed by the bark of a tree closing around her. Caging her in.

It made her want to get out of this house.

Out of the woods.

Out of his life.

She wanted to put as much distance as she could between herself and Hawthorne Fell.

Emeline strode towards the door, avoiding the spilled logs.

"Wait." Swiping a small crimson book off the harvest table, he held it out to her. "Take it."

Emeline stood frozen between him and the door, unsure.

"Please."

His voice shook with anguish, and it was this that made her reach for the book, tucking it into the back pocket of her jeans.

"Good-bye, Hawthorne," she whispered, unable to look at him. And then she walked out of his house and didn't look back.

In the yard, Claw's warning clanged through her mind: *He betrays you in the end!* If Claw mistook the order in which he saw things, the end he foresaw could have easily been two years ago.

A storm of anger and confusion whistled through her body as she strode towards the creek. At the bridge, she remembered the white ring on her finger.

Think of where you want to be, and it will bring you there.

Emeline slowed to a halt.

Home. Her throat burned with unshed tears. *I want to go home.*

The second she thought it, the bridge and the creek and the trees disappeared. One moment, Hawthorne's house stood behind her; the next, she was stepping out of the woods and into Pa's rose garden.

The ring had brought her to Edgewood.

THIRTY-SEVEN

HE MOMENT EMELINE STEPPED inside the house, she found Pa, who stood at the kitchen window. Throwing her arms around his shoulders, she hugged him tight, breathing in his soapy smell and willing his familiar presence to soothe her.

She was safe. The woods and everything in them couldn't touch her here.

Her arms tightened around her grandfather.

"Now, now," Pa murmured, rubbing circles into her back. "Everything's all right."

Maisie looked up from rolling strudel dough across the kitchen table. Her frizzy gray curls were tied back, and white flour speckled her red apron. "Baby girl." Those clear hazel eyes scanned down Emeline. The last time they'd seen each other, Emeline had slain a shadow skin in this very kitchen, then disappeared into the woods. "Are you okay?"

Was she okay? She'd just learned that the boy she loved had stolen something precious from her. Pieces of her past. Pieces of *herself*.

Emeline swallowed, then forced a smile. "I'm fine."

Wrinkles lined Maisie's tan face, like rings on a tree. She studied Emeline as if unconvinced, but didn't press her. "Joel left yesterday."

Emeline winced. *Joel.* She'd fled without telling him where she was going.

Not wanting to date Joel didn't give her license to be a jerk. She would have to make her rudeness up to him somehow.

"He told me to tell you he'll see you in Montreal. Something about your tour?"

Oh no. "What day is it?"

Maisie wiped her hands on her white frilly apron and moved towards the calendar on the wall in the kitchen. "October sixth."

The day before her opening night.

Emeline's blood spiked. "I have to go."

Maisie reached for her hand, lacing her fingers through Emeline's. The smell of flour and cooked sugar wafted off her skin.

"When will you be back?"

She and Maisie had discussed Pa's care while making dinner the other night. While Emeline was on tour Maisie would come twice a day to check in on Pa, and when Emeline was done traveling she'd figure out the best way to keep him in his house.

"Three weeks," said Emeline. "As soon as my tour is over."

In her bedroom, she packed up the few things she'd brought with her, then grabbed her phone from where she'd left it charging on the bedside table. If she could make it to Montreal tonight, she'd have all of tomorrow to go over her set.

But in order to drive the seven hours back to the city, adding an extra hour or two sitting in traffic, she needed to leave now.

Never in her life had she longed for *normal* more. Emeline wanted her apartment full of roommates she barely spoke to. She wanted the lights and the noise and the crowds of the city. She wanted to be up onstage, stringing together chords and turning them into songs, fueled by the audience behind the lights. Their claps and stomps proving that she was, in fact, right where she was supposed to be.

That was her life.

She needed to get back to it.

Forget the woods and the curse and the Wood King. Forget the Vile, who hated the sight of her and wanted her dead. And most of all, forget Hawthorne—who'd betrayed her.

The thought made her want to cry.

After hugging both Maisie and Pa, Emeline slung her bag over her shoulder, grabbed her keys, and got into her car.

She was pulling out of the driveway when Tom wandered up the dirt path from Eshe and Abel's farm, a bushel of yellow apples hoisted in his arms. Seconds, it looked like, from their bruised surfaces. Likely for Maisie's apple strudel. At the sight of Emeline, Tom's brown eyes crinkled, and he lifted his chin in greeting.

Her chest twinged.

I have to tell him about Rose.

It would break his heart.

The thought of it, how it would change things between them, opened a hole in her chest.

It can wait, she decided, not wanting to ruin things yet. *Until I finish touring.*

She didn't stop the car. Only waved to Tom, watching him disappear in the rearview mirror as she turned onto the main road, heading towards the highway.

JUST BEFORE CROSSING THE Quebec border, Emeline stopped to fill up on gas. As she stood at the pump, with the nozzle in, something fell out of her back pocket and onto the pavement behind her.

Thinking it was her phone, she turned to pick it up.

It wasn't her phone; it was the slender book Hawthorne had given her before she left.

Twenty Love Poems and a Song of Despair.

Emeline eyed it warily, then picked it up, still pumping. She'd first noticed this book at his house on the night he made her dinner. Curious despite herself, Emeline thumbed through the pages.

It didn't take long to realize these were exactly what the title described: love poems. Love full of hunger, and sadness, and fire. The words made her temperature rise and her teeth clench.

Emeline slammed the book closed.

She couldn't keep this. A book of love poems from the boy who stole her memories? It was too much.

I'll throw it away, she thought, eyeing the trash can next to the pump.

"Excellent choice," said a deep voice from nearby.

Emeline turned to see a bearded man wearing a black turban pumping gas into his car behind her. He nodded to the book in her hand. "My wife loves Neruda. It's how I wooed her."

Emeline glanced up into gentle brown eyes, which were crinkling in a smile. He had a sweet, grandfatherly demeanor, this man.

"Is she here with you?" Emeline asked, trying to steer the subject away from Hawthorne's book. She glanced to the passenger side of his car, but the seat was empty.

His face fell. "Ah, no."

"I'm sorry," she said quickly, realizing her mistake. By the white of his beard and the deep wrinkles of his forehead, he was probably close to Pa's age.

He tsked gently. "Don't apologize. I love remembering her."

So that's how Emeline passed the next few minutes pumping

gas: listening to him tell her about the love of his life, whom he'd lost five years ago to cancer.

As they went to pay, he opened the glass door for her. "Thank you," he said. "For listening."

She hugged him.

As she walked back to her car a few minutes later, her phone buzzed with a text from her manager.

Want to meet your tour mates tonight?

Her heart skipped. She texted back: *Meet The Perennials? Tonight?*

The thought made her break out in a sweat.

They're grabbing drinks at the Rev. I'll tell them to reserve a seat for you.

A thousand butterflies fluttered through her. In the terror and madness of the past week, there had been no time to be excited for her tour or think about what it would be like to meet the band she'd idolized for years.

If she met The Perennials tonight, they wouldn't be strangers in the green room tomorrow. She wondered what they'd be like. After three weeks on the road together, would they all be friends?

I need friends.

A wisp of memory flickered through her: Hot summer day. Dust sticking to her skin. Legs swinging from the barn beams. And a girl, stretched out beside her, listening to her sing.

Sable.

The memory brought a rush of confusion. She tried to think backwards. Tried to gather other, older memories of Sable from before she ever left Edgewood.

But all that came was a fog. A gap. A *nothing*.

It scared her. She pushed the feeling quickly down, then pocketed her phone. Just before she got into her car, the sight of that same trash can made her pause.

Emeline looked from the trash can to *Twenty Love Poems and a Song of Despair* still gripped in her hand. She could throw it out right now.

But as she moved to do it, all she could think about was the man at the pump and his poetry-loving wife. He spoke of her like she was a radiant sun. One that had set but, like the dusk, still lingered on the horizon where he kept his gaze fixed.

Emeline couldn't help feeling that to throw Neruda's poems in the garbage was to defile the woman's memory, somehow. So she opened her car door, shoved the book in her bag, then pulled out onto the highway and kept driving.

LA RÊVERIE WAS LOUD and warm and crowded as Emeline's leg bounced nervously beneath the table. The members of The Perennials bent their heads close together, making quiet conversation. They were a few years older than her, and since walking in and saying hi, not one band member had attempted to include her in their conversation—despite her several attempts to join.

They had all just flown in from different parts of the country, she told herself. They were obviously a tight-knit group and needed to catch up. Emeline couldn't begrudge them that.

Still. She felt like a third wheel.

Joel wasn't helping. He'd given her the cold shoulder since she arrived—not that she could blame him, seeing as she left him high and dry yesterday. He was currently outside taking a call.

Emeline fidgeted with the ring on her finger, spinning it around and around before remembering who gave it to her.

Hawthorne.

Her hand tightened around her drink, then fell loose. She

wasn't going to think about the king's tithe collector, or anything else in the woods. Hawthorne was a thief. The woods were cursed. And everything in them wanted her dead.

This was where she belonged.

Tomorrow night, she would get up onstage and open for her dream band. It was the culmination of all her hard work. And if she was on her game, Daybreak would sign her. They'd produce her next album. She would have everything she ever wanted before she even turned twenty.

Her biggest, oldest dream was coming true.

"You ready for tomorrow?"

Emeline glanced up to find Edwin McCormick, drummer for The Perennials, watching her. Colorful sleeve tattoos decorated his pale arms and his dark hair was slick, as if he hadn't washed it yet this week.

She smiled. "Of course. I can't wait!" She immediately winced at the sound of her voice—it was too bright and fake. To hide her embarrassment, Emeline took a sip of her root beer. The carbonation fizzed on her tongue.

"Ever played a fourteen-city tour before?"

Edwin's arm was slung casually around the neck of the young woman beside him: Ashley Granger, lead singer. Her bleached-blond bangs were cut straight and short across her forehead, and the rest of her hair was pulled up in a bun, showing off a steep undercut.

"This is my first," said Emeline, her stomach pinching.

"I'm sure you'll do great," said Ashley, studying Emeline from beneath Edwin's arm.

A sudden, cheerful voice interrupted them.

"Emeline Lark!"

The entire table turned to find a curvy blonde with a heart-shaped face and a lipstick-bright smile standing over them. Her dark blue jeans were ripped at the knees and tucked into a pair of cowboy boots.

Chloe Demarche.

Emeline relaxed at the sight of her songwriter, her stomach unpinching.

"I haven't heard from you in *weeks*!! Where have you *been*?"

Emeline's thoughts raced, searching for an answer that didn't sound completely bonkers. "I was . . . taking care of my grandfather."

It was somewhat true.

The light caught in Chloe's bobbing golden curls as she dropped into Joel's empty seat, looking genuinely distressed. "Is he okay?"

"Hey, Chlo?" said Ashley, leaning across the table, her index finger pointing to the chair. "That seat is taken."

"Oh!" Chloe darted to her feet. "Sorry. My friends are over there, anyway." She waved casually across the room, where a group of people were rounding up chairs and taking over an empty table. Chloe turned her attention back to Emeline. "Did you get a chance to listen to those new songs I uploaded to Elegy?"

Emeline had hundreds of unchecked notifications on her phone, all of which she'd accumulated while in the King's City. She shook her head. "Not all of them. But I will tonight. I promise."

"No rush. When you do, let me know what you think." Chloe's cheeks dimpled. "Have fun on your tour!" She lifted her hand in a wave, returning to her friends.

When she was out of hearing distance, Ashley leaned in and said, "Did you hear she's recording an album?"

"What?" said Heidi, their bass player.

"With who?" asked Edwin.

"Daybreak." Ashley snorted, derisively. "Apparently, she signed with them last week."

Emeline shifted uneasily. She scanned the pub, looking for Joel.

Heidi smirked. "Well, that's fitting."

Ashley nodded, glancing across the room and wrinkling her nose. "God, she's so plastic. Just like her songs."

The words turned Emeline's stomach. Chloe's songs were *her* songs too. She sank deeper into her chair.

Across the room, Chloe and her friends chatted happily. *I wish I was over there,* Emeline realized, watching The Perennials lean in towards each other, gossip dripping like jewels from their mouths.

This was one of the things she'd learned to adjust to when she first broke into the scene.

Emeline remembered her first music festival and its afterparty. How excited she'd been as she stepped into the bar after a hot day of stage hopping, hoping to befriend some like-minded newbie.

She'd ended up at a booth, sandwiched between four established musicians, with several more across the table. She'd asked how their sets went, how far they'd traveled, where they were staying. But the conversation quickly dissolved into petty gossip. How much so-and-so had signed their most recent deal for. Whose upcoming album was expected to flop. Who deserved to be on the Polaris short list—and who didn't.

Here, gossip was currency. The more you had, the more power you accrued.

That day, Emeline was a little baby deer thinking she was wandering into a meadow, excited to befriend all the other woodland creatures, when instead she was wandering into oncoming traffic.

Her whole body had hummed with the need to escape that day. But in order to get out of that booth, she would have had to crawl under the table and make a run for it.

She had the same instinct now.

Except this was *The Perennials.* The band she was spending the next three weeks on tour with. And here they were, the night before their tour started, calling Emeline's songwriter a sellout.

What do they think of me?

With that upsetting thought, Emeline rose from her chair and made for the washroom. As the door shut behind her, the loud chatter of the Rev's patrons hushed, leaving her in near silence amid the faint smell of cigarette smoke. The fluorescent lights flickered overhead. Band stickers littered the walls and stall doors.

The familiarity of it made her chest loosen.

She let out a breath.

Okay, she thought, standing at the sinks. *Your tour mates are pretentious dicks. So what? You've dealt with dozens of others just like them.*

Was this why people weren't supposed to meet their heroes?

She ran a faucet, splashing cold water on her face. Someone had put out their cigarette in the ceramic bowl, and the butt lay soggy on the bottom.

Planting her palms at the edge of the sink, Emeline stared at her reflection.

It's only three weeks. You'll survive.

And at the end of those three weeks, she would—she hoped—have a whole lot of EP sales, a whole lot more exposure, and a contract with Daybreak, who would want her to start recording an album ASAP.

Remember why you love this, she told herself.

It was the music she loved. The way the world went quiet and still the moment she started strumming. How she forgot everything she was running from when there was a song in her throat.

I knew a girl once, Hawthorne's voice flickered through her.

Singing was like breathing for her. When she sang, she went some-where no one could touch her.

Emeline's throat tightened. She clutched the sink harder, wanting to purge his rough-soft voice and his leather-pine smell and his river-rock eyes from her memory.

Once she got up onstage tomorrow, it would be a whirlwind of catching flights and checking into hotels and recovering from jet lag—not to mention performing—for weeks. She would have no time to think about Hawthorne Fell, or anything else. Not the cursed forest or its cruel king. Not the monstrous mother who wanted her dead. And especially not the dark power lurking in her depths.

Good riddance, she thought. *To all of it.*

Pushing away from the sinks, she headed out of the washroom.

As she was on her way back to the table, The Perennials clustered even closer together. Joel was still absent, as was Edwin. When she drew nearer, she heard Ashley say, "I give her a year before she drops off the map."

Emeline gritted her teeth. *Still?* What was it about Chloe that irked them so much?

"I dunno, Ash. I mean, she's touring with *us.*"

Emeline slowed.

"Are you kidding me?" Ashley raised a thin, skeptical brow. "The only reason she's touring with us is because she's screwing Joel. And Joel is best buds with Edwin."

Emeline halted, her mouth going dry as cotton. The words were ugly and cruel.

They were also about *her.*

"Joel called in a favor. You know how obsessed he is with her. Emeline Lark has no talent, and everyone knows it. She uses a writer, for Christ's sake."

Emeline stood frozen, several steps away. She told herself to keep walking. To head for the bar and order another root beer, then come back and pretend she hadn't heard.

But Ashley's words had burrowed deep, immobilizing her.

Emeline felt like the one wrong note in the middle of all the right ones. Discordant. Unaligned. As if she was in the wrong song entirely.

No, she told herself sternly. *You belong here.*

She needed to stay strong and get through this.

You've survived worse.

Suddenly, someone bumped her shoulder. A rush of something wet and cold swept up her shirt, stunning her.

"Oh no!" Clutching her now mostly empty glass, Chloe stared at the beer drenching Emeline. "Em, I'm so sorry."

The conversation at the table abruptly halted as the members of The Perennials turned towards them.

Fighting down the lump in her throat, Emeline smiled at Chloe. "Don't worry about it. It's fine." And because they were listening, she touched Chloe's elbow and added, "Congrats on signing with Daybreak, by the way. I'm really proud of you."

Emeline excused herself and walked outside, gulping in the cool evening air, waving her shirt in an effort to dry it. The parking lot was silent except for some smokers huddled on the curb and Joel leaning against the trunk of his car, still on a call. Pressing her back to the brick wall, she slid down to the sidewalk and dialed a number on her phone.

"Hello?"

Emeline closed her eyes at the sound of his voice.

"Hi," she breathed.

"Who is this?"

"Emeline. Your granddaughter. I just . . . I needed to hear your voice."

THIRTY-EIGHT

HE NEXT NIGHT, EMELINE sat on the floor of the Nymph's green room. She pressed her head to the cold plaster wall as fans lined up outside, waiting to get into the venue. Her bare legs were crossed at the ankles, her noise-canceling headphones covered her ears, and her fingers craved the strings of her guitar—which was waiting for her out onstage, along with her ukulele.

She sat alone in this room, which smelled of old coffee and beer. Her foot bobbed nervously as the fluorescent lights *flick-flick-flickered* overhead, humming loudly. The Perennials hadn't arrived yet, but they were notorious for getting onstage late.

Emeline closed her eyes and breathed it all in: her name on the Nymph's marquee, a fourteen-city tour, and (hopefully) a new record deal with a major recording studio. After everything—after grinding out cover songs in dingy bars until 2:00 am, after being perpetually on the road unsure if she could afford her next tank of gas, after busking in the street to make ends meet—here she was. Making it.

And if The Perennials weren't the people she thought they were, so what? It didn't matter. *This* mattered. She was about to go out onstage at the Nymph—a stage where so many of her favorite bands had played before her—and sing before a sold-out show of three hundred people.

She reached into her bag, looking for her phone, wanting to
know how much longer she had before needing to be out there.
Her fingers brushed something stiff and papery: the slender
spine of a book. She pulled it out.

Twenty Love Poems and a Song of Despair.

The cover was red as blood against her black dress.

Emeline was about to shove it right back in when a folded
piece of paper fell out from between its pages.

She stared at the folded note, her heart thundering in her
chest. Summoning her courage, she picked it up, unfolded the
paper, and found a message scrawled in pencil down the lined
page, difficult to read in parts from where the graphite was
smudged and faded.

Emeline,

*If you're reading this, it's because I've finally worked up the
courage to tell you the truth, or you've figured it out for
yourself. I dearly hope it's the former.*

*I've tried writing this letter a hundred times, and
each time, the words are inadequate. What I've done is
unforgivable and any apology insufficient, but please know
that I never meant to cause you pain, only to save you from
it. I realize there's no way to undo what I've done, and no
going back to who we once were, but if there were some way
to atone, some price I could pay to begin to heal the harm
I've caused, trust me: I would pay it.*

*There's a poem in this book that I never understood until
you left. Now I understand it all too well.*

Hawthorne

Emeline's heart flickered in time with the lights.

She glanced to the book of poetry, where the note had been

hidden. One of the pages was dog-eared to mark its importance. Reaching for it, she opened to the page and found a poem staring up at her.

Tonight I can write the saddest lines, it began.

She kept reading.

To think that I do not have her. To feel that I have lost her.

Emeline's pulse thudded hard in her throat.

To hear the immense night, still more immense without her.

She continued on, drinking in the sorrowful words, until one little line made the world go still:

Love is so short, forgetting is so long.

They hit her with a dizzying force, those words. The book slipped from her fingers and fell to her lap.

"'Forgetting Is So Long.'"

It was the name of the locked folder on her Elegy app. The one that contained her old songs.

What if the password is part of the poem?

Emeline grabbed her bag and dug deep. Down at the bottom, her fingers closed around her phone. She drew it out and quickly opened Elegy. A notification popped up.

You haven't accessed FORGETTING IS SO LONG in 553 days. Do you want to delete?

She hit NO. Then tapped the folder.

This folder is password protected, a new notification read. *Enter the password now.*

With only thirty minutes before she needed to be out onstage, Emeline picked up the book, opened to the dog-eared page, and read the poem again.

She tried typing in the title first: *Tonight I Can Write (The Saddest Lines)*

The notification turned red and her phone buzzed.

That password is incorrect.

She tried again—this time with no caps. Then all caps.
More buzzing. More red.

Emeline bared her teeth at the screen. She glanced at the
time. Twenty-five minutes before she needed to go out onstage.

She scanned down the poem until her gaze snagged on that
one little line: *Love is so short, forgetting is so long.*

Hunching over her phone, with the screen inches from her
face, Emeline typed:

love is so short

The folder opened. A list of her old songs popped up—dozens
and dozens of them. Emeline sat frozen, staring at them all. In
almost two years of trying to guess passwords, she'd failed to
open this folder. She hadn't been able to listen to these songs.

With shaking hands, Emeline connected her headphones
and tapped PLAY.

The songs transported her backwards in time, to when she
first wrote them. As each one melted into the next, as her voice
sang lyrics and melodies from her past, memories burst like colors across a blank canvas.

Because inside each and every one of these songs—songs
she'd written before she ever left Edgewood—memories were
hidden.

Emeline choked on them. Hot tears burned in her eyes as
she tapped the next file, and the next, racing through songs and,
with them, memories that had been stolen from her. Images
of a younger Sable flashed before her eyes, interwoven with a
younger Rooke. And someone else.

Hawthorne.

He was everywhere, with his dark hair and strange eyes. Her
songs were so full of him, Emeline felt like she was drowning in
him. Hawthorne, sitting next to the fire, reading a book. Hawthorne, shucking off his shirt and diving into a moonlit pond.

Hawthorne, climbing in through her bedroom window. Kissing her in the dark.

She'd embedded him inside her music.

Because songs were never just songs for Emeline. They were capsules, each one containing a moment trapped inside it.

As the next one started to play through her headphones, an image of a tree rose up in her mind. Emeline could see its thirsty roots; the twisting, twirling gray-brown bark; the gnarly branches stretching towards the sky. A silent sentinel, standing guard at the edge of the woods.

Her tree.

As it rose there in her mind, something snapped.

The Forgetting broke.

All her lost memories came flooding back.

THIRTY-NINE

EMELINE WAS THIRTEEN WHEN *her tree went missing.*
It was a crisp April morning, and everything was frosted with dew. She woke to find Pa on the balcony, staring at the woods, his face marred by a frown.

"They took it," he murmured. She couldn't tell if it was anger that tinged his voice, or fear.

When she looked where he looked—to the space in the hedge— she realized he was talking about her tree.

Which was gone.

They. The things in the woods, he meant. It wasn't a tithing month, though. So why would the Wood King take it?

When Pa left the house for the vineyards, Emeline didn't walk to the bus stop. Instead, despite the warnings of her neighbors, despite their stories clanging through her mind, she went into the woods, looking. As if, maybe, she could find the Wood King and convince him to return her special tree.

But the deeper she went, the woods shifted and changed around her, until they were no longer the woods bordering Edgewood, but something else. The trees were too big and grand, the birdcalls too strange. And the cloying scent of magic was everywhere.

What if she never found her way out?

She didn't find her tree. But something found her. Emeline was lost by the time it seized her, clamping its hand hard over her mouth to stop her scream.

"Be still," her captor whispered. "Unless you'd prefer to be eaten."

Emeline couldn't see her captor's face, only felt him nod towards the river, where a long night-dark shadow was creeping along the dewy bank between the budding trees. It had no eyes and long, sharp talons.

She decided to take her chances with the stranger at her back.

Slowly, his hand fell away from her mouth. Just as slowly, his fingers twined through hers, tugging her quickly through the woods, silent as a tree, until they stepped through the hedge back in Edgewood.

"What's your name?" she asked, turning to memorize his features: maple-dark hair, earth-brown skin, river-rock eyes. He looked roughly the same age as she was.

"Promise to stay out of the woods," he said, memorizing her back, "and I'll tell you."

But now that Emeline knew there weren't just horrors in those trees, she wasn't so sure she could promise that.

"There are things in this forest that will hurt you," he said.

"You're in the forest," she pointed out. "And you didn't hurt me."

"No," he agreed. "But other things will."

Emeline canted her head. "If I stay away, how will I find you again?"

A smile tipped his mouth to the side as he ducked his chin, lowering his gaze. "I'll find you."

"Then I promise," she said. "Now tell me your name."

He paused for a moment, as if he was thinking hard about it. Very softly, he said, "I'm Hawthorne."

HAWTHORNE CAME BACK OFTEN. Soon, his friends tagged along: a shy, sharp-edged girl named Sable and a mischievous boy named Rooke. They were shiftlings from the King's City, deep in the woods. They told her stories of fiery, stampeding ember mares. Of a curmudgeonly dragon forged from stone. More quietly, they spoke about shadow skins and the Vile and the Stain. About a curse that was eating the woods.

Their stories infected her. She wanted to see this world for herself.

But every time she asked, they glanced down and shook their heads.

"Humans aren't allowed anymore. It's too dangerous."

Soon, Sable started visiting on her own. Emeline introduced the girl to all her favorite albums. They'd spend weekends listening to music in her bedroom, gorging themselves on Maisie's apple strudel. Sable especially liked to watch Tom in his forge, working with copper and silver and iron. Sometimes Tom taught Sable how to make things from metal, while Emeline wrote songs on the lawn.

One day, when they were fifteen, Emeline invited Sable to watch her sing at a café not far from Edgewood. The owners needed someone to play live music, and Pa's friend Corny—who was their favorite regular—couldn't stop raving about Emmie Lark and her magic voice. So they asked Emeline to come and play.

Tonight was a trial run: if they and their customers liked her music, she could come every Thursday night. They'd even let her put out a tip jar.

Emeline was terrified.

What if she fumbled her chords or forgot her lyrics? What if no one listened or clapped? What if they hated her songs?

"I can't come," said Sable, looking forlorn. "I'm sorry."

"Shiftlings can't go past the borderlands," Rooke explained.

So Emeline went alone.

She arrived at the café early to set up. The owners gave her free peppermint tea and ginger cookies. Emeline checked and double-checked her mic, then her amp. She tuned and retuned her ukulele. She was so nervous, she felt like throwing up.

All of a sudden, it was seven o'clock.

Time to sing.

"Hi," she said a little too quietly, into the mic, staring out at the tables full of people sipping coffees and digging forks into their desserts. Clearing her throat, she tried again. "Um. I'm Emeline Lark and . . . um . . . I'll be playing some songs tonight."

Obviously. That's why she was sitting on a stool with a ukulele! Her cheeks burned with embarrassment.

A few people paused their conversations to look up at her. Others kept talking. At the very back, Emeline saw Grace Abel sitting alone near the window. Her head was bent over a notebook and her hand moved furiously across the page. Studying, probably. Emeline and Grace weren't in any of the same classes at school, because Grace was in the most advanced ones.

"This song is about my best friend." She'd written it for Sable a few months ago. "I, um . . ." Oh my god! Stop saying "um"! "I hope you like it."

More people looked away, resuming their conversations.

Maybe I can't do this, she thought. Maybe I should say I'm sick and go home. Save myself the humiliation, and spare these poor people.

But there was someone at the back still watching her. Someone who hadn't looked away since she first started talking. A boy with dark hair. He leaned back, one elbow looped around his chair, finger marking his spot in a book, not taking his eyes off her.

Hawthorne Fell.

Emeline hadn't even told him about tonight. Had Sable?

It didn't matter. She had someone to play for.

Emeline started to strum, then sing. She stared at Hawthorne—

the one person in the room who gave her his full attention—focusing only on the warm pleasure in his eyes as he listened.

She immediately hit her stride. Her voice didn't falter. Her fingers didn't tremble. She flew through the songs breezily, as if she were back on the farm with Sable stretched out in the grass beside her.

One after another, heads turned towards her. Conversations grew quiet. People started tapping their toes and bobbing their heads. Even Grace stopped studying to listen.

Emeline kept her eyes on Hawthorne, fearing that if she unhooked her gaze from the one steady thing in this room she might lose her way.

Halfway through her set, after she'd switched out her ukulele for her guitar, another arrival was marked by an earthy, mulchy scent blooming through the air. With it came the faint but steady beat—like that of an ancient heart—thudding beneath the soles of her feet. Keeping time with her songs.

The woods came gently. Respectfully. Like an old friend showing its admiration and support. Their looming presence kept to the edges of the room, listening to her play, and by the time Emeline finished her last song and set her guitar down on its stand she noticed three tiny ferns growing up through the floor, unfurling around her feet.

It was the first time the woods ever came to hear her play.

By the time Emeline finished packing up her gear, the owners had asked her to come back next week. They even gave her cookies for the road.

When she stepped outside, she found Hawthorne leaning against the hood of Pa's truck, waiting for her. Pa, who'd come to pick her up, was inside chatting with some neighbors.

"Hi," said Hawthorne, his dark hair falling into his eyes. He wore pale jeans and a charcoal-gray shirt.

"Hi," she said back, feeling shy now that she'd spent her entire set staring at him from across the café. After hoisting her instru-

ments into the back seat, she said, "Thanks for coming. You didn't have to do that."

The corner of his mouth quirked up. "I wanted to."

A fluttering warmth rushed through her. Like startled butterflies.

It had been like this for a while with Hawthorne. Strange and awkward; stilted conversations full of long pauses; lots of avoiding of eyes.

She shut the door, blushing hard. "Do you want a ride back?" Pa wouldn't mind.

He hesitated, then pointed to a bicycle locked to a nearby tree. "I have one."

"Right." Was that too forward? Offering a ride? *"I'll see you around, then. I guess."*

She opened the passenger side door. Hawthorne pushed off from the hood. But instead of stepping away, he stepped closer, his hand curling around the top of the door as she climbed in.

"You were incredible up there."

She looked up. But Hawthorne had already turned away and was walking towards his bicycle.

"Thanks," she whispered, her heart beating fast.

WHEN SHE WAS SIXTEEN, *Tom bought Emeline tickets to see one of her favorite bands, Death Valley's Little Sister, play in Toronto. But he sprained his ankle a day before the show.*

She had an extra ticket, and since Sable couldn't come, she invited Hawthorne.

As the thick crowd surged towards them, drawn to the stage where Death Valley played, Hawthorne bumped into Emeline. His chest pressed up against her back, sending a jolt down her spine.

She looked over her shoulder to find him scowling at the drunk kids flailing all over the place. Positioning himself between them and Emeline, he leaned in. "Are you all right?"

He'd never been to a concert before. But Emeline was used to shows where the crowd pushed in too close and the only thing to do was hold your ground. Or push back.

She nodded. "I'm good."

A few songs later, the tension in him eased. He stood so close now, Emeline could smell the forest on his skin. It overrode the smell of spilled beer and sweating bodies. She liked the heat of him behind her, warm as sunlight. She liked the way his heart pounded against her spine, louder than the drums.

She was suddenly so aware of him, she stopped focusing on the music. She glanced at several couples around them, noticing how close they stood. What would it feel like to have Hawthorne's arms wrapped around her like that? To be pulled snug against his body? To feel his chin rest on top of her head?

She never found out. Soon, the concert was over, and they were on the train heading home.

Emeline wanted that moment back, so she invited him to the next concert.

And the next.

Each time, he stood a little bit closer.

One night, they were walking back to Union Station from a small, cramped venue called Certain Dark Things. Drunk on the lights and sounds and electric hum of the city, Emeline declared: "I want to do that one day."

Hawthorne looked away from the lit-up buildings around them, his face awash in colors. "Hmm?" he said, as if he'd been deep in thought.

"Make music my life." Traffic honked from the street as they waited for a stoplight to change. She lowered her voice to a whisper, as if admitting some dirty secret. "I can't sleep sometimes, I'm so full of longing. To sing my songs up on a stage. To see my name on a marquee."

Hawthorne watched her closely.

"You will."

He said it like it was a fact. As if it were destined.

The light changed. Stunned by his belief in her, Emeline started walking, then realized he wasn't beside her. She turned back to find him still on the sidewalk, transfixed by the sight of a storefront.

A bookstore, she realized, coming back to his side. A used one.

The Open sign was turned face out.

Books were one of Hawthorne's two great loves, she'd learned from their train ride conversations to and from the city. The other was art.

He pressed his forehead to the glass as he squinted, reading the spines of the antiquated books in the window.

Emeline opened the door for him.

"But we'll miss our train," he said, glancing at her.

"There's another one leaving in an hour."

He smiled like a kid who'd been given permission to pick out a treat. As he stepped through the door, his hand brushed hers as he passed. She followed him in.

They split up immediately, Emeline wandering over to the music section, Hawthorne weaving towards the fiction section. Half an hour later, she found him in Poetry.

"Listen," he said, reaching for her wrist distractedly, eyes on the page of the book as he pulled her closer. Holding the Dark, the title read. By a poet named Melanie Cameron. Emeline leaned back against the shelves, watching him.

"'I didn't know it would go like this,'" he recited. "'I didn't know I would find you in the dark . . .'"

Emeline stared at his mouth, captivated by the cadence of his voice. His expression was hungry as he read on, as if he'd discovered some delicious secret and wanted to feed it to her. Like a ripe red strawberry dipped in chocolate.

"When I lie against you with my eyes closed,
I bring your body with me,
into the darkness,
I bring your whole body inside me.
And in that darkness I know you
so much better than hands and mouth can know,
I know you,
as though you were the darkness inside me."

He glanced up from the page, fixing her in place with that same hungry gaze. Warmth pooled in her belly.

"It's nice," she murmured.

He raised an eyebrow. "Nice?" The corner of his mouth turned up as he lifted his hand, bracing it against the shelf beside her.

She wrinkled her nose at him. "Pretty, then."

"How about tender. And . . ." His eyes dropped to her mouth. "Intimate."

There was the oddest feeling in Emeline's chest. Like a million tiny stars on the cusp of bursting. Sparks crackled in the air between them. Hawthorne seemed about to lean in, to close the gap, when the bookseller called from farther down the aisle, saying the shop was closing in five minutes.

Hawthorne straightened and stepped back.

The sparks fizzled out.

ONE LATE-OCTOBER DAY, EMELINE found Sable and Rooke teasing Hawthorne on the grass beside Eshe and Abel's pond. Hawthorne's sketchbook lay open between them, and Rooke was shaking with laughter as he flopped onto his back.

Hawthorne rolled his eyes. "It's not like that."

"Oh?" Rooke sat up, wiping the tears from his cheeks. "What's it like then?"

Emeline, who'd left to fetch a jug of homemade sun tea and Maisie's cinnamon buns, had clearly missed something good.

"Drawing a human model is no different than drawing a bowl of fruit. There's no . . . It's not like that," he repeated.

"Right," said Rooke, elbowing Sable in the ribs as he winked at Emeline. "Uh-huh."

Sable leaned in towards Hawthorne, a smile quirking her mouth. "You're saying there's absolutely no difference between an apple and a naked woman?"

A naked woman?

At the edge of the pond's bank, brown cattails rustled and bobbed in the breeze. It was mid-autumn, and likely one of the last warm days. Emeline set the basket of food down on the blue quilt, then wandered over to where Hawthorne's sketchbook lay open between Sable and Rooke.

On the page was a youngish woman, extremely pretty, and entirely nude. She was straddling a chair that was faced the wrong way. Her arms were crossed over the chair back and her legs were bent on either side, with her bare feet pressed flat to the floor. Her bold chin tilted upwards as she half closed her eyes, looking down on the viewer.

Emeline thought of Hawthorne's gaze tracing every inch of this woman's body. His pencil marking her every curve and hollow.

Jealousy bit her, sinking its teeth in.

She flipped the pages. There were more sketches of this same person in other poses. Sketches of other models too—men and women, young and old, round and thin.

But her thoughts kept going back to the first.

"I've been taking life drawing classes," Hawthorne explained, not quite looking at Emeline as he pulled the sketchbook away and shut it tight, holding it to his chest. "I saw a poster a few months ago, when we were in the city for a concert."

Rooke was trembling, trying to hold in his laughter.

Hawthorne shot him a piercing look. "You're being awfully immature. Do you have any idea how difficult it is to draw the human form?"

For some reason, this only made Rooke laugh harder. Sable, too, burst into giggles.

Hawthorne threw up his hands. "It's just practice! It's how you get better!"

Giving up on his two friends, he turned to Emeline.

"Anyways. The class is over for the season. It won't start up again until January."

"Oh, whatever will he do?" Rooke crowed.

Hawthorne shook his head.

Suddenly smelling the cinnamon buns, fresh from the oven, Sable and Rooke stood up, still howling as they wandered over to the basket on the quilt.

Emeline couldn't stop seeing the woman on the page, staring her down, a challenge in her heavy-lidded eyes. When Rooke and Sable were out of hearing distance, Emeline heard herself say, "I could pose for you."

Hawthorne turned his head sharply towards her.

Oh god.

Why did she say that?

"I m-mean, unless that's weird," she stammered, feeling her face

flame. "I just . . . um . . . if your class is over and you still wanted to . . . practice."

The wind whipped her hair. She tucked the loose strands behind her ears, wishing she could make herself disappear.

Hawthorne turned fully towards her, his gaze tracing her face. "It's not weird."

She glanced up, staring into those mismatched eyes. "Are you sure?"

As Rooke and Sable stuffed their faces over on the quilt, Hawthorne studied her. "Very sure," he said, voice quiet.

The butterflies were back, fluttering through her. She chewed her lip and glanced to her grandfather's farmhouse in the distance. "We can't do it here. If Pa were to find us . . ."

The thought of Pa accidently walking in on them made her stomach twist. It would be . . . very bad. Pa would lock her up and not let her out of the house until she turned thirty. He would definitely murder Hawthorne. Or at least chase him across the farm with a very big shovel.

Hawthorne nodded, seeing her point. "You can come to my house."

She frowned up at him, planting her hands in the cool green grass. "In the King's City? I thought it isn't allowed." She knew the king no longer permitted those from beyond the woods into his city, on account of a curse.

"It isn't allowed. We'll need to be careful. I'll have to sneak you in."

A tiny thrill whooshed down her spine.

"Are you available tomorrow night?"

Emeline's stomach flip-flopped.

I'll make myself available, she thought, remembering the woman in his sketchbook, yearning to be drawn like that by Hawthorne. His pencil marking out the curves and hollows of her body. His eyes looking at her—all of her—for as long as he liked.

"*Hungry?*" *said Rooke, holding out what appeared to be the last two cinnamon buns to Emeline and Hawthorne.*

She was *hungry.*

But not for cinnamon buns.

To Hawthorne, she whispered, "I'll meet you tomorrow night at the tree line."

The next night, Hawthorne gave her a hooded cloak to wear over her clothes, then smuggled her into the city through a magical entry point. One moment, they were standing in a copse of trees; the next, they were stepping into an alley, surrounded by cracked white walls creeping with green moss.

He'd kept his hand pressed to the small of her back as they walked quickly through the lamplit streets. Emeline snuck glances at the dark city around them, her pulse racing with fear and excitement as she took in the white row houses, the rust-red rooftops, the cobbles beneath her feet. Hawthorne kept close to her whenever someone passed, pulling her hood farther over her face.

And, suddenly, here they were.

Inside his house.

A fire roared in the hearth and before it lay a plush white carpet. Hawthorne stood to the side, setting up his easel, while Emeline hovered around the long table near the windows, humming with nervous energy.

She took off her yellow cardigan first, folding it slowly and placing it on the table. After she took a deep breath, her fingers touched, then fell away from the buttons down the front of her sky-blue sundress.

Is this a mistake? *she wondered.* What if it ruined things between them? What if they couldn't go back to being friends after this?

I don't want to go back to being friends, *she realized.*

"*Are you all right?*"

She glanced up to find Hawthorne watching her. "Um." *Her fingers froze on the uppermost button.* "Yes?"

But even she could hear the lie in her voice.

He straightened, his expression softening. "We don't have to do this. You can change your mind." He walked over, reaching for her folded yellow cardigan. "Maybe this was a bad idea. . . ."

In her mind, Emeline could see him folding up the easel and putting it away. Taking her back to Edgewood. Never bringing her here again.

"I want to," she said, undoing the first button of her dress.

His eyes dropped to her fingers. Something flickered across his face. "Do you . . . want help?" He sounded a little out of breath.

Emeline's heart skipped. Yes, *she thought, dropping her hands to her sides.* I want all the help.

Taking this as permission, he reached for the buttons. Emeline's breath quickened as his fingers brushed her bare skin, working downwards. When he'd unfastened enough to realize she wasn't wearing a bra, his breath drew in and his fingers paused. She could see the pulse in his throat pick up speed.

The dress was loose enough now to pull over her head. Emeline could easily finish this herself.

But she didn't.

She liked watching him move down her, unfastening her clothes. Liked watching the effect it had on him.

When he undid the final button, he glanced up. As he held her gaze, his warm hands slid purposefully beneath the blue fabric and over her skin, along her collarbone, pushing the dress slowly off her shoulders until it fell down to the floor.

When she stood naked before him, Hawthorne's gaze didn't drop. Didn't greedily take her in. Instead, he kept his eyes on her face as he held out his hand. She took it.

His palm was warm and strong and steady against hers as he led her towards the fire. But she could feel the ragged pulse beating beneath his skin.

"What do you want me to do?" she asked when he let go, digging her bare toes into the fluffy white carpet.

"Try . . . lying down?"

Nodding, she lowered herself into the softness and warmth of the carpet.

They tried several poses. Hawthorne stood at a distance, looking for the best angle, making suggestions. Emeline shifted, crooking her knee, bending her elbow beneath her head. But she was too tense and stiff.

"I could strip off my clothes and stand here naked too," he said, sensing her nervousness. "If it would help."

Emeline laughed, certain it would do the opposite, and glanced at him.

"There." His eyes darkened as his attention swept over her. "That's perfect."

She felt vulnerable suddenly, stretched out over the white carpet, with the firelight flickering over her pale skin and dark hair, laying her bare. But she felt powerful, too, watching him take her in.

He drew her over and over, from several angles, his charcoal whispering as it moved across the page. When she started to fidget, he lulled her back to stillness with poetry he'd memorized. Lines from Mary Oliver and Sylvia Plath, Pablo Neruda and Alfred, Lord Tennyson.

They did it again the next week. And the week after that.

Every week, he helped her out of her clothes, his hands lingering longer and longer each time, his expression growing hungrier and hungrier by the end of each session. As Emeline posed, his charcoal scratched in the silence. When she grew restless or itchy or bored, Hawthorne recited more poetry. When he ran out of poems, he recounted stories from the books on his shelves. Tales of Beowulf and Antigone and the Lady of Shalott.

He was an endless font of stories, bewitching her into stillness.

She was growing addicted to the sound of his sketching, and to that moment when she slid off her dress or sweater or jeans and his jaw clenched with restraint. She was growing addicted to his voice soothing her in the firelight. To his ravenous gaze running down her spine and over her hips when she turned her back to pull on her clothes.

It was her favorite secret, these nights.

She never wanted them to end.

On the last day of winter break, they sat side by side before the fire, their hands cupped around mugs of hot cocoa after a drawing session. Emeline, who hadn't dressed yet, was wrapped in a soft quilt from his bed.

"I've been thinking." Hawthorne stared intently into the flames. "Maybe we should stop."

Emeline turned sharply to look at him. "What do you mean?"

He tilted his face to his mug. "You have three singing gigs a week now, not to mention school, and a part-time job. You don't need to keep doing this for me."

She shook her head. This was the best part of her week.

And she didn't do it for him.

"My drawing classes are starting again soon, anyway."

Oh.

This was the real reason, then. He was bored of her. He wanted other people to draw.

That jealous, gnawing feeling was back, sinking its teeth in.

Don't be silly, *she chided. Of course he wanted different bodies to draw. The human form came in every shape and size and he wanted to learn them all. He wanted to get better. It was just like studying different kinds of music.*

But the thought of Hawthorne watching someone else undress made her stomach constrict. A cold sweat dampened her skin.

Emeline didn't know how to make herself unjealous.

Setting down the cocoa, she made her voice sound light and carefree. "Sure. Of course." *Not wanting him to see the thoughts in her eyes, she kept the blanket wrapped around her and rose to her feet, walking to the table where her clothes were folded.*

"What's wrong?" *he asked from behind her.*

"Nothing," *she said quickly.* "It's late. I should get home."

Except there was no one waiting for her at home. Pa was in Cleveland this weekend, playing music with his button box group. She could stay as long as she liked and no one would even know.

"There's another reason for stopping," *he said suddenly.* "The real reason."

Emeline, who was about to let the blanket fall and start pulling on her clothes, turned to find him directly behind her.

"You're not getting anything out of this." *He looked to the darkened windows.* "But I am. Far too much, I'm afraid."

She narrowed her eyes. "What are you talking about?"

His throat worked audibly as he swallowed.

"I never should have accepted your offer. It was wrong of me."

She frowned, holding the blanket closed at her throat. "Wrong?" *Was he ashamed of drawing her? He wasn't ashamed of drawing those other models.*

Maybe she really had ruined things by volunteering herself.

A panicked feeling clawed through her. She didn't want to go back to being only friends. She wanted this. *Whatever this was that they were doing. Her voice came out shaky.* "Why is it wrong?"

He ran both hands through his hair. "Isn't it obvious, Emeline?"

It wasn't obvious to her.

Seeing it, he stepped in closer.

"You're not supposed to want the model you're drawing." *He bent his head to hers.* "You're not supposed to think of her every night before you fall asleep."

His eyes were feverish as he reached to touch her hair, letting the black strands spill through his graphite-stained fingers. His other hand slid behind her neck as he slowly ran his thumb along her jaw, trembling as he traced her.

Oh.

"Is it obvious now?" he whispered.

It was becoming obvious, yes.

Emeline swallowed. Hearing it, he froze. "Do you want me to stop touching you?"

No. Not ever. But Emeline was overcome by an unexpected shyness, and she didn't know how to answer.

Hawthorne pulled away, trying to find the answer in her face. His absence was like a physical ache, and Emeline wanted him back.

She suddenly knew how to answer his question.

Emeline released her grip on the blanket. The fabric rushed through her fingers, falling to her feet. As the cold air raised goose bumps on her skin, she shivered and stepped towards him. Wanting his warmth.

Tangling her fingers in his hair, Emeline pulled his mouth down to hers.

It was a messy, fumbling sort of kiss. Soft and hungry.

Hawthorne quickly recovered from his surprise and pulled her tight against him, his palms sliding over her bare hips and up her back, his mouth tracing her jaw and throat.

Emeline's heart pounded as she greedily traced him back.

The next thing she remembered was staggering to the bedroom with him. And after: her hands sliding beneath his sweater, tugging it up over his head, dropping it to the floor in a heap. And then: stumbling into the bed.

As Emeline lay beneath him, trying to unbutton his jeans, Hawthorne stopped her, bringing her hands up beside her head, trapping her palms beneath his.

"*Wait,*" *he whispered, kissing her throat, her collarbone, her shoulder, then moving farther down, to her hips and thighs and . . .*

Emeline went rigid. "*Hawthorne?*"

"*Mmm?*"

"*What are you doing?*"

His hands cupped her thighs as he looked up at her. "*Do you trust me?*"

Emeline bit her lip. The thought of him kissing her there, between her legs, scared her a little. Did he know what he was getting into?

"*Hey.*" *Hawthorne stopped and came back up, covering her with his whole body, his skin hot against hers, warming her up.* "*We don't have to do this, remember? Say the word and we'll stop.*"

"*No, it's just . . .*" *She wrinkled her nose and turned her face away, feeling embarrassed.* "*I'm afraid you'll be grossed out.*"

He stared at her like she'd grown a second head. "*Is that your only hesitation?*"

Still looking away from him, she nodded.

He turned her face gently back to his, kissing her softly, deeply, making her thoughts go fuzzy. But then he was gone again, moving back down her body. His mouth was warm and wet as he kissed between her thighs. Emeline buried her fingers in his hair as he held on to her, bringing her closer, pushing his tongue deeper in. Emeline gasped.

The warmth went away as Hawthorne's head came up.

"*Are you okay?*"

She nodded fiercely. "*Yes. Are you?*"

There was the hint of a smile. "*Best day of my life.*"

Emeline covered her face with her hands, biting down on a smile.

Soon, she relaxed. As Hawthorne's mouth moved fervently against her, her hips arched, inviting him in. He didn't stop until Emeline's breathing changed and she finally unfurled like a flower, moaning softly with pleasure.

In the aftermath, her body purred with satisfaction like a cat in the sun. Hawthorne came to lie beside her, his hands moving reverently over her skin, memorizing her.

"Where did you learn how to do that?" she whispered.

He smiled against her collarbone.

"I read it," he said, pulling her close. "In a book."

THAT SPRING, SHE SAVED enough money to move to Montreal.

It was June, and the city was calling her. Emeline was seventeen and didn't want to stay in Edgewood any longer. She didn't want to sit in a classroom, watching the clock, waiting for her life to begin. She wanted to be a musician. To make her way in the world, writing and singing her songs, playing them beneath the lights.

One night, she and Hawthorne got caught in a thunderstorm. They were waiting it out on the dusty steps of the barn stairwell.

"I signed a lease," she said, her fingertips tracing his palms in the dark. "I think you should come with me."

He pulled his hands out from under hers, saying nothing. They'd been through this before. Only now it was really happening. And Emeline was determined to convince him.

"You could work in a library. Or a bookstore. You've read more books than anyone I know."

"Emeline."

"They'd hire you in a heartbeat. Or you could—"

"Emeline. Stop."

His weary tone made her fall silent. The darkness was too dark, suddenly.

"I would follow you to the ends of the earth if I could." His voice broke on the words. "But I can't. We've been through this a hundred times."

Because Hawthorne had made a deal with the Wood King—
one that tied him to his king and his court. Whatever Hawthorne
was getting out of this deal he never bothered to say.

Balling her hands into fists, she said, "So that's it?"

His silence was stony, stretching on and on. When he finally
spoke, it wasn't to answer her question.

"I'm bound to the woods." His voice was thin and small. It
scared her a little. "But you're not. You need to go live your life.
This is your dream and I want you to chase it, even if I can't be by
your side when you do."

Her heart sank.

"Is this . . ." Emeline's chin trembled as hot tears welled in her
eyes. "Are you breaking up with me?"

He pulled her to him. Cupping her neck, he nestled her cheek
against his chest, resting his chin on the crown of her head. "I never
want to be the thing that holds you back."

That wasn't an answer to her question.

Before she could say so, he whispered into her hair, "I'll be wait-
ing right here. Always."

"EMELINE?" A VOICE SHATTERED the memories, bringing her
back to the present.

She was in the green room of the Nymph, with its flickering
fluorescent lights and old-coffee smell. Joel stood over her, peeling her headphones away from her ears as The Perennials piled
onto the couches behind him.

"You were supposed to be out onstage fifteen minutes ago."

FORTY

EMELINE WALKED ACROSS THE stage towards the microphone. Her body moved on instinct, her footsteps automatic. Like a confident, seasoned musician.

At least, that's what she hoped she looked like.

On the inside, Emeline was a wreck. Her mind was a dizzying rush of memories, swelling like a storm.

Beneath the bright white of the lights, she blinked, trying to find her bearings. She reached for the mic, her hands shaking a little as she adjusted its height.

"Hello, bonsoir, Montréal!"

Her voice echoed through the speakers, the familiar amplification calming her enough to pull the strap of her Taylor over her head. A round of cheering rose up beyond the lights. She sensed more than saw the faces in the crowd. Heard the coughs and murmurs. Felt the sway of warm bodies.

But Emeline was only half there. Her other half was in the green room, knee-deep in memories she'd only just recovered.

Sensing the chaos swirling inside her, Emeline's brain took over, putting her on autopilot. Telling her body what to do based on all the other gigs she'd ever played.

"Je m'appelle Emeline Lark," she heard herself say. "It's a

pleasure to play for you tonight. C'est un plaisir de jouer pour vous ce soir."

If her voice quavered, no one noticed. The audience clapped and whooped out there in the dark. Somewhere in that crowd, Daybreak reps were watching.

Emeline fastened on a smile as her fingers quickly plucked strings and adjusted tuning pegs. Her set list lay at the base of the mic stand, in perfect view. The titles of the songs Chloe had written for her scrolled in bold black letters down the white.

But before she could even start playing, Hawthorne's voice flooded her mind.

I knew a girl once whose songs helped her stand against all the forces stronger than she was.

The set list at her feet blurred before her.

Sometimes, you remind me of her.

Don't do it, she told herself. *Stay focused. This is everything you've been working towards. Don't screw it up.*

And still, she looked away from the set list and into the lights. Remembering that not so long ago, all she wanted was to sing her own songs up onstage.

She still wanted that.

Pulling her guitar strap back over her head, she set it down on its stand, then picked up her ukulele and quickly tuned it. Her voice was thick in her throat as she said, "This song is about forgetting. And . . . and remembering."

Emeline started to strum. It wasn't one of Chloe's songs; it was one of hers. The one she'd written about her grandfather. Except now, standing on this stage, she realized that wasn't really true.

The song wasn't about Pa. It had never been about Pa.

"Breathing slow and steady
Sleep has settled in

I trace the pathways, midnight blue
That run beneath your skin

Some spirit I have lost somewhere
I search for it in vain
Some beauty I've forgotten
Since you forgot my name

Every time I close my eyes
You're waiting there for me
Rooted in my deepest dreams
Strong and silent as a tree

Some spirit sleeps but never dies
Some beauty never fades
Some love lies dormant underground
Since I forgot your name"

And as she sang, one last memory crashed into her.

THAT FIRST YEAR AWAY *from Edgewood, she did what she needed to make ends meet, playing in whatever venues would pay her—cafés, dive bars, charity fundraisers. When money was tight, she busked in the street.*

She made an EP and used it to apply to music festivals in the fall. She started getting into those festivals. Started seeing her name on their posters. One of the best managers in the business signed her as a client.

But it wasn't enough. No matter how frugal she was, she fell further into debt.

Her manager told her to hire a writer and change up her sound. Fearing this was her one and only chance to make it, she took his advice.

Suddenly, she was getting better gigs—ones that paid her well enough to eat more than instant noodles.

Suddenly, she was doing it; she was building a career.

But there was something else building too: the woods. They came for her at every performance, but not like they used to. Where once their presence was soft and quiet, slipping in through the doors like any other adoring fan, now it was something else entirely. The woods no longer left tokens of appreciation in her guitar case—handfuls of acorns and feathers and maple keys. Instead, they came like a scorned lover: possessive and hostile. Erupting through venues as if they couldn't let her go.

As if they refused to let her forget.

Emeline could ignore the woods if she was careful and clever. What she couldn't ignore was the ache they brought with them, putting down roots in her chest and spreading ever deeper, bit by bit.

At first, she thought it was homesickness. The woods were reminding her of everything she missed: Edgewood. The stars and the quiet and the vast amount of space. Pa and Tom and Maisie and all her old neighbors. Her friends Sable and Rooke.

But you were supposed to get homesick when you moved away. It was a part of growing up.

This was something else. A hole in her life. A deep, dark missing.

She hadn't heard Hawthorne's voice in months—not since the last time she called home and he happened to be visiting Pa. She hadn't seen Hawthorne's face since Christmas, the only time she'd been back since leaving Edgewood last summer.

Every night when she came home from a gig, there was an emp-

tiness in her apartment despite it being full of roommates. The people she lived with were strangers. Polite strangers, but still strangers. There was a space where Hawthorne should have been—reading or drawing or cooking—and wasn't.

More than this, with every new success, the hole in her seemed to widen. Her musical achievements should have fulfilled her. Instead, they left her hungrier than ever.

Emeline might be living her dream. But dreams, she realized now, had shadow sides. Dreams came with costs.

Hers had cost her something precious.

That June, a year after she moved to Montreal, the ache grew into a cavern inside her. She was sitting in a booth at the back of a bar, squished between Joel and his bandmates after a show, watching them giggle and gossip over drinks. It felt like a carousel ride. The painted horses going up and down, around and around. Everyone smiling and laughing and having a good time. But all Emeline wanted to do was get off.

Why am I here? *she kept thinking.* What am I doing?

A few nights later, she packed up her belongings—she had so few, they fit easily into her car—and the next morning she got up to drive all day until she got to Edgewood.

She had no intention of driving back.

It was early evening when she pulled into Pa's lane. Pa was standing on the front patio, looking confused as he squinted at her. She parked in the driveway, left everything in the car, and ran to him.

"I came outside to do something, but I can't remember what it was," he said as she squeezed him. "Did you tell me you were coming for dinner?"

It was odd, the way he phrased it. "Coming for dinner." As if he thought she lived up the road. Emeline shrugged it off and shook her head. "I didn't tell you, no."

"*Well, you have good timing.*" *He kissed the top of her head.* "*Dinner's almost ready.*"

Emeline pulled back. If Pa was out here, who was inside making dinner?

She hauled her suitcase from the trunk of her car and went to find out. Dumping her stuff in the mudroom, she kicked off her flats and headed for the kitchen—where the smell of fresh bread and frying onions wafted out.

A young man stood facing the sink, soapsuds halfway up his arms as he washed and scrubbed the dishes. Emeline paused at the sight of him, her heart leaping into her throat.

Sensing he wasn't alone, Hawthorne turned, hands dripping. He looked different from when she'd seen him at Christmas. Taller. Broader. His dark hair a little longer, curling gently around his ears.

"*Emeline?*"

She nearly burst into tears at the sight of him.

Emeline ran and jumped into his arms. Hawthorne caught her, hiking her up onto his hips. She buried her face in his throat, breathing in his crushed-pine smell. He pressed his face into her hair, doing the same.

You're mine, she thought. You belong with me.

"*What are you doing here?*" *he breathed.*

"*I couldn't stay there.*" *Her arms tightened around his neck, remembering the feel of his body—the solid strength of him—now that he was in her arms.* "*I don't like cities.*"

He let go. Forced to lower herself, Emeline's bare feet landed on the tiled kitchen floor.

"*You love cities.*" *His voice sounded strange.*

She shook her head. "*Maybe I don't.*"

He observed her warily.

Sensing his skepticism, she said, "*It's not my dream if you're not in it, Hawthorne.*"

He turned away from her, his muscles tensing as he reached for a hand towel.

"I'm moving home," she said, more forcefully.

"There's nothing for you here."

"You're here."

He dried his hands on the towel, folded it neatly, but didn't set it down as he turned to face her. "That's not a reason to give up everything you've worked so hard for."

But he didn't know what it was like, achieving success after success only to be rewarded with an ever-growing emptiness.

"I thought you'd be happy to see me."

He opened his mouth to say something, then stopped himself. He turned towards the window over the sink, looking to the woods. "Please don't do this."

Emeline felt like a dropped spool of thread, unraveling across the floor. She'd been gone for too long, she realized. He'd moved on. Moved past her.

If that was true, she needed him to say it.

"Why not?" She balled her hands into fists. "Why can't I do this?"

He didn't turn to look at her, just kept staring out the window. "You'd come to resent me one day. You'd resent yourself. In five or ten years, you'd come to your senses and realize you made a horrifying mistake. One you couldn't take back."

"I'm coming to my senses now!" she shouted at him. "I've already made the mistake, and I'm fixing it!"

He folded in on himself, like a wounded animal. Staring down at his hands, he whispered, "I wish that were true."

He wasn't listening to her.

Why wasn't he listening?

"It's my life, Hawthorne. I get to do what I want with it."

He turned towards her, eyes sharp and piercing. "Fine. But do this, and I will never forgive you for it."

Throwing down the towel on the counter, he walked straight past her and out the door. Cleaving her heart in two.

The next day, after she spent the entire night weeping, something strange happened. Emeline stopped crying, abruptly, and couldn't remember why she started.

Nor could she remember why she came home.

To visit Pa, because she was homesick. Was that it? Or was it to get away from the music scene for a while? It drained her, sometimes— the gossip, the grind, the cutthroat competition. Maybe she should find some friends outside the industry. Nice, well-adjusted ones.

But why was her car packed full of all her stuff? Had she intended to move home? But that was absurd. Her whole life was in Montreal. Her career was on the rise. She couldn't move home.

No matter how hard she tried, Emeline couldn't remember why she was here.

What she did know was that she was booked to play at a music festival the following week. If she didn't head back soon and prepare, she wouldn't be ready in time.

So, the next morning, she threw her suitcase into the trunk, kissed Pa good-bye, and drove back to the city.

Where her life was.

BENEATH THE BRIGHT LIGHTS of the stage, Emeline's fingers stopped strumming. As her song ended, the crowd behind the lights clapped and cheered.

Ever since she was a child, Emeline dreamed of singing her songs onstage. But not long after she moved to Montreal, something changed. *Your songs aren't marketable,* her manager told her. *And you won't be young forever.* If she wanted to pay her bills, if she wanted a rising career instead of a tanking one, she needed to sing different songs and she needed to do it immediately—before her youth ceased to be a selling point and the industry grew bored of her.

So, trusting her manager, she locked her songs away, using poetry for a password.

And then Hawthorne made me forget.

Emeline glanced down at her set list. The music she'd prepared lay right at her feet. The Daybreak reps were in the crowd somewhere. All she had to do was start and keep going. All she had to do was show them what she was capable of.

This was her biggest, oldest dream.

Except . . . was it?

This was what she'd realized two years ago, right before Hawthorne took her memories: *This*—playing someone else's songs, touring with jaded musicians, living so far from what she loved most—was a twisted version of her dream.

It was what the woods had been trying to tell her when they stalked into her performances over the past year, demanding true songs. Nineteen years ago, her grandfather had asked the woods to protect Emeline, and the woods took that responsibility seriously. They *were* protecting her—by reminding her of who she was, and what was important.

You were going to abandon your dreams. You were going to stay. Here. For me.

She understood why Hawthorne did what he did—not that this excused him. He was trying to save her from herself, believing that giving up on her dream would make her miserable in the long run, because he knew how desperately she had wanted a music career.

I still want it.

There was nothing else Emeline would rather be doing than

singing on brightly lit stages or in darkened bars—she simply wanted to do it on her terms. She wanted to sing her own songs.

Maybe I still can.

She'd recovered her old songs. She could sing them right here. Right now. Her manager would be furious, but so what?

The question lifted an invisible weight from her. One she'd been carrying for too long.

Emeline looked out over the silhouetted crowd behind the lights, emboldened. But as she chose her next song—one she'd written for Sable all those years ago—and started to play it, the atmosphere changed. The air thickened, dampening her skin, and the putrid smell of mold seeped up from somewhere nearby. Emeline wrinkled her nose and squinted into the lights, scanning the darkness beyond.

It smelled like . . .

Jagged silver thorns began to sprout from the microphone as something rasped across the stage floor. She looked down to see the floorboards buckle and burst as thick gray roots sprouted up from below, slithering towards her. With them came dozens of leaves, blown by an unnatural breeze, gathering in a pile around her feet. They weren't the vibrant green of healthy leaves. Nor were they the crisp golds and reds of freshly fallen ones.

These were sickly and ashy and gray. Diseased.

The woods had come.

Emeline, they rasped, reaching for her.

She stared in horror at the lethal-looking thorns growing out of the mic, at the snakelike roots headed straight for her. One thick root rose to her full height and, before she could flinch away, brushed across her cheek like a parting caress.

We came to say good-bye.

Good-bye?

Emeline thought of the curse, slowly consuming the forest,

creeping closer and closer to the King's City. She thought of the shadow skins breaching the walls. Thought of Sable and Rooke, forced to resume their true forms, unable to ever change back.

The curse grows more powerful every day, Grace's voice chimed through her. *You need to escape this place before it devours us.*

What had the curse done to the woods? To her friends?

Behind the lights, the audience's cheers fell to murmured alarm as more and more floorboards cracked and burst as twisted roots pushed up through the stage.

I need to go back . . .

Emeline flipped her ukulele over her shoulder, letting it hang on its strap across her back. As the dying woods erupted around her, she reached for the neck of her guitar. Lifting it from its stand, she said, "Thank you, merci. This has been a dream." Taking one last look at the theater beyond the lights, she lowered her voice to a whisper. "But there's somewhere else I need to be. Bonne soirée."

One day, she'd return to this stage—on her terms, singing her songs. She might need to rebuild her career from scratch, but so what? She'd faced down scarier things.

With that thought in her heart and the woods in danger, Emeline strode off the stage and didn't look back.

FORTY-ONE

AS THE DOOR TO the green room swung open and Emeline walked in, every member of The Perennials stopped laughing. Ashley—dressed in black skinny jeans and a red shirt stitched with a barbed-wire heart—sat up from where she sprawled across the couch, her bleached-blond ponytail swishing.

An electric energy pulsed through Emeline as she realized what she'd done. What she was still doing. *Saying good-bye to my tour, and a record deal with Daybreak.*

No. What she was saying good-bye to was spending three weeks with musicians who didn't think she deserved to share a stage with them. She was saying good-bye to recording an album of songs that weren't hers.

Emeline grabbed her bag, buckled her instruments into their cases, then shouldered the door to the green room open and stepped out into the hall.

When it swung shut behind her, Ashley's muffled voice said, "Didn't she *just* go out onstage?"

Emeline should have told them she was leaving. That she was sorry. That she'd find a replacement for tomorrow, even. But she remembered the ugly words they'd spewed about her and Chloe last night and kept walking.

Adieu, jerks.

In the hall, she started to run—past the merch table selling her EPs, past the fans in The Perennials tees loitering against the walls. She ran all the way to the entrance of the Nymph, where a line of rain-streaked cabs waited at the curb. The air was heavy and warm. The city shimmered like glass.

"Emeline!"

Joel's voice.

She winced but didn't turn as the rain came down, speckling her face and hair. Opening the back door of a cab, she tossed her guitar and ukulele cases inside, then ducked into the darkness of the back seat. "Rue Sainte-Catharine Est," she told the driver above the thump of windshield wipers. "S'il vous plaît."

She'd left Hawthorne's ring at her apartment. Not only had she not wanted the reminder, but she never wore jewelry when she played—it only got in the way. Now that ring was her fastest way home.

A hand grabbed the door, stopping her from shutting it.

"What the fuck are you doing?"

Emeline looked up to find Joel's face contorted with anger. He gripped the door so hard, his knuckles were bone white.

"You walked offstage in the middle of your set!"

"I know," she said, reaching for the door handle, thinking of the woods. *We came to say good-bye.* "There's an emergency. I have to get home."

He grabbed her wrist to stop her. "I kissed ass getting you this gig! And you're just throwing it away?! What the hell is wrong with you!"

"I know. I . . ." Emeline tried to twist out of his tightening grip. "Stop it, Joel. You're hurting me."

From the front seat, the cabdriver turned and cussed him out in French.

Glancing to the driver, Joel hesitated. Emeline twisted free, but Joel still had the door in his grip. She couldn't shut it without slamming his fingers.

"If you do this," Joel said, nostrils flaring, "my dad will cut you loose. I can promise you that."

Once, those words would have wrecked her. A few weeks ago, being dropped by her manager would have been one of the worst things that could happen. Now she simply nodded. "I know. Tell him I'm sorry. Really, I am."

Joel's mouth fell open. As his grip loosened on the door, Emeline grabbed the handle and slammed it shut. He withdrew his fingers just in time.

"Imbécile," muttered the cabbie, putting on his blinker and pulling into the street. In the side-view mirror, Emeline glanced from Joel to the Nymph's marquee boasting her name in bold black letters, watching it until it disappeared completely and all that was left was the beat of her heart, thudding in time with the wipers.

IT WAS FULL DARK when Emeline arrived back in Edgewood. The change was disorienting at first, stepping out of the stale air of her cramped apartment and into the crisp, cool breeze on Pa's front lawn. She'd been thinking of Hawthorne when she put on the ring and therefore expected to find herself in the King's City. But maybe the ring could only take you places *beyond* the woods.

She opened the door to Pa's house, intending to cut through it.

Inside, a fire crackled in the woodstove, warming the room. Pa stood at the kitchen window in blue flannel pajamas and slippers. Maisie stood beside him. The two of them stared eerily towards the dark forest, mugs of cocoa cupped in their hands.

"Emeline," said Maisie, her voice hushed. "Come and see."

She stepped up next to them, looking where they did.

The sight set her heart to pounding.

Her tree.

The one Pa planted on the day she was born.

Illuminated by the house lights, she saw its knotted bark and twisting branches. Bloodred berries grew in clusters beneath its dark green leaves. It was rooted in place at the edge of the woods, right where it had always been.

"Your hawthorn," said Pa.

Her stomach clenched like a fist.

That can't be.

But there it was: her hawthorn.

The curse turns everything back to its true form.

Emeline didn't realize she was moving, running, tearing out of the house and down towards the woods, until she stepped across the tree line, avoiding the hawthorn like a horrifying truth she didn't want to face.

The second she stepped inside the forest, she felt the wrongness of it. The trees near the edge, which had always been healthy and strong, were rotting. The moonlight coming through the canopy was soupy and gray.

It no longer smelled like a forest; it smelled like decay.

The Stain had spread all the way here, to the tree line. If it spread this far . . .

Emeline ran. She ran until her lungs burned and her breath was loud and ragged in her ears, and then she kept running.

Emeline, the blighted trees rattled, reaching for her. *You came back. . . .*

Bog guarded the closest entry point into the city, so she went to it first. But when she arrived at its swamp, the stagnant water remained still.

"Bog!"

No muddy head rose up from its depths.

"Bog!"

Only the heavy silence of the Stain answered her.

If Bog had succumbed to the curse, was the entry point gone? Emeline searched for the boardwalk normally hidden beneath the water. But if it was there, it was entirely submerged. And without the entry point, it was a three-day walk to the gate.

From behind her, something *cracked* softly. Like a branch breaking beneath a footstep.

Emeline's spine straightened. A cold sweat broke out over her skin. The knife Sable forged her was taken by the Vile. If this was a shadow skin, she had nothing to defend herself with.

Slowly, she turned around. But the thing waiting for her wasn't a shadow; it was a horse. Her black coat gleamed in the moonlight and her golden eyes glowed like the twisting flames of a fire. The ember mare flicked her ears, staring at Emeline.

"Lament," she breathed.

At the sound of her name, the horse started forward. Emeline reached her arms around Lament's neck, pressing her cheek to that warm, soft coat.

"Can you take me to the city?"

Lament *whuffed* into her hair. As if to say, *Get on.*

THE ONCE-WHITE WALLS SURROUNDING the King's City were cracked and blackened with mold. At the entrance, the copper gate twisted back on its hinges like a broken rib cage.

Emeline shivered as Lament took them through.

The streets beyond were dark and lifeless. A thin sheet of gray dust—like crumbled leaves—caked the cobbles. No hedgemen marched. No faces peeked out of windows.

The city was empty.

Emeline nudged Lament into a gallop.

They rode straight to Grace and Sable's house. At the entrance, Emeline slowed the ember mare, then slid down her warm back. The gate was open, and the sight of the broken latch sent a chill creeping across Emeline's skin.

Emeline didn't bring Lament to the stable. She didn't want the horse trapped, in case any shadow skins lurked nearby.

The night pressed in close as she warily approached the silent house. Lament watched, ears flicking nervously. No plume of smoke issued out of the chimney, and the once-beautiful willow in the yard was white and withered with rot. Taking the dust-covered steps quickly, Emeline knocked on the door. When no one answered, she reached for the crystal knob and turned, only to find it locked.

"Grace!"

No one answered.

She banged, her panic rising.

"It's me! Emeline!"

She was about to bang again when chains clinked from inside and a bolt slid open.

When the door swung in, Emeline relaxed—only to feel the cold, honed tip of a sword pressed to her throat.

At the other end of the shimmering blade stood Grace, both hands clutching the pommel. Her thick black curls were a tangled cloud around her head, and her eyes were dark hollows.

"Move," she said, "and I'll kill you."

FORTY-TWO

EMELINE GULPED, RAISED BOTH hands, and stepped back. Wondering if the curse had somehow poisoned Grace too.

"Hasn't she learned by now?" Grace's voice was rough with fury. "I keep killing you, and you keep coming back, pretending to be people I love."

She thinks I'm a shadow skin.

"You can't trick me," Grace said bitterly. "Everyone I love is gone."

"Grace . . ."

"*Don't speak!*" Grace hissed, coming forward, onto the step. The steel of her blade pressed harder into Emeline's skin.

How do I prove I'm me?

She contemplated the glimmering steel, remembering the times she'd watched a shadow skin die, the way they dissolved like smoke. If Grace killed her, Emeline wouldn't dissolve. She would fall dead to the ground, her blood seeping into the dust-covered earth.

With that image in her mind, Emeline reached for the cold shaft of the blade, gripping it hard, as if she planned to take it. Grace's eyes widened. She yanked the sword back, slicing Emeline's palm.

Emeline winced at the sharp pain, then fisted her hand and held it out between them, letting her fingers slowly uncurl. Blood seeped up from the cut, illuminated by the starlight.

"Shadow skins don't bleed," she said softly.

Blood dripped onto the step between them. Grace sucked in a sharp breath, staring at the drops of red splattering the pale gray dust, then lowered the blade to her side. "Emeline . . . I'm so sorry."

Emeline glanced behind her, checking to see if their voices had drawn trouble, before nudging Grace into the house. "It's fine. Let's get inside."

Emeline bolted the door behind them as Grace sheathed the sword, propping it next to the window, then lifted a candelabra whose flames lit the way.

"Are you alone?"

Grace nodded, silent, moving through the darkened house to peer out the kitchen windows, which overlooked the garden and stables in the back. Checking for threats.

"There's no one left. Sable, Rooke, Hawthorne . . . they're gone. Even the king is gone."

At these words, Emeline's anger at Hawthorne paled in comparison to the wave of grief that crashed over her. The thought of never seeing him again, of never seeing any of them again, felt like gasping for air and finding none.

She was too late; she'd lost them.

Her fingers curled and uncurled. "Is there a way to, I don't know, *undo* it?"

Grace stared blankly. Her normally bright eyes were leaden, and her mouth was pressed into a grim line.

"Well, you can't stay here," said Emeline, burying the horrible weight of it. "You might be able to manage one or two shadow skins, but what happens when *groups* of them come? When they realize you're the last living thing in this city and they decide to swarm the house?"

Sable might have trained Grace to wield a sword, but one girl was no match for a horde of shadow skins. And this house couldn't stand against the Vile and her curse forever.

"I'm taking you back to Edgewood with me."

Grace's brow furrowed. "And if Sable returns?" She shook her head. "I tithed that life. I'm not going back to it. *This* is my home."

"But there's nothing for you here."

The silence following those words hung heavy as a stone between them. It was the same thing Hawthorne said two years ago. It was the reason he took her memories—thinking he knew better than she did.

"I didn't mean that," she said immediately. "But we can't sit here and wait to be devoured."

Grace jutted out her chin. "I wasn't planning on it." Spinning on her heel, she lifted the candelabra in her hand and walked into what looked like a dining room. Emeline followed behind.

Grace veered around a long dinner table circled by upholstered chairs, then stopped abruptly. Emeline came to stand on the opposite side. Between them, across the table's oaken surface, lay the map they'd used to find the Song Mage's house. Emeline, who hadn't gotten a good look at it before, paused as a symbol caught the light of the candle flames. She bent over the map, her gaze trailing past Edgewood on the northern border, past the King's City, to the symbol of a door nestled into the trunk of a giant tree.

Beneath it were the words: *The Heartwood.*

Her brow furrowed. "The Heartwood?"

"It's where the king brings tithes from the borderlands," Grace explained. "To strengthen the woods against the curse."

She reached for the map and started rolling it. "It's where I tithed everything dear to me beyond the forest."

"Okay," said Emeline, not understanding.

"I have one thing left to tithe," Grace explained.

"And what's that?"

"My life," she whispered, still rolling. "The breath in my lungs."

A chill went through Emeline. *"What?"*

Grace gripped the rolled map hard in both hands, staring down at it. "You didn't see how terrified Sable was. She *felt* herself disappearing. She *knew* she'd never be human again." When Grace looked up, tears shone in her eyes. "If I can give that back to her . . ."

Her shoulders started to shake. Dropping the map, she lifted her hands to her face, trying to stifle her sobs.

Emeline's heart cracked open. Moving quickly to Grace's side, she pulled her into a hug. She seemed so soft and small and *lost*.

"Grace," Emeline whispered, swallowing the lump in her throat. "Do you really think Sable will want to return if you aren't waiting for her when she does?"

Grace stiffened, then pulled away. "I've already decided." From the fierce set of her jaw, Emeline knew she would hear no more protests. "I'm going."

Snatching up the map, Grace left the room, leaving the candle burning on the table.

Emeline couldn't let her go out there alone. Not with every horrible thing in the woods on the prowl. So she went after her, certain Grace would realize the folly of this decision. And when she did, Emeline would be there to bring her home to Edgewood.

She may have lost the others, but she could still save Grace.

THEY RODE DEEP INTO the woods. The farther they went, the colder it grew, reminding Emeline of the Song Mage's house. Of that eerie, bone-chilling cold. It stung her skin and made her breath fog the air. Only Lament was warm beneath her.

Beside Emeline, Grace sat astride her own horse, with one of Sable's swords sheathed at her back, scanning the night-dark woods. Around them, pallid trees breathed their rattled, rasping breaths. Beneath the moon, the forest was frost white—the color of corruption.

Sometimes Emeline thought she saw a shadow keeping pace with them, darting in and out of the white trees. But when she looked closer, there was nothing there.

Gripping the reins tighter, Emeline nudged Lament onwards.

Too soon, they found it: a wooden door set into the trunk of a massive oak. Its roots plunged into the earth, thick and thirsty. Its pale bark curled like ropes, reaching upwards to where leafless branches clawed at the cobalt sky.

Emeline dismounted.

"I'll see if it's locked," she said, hoping it was, wondering if she could jam the door if it wasn't. She'd expected Grace to have come to her senses by now. Now she was scrambling to think of another plan.

Grace kept watch as Emeline approached the door. Its copper hinges were rusted blue, and burned into the door's wooden surface was the symbol of a seed.

Before Emeline could reach for the copper doorknob, Grace drew Sable's sword.

At the sound, Emeline turned to find dozens of shadow skins stepping out of the trees, their black shapes stark against the silvery woods. As Grace backed towards Emeline, gripping her blade, Emeline felt the monsters prod at her mind, like dozens of fingers dipping into a still pool, about to plunge into its depths.

Lament reared up, screaming. The unnatural sound pierced Emeline's ears like knives, making her flinch. The ember mare smashed her hooves against the earth, setting it ablaze with red fire.

The shadow skins crept closer.

When Lament reared again, Emeline moved to calm her, but an echoing scream in the distance made her pause. The sound was much louder. Like a roaring sea.

The earth began to tremble beneath their feet.

Emeline turned. In the distance, the orange glow of wildfire swept through the pale trees. Coming straight for them.

No. Not fire.

Horses.

The ember mares were running. Lament had called them.

Emeline grabbed Grace's hand, pulling her towards the oak, hoping to use it as a shield against the flaming bodies barreling down on them from behind. They pressed their backs against the door until their shoulder blades hurt from the pressure.

The earth shuddered and quaked. Their bones shook and their teeth clattered.

Soon, the fire was upon them, hot and roaring.

The ember mares blasted past, parting around the giant oak that sheltered Emeline and Grace. Snorting fire and screaming fury, they formed a wall of flame around both girls as they surged over the shadow skins, pummeling them with their thunderous hooves, drowning them in wildfire, forcing them to retreat.

Emeline pushed away from the door, watching the sea of red-gold wash through the white trees, awestruck as the horses swept into the distance, leaving no trace of the shadow skins behind.

When the woods fell silent, only Lament remained, trotting back to them.

"Come on," said Grace, gripping her shimmering sword and stepping up to the door. It creaked as she swung it open, revealing brown earthen steps woven with thin white roots that disappeared down into the cavernous dark.

"Grace, wait—"

When Emeline stepped inside to stop her, the door swung shut, swallowing them like a hungry mouth and plunging them into blackness. Emeline turned, heart hammering, and reached out her hands, sweeping them through the air until her fingers grazed the wood of the door. Grabbing hold of the copper handle, she tried to turn it.

It wouldn't budge.

Locked.

"No. . . ."

"It won't open until a tithe is given," came Grace's voice from much too far away.

Shit, thought Emeline, running shaky hands through her hair. *What have I done?*

Emeline couldn't see her friend in the darkness, but she heard Grace's footsteps moving ever downwards. Using the dirt walls to guide her, Emeline followed her down the steps.

How would she get Grace out of here now?

As she descended, the air began to glow. Something pulsed through the cool, soft dirt beneath her palms and a damp, earthy smell seeped up. At the bottom of the steps, the glow brightened and Emeline saw the root-infested walls around her.

Grace's silhouette shrank into the distance.

Emeline hurried forward, following her through the glow until the strange pulsing swelled, filling up her chest, and the earthen corridor opened into an orb-shaped chamber, with pale roots trailing like ivy down to the floor.

In the center of the chamber was the source of the glow and

the pulse: huge and white and shaped like a teardrop, a seed thumped like a human heart, suspended in a tangled web of roots instead of arteries.

Beneath it lay a black pool, rippling gently as drops of water fell into it.

The Heartwood.

Emeline imagined the king standing here, offering up the power in Edgewood's tithes, helping the forest fight back the curse. She thought of her father, the Song Mage, making his own sacrifice. Had he stood in this exact spot? Was this where he was transformed from a talented musician into a monstrous mage?

Emeline shivered.

As Grace disappeared around the other side of that beating heart, Emeline felt her last chance slipping away. It was now or never. She would get them both out—by force, if necessary. She would break down that door if she had to. No way was she letting Grace do this.

"You're making a mistake."

Grace ignored her.

"Don't you think Sable would want you to live your life?" Emeline pressed, a little desperately, coming around the other side of the suspended heart. "Don't you think she'd want to know you're alive in the world, sleeping beneath the same sky, thinking about her?"

"She won't know," came Grace's answer. "Because she won't—"

When Emeline came into view, Grace glanced up. Her dark gaze darted to something over Emeline's shoulder and her eyes widened. "Emeline! Watch out!"

When Emeline turned to look, a loud *thud!* clanged in her ears. Pain sparked at the back of her head.

She didn't even feel herself fall before the dark descended.

FORTY-THREE

EMELINE WOKE TO A hazy glow. Her head throbbed, her vision blurred, and a steady *drip drip drip* sounded from somewhere nearby.

She blinked, trying to clear her vision. When that didn't work, she reached for the painful bump at the back of her skull—only she couldn't. She was standing upright while thick, scratchy rope bound her wrists securely above her head.

Whoever had tied her hands had also gagged her. The fabric dug into the corners of her mouth, muffling her voice.

Slowly, the room came into focus. The blur moved to the edges, leaving Emeline staring into a pale face with blue-green veins running like rivers beneath translucent white skin. Bloodshot eyes peered at her, and the same rotten smell of the Stain issued out of the creature's mouth.

The Vile.

My mother.

Her stomach turned over.

In one bony hand, the Vile held a jagged dagger. Dried brown blood crusted along the edge, rusting the steel. In the other, she held a sharpening stone.

Realizing what was about to happen, Emeline struggled, pulling at her bonds. Trying to yank herself loose.

Wait. Where was Grace?

Her gaze swept the cavern until it settled on a crumpled form several paces away. *Grace.* She was curled up on the floor, her wrists bound tightly behind her back.

As Emeline feared the worst, her breath came out panicked and choked—until she saw the subtle rise and fall of her friend's chest. *She's alive.*

But Emeline's relief was short-lived.

"How familiar this feels." The Vile's voice was like wind scraping stone as she studied Emeline, who tore her gaze away from Grace. "His flesh and blood, bound and trapped. Unable to use that pretty voice."

Fear crept down Emeline's spine.

"I made a mistake when I killed him." The Vile lifted the sharpening stone and slid it slowly over the rusted knife. "I forgot that wretched voice of his. He cursed me with it as he died. Me *and* the forest."

The words shocked Emeline. *The curse is the Song Mage's doing?* All this time, she thought the Vile responsible.

"I won't make that same mistake a second time. When I spill your blood, you will have no voice to hurt me with."

The Vile smiled, and it was an eerie, monstrous thing. Emeline saw rows and rows of teeth so sharp, they reminded her of icicles.

"By killing you, I'll silence him forever."

You would kill your own daughter for the sake of revenge? Emeline wanted to ask. But the rope held her fast and the gag muffled her voice. Besides, there was no recognition in the Vile's milky eyes. It made Emeline wonder if she'd gotten it wrong. What if Rose Lark didn't hate the sight of her daughter—a reminder of the Song Mage's horrors—but, rather, didn't remember she had a daughter at all? What if, in transforming her into a monster, the Song Mage's curse made Rose forget her former self, remembering only him and the things he'd done to her?

The thought sickened Emeline. To live life knowing only the worst that had happened to you and never remembering the best . . .

Maybe there's a way to help her remember.

Emeline looked beyond the Vile to Grace, who was still unconscious, then to the massive seed suspended in a web of roots. The Heartwood pulsed, sluggish and exposed beneath the earth, trying to pump life up into the dying trees above.

If the Song Mage had cursed Rose here, in the heart of the forest, using nothing but the magic in his voice, could Emeline break that same curse using nothing but the magic in hers?

My voice is nowhere near as powerful as his.

But her father hadn't always been powerful; he'd had to pay a price for it. He'd tithed something precious to the woods, and the power of that sacrifice poured out of him whenever he sang, transforming him into a Song Mage.

The Wood King's reign was prosperous when the Song Mage was the court minstrel, Grace had told her. *It was a golden age.*

She glanced to her friend's unconscious form and remembered the locked door they'd come in through. One that wouldn't open until a tithe was given.

An idea was blooming through Emeline. Threadbare and tenuous, like the first line of a brand-new song.

But in order to test it, she'd need to get free of this gag. . . .

She pulled once more against her bonds, but the rope around her wrists wouldn't budge.

The Vile sharpened her blade, filing off the brown rust. Emeline drew back, trying in vain to put distance between them. As her shoulders hit the earthen wall behind her, the forest's heart thumped through the dirt and into her body.

It was the life song of the woods, that heartbeat. The woods that always came when she sang, trying to protect her in the only way they could—by helping her remember who she was.

Sing us a true song, Emeline.

She breathed in, glancing to the roots around her rising up towards the trees above. Trees that had helped her several times before.

Help me one last time, she thought. *And I'll sing you every true song I know.*

The Vile's hands quickened to an almost frenzied speed as she sharpened sharpened sharpened. Honing that silvery edge.

Hearing her plea, something surged in the earth wall behind Emeline, brushing against the back of her head like small fingers working at the knot of her gag. She kept herself still as the roots in the wall prodded and tugged. When her gag loosened, they curled around the fabric, grazing her jaw as they pulled it free.

The gag fell loose against her neck.

As more roots worked at the rope knotting her wrists, Emeline peered past the Vile, to the Heartwood. She wasn't going to get another chance.

Her father had used his power for his own selfish whims. He'd ruined things with it.

What if Emeline could do the opposite?

She didn't have to follow in her father's footsteps; nor did she have to run from the power lurking in her depths. She could take that power and walk a different path. She could use it to heal instead of destroy.

But to do that, she needed to offer up something precious.

Emeline swallowed.

And once I do, what's to stop the Vile from plunging her knife into my throat?

She looked to the monster sharpening the blade. Instead of fear this time, pity swelled in Emeline's heart. The Vile had been a woman, once. Kept from the people she loved, abused by a man everyone else esteemed, then corrupted by his curse and trapped here for nineteen years.

What if that woman is still in there, somewhere?

As the rope around her wrists loosened and her gag hung slack around her throat, Emeline said, "I know what he did to you."

The Vile glanced up from her task with an unearthly swiftness. Seeing Emeline free of her bonds, her face contorted with rage. She raised the freshly sharpened blade in her clawed hand, coming closer.

Emeline's heart beat swift and hard.

"It's not okay, what he did." She held that furious gaze. "It's not okay that no one came to help you."

Something flickered across the monster's face. But the Vile didn't stay her hand. "*Stop talking!*" she hissed, raising the knife to Emeline's throat. "Or I'll cut your voice right out of you!"

The steel bit the way frost bites: cold and ruthless.

Emeline swallowed, knowing all it would take was one flick of that pale wrist. But she didn't stop.

"I know who you are, Rose Lark." Her throat grew hot and her voice thick. "You're the daughter of Ewan Lark," she said, eyes prickling. "Beloved of Tomás Pérez." Emeline bit down on her lip, hesitating. "And mother," she whispered, "to *me*."

The Vile hesitated. Those bloodshot eyes flickered over Emeline's face, studying her features, searching for the truth in these words. Searching for *herself.*

As if she feared what she found, the press of cold steel fell away from Emeline's throat as the Vile drew back. "No . . . It can't be."

"He broke things," Emeline whispered. "I'm here to mend them."

Tugging her wrists free of the loosened rope, she lowered her arms and walked past the stunned Vile. Stepping into the glow of the forest's heart, she thought of the words carved into Pa's copper tithing bowl.

The steepest sacrifices make the strongest tithes.

Knowing what she must do pierced her with sorrow. But if it would save her mother, and Grace, and all her friends . . . if it would save the woods and undo the harm her father had caused . . . she would do it.

Tilting her chin, Emeline fisted her hands and summoned all her courage.

"I'm here to give a tithe," she told the Heartwood. "I give you my voice—and with it, my dreams beyond the woods. I'll be your new Song Mage, if you'll have me."

Breathing in sharply, Emeline thought of the cost. She would never again sing her songs beneath the lights. Never walk out on a new stage or record an album she was proud of. She would never get the chance to prove she could make it on her terms.

Emeline breathed out, letting it go.

It hurt when the woods took her offering. Like hands reaching in and plucking out her soul, severing her from her oldest dream.

But when she breathed, something new flooded in.

It felt like the night she sang to the elm tree cage, asking the trees to set Hawthorne free. She'd felt the power in her voice flow out of her that night. This time, though, it was the reverse. Power was flowing *in*. Infusing her marrow and blood. Folding itself into her skin.

It was like Grace said: there was magic in sacrifice. Emeline had tithed the most precious thing she owned, and something equally precious was filling in the gaps.

It coursed through her—thick as honey, bright as starlight.

Pulsing like a blazing-hot sun. Humming like a swarm of contented bees.

Power.

It tasted like sugared sunshine on her tongue.

She laughed at the impossibility of it. And there, standing in the glow, bursting with magic, she started to sing—with both sorrow *and* hope in her heart.

All of her old songs, the ones she'd kept locked away, were set free, flowing easily out of her. With them, power surged. The force swelled in her throat, far stronger than before. It brimmed in the air, heavy and thick with promise.

When the first song ended, she sang another, then another. She didn't grow tired and weak. Emeline found herself an endless font of power. She poured it out: here, in the heart of the forest, for the roots of the trees to soak up.

As her voice filled the cavern, the trees took what she gave them, healing themselves from the bottom up. They joined in her song, passing her magic on to the next, and the next, moving all the way to the edge of the woods.

Driving out the curse.

But it wasn't just the woods she healed.

"Emeline . . . ?"

Her mother's voice was no longer a rasp, but a soft, quivering thing.

Emeline spun to find the Vile behind her, glimmering like a mirage. The air shone, delicate as a cobweb, then *changed*.

Like a butterfly abandoning its chrysalis, the Vile before her fell away, until a monster stood before Emeline no longer. In the monster's place was a middle-aged woman, beautiful as the moon. Her raven-dark hair fell in waves around her shoulders, her eyes were the bright blue of robins' eggs, and down her body spilled a silk dress the color of storm clouds.

Emeline let out a shaky breath.

"Mama?"

Rose Lark dropped the knife and the sharpening stone. They hit the soft earth with a thud. The roots of the cavern immediately grew over them, pulling both blade and stone deep into the earth where they couldn't be retrieved.

Staring at her daughter, Rose took a hesitant step before lifting shaky fingers to Emeline's face.

"I'm so sorry," she whispered as tears trembled down her pale cheeks.

Emeline shook her head furiously, reaching for her. "It wasn't your fault." She wrapped her arms around her mother's frail shoulders, pulling her close. Her hair smelled sweet, like rosewater. Her thin body shook like a sapling in a gale.

Weeping, Rose held her daughter tightly, as if, this time, she didn't intend to let go.

When Emeline pulled away, both of their faces were shiny with tears.

Lacing their fingers together, Emeline drew her mother into the glow and kept singing. She sang her own true songs, and when the very last one spilled from her lips Emeline sobered, thinking of the tree her grandfather planted on the day she was born. A hawthorn rooted at the edge of the woods. She thought of a boy who once quoted poetry to her against the bookshelves, grown into a man who stood at her side when she faced down a king.

He'd gone where she couldn't follow.

When her song ended, when her magic was all sung out, Emeline sent a message to him through the trees.

Come back to me.

FORTY-FOUR

FIVE MONTHS LATER

S THE RED SUN rose over the winter wood, the Song Mage trod the quiet halls of the Wood King's palace, cutting through sleeping gardens and courtyards and promenades, her boots ringing on the tiled floors. Below, the King's City lay like a patchwork quilt, all rust-red rooftops and gray-cobbled streets covered in snow. Beyond the wall, the trees were stripped bare.

Every once in a while, Emeline caught a faint whiff of spring in the air—the smell of buds on the cusp of unfurling, of green things poking up through the snow. Spring was coming.

Perhaps it could thaw her frozen heart.

Five months had passed since she'd sung to the Heartwood and tithed everything that once mattered most to the woods. Since then, the forest had reclaimed itself. The Wood King sat upon his white throne once more, his eyes clear, his spirit uncorrupted. The shiftling court had slowly resumed their human forms, coming back to themselves one by one over the last several months.

Emeline's life here had fallen into an easy rhythm. With her memories returned to her, her friendships with Sable and

Rooke were restored, and she spent most evenings with them and Grace. When she wasn't in the King's City, she visited her grandfather—who lived in his own house again, cared for by shiftling nurses sent by the king and visited regularly by his friends. She spent time at Tom's, where her mother lived, safe from the things in the woods.

Her music career was over before it had even really begun: there were no more stage lights, no more late-night gigs, no more tours. But for the first time in a long time, Emeline was writing and singing her own songs—at The Acorn, for the king.

For herself.

For the first time in a long time, the woods no longer came to claim her; she had claimed the woods.

And though she frequently missed the things she'd lost, more and more Emeline felt that she was where she was supposed to be.

She only wished Hawthorne was where *he* was supposed to be.

She slowed as she passed the crystal room, reminded of long-ago lessons with the king's stoic henchman. Thinking of a starlit dance beneath that sparkling dome.

The memory pricked her with sadness.

Emeline moved quickly on. There was something she needed to do before she rode Lament to Edgewood today.

Finally, she arrived at an arching palace door bordered by thick green ivy. Painted across its surface was the king's crest: a crowned white willow sprouting from a seed. The hedgemen standing guard opened the door and let her pass unimpeded.

Emeline stepped through the door and into a small forest clearing.

Her boots left prints in the snow as the white birches gleamed around her. In the distance she heard the soft *whooo* of an owl, and across the pond ahead, a man perched on a small gray boulder. Three black ravens hopped through the snow at his feet, leaving tracks. He hunched over, murmuring to them, and from his back sprouted half a dozen green saplings growing towards the sky.

"Song Mage."

His voice was still that of a wild, ancient thing. But in the wake of the broken curse, the Wood King seemed . . . tamed. As if the curse had taken him out of himself and he was slowly returning.

"Forgive my intrusion, sire."

At the sound of her voice, all but one of the ravens scattered, taking to the air. The last hopped onto the boulder next to the king.

The king scooped the raven in his hands, cradling it. "You're no intruder here."

She felt like one. Emeline glanced down at her wet boots and torn jeans. She should have changed before coming—this was not the proper attire in which to address a king.

"I came to ask about the hawthorn," she said.

Around them, the wood quieted. The white snow glittered on the banks of the pond between them. From his perch, the king stroked the glossy feathers of his raven companion, waiting for her question.

"It . . . hasn't changed back," she continued.

"Hmm," said the king. "And you're wondering why."

Emeline nodded. Her next words caught strangely in her throat and when she tried to force them out, a sound bubbled up instead. Like a sob she'd imprisoned for months now, trying to make a break for it. She swallowed it down.

The Wood King lifted the raven to one of the saplings growing from his back. As the bird scrambled up into the thin branches, perching there to stare at Emeline, the king leaned forward. "Come here and I'll tell you a story."

The king pointed to the pond between them and Emeline watched in wonder as a layer of pale blue ice crept across its calm surface, crackling and solidifying until it was thick enough to bear her weight.

She stepped onto it, crossing towards him.

"Once," the king began when she stood before him, "there grew a tree on the border of two worlds. It was an unremarkable tree, and if it had been planted anywhere else, it might have lived an unremarkable life.

"But there is power at the edges: that sliver between night and day, the place where winter touches spring, the boundary where forest meets field. Wild magic grows between the cracks in all things.

"On this same border lived a girl with an enchanted voice. She loved to climb into the tree's branches, telling it her secrets and singing it her songs. She did this so often, her voice woke the tree up."

Me? thought Emeline.

"Awakened, her spirit made him long to be human," the king continued. "I heard his pleas echo through the woods, begging me to transform him. So we made a deal: In exchange for my help, he would collect my tithes once a season. For as long as he collected the tithes he could remain human, but to forsake his duty was to forsake his humanity."

I'm bound to the woods, Hawthorne had told Emeline two years ago, when he refused to come with her to Montreal.

This was why.

Emeline's heartbeat quickened. "If you changed him then, couldn't you change him again?"

The king studied her with those strange black eyes. The white pupils were waxing crescents today. "The hawthorn was awake the first time. He asked me to change him."

She frowned. "And now?"

That dark gaze fixed on her sadly, almost piteously. "I can't change a thing that doesn't want to be changed."

Emeline frowned. But that meant . . .

He doesn't want to come back?

"Maybe it's time to move on," the king said kindly.

Emeline turned her face away, trying to hide what those words did to her.

"Moving on doesn't have to mean forgetting, Song Mage."

MUCH LATER, EMELINE SAT in the silence of Hawthorne's empty house. She spent most nights here, despite the row house the king gave her in the heart of the city. At first, she stayed because Hawthorne's smell was on the pillows. When the smell of him left, she stayed to keep it warm for him.

And if I'm keeping it warm for someone who's never coming home?

Emeline sat cross-legged on the white rug before the small, crackling fire. An oil lamp burned beside her, illuminating the book in her lap: a compilation of poems by Christina Rossetti.

His books, these poems—they were a link to him. Her fingers touching pages he had touched, her eyes reading words his had read.

Emeline promised to be at Pa's for dinner tonight, and the sun was already going down. But she couldn't stop thinking of the Wood King's story.

Maybe the king was right. Maybe it was time to stop waiting. To put out the fire and turn out the lights and move on.

But why would Hawthorne not want to come back?

She glanced upwards, to the painting over the fireplace. Fixing her gaze on the artist's depiction of Daphne transforming into a laurel, Emeline remembered the conversation they had last fall.

At least she's safe, Emeline had argued. *As a tree, nothing can hurt her.*

As a tree, her life is forfeit, he'd rebutted. *She'll never be human again. She'll never laugh or sing, ponder or love, again.*

If Hawthorne didn't want this fate for Daphne, how could he want it for himself?

She thought of the note he'd written her, tucked between the pages of Pablo Neruda's poems.

. . . if there were some way to atone, some price I could pay to begin to heal the harm I've caused, trust me: I would pay it.

She sucked in a breath. Was *that* his reasoning? Was he choosing this because, as a tree, he couldn't ever hurt her again?

The more she considered it, the more sense it made. A sudden anger poured through her. Yes, Hawthorne had hurt her. Yes, he never should have stolen her memories, even if his intentions had been good. But he'd acknowledged the wrong he'd done and apologized for it. This refusal to come back to the world—to come back to *her*—wasn't honorable. It was cowardly.

The thought made her rise from the rug. Angrily, she extinguished the lamplight and made for the door, stepping outside and nearly forgetting to shut it behind her.

Didn't she get a say in this? She was the one who'd been hurt, after all.

Fetching Lament from the stables, Emeline mounted up. The ember mare's hooves clattered over the mossy bridge as they left the stone house behind.

Lament took her to the edge of the woods, where her tree stood rooted on the border. Its gnarly, twisted bark flew upwards, breaking into branches. Sprouting dark leaves and red berries.

Emeline swung herself down from the ember mare. Her steps thundered as she approached.

"You're afraid of hurting me again?" she said to the hawthorn. "I hate to break it to you, but that's what humans do: We hurt each other. We fight, and we fail, and we fall short of the standards we set. We're a little bit broken—every one of us. If you can't handle that, then maybe you don't deserve to be human."

The hawthorn stood silent and still. Unresponsive. Because, after all, it was just a tree. Not a boy. Not her Hawthorne.

What did she expect? That a good scolding would change him back?

Tears burned in her eyes.

Enough of this. The king was right. The woods and everything in them might be saved, but the boy she loved was gone.

It was time to move on.

The anger trickled out of her as she realized it, and something fragile and trembling rushed in to replace it. Slumping, Emeline pressed her hands to her tree and closed her eyes against the falling tears. When she stepped in close, her lips brushed the bark as, very softly, she started to sing. Just one last song.

A song for good-bye.

AFTER DINNER, PA'S HOUSE roared with laughter and conversation as the neighbors stayed late into the night. When she finished helping Maisie with the dishes, Emeline noticed three silhouettes sitting in chairs outside. Curious, she grabbed her notepad and pen, then pulled open the door and stepped out.

The air was strangely warm tonight. A heavy fog settled in the trees, giving the sky a misty glow.

Her mother and Tom sat close together on one side, sharing a blanket. Pa sat on the other. Emeline kissed Rose's cheek, then signed *hello* to Tom. Rose and Tom had been taking sign language classes ever since Emeline came out of the woods mute. They'd been teaching her, slowly, but Emeline was nowhere near adept yet.

That's what the notepad was for.

She sat down beside Pa, who sipped the brandy in his hand, the ice cubes *clinking* against the sides of his glass.

"Tell me: Who are you again?"

Emeline looked to find Pa regarding her. She was so used to this question by now, it no longer bothered her.

"She's your granddaughter," said Rose, studying Emeline like she was a small wonder. Emeline often caught her mother staring at her these days, as if trying to memorize the exact shade of her hair, every faint freckle on her nose, the precise curve of her cheekbones. Like an art student seeing van Gogh's *Sunflowers* up close for the first time.

"Ah," Pa said, nodding to himself, leaning in towards Emeline. "I'm getting old, you know." He tapped his temple lightly. "My brain doesn't work like it used to."

It's all right, she wanted to tell him. *I don't mind.*

But she couldn't speak the words. Instead, she reached across the space between them and took his hand in hers. He patted it gently, as if understanding her perfectly, and held on tight.

He might not know her name or recognize her when she entered the room. He might not remember the day she was born or all the nights he carried her to bed as a child or that he'd planted a tree just for her.

But it didn't matter.

His forgetting didn't hurt anymore. He was her Pa, and she was his Emeline, and whether he remembered today or not, that didn't change.

She remembered enough for them both.

FORTY-FIVE

THE STORM STARTED AS she said her good-byes. After she hugged her mother tight, Pa helped Emeline into one of his rain jackets, which was two sizes too big but would keep her dry. She kissed his stubbled cheek, braced herself, then stepped out into the storm.

The rain came down in sheets, drenching her as she moved towards the tree line, where she'd left Lament to graze. A thick gray fog hung over everything, blocking her view of the woods. Unable to make out edges or shapes, she slowed her steps and followed the voices of the trees—which were calling for her.

Emeline, they hushed. *Hurry!*

They sounded frantic. Frowning, she reached her hand through the fog, trying to ensure she didn't walk into something. When her fingertips brushed against trembling cedar needles, she knew she'd reached the hedge. Following it along the tree line, she moved towards the spot where her hawthorn was rooted, calling for Lament.

When the ember mare neither whickered nor trod towards her, Emeline started to worry. Lament always waited when she visited Edgewood and always came when she called.

Cr-crack!

Lightning flashed, illuminating an empty space in the hedge.

Emeline froze.

Her hawthorn was gone.

The earth was ragged and raw, a dark spot against the melting snow around it. As if the tree had pulled itself out—roots and all—leaving a gaping hole behind.

Emeline's pulse quickened.

A raven came out of the fog, soaring towards her though the trees. *Rooke.* He flapped his wings against the deluge of rain, then flew around her head, screeching.

Awk! Awk!

He flew back into the woods.

Emeline raced after him.

The fog sank lower as she moved deeper in, clinging to her waist, then hovering below her knees. The rain had turned the earth to mud beneath her boots, and more than once she slipped.

Rooke flew ahead, fluttering from tree to glistening tree. Half stumbling, she followed after him, until a sound made her stop.

Emeline listened, but all she heard was the rain battering the trees and the river gurgling nearby. When lightning flickered, she saw its shining banks through the branches.

She was about to keep going when she heard it again: a voice calling out. Her heart beat like a wild animal in a cage. Blinking the rain out of her eyes, she turned in a circle, scanning. But all she saw were trees and rain and fog.

Again, the voice called. Louder this time.

Emeline bolted towards it. Her jeans were drenched and splattered in mud now. She ran and slid. She tripped and fell.

And then she saw him.

Hawthorne.

He stood at the bottom of a steep hill. One that dropped off sharply into the river below, the water rising towards him due to all the melt.

Lightning flickered above the woods, shining on his bare skin and dark hair. He was beautiful and naked and covered in mud. Surrounded by thorny brambles, he clung to a birch to keep from sliding farther.

At the top of the hill stood Lament, pawing the ground, whinnying anxiously as she stared down at her rider, unable to get to him.

When Emeline screamed his name above the rain, Hawthorne looked up. Their eyes met—those eyes she loved so much—and Emeline saw he was quaking with cold.

"Hold on. . . ."

Grabbing one tree after another, she slowly made her way down the muddy hill. Halfway down, she slipped and fell, sliding the rest of the way on her bottom.

Planting her feet, Emeline rose unsteadily. Standing only a few paces away from him, she saw the scratches along his legs. Places where the thorns had cut deep and left blood smeared across his skin.

"Don't move, okay?"

Hawthorne stood silent, watching her.

She stepped towards him, tamping down arching strands of thorns with her boots, moving those close to him away with her fingers. Her hands shook. Her whole body shook.

"How did you get yourself into this mess?" she murmured.

She wanted to throw her arms around him, but the thorns between them stopped her.

Except it wasn't just the thorns.

There was something else.

Hawthorne was looking at her the way Pa sometimes did, when he was having trouble placing her. On his very bad days.

When she reached to touch him, he flinched away.

"Who are you?" he asked.

A chill sliced through Emeline at that question. Her fingers quickly retreated.

"You don't remember," she said, not believing it at first.

But the wary look on his face remained.

He didn't know her.

Just get him out of the storm, she told herself, trying to ignore the panic lighting her up inside.

If he didn't remember . . .

Thunder rumbled. Emeline raised her voice above it: "We need to get you somewhere warm!"

She had no idea how long he'd been out in the rain and the cold, had no idea if hypothermia would—or already had—set in.

She trembled and rushed, her hands shakily grabbing at thorns, avoiding those empty eyes. The thorns pricked her, one after another, until her hands were slippery with blood and rain. She tugged and yanked, pulling fiercely, trying to get him free.

"Stop." His voice was rough and soft all at once. "You're hurting yourself."

"It's fine."

He reached for her chin with quivering, ice-cold fingers and raised her eyes to his, studying her as if she were a puzzle he was trying to solve.

"It doesn't look fine to me," he said, his forehead creasing.

Despite the chill of his touch, warmth bloomed beneath her skin. She slid her face out of his grasp and changed the subject. "How long have you been out here?"

But she could tell he didn't remember.

"We have to get you home."

When she finally untangled him from the thorns, she unzipped Pa's jacket and put it on him. Together, they climbed the hill. Emeline grabbed on to the nearest tree, then pulled Hawthorne up; he reached for the next one and did the same for her, until they were at the top. She helped him onto Lament, then followed up behind, looping her arms around his waist.

The whole way back to the city, their bodies convulsed with cold. Emeline clung to him, trying to keep them both warm.

Lament soon flew through the city gate, swift as the wind. When they arrived at the creek near his house, they found the water risen beyond the bank. It rushed across the bridge, flooding over Lament's hooves.

In the yard, Emeline helped Hawthorne down.

"This way," she said, heading towards the house, unable to stop her teeth from chattering. Her wet jeans chafed her skin, her sweater was soaked through, and her hair hung in cold, wet clumps down her back.

Wrapping her arm around his waist, Emeline pulled him against her, trying to lend him what little body heat she had left. He paused, hesitant, then slid his arm across her shoulders. Doing the same.

"What are you doing in the woods at night?" he asked suddenly, his voice washing over her. "In the middle of a storm?"

That voice. Her heart thudded at the sound. She'd thought she'd never hear it again.

"I was looking for someone."

"Someone . . . ?"

"Someone I love."

The thunder quieted as it rolled into the distance and as the rain stopped, the silence grew heavy between them.

She decided to ask his question back to him. "What were *you* doing in the woods tonight?"

"I heard someone singing."

Surprised, she glanced up to find him studying her.

His voice softened. "It was a sad song, like a farewell. It . . . woke me up."

Emeline's lips parted, remembering the king's story.

Hawthorne looked around them. "Where are you taking me?"

Swallowing, she nodded towards the stone house up ahead. "Home." It was no longer dark inside. Instead, the windows glowed warmly, lit from within.

Odd. Emeline had turned down all the lamps before she left earlier.

"Your home?" His teeth clattered loudly.

Emeline pulled him closer, shaking her head. "No. Yours."

They were ten steps away from the door. Then seven. Then four.

His muscles tensed with uncertainty.

Three more steps.

With her cheek against his chest, she felt the strong thump of his heart through Pa's slick jacket. Her hand reached for the knob. Turning it, she pushed the door open.

A fire already crackled in the hearth. Emeline searched for signs of Rooke or Sable, but no one was there. The house was empty.

She stepped inside.

Hawthorne halted in the doorframe, his body going rigid with doubt. When Emeline looked back, she saw the confusion in him.

He didn't know this place. He didn't want to come inside.

"It's all right," she said softly, moving towards the heat of the fire, trying to coax him to follow. If he did have hypothermia, she needed to get him warm.

He stepped back suddenly, out into the cold, wet night. "Are you sure this is my home?"

Seeing his fear, she returned to him. They stood face-to-face on the threshold, drenched and muddy. Hesitantly, she reached for him, and when he didn't flinch away, she brushed the wet hair out of his eyes.

"Everything is going to be all right," she promised.

His uncertain gaze held hers. "How can you know that?"

For a moment, the rain and the woods and the house ceased to exist. It was only Emeline and Hawthorne, standing in the doorway.

"Because," she said softly. "I remember everything."

AUTHOR'S NOTE

I WAS FIRST INTRODUCED TO the concept of ubi sunt in an eleventh grade history class. The Latin fragment, which translates to *Where are . . . ?* (or, as Hawthorne interprets, *Where have they gone?*) is a motif found in literature that meditates on the evanescence of life and our inevitable mortality. You can hear it, for example, ringing all throughout *Beowulf*—an epic poem about the loss of the things of the past, its heroes especially.

When my grandfather—a man who raised me—first started forgetting everyone and everything he loved, the essence of ubi sunt rang through *him*. Standing at the end of his life and looking back, he wanted to know: Where had it all gone? And now that it was gone, what was the point of it? As I watched this hero of mine become less and less himself, I began paying more attention to his questions.

I knew then that I was saying a slow good-bye—not just to him, but to the family he held together and to the home at the edge of the woods where I'd been raised. I knew most of all that I was losing my hero. Not just a grandfather, but a guardian. A pillar in my family, as well as his community. A man who was the example I wanted to set in my own life.

So, the day he first forgot my name, I started writing him

into a story. (Him, and the family I cherished, and the forest that kept drawing me back.) I thought if I put him into a story, perhaps I could keep him. Save him, even. A few years later, as I was revising that early draft in his hospital room, I realized we don't get to save the people we love. Instead, we must become who they inspired us to be and find the strength within ourselves to let them go. Only then can we take the candle they've passed us and carry it into the future.

This story has grown and diverged significantly from that first version, but it's still inspired by my grandfather and his search for meaning.

ACKNOWLEDGMENTS

An abundant amount of thanks is owed to the following people:

Danielle Burby, for believing in this story when I had all but given up on it.

Vicki Lame, for giving *Edgewood* the perfect home at Wednesday Books and helping me make it the best it could be.

The team at Wednesday Books, most especially: Vanessa Aguirre, Angelica Chong, Alexis Neuville, Brant Janeway, Meghan Harrington, Alyssa Gammello, Carla Benton, Lena Shekhter, Barbara Wild, and Devan Norman.

Tara Philips, for the beautiful, romantic rendering of Emeline.

Kerri Resnick, for turning Tara's art into the cover of my dreams.

Tanaz Bhathena, DJ DeSmyter, Jo Hathaway, Rosaria Munda, Eloise Andry, and Emily Smith: for your warmhearted friendship, wisdom, and feedback.

Evelyn Skye, Gita Trelease, Joan He, E. K. Johnston, Tricia Levenseller, and Isabel Ibañez for reading *Edgewood* early and lending your kind words for blurbs.

Emily Gref and Kelly Delaney, for taking a chance on the seed of this story all those years ago.

Heather Flaherty, for everything.

Rudy Klassen, for introducing me to *Beowulf* in eleventh grade. Good teachers make all the difference.

Speaking of good teachers: Dave Hunter, for always believing in me wholeheartedly.

Valérie Mailhot and Annie Duhaime, for correcting my error-ridden French. Merci beaucoup!

Kate Goodwin and Laura Bauman, whose long-distance postpartum support helped me juggle a newborn *and* a book deadline.

Melanie Cameron, along with The Muses' Company, for letting Hawthorne quote *Holding the Dark* in the bookstore scene. (And Jennifer Mains, for introducing me to Melanie's poetry. Looking forward to our next late-night chat by your woodstove.)

Canada Council for the Arts, for helping fund this project.

My family, for your unconditional love and support. (Special thanks to Jolene, Mum, Dad, and Nathan for watching Sibyl while I got my edits done.)

Joseph Bauman, for writing the lyrics to Emeline's song and for reading this story more times than I can count. Your steadfastness is woven through all of these pages, and every time I read them, I find you in them, my love.